RUNES
OF
BATTLE

BOOKS BY G.N. GUDGION

THE RUNE SONG TRILOGY

Hammer of Fate

Runes of Battle

Blood of Wolves

RUNES
OF
BATTLE

G.N. GUDGION

SECOND SKY

Published by Second Sky in 2023

An imprint of Storyfire Ltd.
Carmelite House
50 Victoria Embankment
London EC4Y 0DZ
United Kingdom

www.secondskybooks.com

ISBN: 978-1-83790-182-1
eBook ISBN: 978-1-83790-181-4

For Deborah

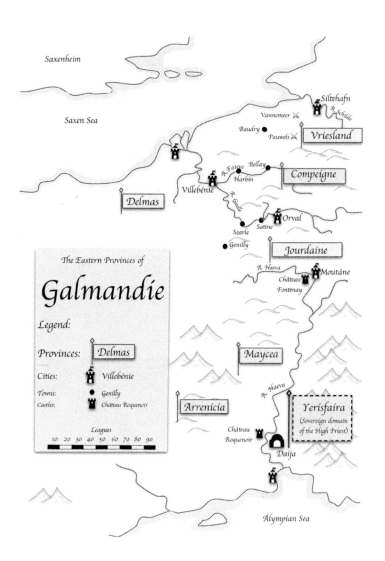

PART ONE

THE HUNTER'S MOON

CHAPTER ONE

1.1 ADELAIS

It was safer to stay away from people. Much safer. But when a sharp stone punched through the thinning sole of her boot, Adelais knew she'd have to risk a town. By that evening she was limping as she made camp beside a stream. She poked her finger through the hole and swore in gutter Vriesian; she could live off the land, in the fat moons of early autumn, but only a cobbler could fix this.

Adelais was nervous about towns. With good reason. She'd walked into a riverside port soon after she'd escaped, hoping to find a boat to take her upriver; the mighty Naeva would carry her almost halfway to Vriesland and she had two gold crowns sewn into her belt, enough to pay her passage. She'd loitered on the wharf, watching for a likely vessel, and all around her the talk was of a Vriesian witch who had killed the high priest. She'd flung a curse into his face, it was said. Killed him on the spot. Then vanished. Just disappeared. The story was told and retold with the relish of a ghost tale around a winter fire, and received with widening eyes and the sign of their god.

There had been a Guardian knight with her, some challenged, so where was he? Ah, that was proof that the Guardians were in league with Kakos, the Destroyer. Heretics, all of them.

Not so, said others; the Guardians were holy men, persecuted by King Aloys for their wealth. Was not the high priest's body burned, as they had been burned? The Vriesian woman was no witch; she was a Blessèd One, wreaking the righteous vengeance of the God. Tall as a man, she was, with hair that shone like the sun and pale blue eyes that could freeze you with a look. No witch could be so fair.

Fragments of the arguments had slopped from waterfront taverns like spilt beer as Adelais had passed. She'd run a finger around the edge of her linen cap to make sure no blonde hair had strayed into sight, tugged her hood forwards and kept walking. Swagger, she'd been told. If you're dressed like a man, walk like there's something between your legs and you're proud of it. There had been soldiers on the quayside, searching people. She'd heard a shout and a scuffle as they seized a beardless, fair-skinned youth and pulled off his cap to see his hair. It wasn't even blonde, just a pale brown, but they made him drop his loin cloth just the same.

Since then Adelais had tramped across country, relying on the sun or the stars to keep her heading north towards Vriesland where a tall, yellow-haired woman was unremarkable. Here in the warm south there were vineyards where the grapes were ripening, and orchards full of apples. She'd scavenged scraps of leather from an outhouse, enough to make a sling, and most days she could kill enough to eat – roosting pigeons or ground-feeding pheasant, mainly. Or sometimes a rabbit grazing near a woodland's margins; they were easier targets than squirrels and better eating. She had flint and char in her scrip and a knife on her belt; she could survive, for now.

But she could not live through the winter, and already it was the hunter's moon; the leaves were brazen with colour and, although the days were still warm, the nights were chill. She might be covering eight to ten leagues in a day, and that probably meant five by the time she'd taken detours around streams and settlements. She guessed she had two hundred leagues to tramp. Perhaps three more moons on the road.

And her sisterhouse boots were disintegrating.

There was a one-temple market town below her on the plain that would have to serve: no walls, no castle, big enough to have a cobbler but probably no soldiers. If she was going to take the risk, it was as good as any. She just had to hope that the king's men had stopped searching.

Adelais prepared well. After more than a moon of living rough she was rank and filthy, so in a cloudless dawn that promised autumnal heat she washed her clothes and spread them over bushes to dry. She had camped where a low waterfall had created a broader pond, too shallow to swim in, but deep enough to cover her body. The stream flowed from a small, sun-baked lake, and she luxuriated in the almost-warm water, lost in her thoughts.

There had been plenty of time for thinking on the way, though she still had no answers. Her grandmother Yrsa had warned her never to sing rune song until she had a true knowledge of it. 'You have power,' she'd said, 'for the blood of your ancestors flows strongly within you, but you have no learning. You are like an infant with a sharp knife.' Yet when Adelais had been hauled before the high priest as a witch, and death had seemed inevitable, she had sung the *thurs* rune of Thor. And as the thunderstorm built she'd felt a power within her as if she were the one hurling thunderbolts. She'd let the high priest think she was an avenging angel, and he'd died. She only meant to frighten him, not kill him. Had that been a coincidence? The storm had been brewing for days and the high priest had looked sick. But if it was her rune song, could she ever do that again? Might she kill by accident?

No answers. She pushed off the log and tipped her head

back underwater, soaking her hair, finger-combing it into the stream. The noise of the waterfall became thunderous. That would mask the sound of anyone approaching, but no matter; she had two pigeons as her guards, huddled together on a branch above. They would fly if a hunter came near, so she let herself relax in a flow that was like an unending caress. It was distracting; her thoughts turned to Arnaud, the lover who'd died trying to protect her. *Sætur Sif*, she missed him.

The birds flew. Adelais spun onto the bank and crouched, streaming water, with one hand splayed on the ground and the other reaching for her staff. A sparrowhawk darted away downhill, weaving through the trees, and she exhaled, straightening. Her clothes were still damp and she squatted by the ashes of her fire with just her cloak pulled around her. She felt she was going wild, living like an animal in this dry, easy season. Dear Arnaud. She wished they could have gone wild together. Adelais flexed her hands, making pretend claws. They were tanned to a reddish gold, darker than the fine hairs on her wrists, but her forearms were pale, the hairs almost invisible.

When the strengthening sun had dried her clothes she began her transformation into Perrin Wilg, itinerant stable boy. No one must suspect her to be Adelais de Vries, fugitive novice of the Daughters of Salazar. Or, as half the country would have her, the Vriesian Witch. If she was caught here in Galmandie, the anakritim would tie her to a stake and burn her.

First, her sling, tied around her waist with enough cloth wadded in its pouch to make a man's bulge over her sex. A loin cloth to bind it in place. Linen strips cut from a shirt to flatten her chest. Thigh-high hose, disintegrating though it was, tied to points hanging from a cloth belt. A man's shirt and the long-sleeved, belted tunic men called a herigaut. A linen cap to cover the pale blonde hair so rare outside Vriesland. She lifted the hood of her herigaut over it to be sure. Her cloak she rolled and tied to the top of her staff as travellers often did on a warm day. She was ready.

A trickle of carts along the road told her it was market day at the town. This was good; she could hide among unknown faces. Adelais put her shoulders back and fell into a man's stride. Being clean, for the first time in weeks, put an extra lift in her step and gave her confidence as she strolled through the crowds, apparently at ease, salivating at pies and cheeses while she looked for a cobbler. She found one by the temple, where a stout man and his scrawny son had set out a trestle table and hung a boot from its edge to announce their trade. They even had a tripod stool where a customer could sit while their shoes were mended.

'First let's see your money, youngster.' The cobbler dropped his eyes from the ripped fabric of Adelais's herigaut to the hose on her legs, now worn into gaping holes.

Adelais showed him a gold crown and the man's eyes widened.

'Come far, have you?'

Adelais named a port at the mouth of the Naeva. 'I was on a ship. We were paid off.' It seemed a plausible reason for a threadbare youth to have gold.

'Don't sound like you come from there.' The man's hands might be shaping leather to her boot, but his eyes were on her.

'I'm Compeignois,' Adelais lied. The accents of Galmandie's northern province were similar.

'Sound more Vriesian to me.'

Adelais shook her head and embellished the lie. 'North Compeigne, over towards Theignault.' This was getting danger-ous. She had only a vague idea of where Theignault was. Perhaps next time she was challenged she'd be Saxen; she'd seen fair-skinned Saxens, and their tongue sounded similar to Vriesian. She even recognised some words.

'My son will put an edge on that fine knife while you wait, if you like.' The cobbler's treadle grinder also had a wheel for sharpening blades.

Adelais looked up. His tone had been a little too keen, though he merely shrugged at her refusal. There was no logical reason why she should suddenly feel threatened, until the cobbler bent to whisper in his son's ear and sent him on an errand. The boy looked hard at her as he left.

'I'll take my boots as soon as you can, please.'

'Not yet you won't.' He lifted a flap of leather and poked his finger through the gap beneath. 'Have a seat, young man. Won't be long.'

Adelais remained standing, stones and grit digging into her feet. She had no choice but to wait. The cobbler began whistling tunelessly, tapping nails slowly into her boot.

'Hurry up, will you?'

'Can't hurry good craftsmanship.'

The market crowds churned around her, ignoring her, yet all her instincts screamed *run*. Adelais turned, scanning the bustle for soldiers, any threat, anyone watching her. Farmers called their produce. Women fingered vegetables stacked for sale. A group listened to a minstrel sawing his bow across the strings of a vielle, and a woman screamed when the minstrel's trained ape tugged at her skirts and held up a cup for coins. Laughter.

And on the steps of the temple, the cobbler's son stood with a priest, pointing her out. Adelais began to back away, wincing as one foot found a sharp stone. The priest started towards her, rolling as he came down the temple steps in the way of an older man; he carried too much weight. Beside Adelais, the cobbler sat with her dismembered boot between his knees, not looking at her, making slow, single taps.

She ran, as best she could. Beyond the market square the road's mud had been baked hard, then crushed to dust in places by wheels and hooves; Adelais hopped and stumbled through the crowd, ignoring the discomfort. She looked over her shoulder, expecting the boy to overtake her easily, but instead saw him back at his father's side. Good. The priest was coming for her, though, and she was moving so slowly that even the fat priest was catching up. He was gesticulating and calling, the tone enquiring and not yet strident, but heads were starting to turn.

Adelais dodged down an alley between two houses, only to find herself in a stable yard, fully enclosed by head-high fences. A tethered nag lifted its head at her, dribbling hay. Adelais flattened herself against a wall, flexing her fingers around her staff as she heard the priest puffing after her. If he'd brought others with him, she had no chance.

He was alone. As the priest ran past her, she slid her staff across his ankles, tripping him, and threw herself on his back as he fell, drawing her dagger as the staff was wrenched from her hands.

'Don't shout, Pateras.' Adelais spoke amiably but held the tip of her blade against his neck.

'I'm a priest, for the love of Ischyros!'

'I'd noticed. And I need your sandals.'

He cursed her as she tied his wrists behind his back and then to his ankles with his own rope belt, and cursed her again as she unlatched his sandals; cursed her so much that she cut a strip from the hem of his robe and gagged him with it to stop the noise. She tried dragging him into an outhouse, but could not shift his bulk. She'd have to be fast away. The priest had a leather flask hanging from his belt that sloshed encouragingly as she shook it, and she took that too. She'd had a moon of going thirsty between streams. If she could escape, this would still be a useful morning. *If.*

The sandals were sturdy enough for her to climb over the fences and out of the yard. Adelais didn't run, not at first;

nothing to excite attention as she made her way through back
ways to the road. But beyond the town's outskirts, when there
was no one in sight, she struck uphill through a vineyard,
crouching low between the vines. From time to time small
stones would work their way between the leather and her feet,
but she kept going, far beyond the forest boundary. The townsfolk would not forgive an attack on their priest; there would be
a pursuit, perhaps with dogs. She found the morning's stream
and worked her way up it, keeping her feet in the water to
drown the scent. When the stream narrowed to a trickle she
found a low-hanging branch, swung herself up on it, climbed
through the tree, and dropped to the ground well clear of the
bank.

Then she ran again, staying in thick forest where mounted
pursuit would be difficult, and not even stopping to hunt. She'd
have a hungry night, but she'd done that before. As the sun was
setting she leaned, exhausted, against a tree on the brow of a hill
where she could watch her trail. The sky was clear and the
night would be cold but she did not light a fire. Instead, she
unstoppered the priest's flask and found it contained a spirit
that spread a burning, gasping warmth within her.

Two towns, and both so nearly a disaster that she knew she
would be foolish to risk more. Adelais sipped, swearing to
herself. *Fjakk*, she was hungry. Could she really walk to Vriesland without meeting people? In a pair of sandals? With winter
coming? She needed help on the way, and there were so few she
could trust. Arnaud was dead. Humbert Blanc, the Guardian
knight who'd become more of a father to her than her own
blood, was in hiding, somewhere. Perhaps his Ischyrian god had
saved him from capture. She'd never find him, anyway. Which
left Agnès, the noblewoman who had befriended her during the
escape from Villebénie, and who by now was probably married
to Leandre de Fontenay. Château Fontenay was somewhere
south of Moutâne and she could find Moutâne; she simply had

to follow the Naeva to the north. Moutâne must be roughly on the way to Vriesland.

More importantly, the hunting lodge where she and Humbert had been captured was near Château Fontenay. Elyse, the castellan's wife there, still secretly followed the old gods and would not betray her. She might even teach her enough rune lore to help her on her journey. But what she really needed was to find her grandmother. Amma Yrsa would look after her. Yrsa was *seidhkona*; she'd learned her skills with runes at her own mother's knee, as the women of their family had done since the gods were young.

Vriesland via Fontenay, then.

Adelais hiccoughed. After a moon drinking nothing but water, the spirits in her empty belly were making the world tumble around her; when the first stars appeared, they seemed to dance in the shining silence of the heavens. Was Arnaud in an Ischyrian heaven, beyond those stars? Had his god accepted him across their bridge of judgement? Could he see her from up there? She lifted her flask to the sky, and woke the night with her shout.

'I'm still here, my love!'

Panicked birds flapped from their roosts.

Adelais drank the dregs, toasting memories.

Would she find Agnès at Château Fontenay? And where was Brother Humbert? Alone in the night on a ridge in Maycea, she longed for some company. She huddled deeper into her cloak, the flask slipping from her fingers, and dreamt that Brother Humbert played the vielle for her. The way his head angled over the bowl of the vielle made him look like a hanged man, yet she danced in slow, courtly steps. Her partner was a man she didn't know, but who screwed his whole face into a lopsided smile to wink at her. Agnès looked on and clapped the time as a trained ape ran among their legs, grinning like a skull. It was dressed in a little white jacket so that it looked like a miniature anakritis. Adelais turned to drop two gold crowns into its cup and found herself looking into the black eyes of Ghislain Barthram, the anakritis-general. She jerked awake into spinning darkness.

1.2 HUMBERT

The word was spreading, to a select few.

This isolated commandery had once been home to a handful of Guardian knights but now belonged to another, less martial order. It lay in a valley where a little-used road crossed a stream, and it served no purpose other than the management of lands scattered across this remote corner of Arrenicia. Travellers on that road would hardly notice the grey-bearded lay brother in the scriptorium. If they claimed a night's bed and board, they might wonder at the respect shown to the old man even by the sworn brothers there. His manner in company was one of quiet sadness, and if they spoke to him they would discover that his work, for his remaining years, was transcribing the Vision of Salazar.

Yet among those who had once served the Guardians, and those whose loyalty was unquestionable, the news had been whispered from mouth to ear: 'the Lord Brother is again among us'. And so his former knights came, in ones and twos, uncertain of the rumour until they could see him for themselves and clasp him, moist-eyed, to their chests. They came humiliated and beaten, sick with the shame of forced confessions, their eyes hollow with remembered agony, and they looked to him for leadership. These were men who had trained for the reconquest of Alympos, and who would accept martyrdom gladly with a chant of Salazar on their lips. They saw not an ageing cleric but their former Grand Commander Humbert Blanc, a lord who would give them back their pride and identity.

They humbled him, these gathering warriors. Humbert's passage through the persecution had been so easy in comparison; he had been visiting the Guardian Commander in Saxenheim when King Aloys's seneschals struck in Galmandie. The Saxens had been openly sceptical about the charges, even refusing to employ torture. Humbert had been imprisoned there at the direction of the high priest, but only after six of his Arrenician Guardians were tortured by the anakritim in Galmandie into saying Humbert had led them into heresy. Any lingering anger Humbert felt towards them had faded when two of those six appeared here at the commandery, dragging their mutilations, begging his forgiveness. He had embraced them fiercely. Who was he to judge, he who had only known imprisonment?

He sent some on their way, back to whatever life they had found, telling them to find others and wait for his word. *Keep the faith. The Guardian vows can never be broken, nor cancelled by a corrupt high priest. The Hand we protected still needs us. We will rise again from the ashes of our brothers' martyrdoms.*

Others stayed with him at the commandery, though not enough to arouse suspicion. They donned the blue hand on white surcoats of this gentler order, which still permitted them to bear arms in the defence of Ischyros. The order's lords in Arrenicia were discreet; they knew there was a price on his head but they also knew the injustices that had been done. They would not betray him.

Yet knowing he was sought, those of his former knights who were permitted to stay organised themselves into a routine of watchfulness. A disused watchtower overlooked the road on a hilltop to the south, and a mill cut the skyline to the north, so his former Guardians now manned these as beacons. One flag signalled caution, that armed men were near; two meant an approach in force.

Traffic on this road had always been light. A small market town lay a day's walk to the north-east, and another almost as far to the south, so the commandery gave hospitality to the occasional wagon passing between the two for market days. Most other visitors were wandering clerics, drawn to a dry bed and hot food in an empty country.

When there were guests, the brothers asked for news, as was the custom, and the events of the outside world were passed around the refectory table as freely as the food they offered in return. They heard that all Galmandie talked of a Vriesian witch who had killed the high priest with a curse, and of the Guardian knight who had been with her. A few travellers lowered their voices as they shared the rumour that the God's retribution would soon be visited upon the king for his persecution of the Lions of Ischyros. She was no witch, but the Lions' Claw. When such tales were told Humbert would sit quietly in the corner, an anonymous greybeard, expressing no opinion.

No one had yet spoken of the Vriesian woman's capture. Humbert hoped, and believed, that she was still free. She had been sent by Ischyros and would be protected by the God, but the ways of Ischyros were mysterious. He had, after all, permitted the persecution of the holy Order of Guardians. The girl had the courage to fight shoulder to shoulder beside knights, and enough backbone to face down the high priest, but that would not save her if the king's men or the anakritim found her.

He prayed for her. He prayed also for the souls of his martyred brethren, and for the continued safe custody of the Hand of Salazar, the most precious relic on earth. Once it had been held in the citadel of the Guardians, the most secure fortress in Ischyrendom; now it must rely on secrecy, somewhere in the care of Lord Leandre de Fontenay. He also prayed for the wellbeing of his living brothers, whose minds sometimes seemed as damaged as their bodies. Humbert prayed a lot.

He was on his knees in the commandery's temple when Brother Thanchere came to him.

'Two flags, Lord Brother.'

Humbert sighed, made the sign of the God, and rose to his feet. There were times when his body ached and he had to force his back and shoulders to straighten. At such times a life as a scribe among the holy texts would have been quite appealing, but Brother Thanchere was pushing a cloak into his arms and ushering him to the door. Thanchere wore light armour only: a quilted gambeson and a bascinet but no chain-mail hauberk. They would need to be fast.

Two horses stood waiting, saddled and provisioned for two days. This too was part of the plan of protection, to allow the Lord Brother to be clear of the commandery before any raid. A few brothers stood nearby, unarmed, though their weapons would be close at hand. Others were assembling in the refectory, where the priest would begin a tutorial on the works of the prophet Salazar. The refectory was also the armoury; they could become a fighting force within a few heartbeats.

A track led through a winding, scrub-filled side valley that hid Humbert and Thanchere from sight within five hundred paces.

'I like this not, Lord Brother.' Thanchere slowed as they climbed into the hills, pacing their horses. 'De Mauriac would have warned us.'

De Mauriac was the local seneschal, a scion of one of Arrenicia's great families and a distant cousin both of its count and of Humbert. Few of the Arrenician nobles had much love for King Aloys, and most still spoke of Arrenicia's lost greatness in the time before Aloys claimed the county for Galmandie. De

Mauriac was an honourable man, as reliable as a Guardian. He would not betray them.

'Have patience, Brother. Our time will come again. I believe it will be soon.'

'But our order is proscribed, on pain of expulsion.'

'So there will be a new order. An order of knighthood as holy as the Guardians, whose mission is to protect the Hand of Salazar.' Thanchere had been one of the Guardians' inner circle, the third degree allowed into the Hand's presence. He had a right to know the vision that Humbert shared with de Fontenay.

'One may hope that the episkopes elect a new high priest that welcomes such an proposal.' Thanchere sounded doubtful.

'There will be many moons of political manoeuvrings. The God struck the high priest down for his greed. Perhaps that will be sufficient motivation for the episkopes to elect a less venal candidate.'

'You were there, Lord Brother. Was she a Blessèd One or a witch?'

Humbert closed his eyes, letting his horse pick its path. His mind's eye flashed a picture of an impish smile in the clear-eyed face of an angel. 'I think she was a girl, just a girl, but the God worked through her as He works through us.'

Thanchere twisted in his saddle, watching the path behind. 'How will we know if the time has come, Lord Brother?'

'With prayer.' Humbert let a hint of reproof into his words. 'When the new high priest is elected I think those of us who were of the third degree, we few who are left, should pay him a visit. Talk to him. Afterwards we will pray together, and if the God tells us the time has come to reveal the Hand, we will visit de Fontenay.'

'And what will you look for, Lord Brother?'

Humbert wheeled his horse and halted. They had reached a

point where they could watch a stretch of the track half a league behind. If there was pursuit, they would see it.

'I would like to discover his vision, and know whether his heart is set on wealth and power or on sharing the love of the God.' Humbert sighed, his eyes on the empty valley behind them. 'Of one thing I am sure, the Hand is too holy to be used for personal gain. It will strike down any who wield it for base purposes. Our new order must be its spiritual protector as well as its physical protector.'

'*Amín*, Lord Brother.'

They spent the night in a shepherd's cot, one of their agreed hiding places, high enough for the first dawn frosts of autumn to crisp the grass in the hollows. A brother found them the next morning around the time of the second office, when the sun was gilding the hilltops but leaving the valleys in shadow.

'King's men,' he announced. 'Random search, asking for the Lord Brother and Adelais de Vries by name and descriptions. They seemed more interested in the woman.' He sounded slightly offended. 'They found nothing and left.'

'You are disappointed?' Humbert asked gently.

The knight flexed his right hand as if grasping for a sword.

'It was like the day they came for us, five years ago.' He hunched within his gambeson. 'Back then we thought there must have been a mistake. We went with them willingly. Never thought to fight.' He looked down at his other hand. His left would no longer flex, not since the anakritim's tormentors had broken it, bone by bone. For the rest of his days he would carry the shame of the false confession that had earned him his release.

'Your chance for battle will come, Brother.' Humbert knew this one would never be admitted to the third degree. That was only for those who had proven faithful even under torture. But an order of knights with such anger would be invincible in battle.

'When, Lord Brother?' Like all the survivors, this knight would fight to the death to prove his worth to his brethren, his God, and himself.

'Soon, Brother. Soon.'

1.3 TAILLEFER

Mid-autumn hunts could be the finest of the year; the sun shone but there was enough chill in the morning air to set the horses dancing, and now that the peasants' harvesting was done Taillefer de Remy could gallop without the guilt of riding down their crops. It would have been perfect if he hadn't been forced to share the day with the king's entourage, with their ever-present reminder of that morning's vicious King's Council.

They rode the fringes of the vast Forest of Harbin, King Aloys's favourite hunting ground. Perhaps that was why his brother Othon had used his influence as chancellor to secure Taillefer the rich diakonerie of Harbin, for Taillefer rode as well as any courtier, and at the end of a day's hunting the closest lodging worthy of the king was the palace of the diakonos. Hosting the king and his court was punitively expensive but it was an opportunity for the de Remys to extend their influence.

Yet Taillefer hoped the politics would be shelved until the evening. This was a day for pleasant riding, if not for much sport. If anyone had a successful hunt, it would be the king, who rode on ahead with his huntsmen, working into the wind where the quarry's scent would carry to his hounds. King Aloys had no wish for his entourage to ride close enough for their noise to spoil his own hunt, so hunting with the king was no hunt at all. When the horns called that a quarry had broken cover, the court would gallop together, in a multicoloured blend of allies and foes, well behind the king. No one would pass His Majesty to chase a boar or a stag.

Not everyone enjoyed these days in the saddle. Othon was with them only to be near the king, sticking as close, it was said, as shit to a blanket. Years of desk work and courtly manoeuvrings had blunted whatever riding skills Othon might have had, while Taillefer still rode for pleasure. His vows denied him women, and his role as diakonos demanded he set an example by eating and drinking in moderation, but there was nothing in the holy texts that banned the joy of a strong horse between his knees. Othon plodded along on a steady, safe mount and found it hard to keep up, a fact his enemies among the warrior lords were keen to exploit. Hunting was, after all, a test of horsemanship, as well as courage and skill with the spear, or the short hunter's sword.

Thankfully the most dangerous man at court, Anakritis-General Ghislain Barthram, did not hunt at all. The priest charged with the purity of the faith wielded a different kind of blade.

Taillefer's mare pricked up her ears at the sound of horns, breaking into a canter before any touch of his spur. She was keen, this mare; fit enough to be ridden all day, and she made the madness of the chase glorious. For he and she became one, joined at hand and leg, at finger and mind; a surging, leaping, twisting joy. He could believe that the same hunter's blood pumped in his veins as flowed in the beast beneath him.

It was a long chase, or at least a long trail from where they picked up the scent; long enough for him to forget the poisonous politics around him, even to forget he was a priest; he was young, fit, superbly mounted, and the horns were calling him on.

Outrunning Othon was a mistake. Taillefer had not realised who was ahead of him; he'd only seen the confection of a noble's hat above a flapping blue cloak, and in the wild exhilaration of the gallop he gave chase. He leapt a fallen tree side by side with blue-cloak, whooping at that glorious moment of weightlessness, and it was only when Taillefer glanced sideways at his competitor that he recognised Duke Gervais of Delmas, the king's brother. Delmas took up the challenge. They ran neck and neck until they burst into a clearing where hounds were milling back and forwards, noses to the ground, and the king himself bellowed at them to back off before they spoiled the scent.

'A galloping diakonos, no less!' Delmas was unconcerned by his royal brother's ire. He patted his horse's sweat-streaked neck, calming the beast. Delmas was large, still muscled enough for armour, though running to fat after his forty-fifth summer, and his horse was blown. 'You are young to wear scarlet. Have we met?'

'I am Taillefer, Diakonos of Harbin, Your Highness.' Taillefer breathed deeply, wishing he'd stayed alongside his own brother. Diakonos he might be, with thirty temples and fifty priests under his rule, but until Othon taught him the ways of court politics he was still the young innocent.

Delmas's smile faded. Other nobles were arriving, slowing their mounts as they saw Delmas's horse standing head down, blowing, and the king beyond. 'Look, de Fontenay,' Delmas called to a dark, broad-shouldered knight, 'the de Remys are multiplying. And this one can ride.'

De Fontenay nodded, his eyes hooded and hostile, his attention more focused on keeping his horse out of the path of Prince Lancelin, the king's son. Lancelin rode with his face pursed by a malice that Taillefer did not understand, at first. Had Taillefer committed some terrible breach of protocol by riding in front of him? Surely the rules of precedence did not apply on a hunt? Taillefer was slightly relieved when he realised Lancelin's evil stare was not at him but at Delmas. He had so much to learn about the tensions of the court.

'I give you one piece of advice, young de Remy,' Delmas continued, loud enough for all around them to hear. 'Consider it a reward for besting me just now. Plan for a future without your brother's protection. Othon de Remy will fall, and his fall will take down anyone who has no stronger support.'

Taillefer did not know how to respond. How could he, a newly appointed diakonos, challenge the king's brother? Someone more used to the ways of the court would know how to turn such a remark with a jest, but Taillefer could only incline his head, acknowledging but not accepting. He felt like a tongue-tied fool. Even de Fontenay curled his lip at him in distain. Taillefer backed his horse away, letting the passing court come between him and Delmas. He waited until he could fall in beside Othon.

'So what did Delmas want?' Taillefer's brother had a way of asking questions quietly, as if they were of no consequence, much as he would sometimes balance a dagger across his fingers and bounce its tip against a table; a little drum roll of menace.

'He predicts your fall, brother.'

Othon snorted. 'The great nobles still seethe about the withdrawal from Vriesland. They snap at the king's heels and plot against me.'

'Yet the king himself ordered the withdrawal, did he not?'

'Our illustrious king is frightened, little brother, but I cannot afford to let him lose the support of the nobles.'

'Frightened?' Taillefer turned to ensure no one was within hearing.

'The Guardian grand master cursed him and the high priest from within the flames of his execution. He called on them to meet him before the God. Less than two moons later the high priest dies, cursed to his face by a witch who ripped a crossbow bolt from her own belly and lived. Now King Aloys wets himself at the sight of a Vriesian army.'

'He is our liege lord, brother, but do you have to take the blame upon yourself?'

'If Aloys falls, who will succeed?' Othon gestured towards the nobles ahead of them.

'Prince Lancelin, of course.'

'Watch him. Tell me what you see.'

Taillefer studied the prince. Instinctively, Taillefer did not trust him, nor any of the young lords who danced attendance upon him. They all seemed to sneer at anyone outside their own twittering clique, and Lancelin set the tone. He'd look at other courtiers and whisper remarks out of the side of his mouth so that only his sycophants could hear, but which set them tittering.

'He is well-favoured, but his tongue is as sharp.' Taillefer hesitated to call his future king a 'bitch'. 'He and the Duke of Delmas loathe each other.' Delmas was foul-mouthed and outspoken. As the king's brother he could escape censure for remarks that would have a lesser noble banished from court.

'True. And?'

'He likes fine clothes?' Lancelin was brushing a spot of mud from the skirt of his exquisitely cut cote-hardie with the back of his hand. He shaped the fashions for the young nobility of Villebénie.

Othon nodded. 'More importantly, he is weak. He does not have the respect of warrior nobles like Delmas and de Fontenay, so he both fears and resents them. There are whispers that if Aloys dies, the nobles will refuse to acclaim Lancelin, and Delmas will seize the throne.'

'And Delmas despises you.'

'To Delmas I am a base-born upstart who has too much

power. If he were king, neither you nor I would survive a moon. But if we give the king the witch, and prove that she and the Guardians were in league with Kakos, then all will be well. And I intend to do that before Ghislain Barthram and his anakritim get their hands on her.'

'Surely you and the anakritim have common cause?' Taillefer did not understand the friction between Othon and Barthram.

'It is all about power, little brother, and that rat Barthram already has too much of it, whispering poison into the ear of the king. If he gives the king the witch, he will be unassailable, so he has every priest and every anakritis in the land looking for her. I too have people. Soldiers. Agents. Someone, one day soon, will capture her. I intend it to be me who gives the king the pleasure of watching her burn.'

'But the stories one hears are so confused. You've said so yourself. When she is caught, should there not first be a trial?'

Othon had a way of smiling that would frighten children. 'Sometimes, my brother, you are so touchingly innocent.'

1.4 BARTHRAM

For Pateras Ghislain Barthram, horses were a means of transport, a necessary discomfort between places where he could do the work of the God. He allowed himself a massive destrier nonetheless, though his was old enough for the fire in its belly to be dampening safely. He had acquired a similarly ageing beast for his escort, but for him it was a necessity: Pateras Octave stood a head taller than most men, had the build of a wrestler, and needed a knight's mount to carry his weight.

Barthram trusted few men, and no women, but Octave was useful. There were rumours, especially since the debacle of the grand master's execution, that some might seek vengeance for a tortured relative, even if the cost of that vengeance was an eternity in the pit of Kakos for the sin of killing a priest. Barthram did not fear death; his passage over the bridge of judgement was, after all, assured. But he feared disruption to the work of the God, so Pateras Octave was his constant companion, wearing a chain-mail hauberk beneath his habit and cradling an iron-bound, lead-weighted staff.

Octave was so much more useful than the last fool. He asked no philosophical questions. He had no doubts about the rectitude of their work, and he was just about intelligent enough to act as a sounding board. He also knew when to keep quiet and let Barthram think.

The King's Council had concerned Barthram. Or rather the king concerned him, for the king was Galmandie personified, anointed by the God. When the king faltered, the whole realm stumbled. And he needed this king. Barthram had served him well, even though his allegiance was nominally to the high priest. But the high priest was dead. He'd been weak when he was alive, and far away in Daija, while the king was here in Villebénie and the source of all temporal power. Sometimes a priest needed power to do the work of Ischyros, and the influence of the anakritim had grown very satisfactorily in the reign of King Aloys.

Deservedly so. Barthram and his anakritim had delivered the Order of Guardians, trussed and bound with enough of them squealing their confessions for their fate to be sure. The Guardians had grown too rich, all the while hiding perversions and heresies behind their facade of piety. The 'Lions of Ischyros', indeed. Such arrogance. Their wealth, in Aloys's hands, had advanced the borders of Ischyrendom more than their knights ever did in battle.

Now all this achievement was at risk. Barthram sighed, lifting his eyes from the road to the horizon, where the smoke of the capital's fires rose straight into the still air, then bent to the west in some breeze flowing high above the ground. The setting sun gilded the underside of the clouds and at a distance the scene was uplifting, like incense rising to the God. A league closer and the truth of Villebénie would come clear, like a smoking dungheap. Their journey was nearly over.

'A troublesome Council, Pateras?' Octave had recognised Barthram's sigh as an invitation to speak.

'Our illustrious king is shitting himself. He fears he has offended the God.' Barthram could voice the unspeakable with

Octave, who was, of course, totally discreet. He was of the anakritim.

'Because of the Vriesian Witch?'

'A witch so evil that she could rip a crossbow bolt from her own belly and live, and then kill the high priest in fulfilment of the Guardian's curse. A curse that included the king.'

'And the solution is?'

'We must prove that the Guardians were heretics in league with the Destroyer, and so deserving of their fate. We must give the king the witch and prove her witchcraft, and we must do it before dissent among the nobles boils over.' *And while I still have some influence with the king.* His position was no longer secure; the witch had been in his hands when she escaped, or at least in the custody of his idiot assistant Malory d'Eivet. It was essential that he, *he* recapture her.

'Yet the whole realm is searching, Pateras.'

'So it is time for us to employ more subtle methods.' It had taken a whole day's riding for Barthram to think this plan through. 'Methods that some may think duplicitous, even un-Ischyrian.'

Octave rode for several strides of his horse before answering.

'The apothecary's most effective drugs are vile, Pateras. If the potion is administered with prayer, and healing follows, the God will pardon the foulest taste.'

Oh, Barthram liked this priest.

The following morning the rising sun was sharp in Barthram's eyes as he left his small house within the temple grounds to walk to the Black Tower. This castle-turned-prison lay along the right bank of the River Gaelle, frowning down at the water. Few entered its dread gates by choice. People even made the sign of the God as they passed it, though Barthram saw this as foolish superstition; it was a place of work, no more and no less than the rabble's shops and tanneries. The screams that sometimes found their way through slits in its massive walls were as much the sound of industry as the tinkling of the silversmiths' hammers in their booths on the Great Bridge, from the Isle to the northern bank. And the men who greeted Barthram were no mere gaolers; their craft earned them a label in the way that other master craftsmen could be armourers or weavers or saddlers. These were *tormentors*.

Barthram stood by a heavy door in the guardroom, waiting to be escorted into the depths, and knowing the sounds and smells that would come. It always began the same, like a choir that knows few songs; at the snap of the bolt there would be a collective gasp from below, and palpable tension would rise up the steps with the stink of unwashed bodies.

Three tormentors led him down the spiral staircase into the cells at the base of the tower, lighting his way with pitch-covered torches while their nailed boots grated on the stone. Barthram knew that the prisoners counted their footsteps, straining to hear how many were coming. Mere gaolers went down in pairs, one carrying buckets of bread or water or a gruel slop, the other a mace in case any of the prisoners was foolish enough to attempt an escape; two sets of boots on the stairs often signalled food. The gasps would subside. But tormentors went down in threes; one would hang his torch in a sconce outside a cell before stepping back, tapping the head of his mace intimidatingly into his gauntleted palm, while the other two entered to seize a prisoner. They'd lay about them until they cleared a way to the one they wanted, and they'd seize him under the arms and pull him out as if he were some floundering carp, dragged from a drying fishpond and gaffed through the gills. Most victims would pray as they were taken. Some would beg and cry, all dignity gone, all honour forgotten. A few would piss themselves.

This day Barthram heard the sighing music of three rise up to greet him, so much higher and more desperate than the tempo of two. He himself wore soft leather shoes, and bundled the skirts of his habit into his arms, both to keep it out of the filth and to prevent even the susurration of cloth against stone from warning of his presence. For when the cell door was opened, and he was recognised, the panting would start. *The Angel of Death himself is come*, and there'd be the frenetic wind of thirty mouths blowing fragments of muttered prayer, all overlapping.

Blessèd Salazar, pray for us in the hour of our death...

All ways of saying *please, not me. Not today. I'll spend my life on my knees, I'll crawl to the holy sites on pilgrimage, just spare me today...*

It was not cruelty that made him reveal himself thus, it was only efficiency. Those who are already fearful speak more readily than those who harbour some vestige of hope. In a way, he was instilling terror to spare them later pain.

Two tormentors entered before him, their flares touching the cavern's vaulted ceiling with dancing warmth. Nearly thirty faces stared back at him, wincing at the torchlight; most sat in the filth of the floor, though some were on their feet and backing away. Others tried to hide behind their fellows' backs. It must be a gamble for them; those nearest the door would be nearest the food, when it came, but oh so visible to the tormentors. Barthram searched the faces, watching them hunch and shrink. Only one stood to face him without fear: his former assistant, Malory d'Eivet. He'd been stripped of his anakritim robe and wore the garb of a humble cleric. His dark curls were now matted, yet he smiled a little in a way that said he accepted his penance. D'Eivet even spread his arms wide as if to say he would accept any end if it was the will of the God that it should be this day.

Fool. Barthram ignored him; he didn't want d'Eivet. Barthram had thrown him in here in the hope that the former

Guardians in the cell would kill him and spare Barthram the problem. D'Eivet was too well connected to execute, even though he'd let the Vriesian Witch escape. But here he was, still alive, and by all accounts even ministering to his fellow prisoners.

Barthram pointed beyond d'Eivet into the shadows. 'That one. Fulke d'Aurillac.' He launched his tormentors, and a mass sigh hissed around him, the sigh of men who will live another day.

Yet d'Aurillac actually stood. Not only stood, he limped towards the door until the tormentors seized him. It was only when he called out that his fear showed, heard – not seen – in a faltering cry.

'Remember me, Brothers!'

D'Eivet made the sign of the God's blessing as d'Aurillac was dragged past him, and as the last tormentor slammed the cell door, several prisoners began to chant.

'*Ischyros be merciful and shine upon us, and lift his hand to bless us.*'

Barthram recognised the sixth book of Salazar, chapter three.

'*That the way of truth may be known among all nations*'

The Guardians' prayer.

'*Thy saving health among Thy faithful.*'

It irritated Barthram when heretics used the holy texts.

'*Let all the people praise thee!*'

And sounded as if they meant them.

They climbed slowly to the guardroom, hampered by the prisoner's limp. There the Guardian was blinded by the light, blundering with his face screwed into his arm, until the tormentors lost patience and carried him between them. They spiralled onwards, up a stairway cut into the tower's wall, and threw d'Aurillac onto a bench in a high chamber. He gasped as his injured foot struck the floor.

'Shall I fetch the boot, Pateras?'

D'Aurillac whimpered and drew his injured foot under him. The 'boot' had been such a simple but effective innovation: an oak-lined, open-fronted iron box large enough to take a man's foot. Tormentors would fill the gap around the foot with flat pieces of oak, and at Barthram's signal would tap wedges to force the slabs against the foot, crushing it a little more with each blow of a mallet.

The last time Barthram had talked to this prisoner the need for information had been urgent, for d'Aurillac was the only Arrenician Guardian still alive and in custody, and Barthram wanted to know more about d'Aurillac's former commander, Humbert Blanc.

'The boot, Pateras?'

Barthram started out of his reverie. He'd been staring at his prisoner's naked foot. It looked normal enough. Certainly filthy. A bit twisted, maybe. No bruising, but then it had been allowed to heal for over a moon.

'Not today.' Barthram sat down in a window seat over-looking the central courtyard. Now he needed to wait for Pateras Octave to bring his other 'guest' into view, and it was easier to wait in comfort where fresh air pushed away d'Auril-lac's smell. And by Tanguy he stank.

D'Aurillac still couldn't open his eyes fully; they were screwed into fluttering slits. He was panting, like a dog, and when a tormentor came between d'Aurillac and the light he threw up a protective hand. With its broken little finger, perma-nently locked in a deformed curve, that hand reminded Barthram of a small monkey's, of the kind that is brought back from distant lands to be a lady's pet; it was brown with dirt but almost human.

There was movement in the courtyard below. Barthram stood.

'Bring him.' Barthram waited until d'Aurillac also stood at

the window, held between two tormentors. 'Look, Guardian.'

D'Aurillac stared upwards, his eyes now wholly open, and his face stretched in wonder. He actually began to laugh as if he'd seen a celestial vision.

'What year is this, Pateras?'

The tormentors gripped d'Aurillac's arms more tightly and looked to Barthram, but he shook his head. This was not a normal questioning. The prisoner need not be struck.

'It is the twenty-second year of the reign of King Aloys.' Barthram also looked upwards to see what had so distracted his prisoner, yet all there was to see above the battlements was the conical roof of another tower. Beyond that were clouds. Nothing remarkable.

D'Aurillac's eyes filled. 'It is five years since I have seen the sky. Thank you, Pateras. This is truly a blessing.'

Barthram snorted. 'Look down. Tell me what you see.'

Sunlight streamed across the wall opposite them, illuminating one corner of the courtyard. In that corner Octave walked with a dark-haired youth, a noble by his clothing, with the first shadow of manhood on his lip, though the anakritis's great bulk beside him made him look smaller and younger. They turned, with Octave gripping the boy's shoulders, angling him towards their window. D'Aurillac merely frowned and for a moment Barthram feared that they had seized the wrong boy.

'Look again, Guardian. Do you not recognise him?'

The boy turned to talk to Octave, putting his face at a new, questioning angle, and even Barthram saw the similarity; that lift of the nose and broadening of the shoulders as a question was asked, the shape of the jaw.

D'Aurillac tensed, straining towards the window so the tormentors had to push him back.

'Gaultier?' And again, shouting now. '*Gaultier!*'

The boy turned sharply, hearing his name, his eyes

searching the battlements. 'Fulke?' The cry echoed around the courtyard.

D'Aurillac's next shout was punched into a groan by a tormentor's fist to his belly. At a sign from Barthram he was dragged back to the bench.

'There.' Barthram masked his relief. 'Your little brother has grown in the last five years, has he not?'

'Why?' D'Aurillac's eyes were now wide with shock. 'I've told you all I know.' He had to gasp for air between words.

'And I believe you.' Barthram settled back into the window seat, ignoring the fading cries bouncing between the walls of the courtyard. 'You are of no more use to me here.'

'Why Gaultier? He will be... sixteen? Seventeen? What crimes can he have committed?'

'None, as far as we are aware. He is a studious boy, by all accounts. His professors at the university speak highly of him.'

'Yet you have him in the Black Tower.'

'He will be well-treated, if you do as I ask.'

Oh, the terror in that face. A different terror, Barthram noticed, to imminent torture. Agony is known. Predictable. Here was fear of the unknown.

'You confessed to heresy, did you not, Guardian?'

D'Aurillac lifted his right hand with the deformed finger. That would have been in the early days after his arrest. One of the tormentors specialised in the breaking and constant re-breaking of the same bones; apparently it hurts more. 'I would have confessed to anything to stop the pain.'

Barthram recalled that it had taken several weeks. On the day that d'Aurillac broke, a tormentor had been twisting the shattered bones and taunting him with songs his nurse might have sung. *This little lady went to market...* Barthram now knew that fire produced quicker results. He'd learned his craft. 'And you retracted your confession in front of the high priest's commission.'

'I told them the truth.'

'In the eyes of the law you are a relapsed heretic. You are fortunate to be alive.' They had burned the others en masse, all fifty-four who had retracted. D'Aurillac was being questioned that day, and so had escaped. Barthram now planned to make use of that oversight.

'Fortunate?' D'Aurillac shrugged. The man had courage. 'The Black Tower is not life. What do you want with Gaultier?'

'I have a choice to make, Guardian. Either I have you burned or I make use of you. I have an errand in mind, but I need surety that you will obey.'

'Errand?' That fearful look was back.

'Call it an opportunity. I am minded to release you.' Barthram watched in vain for a reaction. 'While young Gaultier will be the guest of the king to ensure your good conduct.'

'Good conduct, Pateras?' *By Tanguy, this repetition is irritating.* D'Aurillac lifted his right hand and tried to make a fist. The hand would not fully close and the deformed little finger hooked the air. 'A sword would be knocked from my hand.'

'Though your foot is healing.'

'I'll never run again.'

'Run. Quite. Since you know I can have you burned, I fear you might disappear beyond the borders of Galmandie. We wouldn't want that, would we?' Barthram spoke like a father with an errant child. 'So you have a choice. Perform a small task for me and both you and Gaultier go free. Or run, and Gaultier burns in your place. I will then hunt you down and burn you, too.'

'My brother Roche would never allow this. He is the Seigneur d'Aurillac. He will appeal to the king.'

'Of course, you cannot know. Roche is dead. Two years ago. A hunting accident, I believe.' Barthram watched d'Aurillac's eyes widen. 'So there is no big brother to protect either of you, Guardian. The future of the d'Aurillacs is in your hands.'

D'Aurillac closed his eyes, his face stricken. Barthram let him absorb the news in silence.

'What do you want?' D'Aurillac's voice was flat.

'You will be released from your vows. The only rule I want you obeying is mine. I will give you a horse and enough money to journey to your lands. So that you may travel as befits your station I will even give you a sword and have a seamstress prepare a surcoat with your arms. Blue with three silver birds, is it not?'

'And then?'

'You will seek out Humbert Blanc, who was your commander. It may take a Guardian to find a Guardian. We believe he is hiding in Arrenicia.'

The eyes flew open. 'No. I will not betray him.'

'But you already have. You confessed he defamed Salazar at your induction into the Guardians.'

'Under torture, and you gave me the words to say. I will not betray him again.'

Barthram shrugged. 'No matter. Our interest is not in Blanc.' Sometimes it was necessary to dissemble a little for the good of Ischyros.

'What, then?'

'Your father was killed at Pauwels, was he not?'

D'Aurillac stared at him and nodded slowly.

'Pulled into the mire from his destrier and cudgelled to death by Vriesian peasants.'

'Along with five hundred other knights.' D'Aurillac sounded defensive.

'And hardly an honourable death. I am going to give you an opportunity for vengeance. I simply ask that you talk to Brother Humbert. Win his confidence. We are much more interested in a woman of his acquaintance.'

D'Aurillac frowned, clearly confused. 'Guardians do not consort with women.'

'Your former commander spent more than a moon in a woman's company. We believe he became quite foolishly attached to her.' Barthram breathed deeply, mastering the loathing that threatened to show itself in such an undignified way. 'A Vriesian woman. A witch.'

Barthram looked down. His hands had fisted until the knuckles whitened. He forced them open in his lap, as if releasing a burden.

'So this is your task, Seigneur, for as of today *you* are the Seigneur d'Aurillac. Find Humbert Blanc, befriend him, and find the witch. She may be with him, she may be elsewhere. When I have her, your brother will be freed and you will have my pardon.'

Barthram saw the first dawning of hope in d'Aurillac's eyes; the look of a man so desperate for the world outside the Black Tower that he could smell the Gaelle and think it sweet as incense.

'If I find her, how will I tell you?'

'Will', not 'would'. He would do it.

'Any priest will pass a message. An anakritis, ideally.'

'And when I have found her?'

'Find an excuse to stay with her until you can tell a priest. Do not alarm her, for she has already escaped once.'

'And then?'

'Do not leave her side until she is arrested. Come to Ville-bénie and escort your brother home. He will be released on my order.'

Barthram stood, ending the interrogation. D'Aurillac looked back at him, his mouth open with disbelief, clearly uncertain what should happen now. Barthram nodded towards the steps leading down and away. 'I suggest you begin with a wash.'

The tormentors seemed as stunned as d'Aurillac. Barthram had to wave all of them out of the chamber. He remained at the window, thinking.

He had no need to tell Chancellor de Remy about d'Auril-lac, not yet. If d'Aurillac succeeded, de Remy would try to take the credit, and Barthram needed to be sure the king knew who'd won the prize.

And no one, not even the king, had any concept of the forces he was about to launch behind d'Aurillac. So apparently insignificant, yet capable of equipping Barthram with godlike knowledge.

First, he must find the enemy. Then he could control the game.

And they wouldn't even know how.

1.5 ADELAIS

Adelais walked in a trance, light-headed with hunger. Some part of her still watched for hazards and planned where her steps must fall, but such movement required no thought. Alone on a mountainside her thinking was all about friends; she wove their names into a whispered chant, endlessly repeated in time with her tramping feet.

One, two, where-is-Hum-bert? Three, four, I-miss-Ag-nès.

From time to time she had to break her rhythm where the bed of a dry rivulet crossed her path, and the little rush of faster footsteps down its banks would trip her thoughts into a new pattern, like grace notes enriching the chant.

How-many-steps-to-Vries-land?

She'd evaded the searches in the lowlands by climbing into the hills to the west of the Naeva; no chase would follow her up here unless they had dogs and were tracking her scent. She'd climbed so high that until that morning she'd been able to see right across the great river's valley to the mountain range far to the east. It lay like a bank of cloud, low on the horizon. Some of those distant peaks were already capped with snow. If she kept those on her right she would be walking north, towards Vriesland.

Yet for half a day now she'd marched through cloud that robbed her of her guiding mountains and dissolved her world into a procession of trees. They emerged from the mist, became solid, and faded behind her. She took her direction from the moss on the shaded side of their trunks, moss that trapped enough moisture from the cloud or dew for her to moisten her lips and stave off the worst of the thirst.

The silence was so complete she might touch it; push her fingers through it like the damp skeins of spiderwebs. Her ears strained in vain for the call of a bird or the scramble of a squirrel that she could hunt. Or, just as necessary, for the sound of water. There had been just one trickling stream in the foothills where she had filled the priest's flask, but she'd finished the water the day before. This high in the hills, before the autumn rains, the stream beds were all dry stones.

Perhaps the silence was not complete. She could hear her own breathing and footfalls.

Five, six, Am-ma-Yr-sa.

Her grandmother Yrsa was often on her mind. In far-off Vriesland she'd be singing rune song to bring Adelais home. Each time Adelais thought of Amma Yrsa, she'd touch her scrip to feel the familiar hardness of her grandmother's charm in its secret pocket in the lining. It was a thin piece of wood, not much larger than a thumbnail, with rune carved upon rune to make a single, composite bind-rune. As Yrsa had carved it she'd sung rune song in a high, keening voice that seemed to come from the lips of spirits, not her beloved grandmother. She'd stained these runes with her own blood to forge a *taufr*, a talisman whose fate was to bring Adelais home, that she might teach her the ways of the gods. And if this *taufr* was found in her possession in Galmandie, its fate would be to have her burned as a witch, even if she hadn't killed their high priest.

It's bringing me home, Amma, one step at a time.
One, two, how-many-steps-to-Vries-land?

The ground had been rising for some time, slowing her pace and forcing her to lean into the slope. There was a lightness to the cloud that hinted at sunshine above. At the limit of her vision a dead tree trailed a single, leafless limb like a mighty *lœgr* rune.

ᚱ

Its dry bark held no moss, no moisture, turning the rune into a jest. What if she murmured rune song as she walked? *Lœgr* was the water-rune. When Yrsa worked *seidhr*, the magic of the old gods, she'd sing and beat the ground with her staff at about this steady, hill-climbing pace.

Lœgr-er-vellanda vatn.

Lœgr is the eddying stream.

Ok vidthr ketill.

And broad fountain.

Ok gloemmungr grund.

And land of the fish.

She was forgetting herself. Mustn't sing rune song. Had she just sung the *lœgr* rune or only thought it? By Odhinn, she was thirsty.

One, two, Am-ma-Yr-sa.

She would dream of walking this night, if thirst and hunger let her sleep.

There was movement ahead at the edge of her vision, enough for her to pause, wind the thongs of her sling around her fingers, and flick her cloak away from her right arm. An animal. Large. Appearing and disappearing as it trotted across her path, heading directly up the slope. The hazy movement suggested a fox, or a dog, but the size said wolf. Yet sizes can be deceptive in cloud or fog.

The creature stopped. Adelais stepped a little closer, her left hand holding both her staff and the stone in the sling's pouch, leaving the right ready to swing and loose. Wolf. A big one. Still indistinct, but she had no doubt. It was aware of her, looking back over its shoulder; a posture that did not threaten. Adelais put her sling away, remembering another wolf outside the sisterhouse at Montbeauvoir; a wolf that had come between her and a cache of clothes and so prevented her escaping that day. In a way, her fate had been shaped by that wolf. Yrsa's ancestors were the people of the wolf; their warriors wore wolf-skins into battle. A lone wolf would be seen as a portent. Adelais wasn't sure, but she had the strange notion that it was waiting for her. When it turned away and faded into the cloud she followed it, turning west rather than north, fully aware that she was no longer being sensible. You don't mess with wolves. Were there others? She'd heard no baying. It had left no tracks in the stony ground but had been taking the steepest line up the slope.

The cloud was ever brighter as she climbed. Soon the low scrub trees on the hillside cast a faint shadow, and the limit of her vision broadened. In another hundred paces she had climbed into sunlight and was met with a view of the horizon. The mountains rose ever higher to the north, but in front and a little above her to the west was a ridge so sharp against the blue that she might be looking at the edge of the world. Adelais climbed upwards, and turned. There was no sign of the wolf, and she felt a little foolish for following it. Either side of her an endless sea of cloud lapped against the hills, making a shining shoreline. She stretched out her arms, and in her hunger she felt she might soar over it like an eagle, feather-light, free of the pull of her body. Yet she merely spun, giggling, rooted, until she saw what lay beyond.

The hills held back the cloud from a plateau that stretched away, gently rising and falling, one curve after another into the furthest distance. It was empty of all sign of people but, wonder of wonders, five hundred paces below her where this gentle plain met the hill was a lake, scooped out of the ground the way she might slice the top off an egg. Adelais laughed aloud with the joy of it and ran whooping down the slope.

She slowed as she approached the water, for she'd seen the surface broken by the overlapping arrowhead trails of ducks. They seemed ridiculously tame, eyeing her without fear as she loaded, swung, and loosed. As the stone struck, the flock erupted into a frantic rattle of wings against water, leaving one of their number beating the surface with a broken wing, circling erratically.

Adelais threw off her boots and clothes, dancing in her eagerness, and waded into the water. It was cold enough to cut at her throat and belly, for she drank as she swam, laughing madly. She seized the duck from beneath with both hands like a great predator fish, dragging it under. They drank together until its struggles ceased. It was necessary.

Adelais shook with cold, wet and naked under her cloak, as she foraged for firewood. She found a patch of dead, prickly shrub that snapped easily, releasing the spicy aroma of juniper, and she gathered enough for a blaze. She camped in the hollow created by the fall of a great fir tree, with its roots shielding her back. They too made good firewood and soon she squatted beside an intense, scented blaze. Adelais lifted her cloak-wrapped arms around the flames, bat-like, letting the heat bathe her skin. Sometimes she felt more like a two-legged animal than a woman.

Later, baked, clothed, and feasted, she found cloudberries in the peaty ground further along the lakeshore; most of them were over-ripe and sweet, others tart and fresh enough to cut through the savour of duck in her mouth. Sitting beside her fire, feeding it fir roots and juniper, she wondered whether to rest there for a few days. There was food in plenty, and water. It would be easy to build a shelter of sorts in the fir's hollow.

The cold woke her while it was still dark, gnawing its way up through the bracken she'd cut as a bed, and pressing down through her cloak until the thick wool seemed as light as fine linen. Adelais lay with her knees drawn up like a newborn babe, shaking, reluctant to let sleep go. She'd slept lightly, not sure whether she should be grateful to that wolf or fear its prowling presence.

She woke fully at the thought of the wolf and sat up, pushing the cloak back from her face. Her fire had burned out; an all-night fire, even if banked, would need thicker wood than her knife could cut. At least her kindling hadn't been dampened by rain, but she shook uncontrollably as she struck sparks from her flint.

By dawn Adelais had emptied the flask of water and was thirsty again. She'd eaten the whole duck, mostly out of hunger but also to avoid leaving scraps to attract predators, particularly if there were wolves about. She'd even burned its carcass. The fallen fir tree stretched out into the lake, and she lay along its trunk and sipped clean water from beyond the shoreline. She drank her fill and then drank more, saturating her body as well as refilling the flask. She lay there afterwards, watching the drops that fell from her lips. They hit the water with the faintest plop, launching ripples that arced out and were swallowed by a light mist. It lay in a fine layer over the lake, ghost-grey, surrounding her; she might have been the only living thing in a spirit world. If it had not been for the coarse bark against her cheek and fingers, she might have imagined herself already dead; the boundary between this world and another seemed thin in this place. Perhaps not even a boundary, more a dream-space between sleeping and waking; as real yet insubstantial as the fog of a winter's breath that is exhaled and rebreathed, then fades into the unknown.

The mist lay so close to the surface that when she climbed back to her camp the shoreline between water and land did not exist. The lake lay beneath a thin, opaque blanket, yet above it the plateau stretched to the horizon, charcoal-dark against the lightening sky, horizon upon horizon. Empty.

Was this what Amma Yrsa had meant about being in touch with the gods? Ischyrians believed their god lived beyond the stars and this was the world of men and Kakos the Destroyer. It was written. But Yrsa said the gods walk this world; they live alongside us as the bear lives among the lesser beasts. The gods, she'd said, need no temples. They cannot be confined within walls, you feel them in the forest vastness. You open your heart and know that you stand in a sacred place.

Adelais closed her eyes, turning her hands palm-out as she had seen Yrsa do, listening with every fragment of her being, for this felt a holy place where the gods might hear her. She needed help, even though Yrsa had always said that you do not beg the gods. They honour courage but will let our fates run their course.

Yet Yrsa also said that our fate was not fixed. It was woven as we live, and by how we live. Those with knowledge could even harness the wisdom of Freyja and Odhinn to alter fates. That was Yrsa's skill, when she wove *seidhr*-magic. This power Adelais knew to be true, though she knew so little of rune lore. It excited and frightened her. Yet the day before she'd simply thought of the rune song of *lœgr*, and found water. Or had the wolf led her to it? Adelais lowered her hands and opened her eyes.

The wolf was staring at her. It sat on its haunches perhaps ten paces away, with its hind legs spread in a way that reminded Adelais of Yrsa, sitting on her stool with her knees wide so that the skirts of her kirtle made a valley between her legs. A she-wolf, Adelais saw, and old enough for her joints to make sharp angles in a pelt as grey as a dove's wing and streaked in places with brown. A snowy bib tumbled down her chest.

Adelais did not feel threatened. The wolf's posture was more like that of a patient hound than a hunting beast. It watched her as if it knew her and was waiting for her, and not like a subservient dog with its head lowered, but with the steady gaze of an equal; exactly how another wolf had looked at her, below the sisterhouse.

It had to be another wolf. Wolves do not range that far.

Do they?

Something was not right. The wolf's eyes were ice-blue, a reflection of the dawn. Wolves don't have blue eyes. Nor did they look so kindly.

But Yrsa did.

A terrible doubt began to gnaw at Adelais's heart.

'Amma? Amma Yrsa?'

The teeth bared briefly behind black-rimmed lips. Can a wolf smile?

Adelais took a step forwards, but the wolf rose and trotted away to the north.

'Amma!' Adelais shouted after it, but it did not stop until it was almost out of sight, a grey movement against grey mist. There it paused and looked over its shoulder as if to say *'what are you waiting for?'*

It had been a wolf. Just a wolf. But why did she feel this kinship? And why had it led her to water and food? And how could a wolf remind her so powerfully of her grandmother?

Could Yrsa send a wolf? She'd never spoken of such power. But there were folk tales of *fylgjur;* the newly dead who inhab-ited the bodies of animals so they could protect a living relative... Adelais fumbled as she gathered her cloak, scrip and staff, her breathing coming in short bursts, sweat pricking at her hairline despite the chill, doubt gnawing at her and the weight of a dreaded thought descending upon her. *No. Not Yrsa. She can't be.*

But Adelais was sure she'd been given a message; she'd been shown a refuge, not a place to stay. Soon the dawns would be this cold down in the valley and there would be snow here in the hills. And all she had on her feet were the priest's sandals. The wolf knew her. It was urging her on.

She collected herself enough to fell another duck and fill her scrip with berries. But as she made these preparations, doubt gradually gave way to certainty, and she allowed herself pause to embrace the crushing grief enveloping her heart. Grief not only for her beloved grandmother, but for the wealth of rune-lore that Yrsa would now never teach.

PART TWO

THE BLOOD MOON

CHAPTER TWO

2.1 HUMBERT

'One flag, Lord Brother!'

Humbert Blanc looked up from his desk in the small scrip-torium, taking advantage of the interruption to roll the strain out of his shoulders. These days he had to read at arm's length, with the aid of a polished wood pointer, yet the single flag flying from the tower on the horizon was crystal clear.

One flag. Caution: armed man, or men.

'So I see.'

Humbert looked back to his work. The commandery's copy of the *Vision of Salazar* lay open in front of Humbert under the window, held down by fine leather straps lest a breeze lift and damage its precious pages, and the words of the prophet were speaking to him. *Resentment is a poison of which men drink their fill, though it never slays the object of their resentment.* Resentment? How could one not feel anger for the destruction of the Guardians, the Lions of Ischyros? They had been brought down by the greed of a king and the weakness of a high priest, but it was not for them that his fiercest anger burned, it was for the anakritim. The order charged with the purity of the faith had committed its worst atrocities, all in the name of the God, and all for the sake of power. Yes, he felt resentment.

He struggled with this fury. It might cloud his judgement. If the Guardians were to rise from the ashes, if he and de Fontenay were to found a new order to protect the Hand of Salazar, it would need to be righteous. That did not preclude his anger, but vengeance belonged to Ischyros; the God he found on his knees in the temple, not the God of anakritim who saw torture as an act of love.

The new order must hold to the pure principles of the Guardians and be humble to the will of the God. He must learn to shed this anger, and perhaps his pride. More killing would not resurrect his brothers from the ashes, and if it was His will that a grand commander who had ruled seventy knights and as many manors should spend the rest of his days copying the holy texts, then His will be done. He prayed often, as humbly as he knew. The God would show them when the time was right and it would be soon, he was sure; the Hand had been hidden in the Guardians' care for two hundred years, but in the delirium of hunger he himself had exclaimed its existence. Ghislain Barthram had heard and it would no longer rest peacefully. It would need protection.

Humbert pinched the bridge of his nose, trying to massage away a headache, and eyed the flag on the horizon.

In truth he welcomed the single flags, for those who travelled well-armed would be knights or men-at-arms, and they were usually better informed than merchants or mendicant clerics. And after each such visitor he would give thanks in the temple that they had brought no news of the arrest of Adelais de Vries. If there were knights nearby he would not hide when 'one flag' was called but would stay among the holy books and parchments in the scriptorium. From there he could observe the newcomers and choose whether to be seen; his desk had a good

view of the road to the south, and beyond the door was the
courtyard and the road to the north.

The coming winter was bringing new challenges; his adoptive
order could not afford glass, only waxed linen, and he needed
the window open to have enough light to read or write. The
draught was chill, and he blew on his fingers, flexing them as he
watched a solitary figure ride slowly towards him out of the
south; a daub of heraldic blue against the grey-brown dust of the
road. Beneath the blue, a bay destrier drooped its head, plod-
ding towards water and rest. A riderless packhorse followed on
a lead rein. The rider was close, within a bowshot, before the
blue resolved into a noble's surcoat charged with three silver
birds.

From where did he know that device?

The rider swung stiffly out of the saddle, landing with all
his weight on his right foot before gently lowering his left. He
wore a long, hand-and-a-half sword and, unusually, had the
small, round buckler shield of a common foot soldier hanging
from his saddle, not the lance-stopping shield of a noble.

Blue, with three silver birds; the merlettes of heraldry. The
arms of d'Aurillac. Yet the rider did not wear the golden spurs of
knighthood, so this could not be Roche, the seigneur. And
hadn't he heard that Roche was dead? This d'Aurillac lifted a
hand to sweep the hood from his face, and Humbert finally
recognised the visitor. Fulke. By Salazar, *Fulke*. It had been
nearly six years.

He left the scriptorium smiling, with his arms wide in
welcome for his old comrade in arms.

2.2 ADELAIS

There were watchers at the gates of Château Fontenay. Anakritim, no less.

Adelais had learned to hate the anakritim; hard-eyed men who would inflict unspeakable agony in their quest for heresies, while believing they did their god's work. They stared at people in that penetrating, unsmiling way that judged and said '*I see a sinner*'. They were like insects in their cloaks, black as a beetle's wings, and they appeared every time she came close to a road, as if some foul nest had newly hatched. And, by Odhinn, they could sting.

This pair were too obvious; it would be easy to slip around them. But that probably meant there were other watchers inside that she wouldn't see. And no one, least of all the ragged urchin that she must seem, would be allowed close to a member of the mighty de Fontenay family without explaining themselves. So Adelais squatted, watching, not even breaking from safe cover when Agnès herself rode up the hill into the château like a queen, with a falcon on her wrist and a colourful party of ladies and grooms in attendance.

Perhaps she should move on and look for the hunting lodge

where she'd been captured, and where Elyse, the castellan's wife, would surely help her. It would be in the forests somewhere to the north, beyond the River Naeva, and she might wander for half a moon without finding it. Better perhaps to wait until someone she trusted came out: Agnès's servant Mathilde, Guy Carelet, even Agnès herself. Either way she had to find shelter, soon. Already she woke shaking with cold every night when her fire burned down; she would not survive far into winter.

Château Fontenay taunted her from across the valley; it rose along the crest of a ridge, tower after pinnacled tower, its stone shining bone-white in the sunlight, more of a fortified town than a castle. It floated above her on tendrils of mist, a cloud castle. Unreachable.

Adelais stood as a man-at-arms led a small group of mounted squires and pages from the château down to a meadow in the valley bottom, below her hiding place. Even at a distance she recognised Humbert Blanc's destrier; a dark bay, almost pure-black stallion with a distinctive hazel lightening around the muzzle. As they came closer she recognised its rider as Arnaud's former apprentice, Guy Carelet. His horsemanship must have improved over the summer to be trusted with such a fine beast.

Adelais watched retainers unpack a laden cart, hammer posts chest-high into the ground, and stretch a rope between them until they formed a straight line perhaps forty paces long. They draped cloaks over the rope to turn it into a makeshift barrier, and Adelais puzzled at its purpose until the squires began to arm themselves with gambesons, hauberks, mail coifs and great helms. It seemed the man-at-arms was about to give his juniors a jousting lesson.

Adelais eased her way back into the trees, calculating her line of approach. Much of the meadow would be hidden from the anakritim by the houses at the crossroads. If she could drop into the valley without being seen, there were vineyards to mask her approach all the way to the cart. The vines were almost bare of leaves now, but together they would offer enough cover, and her cloak was now almost the colour of the earth.

The men were already jousting by the time she reached the meadow, riding at each other with blunted lances down opposite sides of the roped line. She'd hoped to use the cart as a screen, but a servant told her to 'go shaft yourself, boy', his lip curled in distaste, and she moved to squat at the edge of the vines. Other wastrels were drifting towards the field to enjoy the sport, though none came near her.

Boy. These days she'd be more surprised, and worried, if someone called her 'girl'. She inhabited a different body when she came near people, holding her shoulders wide and moving in a masculine, long-stepping way that was now almost natural.

Humbert's destrier recognised her, though. Guy, hunched behind a plain shield and anonymous inside a borrowed great helm, was tilting at a squire who wore the retainer's badge of de Fontenay on his surcoat. In the last few strides before they struck, the destrier's eyes locked onto Adelais. His ears went forward, and he danced sideways towards her, drifting off his line. Guy's lance went wide, though the squire managed to shift his aim and hit Guy's shield. The crack of steel on leather-wrapped wood rocked Guy in his saddle, but it was a glancing blow and did no damage.

'Keep your leg on him!' The man-at-arms sat astride his destrier opposite her, in the middle of the roped line. He wore a sword on his hip but otherwise had not donned armour. 'He's napping away from the impact. Use your spur to hold him to the line. Again!'

Humbert's destrier wouldn't shy from contact, Adelais knew. He knew his job; she'd seen him hurl himself head-on at charging cavalry. Guy's line was spoiled by his weak riding and the horse's glimpse of an old friend. She could see the beast roll

his eyes towards her, even as Guy cursed and yanked at the
bridle, turning him at the end of the barrier.

This time, on the opposite side of the rope, Guy held his
line but he was no match for the squire. Perhaps the squire was
keen to prove it. Adelais could see Guy struggle as they
launched into the charge; struggle to guide his mount, struggle
to hold his lance steady, and struggle to strike his mark, while
the squire made it all look easy. A heartbeat before impact he
leaned forwards in his saddle, gaining extra reach, and lifted his
aim from Guy's shield so that his point clanged against Guy's
helmet, like a blacksmith's hammer hitting an anvil. Guy
dropped his lance, swayed in the saddle, and toppled sideways
to thump heavily into the grass. He lay still for a moment, but as
the servants rushed to help he rolled onto his hands and knees
with his great helm hanging low between his shoulders.

The man-at-arms seemed unconcerned. 'Well struck,
Maurice! Guy, rest. We'll try you against targets for a while.
Etienne, you're next.'

Humbert's destrier, now loose, stopped his run at the end of
the rope line, turned, and walked towards Adelais, keeping his
head low enough to rub it against her body when he reached
her.

'Hello, Allier.' She remembered that Humbert had named
him after a swift-flowing river of Arrenicia. She gathered the
trailing reins and stroked the horse's neck, whispering endear-
ments, but her eyes were on Guy. The meadow's grass was long
and thick with fallen leaves, but such a fall could still be
dangerous.

Guy staggered to his feet, unbuckling his great helm. When
he lifted it off his head, his face was grim with anger and humiliation. He breathed deeply, rolled his shoulders, and strode
towards Adelais and his horse.

He didn't recognise her. Adelais waited until he was about
to snatch the reins from her fingers.

'Are you hurt, Guy Carelet?'

He stopped as if he'd been struck again. 'You!' He looked over his shoulder. No one else was close enough to hear. Another worried-looking page was being helped into the saddle to face the victorious Maurice. A servant stood at his stirrup holding up a great helm.

'It's good to see you, too, Guy.'

'All of Galmandie is looking for you. There's a hundred in gold on your head. We can't talk here.'

'Where, then?' Adelais had quite fond memories of Guy, the way she might for a slightly irritating younger brother. They were fading fast.

'Dunno. There's people watching...'

'Anakritim. I've seen them.'

'And others. Look, you'll spoil everything.'

In those few, whining words Adelais understood a great deal. She guessed that Guy had a good position in the de Fontenay household, a position he didn't want to lose. He was safe. No one else had connected him with Humbert and Agnès's flight from Villebénie, and therefore with the Vriesian Witch. He was being trained as a man-at-arms. And he wanted her to go away before she threatened all that.

'Where do I find the hunting lodge where I was captured?'

'Take the Moutâne road, and the first left fork.' Guy looked around again. The man-at-arms was now watching them curiously. 'There's a bridge over the Naeva three leagues away. It's about two leagues north of that.' He was gabbling, keen to break away.

'Then take a message to Lady Agnès for me. I will wait there seven nights. If she does not come or send word, I will know it is not safe for her, and I will understand.'

Guy snatched the reins from her and dragged the horse away.

Nearly three moons on the road. She'd tramped her feet raw

and her clothes into tatters. She'd lived rough and she'd fought hard, and Guy hadn't even asked her how she was. '*Fjakk* you, Carelet!' She swore at him in filthy Vriesian and he looked over his shoulder, not understanding.

'Farewell, Guy Carelet.'

Her voice was hard. Across the field the man-at-arms called to Guy, his voice imperative, and Guy hunched his shoulders, tugging at the horse. Allier looked back at her as he was led away, straining towards her until the edge of his eyes showed white.

2.3 BARTHRAM

Pateras Ghislain Barthram knelt in a side chapel of the great fire temple of Villebénie, watching the sun through the temple's glass. Artisans had found a way of staining the glass with reds and yellows, and had built the windows with lead-framed fragments in the shapes of flames. It was one of the wonders of Villebénie. Important ceremonies would be timed so that this rich light fell upon the golden head that encased the skull of Tanguy, the First Disciple of Salazar, but not today. This was a simple second office on a working day.

Around Barthram a light scattering of worshippers, mainly temple staff and clerics, also listened to the chanting of a nervous priest. Sometimes Barthram found the terror he inspired as anakritis-general useful, at others it was an irritation. This morning the officiating priest made frequent glances in his direction, as if for reassurance, and that marred the tranquillity of the moment. Barthram needed peace, a time for reflection when the great issues facing him could be allowed to form in his mind, be defined, and then laid before the God.

He was ever more worried for the king. Barthram knew, as only the king's pardoner could know, the burden King Aloys felt for sending the last grand master of the Guardians to the stake. This surprised Barthram; political expedience meant kings eliminated opposition to advance the realm, and did so without regret; in the twenty-two years of his reign Aloys had left a trail of dead behind him as he built Galmandie to a kingdom greater than ever before. Yet Aloys felt huge guilt for the grand master's death. Guilt and fear, for that curse from the stake had not simply struck down the high priest, it had destroyed his body.

The evil forces of Kakos were powerful indeed, always seeking to destroy the works of the God; it was time for men of Ischyros to show their strength. Meanwhile the king was nervous beyond any unburdening, and all Galmandie was rife with stories of the witch who had hurled the fatal curse into the high priest's face. A witch so powerful that she could persuade a priest, an *anakritis* at that, to stand aside and let her and Humbert Blanc walk to freedom. A priest who still behaved as if that had been a holy act rather than a sin. Barthram was vaguely aware that those watching would interpret his frowns as intense prayer.

In the aftermath of that terrible day the world seemed to have forgotten why they'd been chasing Blanc in the first place; the desecration of a temple and the possible theft of a relic. Barthram hadn't forgotten. He'd heard Blanc say the witch had touched the Hand of Salazar, and if that impossibly precious relic existed it would change the world. Pilgrims would flock to see it, bringing wealth that would fuel the growth of Ischyrendom. And for the priest who found it, with unquestionable provenance, there would be the purple robe of an episkopos. Perhaps, even, the highest office, for the seat of the high priest was still unfilled.

The Hand, he was sure, was now hidden by Leandre de Fontenay, a man too powerful to arrest without evidence.

Humbert Blanc could provide that evidence, if they caught him, but he would probably endure torture rather than speak.

Though he might well talk to save someone dear to him. So, the witch was the key. The anakritis-general lifted his face to the light, spreading his arms wide to let the patterns of colour wash over him like a blessing. *Blessèd Tanguy, for Ischyros's sake, give me the witch.*

When he rose and turned, a dark, leathery-faced figure waited for him, bobbing his head deferentially. The man's head would have fitted more suitably under a Saradim turban than the labourer's cap he wore, and the departing worshippers parted to flow around him as if he had some contagion.

'There is news, Kasim?'

The man bobbed his head again. Kasim could not speak; Barthram had made sure of that, though Kasim would never know who'd ordered his tongue to be cut out. To Kasim, Barthram was his saviour, the priest who'd released him from prison and shown him the love of Ischyros. Once he could tell no secrets, of course.

For Kasim had a rare gift, one that none could know. He'd been arrested in a remote Guardian commandery where he'd been sent from a citadel on the borders of far-off Alympos to start an experiment. The Guardians on that frontier of Ischyrendom had learned that the Saradim had discovered the art of training doves or pigeons to carry news. The commandery's Guardians had seen no reason to disguise their activity from Barthram; there was no heresy in breeding pigeons. Just think, they'd said, if a Saradim fleet sailed to attack Galmandie, you could know in a day rather than wait for the fleet to arrive off the coast.

Barthram had seen the potential immediately. Such power should belong to the faith, not to any secular authority. To know great events even before kings was power indeed; such knowledge would seem divine, the whispered word of Ischyros.

He had everyone from that commandery killed; a necessary evil for a greater good.

Except, of course, for a muted Kasim and his cage of breeding pigeons.

One of which, it seemed, had just come home to roost.

Barthram's position as anakritis-general earned him a modest house with a small garden in the temple grounds, and it was here that Kasim had been allowed to design the cages for his birds, next to an area bounded by fine netting where they could fly. Barthram's garden was always filled with their cooing and bubbling, and from here Kasim trained them, carrying them ever further distances from the garden in wicker cages. He identified the bloodlines of those that flew fast and sure, and marked the ones that did not. Visitors to the house were astonished to see the most feared cleric in Galmandie cradling the birds, and to see them accept his hands. 'Like a Blessèd One,' they said, seeing a sign of gentle holiness.

'Oh, they serve a purpose,' he'd respond, offering his guests dainty pies filled with the meat of the birds that Kasim had rejected.

Barthram was learning the practicalities of the birds; they could not be told where to fly, they could only learn their home and be released to fly back to it. They could not be kept too long caged, unable to fly, and they could not be allowed to find another place so comfortable that it became their new home. Every six days a junior cleric left Villebénie, not knowing why he must ride to a brotherhouse in Arrenicia with one of Kasim's baskets, a return journey of at least half a moon. An anakritis at that distant brotherhouse had been trained to attach a message and release a bird when a replacement arrived. At such a distance Barthram had to keep two or three of his precious trained birds on the road to have one always ready to fly in Arrenicia. The best birds could fly home in under a day.

Other than Barthram, only four men knew of this great

secret. Two anakritim had been taught how to attach messages; one he'd sent to Arrenicia and the other to Jourdaine, to await instructions. He did not have enough birds to keep both stocked. Pateras Octave knew. So, of course, did Kasim, who now led him towards his aviary, ducking his head like one of his own birds. Kasim reached into the 'arrivals' box where the bird would have found food and water, and pulled it gently out.

The bird struggled a little as Barthram reached for the tiny, hollow tube tied between its shoulders, sealed with hard wax and scarcely thicker than a reed, but at the sound of Kasim's voice it settled back into his palm.

The paper within was as fine as the maker's art could create, too fine for any lasting document, and written in tiny script that Barthram had to lift to his face to read.

The silver birds have found their nest at the commandery of Saillac.

Barthram closed his eyes and gave thanks to the Blessèd Tanguy. His prayer had been answered as soon as it was made. The fool d'Aurillac, riding round the country in his noble surcoat, could not know that every anakritis and many clerics watched for him. He didn't have to do anything, just find his master. His nest.

Barthram would have the commandery watched, but he wouldn't move, not yet.

He wanted the witch. He wanted both of them.

2.4 ADELAIS

Adelais paused in sight of the Naeva, which now ran from the west, blocking her way north. The town of Moutâne, smoking the horizon to her east, must lie in the elbow of a great bend of the river where it swung south towards the distant sea. It was narrower here, perhaps two hundred meandering leagues from its mouth, but still a mighty barrier. Two bored soldiers guarded a five-span stone bridge, pushing themselves off the parapet to check all travellers. Adelais watched them for long enough to realise they were more concerned with traffic flowing towards Château Fontenay rather than away from it. To be safe, Adelais looped back half a league and fell in with a peasant driving cattle northwards. There's an easy camaraderie on the road, for those who have far to tramp, and the cowherd accepted Adelais's company after she used her staff to return a stray to the path. She made a show of herding the cattle onto the bridge, calling to them as if she'd tended them all her life, and the soldiers didn't even look at her. The peasant seemed quite disappointed when she left him, and showed his thanks by letting her drink from one that was in milk. The taste was rich and creamy, and she laughed aloud with the joy of it.

From the Naeva northwards she recognised the landscape; soldiers had brought her this way to the river in the summer, en route to Château Roquenoir and the anakritis-general. Then, she'd been carried in a pallet, unable to walk, her body bruised and scarcely holding together where a crossbow bolt had struck her, or rather struck the stone she'd tied under her loin cloth to give her a man's shape. The stone had saved her from a mortal wound, though it had been punched deep into her belly and she'd almost died from the bleeding that followed. Her memories of that journey were heavy with grief, for Arnaud had been cut down trying to save her, and she'd lost the child so newly seeded within her. Grief, and growing terror at the thought of the anakritim who waited for her. Now she retraced the soldiers' route, taking deliberately masculine strides on the open road but allowing herself to relax when her path branched off into the forest and she was alone.

In the late afternoon Adelais paused where the track to the hunting lodge forded the stream. The scene brought back painful memories, although the donjon tower looked benign in the fading light. A pair of ravens flapped around the empty battlements. She had forgotten the ravens. Elyse, the castellan's wife, fed them scraps and they came to her like the legendary messenger birds of Odhinn. In the summer, they had seemed harbingers of doom, cawing their warning as the banner of de Fontenay lured Adelais into a trap. Now, they seemed to welcome her. One of them even swooped down to a nearby branch and looked at her, its head canted to one side, before flying off to settle nearer the walls.

But for the bird, Adelais would not have seen Elyse. She was weeding rows of winter vegetables on the south-facing slope between the curtain wall and the stream. Elyse seemed part of the earth, almost fading into it; her ankle-length kirtle, tanned skin, and even the apron at her waist were all shades of brown. Her hair, the grey-brown of a mouse, was loosely tied at her nape and tumbled down her back as naturally as a horse's tail.

Elyse bobbed in a steady, repetitive motion, scraping a hoe around the crop. When the raven landed near her she straightened, looking at it, with one hand on the small of her back, stretching away the aches of her labour. The bird bobbed its head, and Adelais had the strange notion that it and Elyse were talking to each other.

Elyse turned and stared at Adelais curiously, frowning until recognition dawned into wide-eyed disbelief. She let out the whoop of a girl twenty years younger and hitched her skirts to run until she could envelop Adelais in her arms. The little, round woman who scarcely came up to Adelais's chin had the strength to lift her from her feet. When Elyse pulled back to look at arm's length, her face had creased into the soft folds of winter-stored apples.

'Come, child.' Elyse tugged her up the path while their greetings were hardly started. 'Let's get you out of sight. Were you followed? Did anyone see you? All the world is looking for you. Such things they say you have done!'

Adelais let herself be led, saying little, relishing the sense of being known. On the road she had been a nameless boy when she could, or Perrin Wilg when a name was demanded, and suddenly she was Adelais again. Elyse banished Sennet, the smiling castellan, from the kitchen after the briefest of welcomes, and proceeded to help Adelais shed all trace of rough living. She filled a half-barrel with water warmed in the great cauldron by the fire, and peeled the stinking cote-hardie from Adelais's body as if it were the skin of an onion. Adelais squatted in the barrel, relishing the warm water and feeling like a woman again, and inhaling the aromas of heating stew while Elyse gently wiped the road from her back.

'Stand up, child, show me the place where it hit.'

Adelais stood, unashamed, and let Elyse rest her fingertips

low on her belly, just above the golden tuft of her sex. The bruising had long since faded, but Elyse had tended her in the days after the wound, and knew precisely where the damage had been.

'No wonder the Ischyrians are calling that a miracle.'

'Or witchcraft, Aunty,' she said, hoping the endearment hit the right balance of respect and affection. 'But remember I'd hung a stone there, inside a sling. It was luck. Just that.'

'Mayhap, child. But it was not your fate to die that day.' Her fingers traced the place, pushing a little harder as she watched Adelais's face for signs of pain. Adelais did not mind the probing; Elyse was a healer and knew the lore of the old gods.

'Does that hurt?'

Adelais shook her head. 'My courses are painful. Very. Otherwise all is well.'

'Have you lain with a man, since?' It was a healer's question, not intrusive.

'No.' Though she'd ached with longing at the thought of Arnaud.

'Make sure he's a gentle one, when you do.' Elyse stood back to look her up and down. 'Why, my sweeting, there's nothing of you.'

Adelais put her hand on her navel, knowing that she was lean as a she-wolf in winter. 'I have walked far, and had little coin for feasting.' In fact, she rather enjoyed being this slender; in the longer days of summer she'd walked ten leagues on a good day and still had time and energy to make camp and to hunt.

'Then let us eat. Put some flesh back on you.'

Elyse bustled away to fetch a chemise and her own feast-day kirtle, which barely reached to Adelais's shins, but fresh clothes on clean skin were luxuries Adelais had not known for moons.

'You saved me twice, Aunt Elyse. Once here, when you sang the rune songs of healing.' Adelais could still remember the soft drumbeat that willed her to live. *Úr er skýja grátr, ok skára thverrir...* *Úruz*, the legged rune of healing that could sing the strength of the auroch cattle into a sufferer.

'And the second?' Elyse struggled to button the cuffs of the chemise's too-short sleeves. She was dressing Adelais as if she were a child about to meet a lord.

'The potion you gave me, for the pain, or...' Adelais left the words unsaid. They both knew that its main purpose was to save her having to face torture. Ever. 'The guards drank it, in wine that I was about to drink.'

'It worked, did it?' Elyse's face hardened with mirthless humour. She despaired of fastening the cuff and rolled it back as if they were about to bake bread.

'You carved the *thurs* rune into its seal.' Adelais shut her eyes at the memory of that little bottle in her hands, smooth under her fingers in the moment when she'd chosen self-murder rather than a slow, agonising death. By then she'd already broken the seal, but the image of the rune had been strong in her mind.

'I sang the rune song of Thor that day.' Adelais would not have admitted that to anyone else, except Yrsa.

Elyse looked up, sharply. 'And?'

'There was a thunderstorm. The high priest of Ischyros died.' Adelais did not have the words to describe the awe of that moment. 'They were going to kill us, but the guards drank the wine and Brother Humbert and I walked free.'

'I said you had power. The threads of many fates run through you. You also carried a bind-rune *taufr* that your grandmother carved. You still have it?'

Adelais fingered the scrip hanging from her belt, and nodded. 'Though I fear Amma Yrsa is dead.' Adelais clenched her teeth, fighting back tears; this was the first time she'd said that out loud. She had to take a deep breath before she could say more. 'Will it have lost its strength?'

Elyse touched the scrip gently, as if listening with her fingers, and shook her head. 'Your amma gave it its own destiny. Why do you think she is dead?'

'She came from the Wolf People of the far north, and a wolf guided me on my way. Led me to food and water.'

Elyse frowned, listening intently. 'And?'

'Once, it came close. Its eyes were blue, like Yrsa's. Who ever heard of a blue-eyed wolf?'

Elyse breathed deeply and exhaled slowly before she answered. 'Did Yrsa ever talk to you about *fylgjur*?'

Adelais shook her head. 'Though I have heard tales.'

'Then we will talk, later. First let's eat. I will call Sennet.'

Adelais was fighting off sleep when she and Elyse were next alone, sitting at the great table in the kitchen. Adelais blinked at the steaming mug of milk in her hands. She was warm, and her belly was full of good food. She was safe. Only her need to understand the wolf kept her awake.

'How often have you seen this wolf?' Elyse asked.

'Three times. Once it stopped me running away from the sisterhouse.'

'Then your fate lay on another path. And?'

'After Brother Humbert and I escaped, a wolf seemed to call me to go north.'

'Perhaps to shelter, here.'

'And once it led me to food and water when I was starving. That's when I saw its eyes.'

'Well, my sweeting, if the wolf truly was a *fylgja*, your guardian spirit, then yes, I think your amma is dead,' Elyse began gently. 'Some say that a *fylgja* is just a spirit, appearing to our eyes in animal form, but as insubstantial as a ghost.'

Adelais shook her head, remembering the detail of the wolf's coat and the way the fur had moved. It had been real.

'Others say an ancestor can inhabit the body of a living animal. Either way, they tell of the animal showing some small trace of the dead, usually in the eyes.'

'The dead?' Adelais prompted.

'Aye, my sweeting. The Ischyrian priests talk of witches inhabiting wolves or eagles so they can roam the world far from their living bodies, but these are tales to scare folk. A *fylgja* is spirit, and its fate is to protect or guide a loved one.'

Adelais had known, in her heart. She felt no wave of new sadness, only a quiet certainty. In a way, it was comforting. Yrsa had been close to her on her journey. Perhaps she still was.

'Amma Yrsa was going to teach me rune lore.' Was it selfish to think that way? 'She so wanted me to know the ways of the old gods. She said I had power but no learning.'

Elyse nodded. 'Your power is wild, like the lightning. You don't know how to call it, nor how to use it. I told you once that you are like wildfire, a danger to good as well as bad.' Elyse's face was gentle, and soft as old leather around the eyes.

'You also once offered to teach me. Will you do that, Aunty, please?' If Yrsa was dead, who else but Elyse could give her that wisdom?

Elyse hunched a little. Caution showed in her eyes and shoulders before she spoke. 'That would take years, sweeting. You need to live with a *seidhkona* in a realm that lets her practise the mysteries.'

'But you are *seidhkona*. You asked me to come back to you.

You thought it might be your fate to pass on your learning. Perhaps just a little, enough to help me reach Vriesland?' The thought of that journey, alone and in winter, was frightening.

Elyse's jaw tightened. 'In the spring the anakritim were hunting a relic. Now you've killed their high priest and they're hunting you. There's enough gold on your head to tempt anyone. Let us ask Lady Agnès. For me, it would be a joy to have you here. But just think what it would mean to her and Lord Leandre if you were captured; the most wanted woman in Galmandie being given succour under their roof. The king would destroy them and take their lands.'

Of course. Fool that she was, on the road Adelais had savoured a vision of food and laughter, friendship and comfort. She'd built a world in her mind where she and Agnès strolled arm in arm through the grounds of a fair château; Agnès, who'd promised to teach her to read; Agnès, the jolly, hard-drinking aristocrat who'd become a true friend on the bloody flight from Villebénie. Such dreams had warmed her on cold nights and softened hunger into appetite on days when the hunting failed. Now she saw the reality.

Something must have shown in Adelais's face, and Elyse folded her into another hug. 'Hush, my sweeting! We will ask her.'

But Adelais now accepted the truth that she'd been pushing away: there could be no home for her with Agnès without risking her friend's life.

2.5 ADELAIS

After moons of sleeping on bracken, a feather bed was too soft for comfort. Adelais woke early and opened the shutters to a milky dawn. Elyse had given her the room where she'd recovered from her wound, high enough in the tower to see over the curtain wall to the woods beyond. The nearest trees were charcoal lines drawn on the mist, smudged with the cold orange of late autumn; Adelais had woken into a dream world where she need not run, need not start awake at movement in the forest. A world where she was dry and warm, where her belly still knew the weight of the last night's stew, and where logs and kindling lay ready by the still-warm ashes of a fire.

One of Elyse's ravens landed on the ledge and tilted its head, scrutinising her.

'You tried to warn me,' she whispered. Ravens had flown into her face as she and her friends rode into the courtyard below on the day they were ambushed.

The bird rapped its beak on the stone. Perhaps it simply wanted corn. What was it Elyse had said? *You hear, but you are not listening.* She had so much to learn. Runes. Portents, whether they were wolves or ravens. The bird flew when she wrapped her cloak about her shoulders and buckled the priest's sandals onto her feet.

Sennet the castellan found her standing near the ruins of the temple outside the lodge. Once there had been a village here, in the days when the lodge was a minor fortress and had a garrison. Now trees grew through disintegrating walls. And two new graves humped the ground near the ring of rubble that once would have supported the temple's dome. Adelais stood between them, at their feet, wondering if she could sense which one was Arnaud's.

'That one.' Sennet pointed. 'The other is the man who betrayed you.'

Adelais glanced at him, wishing he had let her decide and then told her if she was wrong. He was perhaps a finger shorter than her, with thinning hair and the florid complexion of one too fond of wine. His beard was amiably curly, hazel brown on his upper lip and silver elsewhere.

'Elyse bids you come and break your fast.' Sennet spread both hands across his belly as if in anticipation. His smile seemed kindly, crinkling his eyes and tufting his beard. Adelais wondered if he, too, followed the old gods. Perhaps that was why the two of them were content to live in this isolated place, far from prying eyes.

Before noon the ravens warned them of people approaching, becoming agitated and flying backwards and forwards between the gatehouse and the lodge's tower. Adelais looked up from chopping wood in the courtyard, wondering at the cause. Sennet came down the steps, fumbling as he buckled on a sword, as if this was a rare event. He muttered 'must get them gates fixed' as he passed her. The former fortress's twin doors were useless; one had been slumped against the gatehouse wall on buckled hinges for so long that weeds grew around it.

Adelais sensed that Sennet was a man who spoke often of things to do but took a while to do them. She began to back away, wondering if she should hide. Her linen cap was still drying by the kitchen range; she was visibly a yellow-haired woman in borrowed clothes.

'They're just excited.' Elyse stood at the top of the steps, flour-dusted and smiling. 'Friends are coming.'

Two men rode beneath the portcullis, one fearsome-looking, with a sword at his side and a disfiguring scar across his face, and the other a gangly youth in the spotty, thin-bearded stage of adolescence. He led a third horse, loaded with baggage, and Adelais's heart leapt to see the gelding she'd ridden across Galmandie in her escape. These men must come from Agnès. She ran to hold a bridle, smiling up at the first rider and trying not to look at his wound; the long-healed cleft ran from an empty left eye socket down across the cheek and jaw, giving him a permanent grimace.

'You must be Mistress Adelais.' There was no warmth in his greeting. 'I am Rossignol.' As he swung out of the saddle she saw a large, soft leather bag slung on his back. It made a hollow, incongruously tuneful sound against his back as he landed lightly on his feet. 'I am sent by Lady Agnès.' He did not sound as if he welcomed the task. They untacked and stabled the horses together, but Rossignol answered her questions with as few words as possible. Yes, Lady Agnès had married Lord Leandre and was now Lady de Fontenay. Yes, she was well. Yes, Lord Leandre was away with the court. And they would talk when they were all together. They carried the bags into the lodge in uneasy silence.

They met around the great table in the lodge's kitchen, where the atmosphere was much more convivial; the youth, Eloi, was Sennet and Elyse's son. Sennet poured wine like an affable innkeeper, Eloi sat by his mother, embarrassed by her affection, while Rossignol took the end of the table, his one eye staring down its length at Adelais.

'Lady Agnès sends greetings,' Rossignol began. 'She will come as soon as it is safe. She is working to create reasons for her absence but for now there are too many eyes in Fontenay.' He spoke in short, clipped tones, his words prepared and directed at Adelais. 'You are to trust only the people around this table, and Guy Carelet. I will remain here. Eloi will be a messenger between this lodge and the château. You are to avoid all other contact. Do you understand?'

Adelais nodded, sure that Agnès would have delivered that message in warmer tones.

'Lady Agnès sends you the gelding, but asks that you remain here, or nearby in the forest, until she can equip you for your onward journey. It is sent now so that you may escape swiftly if necessary.'

Adelais shivered with excitement. She and the gelding had bonded on their travels.

'If you fear you have been discovered, you are to go without waiting for farewells. At all costs you must avoid implicating the de Fontenays.'

Surely those were his words.

'Guy Carelet told Lady Agnès that you are in need of boots and clothes. Some she sends with me; she has guessed your size. Others she will order to be made. Eloi will take measurements and draw the outline of your feet on leather. And I bring a gift of my own.'

'Indeed?' Adelais inclined her head in surprise.

'When you leave here, Lady Agnès suggests you leave as a gentle: mounted, dressed as a man, with gold in your purse and a sword at your side. My gift to you is to teach you to use it.'

'I am honoured, messire...'

'Just Rossignol. I am no lord. And I suggest we start now, while Sennet, Elyse, and Eloi are reacquainting.' Adelais smiled at Elyse; she could stay, for now. She would travel onwards with warm clothes, and mounted on a horse she knew and loved.

And she would have time to learn a little more rune lore.

Rossignol carried two blunted practice swords and one chain-mail coif out into the courtyard. He also cradled two bucklers to his chest – round, slightly conical shields about the width of her forearm, both with a spike at their centre. He tossed a sword to Adelais.

'Catch, mudlark!'

The sword and scabbard smacked into Adelais's palm like a kick, but she was more angered by the insult. It dated from the battle of Pauwels, when the Galman cavalry became mired in mud before they could complete their charge. Five hundred knights were pulled from their horses and clubbed on the ground by 'a bunch of fucking mudlarks' as the Duke of Delmas had famously described them.

'In Vriesland that is a term of great respect,' Adelais told him stiffly. Vriesians who had fought that day proudly called themselves 'mudlarks'. To the Galmans, it was a generic insult for the whole Vriesian people.

Rossignol jabbed his thumb at his empty eye socket. 'A Vriesian sword did this at Vannemeer. And if you poke out the other one, I'll tan your backside, little mudlark. Not that you'll ever come close.'

So he was not without humour.

'And do you know what we Vriesians call Galman knights?' she asked him.

'Tell me.' His one-eyed smile was terrible.

'*Gykes.*'

'And what does that mean?'

'Learn Vriesian and you'll find out.' It was a term they also applied to their own Galman-speaking nobility. It had connotations of weakness or effeminacy, and was spoken with all the contempt of homespun-clad yeomen for silken courtiers.

Rossignol grinned at her without humour. Battle was already joined. 'Then listen, mudlark. If you try to fight an armed soldier on his terms you will die. *Gyke* or not, he will have training and armour. He will probably have a shield. You only have speed. So listen. What I say may save your life.' He pulled her sword from its scabbard and handed it to Adelais hilt-first, standing at her shoulder so that the blade pointed away from them both. He touched her sword's cross guard. 'This is the quillon. It protects your hand, but if your grip is close beneath it, it restricts your movement. Hold your hand lower.' He moved her hand back until the heel of her palm rested against the pommel. 'That also gives you a little extra length. You should fight with your wrist, not your shoulder.'

Adelais moved the point in circles. It took effort to move the weight of steel with the wrist alone and she could feel the pull on the muscles of her forearm.

'Looser, mudlark. Thus.' Rossignol kept his fingers over hers as he demonstrated; long fingers that made Adelais look up at their surprisingly gentle touch. She resisted flinching away at the closeness of the terrible scar across his face.

'Put on the coif.'

'These swords are blunted.'

'A blow will still knock you senseless or crush your throat. Then pick up a buckler.'

'But you aren't wearing one?'

'I told you: you won't touch me, mudlark.'

Adelais snorted as Rossignol drew a practice sword and tapped her buckler with his blade. 'What do you think the spike is for?'

'To stab your enemy?' Adelais pushed it slightly towards him.

'No. It is to trap your enemy's blade. Lunge towards me, but slowly. I will show you.'

The chain mail lay heavily on her shoulders as Rossignol crouched in a defensive posture with his blade towards her, angled slightly upwards so that the point was level with her eyes. He'd bent his body at the waist and held both arms outstretched so that his buckler was protecting his sword-hand.

Adelais thrust at Rossignol's face, expecting him to flinch away, and in a single heartbeat found her sword pinned downwards by Rossignol's buckler, useless, while the edge of his blade lay against her throat.

'I said slowly! How else will you learn? Do it again.'

Humbled, Adelais retreated and recovered her guard. She repeated the thrust, slowly this time. Rossignol pushed her sword aside with his own – 'Deflect, don't block; it takes less effort ' – and rolled his blade over hers so he could push it downwards. His buckler moved with his sword so that the spike also lay on top of her blade.

'This is called an overbind. Your sword is pinned there, useless. Your best escape is to dance backwards.'

Adelais started to move, but Rossignol twisted his sword with his wrist, flicking the blade upwards to touch her neck while his buckler still trapped her weapon.

'But the wrist and sword can move faster than the feet. One flick of the wrist and you can kill while your enemy's blade is useless.'

He released her, straightened, and tapped his blade with the edge of his buckler. 'You must aim to wound with the last handspan of the sword. Swing the tip to the skin and let the blade's weight do the work. Don't hack.'

He made her do it again. And again. And again, each time a little faster. Her wrist and forearm hurt long before Rossignol called a halt. She shook her hand, loose-fingered, trying to ease the ache.

'So what if my opponent wears mail around his neck, like this?' Adelais poked a thumb at her coif.

'You stab for the eyes, or cut for the arm or leg. When we are wearing great helms I will show you. I will teach you one trick every day that you are here, and you will practice until you do not feel the weight of that sword. Agreed, mudlark?'

'Agreed.' This might be invaluable on the road to Vriesland. '*Gyke.*'

PART THREE

THE FROST MOON

CHAPTER THREE

3.1 ADELAIS

The weather broke with the frost moon. A driving rain blew out of the north-west, cold enough to hint at sleet in the hills. It stripped the last of the leaves from the trees and scattered them in a brown pulp over the meadow. Rossignol moved her lessons from the courtyard into the lodge's hall, shoving the table to the wall to give them space. At dusk on a day when the wind rattled the shutters and sucked at the chimneys, Sennet and Rossignol sat upstairs in the hall, drinking wine, while Elyse and Adelais sat downstairs by the kitchen range with Elyse's bag of rune staves.

Agnès still had not come, and Adelais fretted almost as much as her younger self had fretted for the sight of Jan, her first love. Ridiculous, of course. Jan was a man. Adelais didn't *desire* Agnès in that way, but she longed to repeat the easy warmth of the evenings they'd talked away together in the summer, sharing a bed like sisters when they had shelter. Agnès was a different kind of loving; the loving of sparkling eyes and rich, earthy laughter. The warmth of skin on skin, of friendship without passion. No barriers between them. No secrets.

Well, one secret. One big one. Adelais followed the old

gods, not Ischyros. And there was the little matter of rune lore that Elyse was teaching her. And how would Agnès react if she knew? The law would have them both burned as witches if they were discovered.

'The stave is but a picture,' Elyse said, laying the lightning-stroke *ihwaz* rune on the table. It made a slight click against the oak.

'*Ihwaz* is the yew-rune. It is the sign of the world tree, Yggdrasil. Some say Yggdrasil is an ash, but I hold to it being a yew. Ash trees grow old and die, while yews live forever unless fate blows them a storm. Odhinn hung on Yggdrasil to learn the wisdom of the runes, so *ihwaz* is also the rune of wisdom. The yew is evergreen, so it is also the rune of life and of endurance through the trials of winter.'

Adelais picked up the rune stave. She would need such endurance if she journeyed on in this weather.

'It is also a song. *Ýr er bendr bogi...*'

'*Ok brotgjarnt járn...*' Adelais added the words for her.

'Not yet, my sweeting. You must learn the mysteries behind the runes before you sing their songs, for runes work in harmony, the way a weaver needs a blue dye and a yellow to make a green. Did Yrsa ever initiate you into the way of the old gods?'

Adelais shook her head. Her father was Ischyrian and had forbidden it.

'It is like the Ischyrian rite of naming. It simply presents you to the gods and asks their blessing. When you have learned all the runes' meanings on their own I will do this for you. Then we will progress to learning their meanings when combined.'

Adelais smiled. She liked this idea.

. . .

The sounds of a sweeter music came to them from the hall above; Rossignol, it seemed, could play the lute. And sing. *'I pledged my troth in the flower moon / two hearts now will be one full soon...'*

They both looked up, smiling. Elyse sighed. 'He were a lovely lad before the sword took his face.'

The music stopped abruptly as hooves clattered in the yard. Elyse scooped her runes into their bag and pushed them behind a loose stone in the wall. Above, the men's boots sounded on the stairs.

'The ravens?' Adelais asked. She was used to their warnings.

'They'll not be out on a night like this. Too sensible.' Elyse listened intently, then relaxed, beaming. 'Eloi.'

Adelais knew that there would be no more rune lore that day. Elyse would want to spend the evening doting on her son. It would be a time for sharing a single fire, and wine, and Rossignol's music, not rune song.

Adelais slept poorly that night, still unused to a soft bed, and impatient to see Agnès; Eloi had said that she would come on the morrow. In the morning she found it hard to concentrate during her sword lessons and by noon was pacing the hall. Elyse had almost finished adapting a padded, short-sleeved *jacquet* from old, quilted-cloth armour. It was laced tight to her body over her chest, but hung loose enough below to thicken her waist. It was similar to the gambeson she'd worn to escape from Villebénie in the spring, but Elyse had cut and sown this one to fit.

'Turn.' Elyse lifted her hand, trailing heavy-duty thread,

and made a circular motion with her needle. She eyed Adelais critically.

Adelais obeyed. Below the hips she was dressed in a cleaner, smarter version of her clothes during the months of her escape. New hose sheathed her legs. Her sling, wadded with linen, pushed a loin cloth into a modest bulge over her sex.

'Now walk. Swing your arms.'

A few strides took Adelais to the end of the hall where she turned, putting her shoulders back.

'It's indecent to see a woman like that.' Elyse said. Nonetheless she held out another gift from Agnès – a calf-length winter cote-hardie that might once have graced a merchant. Adelais pulled it over her head.

'Don't buckle the belt so tight. It still gives you too much waist. Let it hang lower. Better.'

The soldier's dagger, newly-honed, was a familiar weight on Adelais's left side. Her drawstring leather scrip, with Amma Yrsa's *taufr* talisman concealed within, hung on the right.

Elyse tugged down the cote-hardie's skirts and stepped back to admire her creation. 'You'll do. In fact you'd break a girl's heart. I still think it's shameful, though.'

'I cannot go out as a woman, Aunty. Not alone.'

'Risky for any woman, and doubly so for you.' Elyse tucked a wayward strand of Adelais's yellow hair back inside a linen cap, and pulled her hood forwards. 'Best you do not go out at all. Wait for my lady to come.'

'I am like a caged bird here, for all your care.' She wasn't ungrateful, but she longed to go beyond the lodge's walls. 'And why else would Lady Agnès have left me a horse, if not to ride out?'

'Except now, if you're captured, you'll bring down Lady Agnès and the de Fontenays,' Rossignol growled from the top of the stairs. She hadn't heard him come.

'Then come with me, Rossignol! I'm only riding to greet her

on the forest road. Not beyond the forest edge. That was her request. Please, let me fly free for a while?'

Rossignol's lopsided expression was hard to read, but Adelais sensed her disguise had his grudging approval. She saw the hesitation on their faces and bent to kiss Elyse on the cheek.

Rossignol sighed, relenting. 'I will ride ahead, and make sure the road is clear.'

Adelais was already running for the stairs. She whooped as she jumped the last four steps.

At first Adelais let her horse walk, but perhaps the little gelding thought they were heading towards Fontenay and his usual stable. Perhaps the wind through his tail made him restive; it blew her cloak forwards from her shoulders like a banner. It may just have been that Adelais's joy at being out and alone on a grassy road, and on horseback, inspired him to run; Rossignol would, after all, be somewhere ahead of them. Whichever it was, they were in full gallop with Adelais crouched over his neck and shouting her encouragement towards his ears when she rounded a corner and there was Agnès coming towards her, a hundred paces away, with Rossignol another hundred paces behind. At the sight of her Agnès spurred her own mount forwards as if they were jousting knights, and they passed with hands outstretched to touch before coming to a bounding, hard-hauling turn. Both horses curvetted with excitement, dancing side by side, before they brought them under control. Agnès's face was shining as they clasped hands.

'It is so good to see you—'

'I would have come earlier—' The words were tumbling out. They both stood in their stirrups and leaned over to kiss. When they sank back into their saddles they were laughing; at nothing, at each other, at everything.

'Where has Rossignol gone?' Adelais twisted to watch the minstrel turn his horse to retrace Agnès's path.

'He'll watch the track behind us.' Agnès was bouncing with her horse, breathless. 'Guy Carelet is back there somewhere too. Rossignol is nervous for my safety.'

Adelais pushed her hood and cap back, and shook her head, gloriously liberated, and grinned at her friend. With the lodge ahead of them and two guards behind, she could let herself feel the wind through her hair, even though it was blowing icy spatters into her face from the trees. They reached out to touch again, their fingers promising the hugs to come.

'You are flushed, *kjúkling*.' Agnès used the Vriesian endearment she'd learned from Adelais. *Chick*. Her accent was still terrible. 'The last time I saw you like that, you'd just spent a night with Arnaud.'

'You once told me that a gallop can be almost as good as a coupling.' It was strange how naturally they fell into easy intimacy, she and Agnès. Their cares were left behind them on the road, like Guy and Rossignol; there, acknowledged, but somehow less relevant than the leaf-mould smell of early winter and the thump of hooves on turf.

'Coupling? By the God, I wish!' Agnès let out a long sigh.

'De Fontenay does not please you?'

Agnès looked over her shoulder. 'Tell you later. We have so much news to tell!'

Adelais also twisted. Rossignol and Guy had closed to within a hundred paces. They too were looking behind them.

'You are watched?'

'Always, *kjúkling*. When you are a de Fontenay, everyone's eyes are upon you. Some are merely doing their duty, for there are estates to govern and in the absence of de Fontenay I must administer justice. Others have purposes I can only guess at.'

'But *followed*? Because of me?'

'Probably. There are anakritim everywhere. But I've given

them the slip today!' Agnès grinned at Adelais as if they were young girls, complicit in some petty naughtiness. 'A girl I grew up with married a minor lord near Moutâne. She is heavy with child and lacks company while her lord is away with the duke in Alympos. I've had to visit her twice so that watchers think it normal for me to spend nights away.'

'But what if someone sent for you there?'

'She would say I'd gone hunting. She believes I have taken a lover.'

'Does your friend not think ill of you? For taking a lover?' Adelais was humbled that Agnès would compromise her honour to be with her.

'It happens, though usually ladies wait until they have provided their lord with an heir or two. Lords like to see their own features on their firstborn.'

'I do not want to put you in danger.' Adelais was used to being hunted; there was no reason for Agnès to risk all.

'Nonsense. We have lots to think about. And I have a plan.'

3.2 HUMBERT

Humbert Blanc was concerned for Fulke d'Aurillac. He saw a man at war with himself, even though Fulke's bodily strength was returning after nearly a moon of good food and exercise at the commandery. His skill at arms might also come back, but never in the same form. Before the persecution d'Aurillac had been one of his most promising men-at-arms, skilled with sword, lance, and destrier. Now he could not hold a lance, and had to use a hand-and-a-half sword so he could steady the grip with his left hand.

But it was his mind that was most concerning; there was so much anger there, and at its heart was self-loathing. Humbert had seen this before, in all – *all* – of those who had survived torture. The remembered degradation, the false confessions pressed out by agony, the enduring guilt at what they saw as their own weakness. In most brothers it faded in the gentle comradeship of others who had suffered, and in pardon and understanding. Or maybe it was only buried. Time would tell. In Fulke it still raged. He was like a knight who swung his sword at shadows, fighting an enemy that only he could see.

Fulke held himself apart, even from the love of his former brethren of the Guardians. His manner pushed them away.

He was wielding that great sword now, in a practice bout with one of the brothers in the commandery's courtyard. Either side of Humbert, a ring of former Guardians formed a loose and critical boundary around the sparring men-at-arms. All were identically clad in the dark blue cloaks of their adoptive order; the chill wind hinted at snow on the high peaks. At the commandery's gate, two passing travellers had paused to watch: an itinerant mason, carrying the tools of his trade on his back, and an elderly cleric, smiling benignly beneath thin grey hair that was pressed into a halo by the blood-red cap of a pardoner. The afternoon sun was sinking, so both would probably claim a night's board and rest, as was their right.

It was an unequal fight. In battle the brother would have an easy win, but this match was to help d'Aurillac, not to humble him. Both men had been trained from childhood to fight with a single-handed sword, in chain mail and great helm, and with a heavy shield strapped to their left arm. Success demanded landing a blow around the opponent's shield hard enough to break a limb through mail, or finding the opening to punch the sword's point clear through the mail and the padded gambeson beneath. Now, with that hand-and-a-half, Fulke had a longer blade but no shield, only the smaller buckler. He'd had an armourer adjust the buckler's grip to fit so snugly to the sword's hilt that he could either wield the sword two-handed or deflect a side blow with just the buckler.

That was one weakness; a round buckler just twice the size of a spread hand could only deflect, not block a heavy blow. It was a style of fighting closer to that of a lightly armoured foot soldier, but Fulke lacked the agility it demanded. He tended to plant his injured foot in one spot and fight around it, so his attack was weak. He was a chained bear of a knight, roaring his fury but unable to run down the dogs that baited him.

The brother was leading with his shielded shoulder, making himself a walking fortress. With his skill, he'd be able sweep aside Fulke's blade with the shield and probe with his sword past that little buckler, but so far he hadn't pressed home his advantage, allowing Fulke to block his thrusts. Both men wore full suits of mail: coifs, hauberks, and chausses, but no great helms. Despite the cold, sweat glistened on their faces.

The brother briefly broke off contact to touch the soft, unarmoured inside of his gauntlet to his forehead, un-sighting himself and lifting his sword high over his head. In the moment that his opponent was blinded, d'Aurillac lunged forwards and touched his sword point to his opponent's side, just under the armpit; not enough to wound, just enough to prove that he could have killed.

The brother scowled, for this was not serious combat, this was a practice; a testing and honing of skills, warrior to warrior, brother to one who was once also a brother. In combat they'd both be wearing great helms, and you can't wipe sweat inside a great helm, you have to live with it. The watchers didn't like the strike either; their heads moved closer together, murmuring about tactics. They enjoyed a fight, these warriors without a war, and this one was starting to become personal.

In that small interaction Humbert saw the essence of the problem with Fulke: he alienated the brethren. Even Fulke's clothes set him apart; he fought in the blue surcoat of the d'Aurillacs, blue with three silver merlettes, not the simple blue hand on white of the order. He was the gaudy outsider in their midst, and now even the most forgiving of the brethren wanted to see him beaten. They made calls of encouragement as their champion half-crouched, readying himself behind his shield.

The brother's shoulders showed a new aggression as he moved on d'Aurillac, trying to close to a distance where d'Aurillac's longer blade would be a disadvantage, and it looked as if he would succeed; Fulke appeared anchored by his damaged foot.

Soon that would make him stumble, and his attacker's blade would be inside the buckler's guard. For a long moment they stared at each other, until Fulke feinted high, making his opponent lift his shield. Fulke used that moment of blindness to move his damaged left foot a whole stride backwards. He feinted again, and put his whole weight on his injured foot to step backwards with his right, breaking contact enough for him to bring a two-handed, scything swipe *under* his opponent's shield and across the shins.

There was a crack as Fulke's sword's point struck the greaves, carving deep into the hard leather. At the last instant Fulke seemed to pull the stroke, just enough to avoid breaking the leg.

Fulke stood back, resting his sword, as his opponent swore an unholy word and danced a limping circle. He came to a halt and glared at Fulke, slowly and reluctantly lifting his sword in salute, accepting defeat. In real combat, he'd now be on the ground, his leg shattered, awaiting the final blow. The watching brethren took a deep breath, all together, and began to mutter their disapproval.

'Enough!' Humbert stepped between them, placing a restraining hand on Fulke's arm. 'Before you kill each other.' He didn't like to show leadership with strangers watching, but this was going too far.

Fulke sheathed his sword, pulled off his gauntlet, and offered his hand to his opponent. 'That was too severe a blow. Will you accept my apology, brother?'

The nod was reluctant; the eyes still blazed their fury.

Humbert tugged at Fulke's arm. 'A word with you, Messire d'Aurillac.'

Fulke allowed himself to be led away, his face resigned to the rebuke that must come.

'Have you decided what you wish to do with your life, Brother Fulke?' Humbert still called Fulke 'brother', even though he'd been released from his vows. 'You sought us out, those of us who are left, and we are giving you time to recover your strength. Yet there are times when you seem to rage against our hospitality.' Humbert kept his tone mild, even though Fulke had nearly crippled one of his hosts.

'I rage against myself, Lord Brother. Sometimes that fury spills over, and I am shamed by it.'

'Let us sit.' Humbert led Fulke to a stone bench on the hillside. Generations before, a channel had been cut from a little higher up the valley to divert the stream to a garden where the brothers grew vegetables. The outfall was a peaceful place where conversations might happen amidst the music of trickling water. A leather beaker sat ready at the fountain's rim. Humbert filled it and offered it to Fulke, who drank as only a man who has fought in quilted gambeson and mail can drink.

Humbert needed to push Fulke towards a decision. No-one's hospitality can be endless, even to a former brother, and Fulke's presence was becoming unsettling. He had to go. 'I sense you are not yet ready to renew your vows,' he prompted. The only justification for living indefinitely at the commandery would be to join the order, but first, Humbert sensed, Fulke would need to be more comfortable in his own skin.

'When I made my vows as a Guardian, Lord Brother, I was filled with the joy of a holy purpose; I aspired to recover Alympos for the faith, or die in the attempt.'

Humbert remembered that zeal. He'd shared it, years ago, when many still believed they might retake the land of Salazar.

'But I fear the tormentors crushed a part of my soul, as well as my hand and foot, and they did it in the name of the faith. Now that divine fire has gone. I will not make vows in which I cannot believe.'

Humbert took back the beaker, refilled it, and sipped. The water was icy cold and carried flavours of earth and the leather's tannin, like thinned wine. He understood, only too well. He also still felt some responsibility for this man, who had once been one of his own. The habit of leadership was still there; *true* leadership, which was service to those who followed him as much as service to the God. He'd like to help Fulke find himself again and be reconciled with who he was. The silence stretched as he thought. Beyond the road, four peasants harvested a field of cabbage, plucking at the earth like pigeons. The wind blew fragments of a slow, undulating song up the hillside to the seat.

'So will you return to your lands? You are now the Seigneur d'Aurillac, are you not?'

Four boys followed the harvesters, gathering the crop into baskets and staggering with them to a cart on the road. Boys only, from a hamlet down the valley; no women or maids, for this was the land of an order where temptations of the flesh must be kept at a distance.

Where, Humbert wondered, was young Adelais at this moment?

'Not yet, Lord Brother. There is a restlessness within me...'

'There is too much anger in you, d'Aurillac. And I think you need to forgive yourself.'

'I betrayed the order, and I betrayed you.' Fulke held up his sword-hand, with the curved, rigid finger. 'Such a small part of the body, yet it can yield such pain. I lost count of the days, but there came a time when I would indeed have denied Salazar to have ended it.'

'There are others here who have suffered. No one condemns you.'

Fulke's sigh told Humbert that it was not the condemnation of others that troubled Fulke, it was an inability to pardon himself. Fulke's soul was as bare and churned as the earth behind the harvesters.

'I confessed to heresies as they required me to confess. I implicated you, Lord Brother.'

'I was fortunate to be imprisoned in Saxenheim, where they

took a less rigorous approach. And you know that, for me, there is nothing to forgive.'

Fulke tried to close his sword-hand, straining against the wrecked, rigid fingers. He winced at the pain and Humbert understood that this was a form of self-punishment, the way some clerics flailed themselves as they prayed.

'Yet my failures weigh more heavily upon me than this mail, Lord Brother.'

'Have you made your unburdening and sought pardon?'

'Pardoning is for sin, and yes, I have made my peace with Ischyros. I also need atonement for my shame, and for that no words are enough, however holy.'

'And what would bring you atonement, Brother? For I still think of you as my brother.'

'I would like to take up arms against those who brought down our order. The chancellor, de Remy. The anakritis-general, for all that he is a priest. Even King Aloys himself. I would like to find an honourable death.'

'Do not rush to die, my friend. Ischyros has a purpose for us all.'

Fulke closed his eyes, grimacing once more.

Humbert refilled the beaker and offered it to him. 'Can I trust you, my brother?'

Fulke breathed deeply before his response burst from his chest. '*No*! Never trust me, Lord Brother. I have already betrayed you, and the order, when I told them you were a heretic. I was mad with the pain...'

That vehemence convinced Humbert. 'And now you seek atonement. Would you make a journey for me, to carry words that I dare not commit to writing? I need a messenger I can trust.'

Fulke's hand shook enough to spill water into his lap. He'd have to clean and oil his hauberk against rust.

'Are you not frightened that I will betray you again, Lord Brother?'

'You have been here almost a moon, and all that time you have been free to come and go. If you were planning to betray me, the king's men would already be here.'

'I would go to the ends of the earth for you, Lord Brother.'

'Good. You know of the de Fontenays of Jourdaine? Leandre de Fontenay recently married my niece Agnès de Molinot.'

There were cries of glee from the field as a rabbit broke cover and bounded away. Humbert turned to watch as boys whirled slings, sending stones after it. He remembered Adelais's courage as she crept towards a guard above a gate, her mouth working as she whirled her sling. *One. Two. Release.*

There was a grunt of assent beside him.

'Then my request is that you ride to Château Fontenay. There is a debt I wish to repay, to a young Vriesian woman.'

When Fulke did not answer, Humbert turned to look at him. Fulke's face was folded with pain. He'd hunched over his hand, which was shaking with the effort to form a grip.

3.3 ADELAIS

'I was only trying to frighten him. Honest.' Adelais made a sweeping gesture with her goblet, spilling wine. 'Oops.' She licked it from her fingers. Agnès de Molinot, now Lady Agnès de Fontenay, watched her wide-eyed from the great bed in the lord's chamber of the hunting lodge, where she rested with her back against a bolster. Adelais stood by the fire burning in the grate, relishing its heat on the back of her legs; the room was warm enough for them to be barefoot, in undershirts.

'Then there was this great clap of thunder and the high priest went all goggle-eyed and gasping, like a stranded fish.' Tales that had been told with much flourishing of a capon's leg were being retold over wine. So why was she jesting, like it was some great adventure? Had it been coincidence, or did she really have the ability to cast death? 'Perhaps I really am a witch.'

Adelais stopped herself saying more. She couldn't tell Agnès she'd chanted rune song and, for a moment, had felt a terrible power within her.

Agnès looked sympathetic rather than alarmed. 'Just

because things happen around you doesn't make you evil. Do you know what the surviving Guardian knights are calling you?'

'The Vriesian Witch. I heard.'

'No, *kjúkling*. To those who still believe in the Guardians' innocence, you are the Lions' Claw, the one who hurled the grand master's curse in the high priest's face. The word from court is that the king is shitting himself while you are still free.'

'I like that. The weaver's daughter who makes a king *skit* in his loin cloth.' Adelais clawed her spare hand and made a pretend growl towards the bed. Behind her the fire flared with the suck of the wind, sending a wave of delicious heat under the tails of her shirt. 'The Lions' Claw. One of the Blessèd Ones.' Disbelief lightened her voice.

'And the king thinks you're the spawn of Kakos. Stay with the Blessèd. Be an angel.'

'It's no fun being an angel. No one wants to *fjakk* an angel.' Adelais closed her eyes, remembering another feather bed with Arnaud's body poised over her and his manhood reaching for her. Must be the wine. She placed her goblet on the floor with exaggerated care, and stumbled a little as she straightened. *Sætur Sif*, it was good to talk, and even better to feel safe.

'Come.' Agnès patted the bed beside her. 'Sit here before you fall over.'

'Not used to wine.' Adelais crawled up the bed on hands and knees. 'Drank from streams. Wine gone to my head. I'm staggering like a tavern harlot.' She flopped over to lie shoulder to shoulder with Agnès. Adelais let her arm fall palm-up on Agnès's thigh, asking to be held. There were spots of wine on her cuff, like blood.

'Do you still miss him?' Agnès dropped her hand onto hers.

'As the winter misses the sun.' She had not known that she could feel so fully alive until that gentle armourer unlocked wonder.

Yet there had been a deeper sadness in Agnès's voice; some

signal a friend should hear. 'Things are not well between you and Lord Leandre? He does not please you?'

'I do not think we please each other. He did not even take me to Villebénie when he went to attend upon the king.'

Adelais rolled onto her side to face Agnès. 'Oh my poor friend, I am so sorry. But you are beautiful. You are witty. You are fun to be with. How can he not love you?'

'Tell that to Leandre. It seems he prefers the company of his knights to our marriage bed.'

Adelais squeezed her hand. 'Has he ever...?'

'Lain with me? Once, yes. Enough to say our union was consummated, but it was difficult for him and it gave me no pleasure. By Salazar, I had to listen to you and Arnaud so I know what a good coupling sounds like. I think de Fontenay was almost relieved when he was called to Villebénie to discuss taxes for war.'

'There is to be war? With whom?'

'Was to be, though it seems nothing came of it. Your Duke Ragener doesn't accept King Aloys's sovereignty. The armies faced each other near a town called Baudry, wherever that is, but did not fight.'

'Oh.' Adelais was more surprised by her own ignorance than by the fact of war. All her life troubles had simmered between Vriesland and Galmandie, sometimes boiling over into battle. The people had danced in the streets when the news came of the victory at Pauwels. There was no dancing after Vannemeer.

'Apparently our army marched all the way to Baudry and came back again. There's a story going round that the Vriesians dressed a woman up as you, and had her call on Aloys to come and receive the judgement of the Guardians. Aloys turned tail and ran back to Villebénie. Some say the chancellor persuaded the king not to keep an expensive army in the field over the winter months, but the nobles think Aloys is scared.'

Adelais caught a glimpse of a wider world, beyond this shut-tered warmth; a world of kings and dukes and politics. 'Does de Fontenay know I am here?' she asked.

Agnès shook her head. 'No, and I can't tell him, in case my letter is intercepted. He seems in no hurry to return. Since the events of the spring he is out of favour with Chancellor de Remy and therefore with the king. He is staying in Villebénie, building an alliance with the king's brother, Duke Gervais of Delmas. The duke detests de Remy. *My enemy's enemy*, and all that. And while he's away I have to make all the decisions.'

Agnès sipped her wine, looking at Adelais over the rim of her goblet. 'So what do you want, *kjúkling*? What now?'

Adelais rolled onto her back, thinking. The beams above seemed to dance in the candlelight. The muffled sound of voices came through the floorboards; Guy, Rossignol, Elyse, and Sennet were also talking late into the evening in the lodge's hall below.

'What I want and what I can have are different.'

'So what do you *want*?'

'To live openly as a woman.' Adelais squirmed her back into the bolster, luxuriating in its softness. 'I'm tired of being a boy who lives in the woods. I've had enough of shitting in bushes and wiping my *rass* with dock leaves. I want to be clean.' She stared at the stubborn traces of grime under her fingernails. 'I want to wear women's clothes,' she moved her bare legs against the linen beneath them, 'and talk to people. I think that can only happen in Vriesland.'

Adelais let her dream take shape, knowing it could only ever be a dream. 'But while I'm here I'd like to walk into your hall, and be bright and witty.' She pictured a glittering hall full of knights and ladies. 'I might even flirt with your courtiers.' Adelais looked up at Agnès and fluttered her eyelashes.

'If you came to Fontenay you would soon be discovered. Hold that.' Agnès passed Adelais her own goblet of wine, and turned to kneel astride her, looking at her critically. She combed her fingers through Adelais's hair, stretched a strand to its full length, and let it drop. It had grown a little since the sisterhouse but still barely reached her shoulders. Adelais puffed a strand away from her nose and took a sip of Agnès's wine. They'd shared a cup often enough before. That was another thing she wanted. Long hair. Before she'd been sent to the sisterhouse it had fallen to her waist; her grandmother used to brush the cascade and call her *mynn litla Sif* after Sif, the golden-haired wife of Thor.

'Your hair is the problem.' Agnès sat back, her weight now resting on Adelais's thighs. Why, Adelais wondered, had the gods given such curves to Agnès, but left her with so little? Agnès reminded Adelais of ships she'd seen on the Schilde as a child, blowing in from the sea with their sails full.

Agnès took her wine, gulped, and gave it back. 'All the world seeks a tall, slender woman with blue eyes and short, yellow hair. We can dress you like a man.' Agnès bent to stretch Adelais's chemise tight against her body, shaping her, frowning. Adelais pushed her chest out and pouted, pretend-saucy, even though her own sails would be forever furled. 'But the squires all live together in a dormitory. You'd be discovered on the first night.' It was the custom to sleep naked. 'Earlier if you took a piss.'

Adelais sighed. It had been wonderful to dream, and to dream together, if only for a moment. 'Impossible, I know. It has to be Vriesland, where yellow-haired women are common and King Aloys holds little sway. But I shall miss you, Agnès.' She let one hand fall on her friend's leg.

'Take the gelding when you go. You could be in Vriesland in half a moon.'

Adelais squeezed her thanks, feeling her eyes moisten with gratitude. No words were enough. On horseback she might cover ten leagues a day even in winter. And if she was well-mounted and well-disguised, there would be no time lost avoiding people and towns.

'But I think you could stay here,' Agnès added, 'at least for the worst moons of winter.'

'But you are watched...'

'I'm watched at Fontenay. You'd be safe here. It's empty forest; the de Fontenay hunting ground. Nobody comes here, especially in winter.'

'I don't want you to risk so much for me.' Adelais heard the regret in her own voice. She was safe and warm, and there was food in her belly.

'Besides, you can't go yet. I'm having boots made to the pattern that Eloi took. And you should ride dressed as a gentle, lest anyone think you stole the horse. I will bring proper clothes. And you must have gold in your purse, for a gentle would lodge at an inn, not sleep under a hedge.'

'How can I thank you, Agnès?'

'Just by being you, and by being here for a little longer.' For a moment Adelais saw a vulnerable woman behind the noble facade. 'Actually I'm being selfish, *kjúkling*. Everyone around me has their own purpose. Money. Influence. Power. And in the absence of de Fontenay they press upon me. Your only purpose is friendship. You have no idea how refreshing that is, even if I can only risk your company for three or four nights in a moon.'

'My purpose is survival. Yours as well as mine. I would be no good friend if I caused you harm.' Yet so much of the pull to Vriesland had been a pull to Yrsa. Who but Elyse could teach her rune lore, now? Adelais wondered if she, too, was being selfish in thinking about staying.

Agnès threw herself back on the bed and took Adelais's hand.

'We'll have snow soon. The roads will be foul. But it doesn't last long in Jourdaine. Why not wait for the thaw?'

By the gods, it was tempting. 'If you're sure I'm not putting you in danger?'

'Please, *kjúkling*, for my sake. You wouldn't believe how lonely a great château can be. But with you I can laugh, I can drink as much as I want, I can be myself. Here no one judges me, no one watches me.'

Adelais stared upwards, dizzy with wine and friendship, to where the flickering firelight painted the *fehu* rune over the roof beams.

Fehu, the rune of abundance. A sign that it was time to gather the fruits of effort. A rune of endings and beginnings.

Fé er frænda róg, ok flædhar viti, ok grafseidhs gata...

Lute music floated up through the floorboards like magical sparks from the fire. Adelais's head spun as if she were swaying in a ronde. Beside her Agnès's breathing softened towards sleep.

'I'll stay,' she whispered. 'Until the thaw.'

She let the night claim her.

CHAPTER FOUR

4.1 BARTHRAM

Ghislain Barthram had a routine, when the affairs of state allowed; a daily pattern as regular as the offices of worship, and the most precious element of this pattern was to walk in his garden after the Lighting of the Lamps. The fading day made reading difficult, so it was a time to reflect on the day's successes and challenges, and plan the morrow. There was just enough space for a steady circuit on paved ground, and the repetitions were as soothing as a chant. It was the evening's balance to the morning's reflections at the dawn office. Always, now, his primary concern was the witch. In this matter the God's will, the king's will, and his own will were the same. She would be living proof of the Guardians' pact with Kakos and of the king's righteousness in bringing them down. And she might just be the key to finding the most precious relic on earth.

There had been sightings. One recent and credible, from the Jourdaine–Maycea border where a priest had been attacked for so trifling a thing as his sandals. The witch still in Galmandie, near the Naeva, and working her way north.

The fluttering of wings as a bird returned sounded like a messenger from the God. Barthram saw it peck at the one-way flap into Kasim's dovecote, and he resisted the urge to rush towards it. He knew not to scare the bird away. The birds must enter peacefully and willingly, and be rewarded with the food beyond. Only then could they be handled. Besides, such speed would be unseemly, like a child running for offered sugar. Barthram closed his eyes again, forcing himself to be still, and to keep them closed as if in prayer, even when Kasim waited beside him. His prayer for news had been answered. Now, by Tanguy, let it be *useful* news.

Barthram waited until Kasim coughed, quietly, then held out his hand for the tiny container in a way that let Kasim think he was interrupting. The wax seal was unbroken, though it would matter little if it was, since Kasim could not read. He was indeed the perfect servant: illiterate, incapable of speech, yet skilled and fully able to understand instructions.

The light was too poor and the writing too fine to read, so Barthram sent Kasim for a lantern, and in its flickering light read the simple message. *The silver birds have flown east towards Jourdaine.*

Barthram held the scrap of paper in the flame, and nodded his dismissal. So d'Aurillac had been moved on, towards Jourdaine. There was only one logical place where the witch would hide in Jourdaine – with her friend Agnès de Molinot, now Agnès de Fontenay. The search was narrowing and he would send no more of his precious birds to Arrenicia; he had enough to sustain messengers at one post, and one only, which would now be an anakritim brotherhouse near Moutâne, barely two hours' ride from Château Fontenay.

He would send the next birds there, on the saddle of another anakritis he had trained to the task; the brother would be there in eight or nine days. He would know about the blue d'Aurillac surcoat and would alert all anakritim and trusted clerics to watch also. The anakritis would leave that day. Barthram could do no more.

His more pressing problem was what to do with Humbert Blanc.

The witch could not be with him. No commandery would tolerate a woman's presence, be they Guardian or any other order, and nor would Blanc sully his hosts' welcome and his own reputation by concealing one. So they had separated. If Blanc had sent Fulke d'Aurillac to the witch, he had served his purpose and could be arrested. Indeed, if allowed to remain free, he might disappear again. It was time to bring him in, and extract what information they could.

But Blanc was protected, and the roads to the commandery watched. If enough force was sent to ensure his arrest, it would be seen and Blanc would escape. Arrenicia had only been brought within the rule of Galmandie in the reign of King Aloys, and local allegiances were unsure. There would be many lords in that vast region who would give Blanc shelter. He might never be found.

Then there were the practicalities of arrest to be considered; with the Order of Guardians gone, the only trained warriors in Galmandie who owed allegiance to the faith rather than a temporal lord were now the members of the order that was concealing him. Which meant that the local seneschal must make the arrest. This in turn required Barthram to share his knowledge with Othon de Remy, the chancellor, who alone could command the seneschals in the name of the king. If they succeeded, de Remy would try to take all the glory, but an arrest in Arrenicia could not be achieved without him.

If they needed to arrest the witch at Fontenay, they would have similar problems, for there Leandre de Fontenay himself was the seneschal.

And de Remy would have his own spies watching for Blanc and the witch. In time, they'd find Blanc, and then Barthram's chance of restoring his position with the king would be lost. Regrettably, telling de Remy was the only way. At least

Barthram did not have to share how swiftly he had the information. A messenger might have spent ten nights on the road. Longer, perhaps, from deepest Arrenicia. No one need know that he had the news in a day, tied to the back of a bird. *That* secret was safe. De Remy would surely have spies within Château Fontenay and in the area, but none so likely to succeed as d'Aurillac. De Remy would also have to wait seven or eight days for a messenger to deliver news that Barthram would have in a day. There he'd have the advantage.

But how best to take Blanc? Barthram began to pray again, seeking inspiration. As so often happened, when he opened his mind to the God, the answer came. It was so brilliantly simple that he wished he'd thought of it before.

If Blanc was protected by a clerical order, his protection must be neutralised.

And Pateras Ghislain Barthram knew exactly how to do that. This would be wonderful.

For Blanc, it would be like being smitten by Salazar Himself.

It was such a pity Barthram couldn't be there to watch.

4.2 ADELAIS

Adelais had nightmares every moon just before her courses began, whether she slept on a bracken mat or a feather bed. Gripping pains in her womb would fold her over yet would not let her wake, as if she were pinned into slumber through her belly. Each time the turmoil's beginning was the same; she saw the Nornir, three goddesses spinning the threads of fate, each thread a life, and one of those threads was being pulled from her belly. On looms of power made from warriors' bones they were weaving the blood-soaked cloth of battle, and the agony as her own life was pulled into that warp and weft was like a mighty beast's jaws sunk deep in her guts.

Her grandmother's bind-rune *taufr* dangled from her thread, dancing, and Adelais knew that if she could only reach the talisman she would be saved. Yet each time she stretched for it, it was tugged away from her faster than she could crawl, the way a child might tease a kitten by pulling a lure. She stood up, swaying, and immediately knew a different pain, the heart-sick pain of betrayal, as she saw that Agnès jerked the thread. Still she staggered forwards, pleading, until another pain stopped her as violently as a spear thrust.

Adelais looked down, newly aware of her own nakedness, to see the copper flights of a crossbow bolt protruding from her belly between her navel and her bush. Her panting gave the shaft a sick, bobbing, masculine life. Beyond it, her own life's blood streamed down her legs. In her agony she creased over it, craning her neck upwards to see who had fired that fatal shaft, and found herself staring into the skull-like face of Ghislain Barthram. He cradled an empty crossbow and watched her with those black, implacable eyes. They told her that this was only the beginning; they promised her pain to come beyond her wildest imaginings.

This moon the nightmare changed, unfolding in new ways. Now a she-wolf stood beside her, fangs bared at the Angel of Death. And with the certainty of dreams Adelais knew that Amma Yrsa was dead, and that this was indeed her *fylgja*, protecting her in spirit form. Yet Ghislain Barthram merely smiled, and waved forwards an Ischyrian priest to seize her. Worse still, the wolf backed away, head lowered, snarling, defeated, allowing the priest to reach for her in arms that were clad in the shining red silk of a diakonos.

Adelais moved to cover herself, shamed by her nakedness. Her palm brushed against her bush and her fingers felt the stickiness of blood between her legs. *This is real.* But her forearm touched no bolt above her sex. The wolf's snarling sharpened into a harsh croak, more bird than animal. *Is that real?* And her amma's *fylgja* disintegrated into a flapping burst of black wings.

Adelais lay panting in the darkness, unsure if she was awake or still dreaming. A faint dawn light outlined the shutters; a light tapping noise against them ended with a flutter and the caw of a raven. She let her head sink back into the bolster, swallowing with relief, her heart pounding. Still her eyes probed the corners of the room, half-expecting to see the white of an anakritim robe. It took courage to leave the bed, fumble her way to the window, and throw wide the shutters. Biting cold air spilt into the room and her breathing slowed as the room's shadows took empty form.

The dawn was still milky grey, dark enough for the woods to be a continuous mass rather than individual trees, and for the setting moon to glow above them in as fine a curve as a scribe might shave from a quill. It shone through thin cloud that promised rain, perhaps sleet. The black outline of a solitary raven hopped along the battlements near the gatehouse. Adelais stayed at the window, letting the cold air cleanse the memories of the night, until the stickiness on her thigh told her she needed to find a rag and dab at the first trickle of her courses.

Yet the sense of dread remained. If Agnès had been there Adelais would have woken her and shared her fears, but Agnès was back at Château Fontenay. Elyse was below with Sennet, in their room off the kitchen, but Adelais would not wake her like an infant crying for her mother. Nor could she sleep. She dressed, left the tower as quietly as she could, and stood under the arch of the gateway. The bared fangs of the portcullis, black against the lightening sky, turned the arch into a gaping mouth. The gates still hung open, weed-choked and rusted.

The portcullis heightened her sense of dread. It had been dropped to trap them on the day that Arnaud died. Adelais moved beyond, where the water meadow stretched ghost-grey towards the trees. If Amma Yrsa had been here, she'd have held her and sung rune song for protection. Adelais could picture her, shoulders wide, straight-backed, beating time in the earth with her staff. The song of *ihwaz*, perhaps; the yew-rune, the life-affirming rune of protection, a strength-giver.

Ýr er bendr bogi, ok brotgjarnt járn, or fífu fárbauti...

She had not spoken the words out loud, yet there was a shuffling of feathers from the gatehouse. A gathering of ravens. Adelais knew they were listening, but did not know how she knew.

Adelais stared at the far edge of the meadow, hoping in vain to see the shadow of a wolf. *Are you there, Amma?* Amma Yrsa would not have been content with mere protection, she'd have woven the threads of fate. The *naudhiz* rune, then. *Naudhiz*, the need-rune, the shaper of destiny.

Naudh er thýjar thrá, ok thungr kostr, ok vássamlig verk...

'You are playing with fire, child.'

Adelais turned. She had not heard Elyse arrive behind her. She'd pulled on a loose robe and had pushed her feet into house shoes as if she'd come in a hurry.

'I said nothing, Aunty.'

'Nothing a person's ear might hear, but the ravens knew.'

'I'm frightened, Aunty. I feel like a child who has woken in a great, dark hall that has been empty for generations.'

'Yet beware your power, my sweeting. You may find there are giants in that hall. Do not wake them before you know they will do your bidding.'

'Always the dreams and pains come with my courses, but this moon they are worse. Much worse. I'm grasping for runes the way a knight might reach for his sword. I crave for you to teach me more.'

'I teach what I can, while I can. But it would take years, my sweeting, and you will soon be gone.'

'But what is this fear within me? This is like my days as a captive, waiting to be tortured. There is a menace growing around me.'

Elyse put her arms around Adelais and held her close. Her hug was almost as good as Yrsa's.

'I feel it too, sweeting.' Elyse spoke into Adelais's chest. 'And I fear for you. I fear for all of us. But blundering into rune song could make it worse. Much worse.' Elyse pushed Adelais back and looked up at her. Her face was hard to read in the half-light. She sighed as if she had come to a decision.

'I think you are ready to be initiated into the ways of the gods. Mayhap it will help. It may strengthen your rune song, when you use it. Wait here. I will gather what is necessary and tell Sennet to keep Rossignol here.'

'You want to do it now?'

'The dawn is the best time. And Rossignol still sleeps.'

Elyse led Adelais along a path beside the stream, far enough from the lodge for the forest to have closed around them. She carried a sack over her shoulder and walked with a rune-carved staff that marked her as a *seidhkona*, a staff-woman of the old gods. The mere possession of that would have her burned if she was caught. She stopped where the stream looped around a small clearing, leaving a flat area of river sand at its centre. Elyse swung the sack onto a stump at the clearing's edge, pulled out a tinderbox and a handful of kindling and lit a fire. She set a pot of water in its flames.

While the water was heating Elyse used a bundle of twigs to sweep the clearing's sand until its surface was parchment-fine. When she was satisfied she stood at its centre and used her staff to inscribe a circle.

'Watch, listen, and learn, child. This will become our *vé*, our sacred place.' Elyse bent to draw eight lines radiating from the centre, and chanted in Galman as she drew, not the Old Tongue of rune song.

'Come forth, mighty Fimbultyr,
From the eight heavenly worlds.
Let Sleipnir be saddled
And bring you swiftly to us, Galdrsfadhir.'

They were just words, at first. Adelais expected to feel more magic in the moment. Elyse began to inscribe runes around the edge of the circle, three for each of the eight divisions. *Fehu, úruz, thurs, ansuz...*

Let the hooves of Hangatyr's steed strike mighty
streams of rune-strength, through staves of
mystic power...

Adelais had no hope of remembering the chant. Elyse worked steadily, with a quiet respect. When she was done, she measured a small quantity of flaky dust into the now-steaming water, stirred, and poured the concoction into an earthenware beaker. She handed it to Adelais.

'Drink.'

Adelais inhaled the steam. It smelt of mushrooms. The dust was gritty in her mouth, and she licked the residue from her lips as she finished.

'Good. Naked you came into the world, and naked you must enter the domain of the gods. Strip, girl.'

Adelais hoped the ceremony would be a short one. She was shaking with cold as she stepped into the circle, though the potion was spreading a numbness within her. The sand was icy under her backside when Elyse sat her cross-legged in the centre of the circle. The cloud had thickened and now leaked a mist of rain so fine that it settled on her skin as gently as butterflies, so cold it smelt of snow.

She did not remember the ceremony. She knew only that there had been more chanting, and rune song in the Old

Tongue. Water, too, sprinkled over her like an icy benediction. What she remembered was feeling wonderfully *aware*, with all her senses tuned. The air no longer felt cold. It was a little like the time in the stream below the waterfall; the droplets of rain falling on her knees, her hands, her breasts, her upturned face, were fragments of the great world that reached out to touch and claim her. She was one with them.

And for a moment she glimpsed a great wisdom; she knew herself to be stronger than all the armies of the world, and female in the way that the earth is female, receiving seed and nurturing all that grows and lives upon it. Yet that knowledge faded, and she sensed that such wisdom could never be grasped, only received as a gift.

Her head fell forwards. Jewels of moisture had formed on the fine hairs of her arms, as many as the stars on a shining night. They formed tiny rivulets in the creases of her hands and she moved her fingers in wonder until a single drop formed in her palm, trickled, and fell to the sand. It was all so exquisitely *pure*.

The world began to spin as if she sat motionless at the centre of a whirlpool. She lifted her eyes, expecting to see the clearing moving around her, but there was only the stream and the trees, and Elyse sitting on the stump steadily beating the ground with her staff as she chanted. Adelais felt the rhythm through her body as if the earth itself sang at a level just beyond her hearing.

And at the edge of the clearing, a great grey she-wolf grinned its approval. Adelais laughed with the joy of the moment and the certainty of her amma's presence.

She must have slept. Adelais woke with her head slumped downwards and her hands slack across her thighs. She was not thinking well; it was like the morning after too much wine, although her head did not hurt. She was cold, now, even within the fur-lined cloak that Elyse had draped around her shoulders.

Adelais knew that the fur would be cat skin in honour of Freyja, goddess of the Vanir, mistress of the runes, whose chariot was drawn by cats. Adelais tugged it closer around her as she began to shiver. At the edge of her vision Elyse swept away the last signs of her circle, waiting. Adelais straightened her back, letting out a small groan.

'It is done. You can dress. Quickly now; the world is awake. Rossignol will be waiting to teach you swordcraft. He may come looking, for all Sennet's assurances.'

Adelais stood, shivering uncontrollably as she brushed damp sand from her legs and backside. She realised she was hungry. Very hungry.

'There is bread and cheese in the sack.'

How had Elyse known?

'You sang the *lœgr* rune, Aunty.' Adelais pulled on clothes. Warmth before food.

'You know it?'

'On my journey it came to my mind when I was thirsty, and I was led to water by my amma's *fylgja*.'

Elyse nodded, apparently content. '*Lœgr* is good for developing the inner sight.'

'She was here, today, too. Whatever you gave me to drink helped me to see her.'

'And is she pleased?'

Adelais grinned through a mouthful of bread and cheese. She swallowed rapidly as Elyse folded her into a hug.

'Then welcome to the way of the gods, my sweeting. I will care for you as she would, while I can. And now we will start learning the way the runes speak to each other and change their meanings.'

4.3 TAILLEFER

Taillefer de Remy did not know why his brother had summoned him. Othon's 'invitation' was couched in terms that implied urgency, and, besides, one did not refuse the Chancellor of Galmandie, brother or not.

He had expected the meeting to be private. The sight of the anakritis-general in the chancellor's office was enough to make Taillefer stop at the threshold, consciously wiping all emotion from his face. Ghislain Barthram sat at his brother's table, watching Taillefer with the kind of unblinking stare that could unnerve even the holiest of men. Taillefer might now be a diakonos, with responsibility for a province of clerics and their temples, but, by Salazar, this man was dangerous.

'Come in, my brother!' Othon de Remy sat in a carved, throne-like chair at the head of the table, to Barthram's left. He did not rise, but sounded affable. 'If you please!' Othon waved to a lesser chair beside him, opposite the anakritis. The lack of titles or honorifics told Taillefer it was to be an informal talk, yet there could be no insignificant meetings with either of these men. Taillefer glanced round as he crossed the room, to see who else might be there, but no clerk waited in the shadows to record their words.

Taillefer sat, forcing himself to appear at ease, even though Ghislain Barthram seemed to look into him, rather than at him. Othon merely frowned, apparently gathering his thoughts, and the silence stretched uncomfortably. Beyond his brother's shoulder was a window-lit desk, covered in documents. The windows were glazed with real glass, not waxed linen, so shafts of light reached into the room as if the windows were wide open.

'You asked to see me, brother.' Taillefer was not some boy to be left to squirm.

Othon tapped the table and looked up. 'We have need of a diakonos.'

'We?' Taillefer looked between the two of them. The anakritis-general and the chancellor were not known for their closeness. In fact they fought like stags in the rut. Both competed for the king's attention, although at present Barthram's standing was reportedly low. He had, after all, lost the witch. Othon too had his problems; the king's brother the Duke of Delmas had lately accused him of taking bribes from the Vriesians in return for engineering the withdrawal from Baudry.

'You were at the King's Council in Harbin, after our return from Vriesland. You will have noted the king's obsession with the Vriesian Witch. I tell you truly, brother, that today there is no more important issue in Galmandie.' Othon rose to his feet and poured wine from a jug. 'More important even than quelling the rebellion in Vriesland.' He placed goblets in front of them and carried his own to a window. He spoke outwards, towards the Gaelle.

'The high priest's death,' Othon continued, 'was unfortu-nate, coming so soon after Grand Master Guerin cursed him and the king from the flames. The people are now watching all who were instrumental in the Guardians' demise, in particular the king, me, and Pateras Ghislain here.'

Taillefer glanced at Barthram. The man's skin was pale as pastry yet his eyebrows and close-cropped hair were black as his cloak, so his face seemed part of his anakritim robes. The pink tip of the tongue, glimpsed before he spoke, was too alive for those bloodless lips.

'I gather there are wagers in the taverns about who will be next, like a game of dice.' Barthram lifted his nose, as if to smell Taillefer's reaction.

'The curse was the deed of a man in agony.' Taillefer could not believe that the king would give credence to such tales. 'And the high priest's death was a coincidence. I'm told he was already sick.'

'Perhaps.' Othon was clearly unconvinced. 'But the king requires that the witch be caught and burned.'

'I was there, as you say.' Taillefer still didn't see where this conversation was leading. 'So what is my part in this?'

'You can help us capture the witch.' Othon turned to face him. 'I want you to expel her. And the Guardian who was with her.'

Taillefer placed his goblet on the table slowly, thinking fast. Expulsion. The most severe censure open to the faith, for it condemned a soul to the pit of Kakos for eternity. 'There is a process for expulsion. It requires a trial, with witnesses. The accused must be offered the chance to plead or confess—'

'We do not have time for a trial.' Again, the anakritis-general lifted his nose, like a sniffing rat. 'It needs to be done today.'

'Why?' That simple question was the bravest word he had ever spoken. Both the anakritis-general and the chancellor broadened and tightened their shoulders like archers drawing their bows.

Othon exhaled slowly, showing how much Taillefer was testing his patience. 'Pateras Ghislain has discovered the where-abouts of Humbert Blanc, the Guardian who was with the witch in front of the high priest. An itinerant cleric spotted him in a commandery in Arrenicia. He is protected and he would escape if we sent excessive force. However, if the expulsion also applies automatically to anyone giving succour to the witch or to Blanc, we will flush them out of hiding. Give them nowhere to hide.'

'Is the witch with him?' Taillefer played for time.

'Apparently not.' Barthram sniffed again. Did he never blink?

'Expulsion is a censure,' Taillefer prevaricated. 'A *medicinal* penalty, not a military tactic.'

'I would say it is a proper penalty. The only possible penal-ty.' Othon's voice rose. This was rare enough to be a dangerous sign, to those who knew him well. 'I wish we had thought of it before.'

'On what charge?'

'Sorcery leading to the death of the high priest of Ischyros.' Barthram sounded calmly calculating.

'Then they should be brought to trial where evidence can be presented and tested. I cannot expel on the basis of rumour. Who actually saw and heard? Who was there?'

'I was.' Ghislain Barthram's stare was hard and unblinking. 'Do you doubt my word?'

'Who else?' Taillefer's unease was growing. The anakritis-general knew the process better than anyone. He should be the last priest to break temple law. This demand stank worse than the river outside the window.

'The high priest's secretary. Soldiers. Malory d'Eivet, my own assistant. He says she offered him pardon. *A woman*. That alone is grounds for expulsion.'

'And where is this Malory d'Eivet?'

'Deep in the Black Tower where he belongs. He let them escape.'

'D'Eivet. Would he by any chance be related to *Episkopos* d'Eivet?'

'His "nephew". He may even be his son.' Barthram sneered his disapproval. 'That is why young Malory has been allowed to live.'

'And Episkopos d'Eivet is my immediate superior. I must act sensitively.' Taillefer turned to his brother. When Othon was angry his eyebrows met above his nose, and the bunching muscles in his jaw made his face even more square. 'Again, why the urgency, brother?'

'It will take seven or eight days for a messenger to reach the nearest seneschal to Blanc's hiding place in Arrenicia. The longer we delay, the more likely Blanc is to have moved on.'

Taillefer closed his eyes. He even prayed, and the answer came to him in that moment of calm. He had a way out.

'I do not have jurisdiction. Neither the crime nor the perpetrators are within my diakonerie of Harbin.'

Taillefer's eyes flew open. His brother had struck the table hard enough for a goblet to dance, slopping wine, and he found himself staring into Othon's face. He hadn't even heard him cross the room. Taillefer could smell the spices that had flavoured the chancellor's last meal above the scent of newly spilt candle wax.

'I made you, brother, and I can un-make you, before you even have time to discover that the pinnacle of power is slick with blood and shit. Just do it. Cast them out. Crush them with the full weight of Ischyros's curse. Starve them of help.'

Taillefer looked his brother in the eye and breathed deeply. 'No.' He swallowed, steeling himself against Othon's building fury. 'I will follow temple law and listen to evidence. I will talk with Pateras Malory d'Eivet before I make a decision.'

Othon de Remy leaned on his knuckles across the table from Taillefer, so close that their foreheads almost touched.

'I give you one day, brother. Then come to the right decision or, by Tanguy's bones you'll be stripped of that diakonerie before you can return to Harbin.'

4.4 ADELAIS

Adelais felt light-headed after the ceremony by the stream, as if she floated a little above the ground, dancing despite the weight of the chain-mail coif on her shoulders. She was still at one with the world, willing to like even Rossignol, who seemed keen that she should stay firmly grounded in a fighting stance.

'If you hold your sword too tightly it will restrict your move-ment. Remember you will kill with your wrist and forearm, not your shoulder.'

Adelais corrected her grip.

'And if you hold it too loosely it will be knocked from your hand.'

Fjakk him, she thought amiably.

'Put your weight on the balls of your feet and lean forwards. Sword pointing slightly upwards, like this.'

Rossignol corrected her.

'Now put your buckler out so it protects your sword-hand and forearm. Remember you want to deflect, not block. You cannot deflect if it is against your chest.'

It felt wrong to have both hands extended forwards; her

instinct was to lead with the shield arm so the sword could cut or thrust through.

'Crouch a little. Good. Now you are in the half-shield position. Your sword and buckler can work together.'

But the crouch meant her *rass* was sticking out. The skirts of a woman's kirtle were too restrictive for the footwork of a sword fight, so she wore the man's cote-hardie that Agnès had given her over her shirt. It hung below her knee but there was still a cold wind beneath when she stood like this; the dawn's icy rain had eased but the day was chill. Elyse expected snow at nightfall.

'Today, mudlark, you are going to learn about distance. "In distance" means you can wound or be wounded. You want to be *just* in distance so your blade's tip can do its work. No more.' Rossignol took up his half-shield position in front of her. 'Now come at me. Try to touch my neck with your sword.'

Adelais tried, and kept on trying. Each time he'd dance easily *out* of distance or deflect her blade. He wasn't even trying to attack her. Adelais's goodwill began to fade. She lost patience and moved closer, swinging.

And found his point prodding her breast through the cote-hardie. She backed off, wincing, pushing her arm against her chest. *That hurt.*

'Remember the hands move faster than the feet. Since you must move your feet to move into distance, it is easier to defend than to attack.'

She crouched again into half-shield, glaring at him. 'So how does a minstrel know so much about sword fighting, Sir *Gyke*?'

Rossignol shrugged without dropping his guard. 'My parents were minstrels and trained me well, but I ran away to war. I wanted to be the knight throwing coins, not the boy scrabbling for them in the rushes.' He spoke without warmth. 'All went well until a Vriesian sword took my eye at Vannemeer.

Now I don't even see the coins being thrown half the time. Try again, mudlark.'

'My brother fought at Vannemeer.' Adelais saw his eyes narrow, and took her chance to lunge forwards.

Rossignol danced sideways, evading her easily, and stamped on the back of her leg as she passed. Adelais was thrown forwards onto her knees, and a back-handed blow with the pommel of his sword between her shoulders sent her sprawling face-down in the courtyard's mud. *He always swerves left*, she realised, to stay sighted. One day she'd use that knowledge. The cold air also told her that her cote-hardie had ridden up her body. She was bringing her elbows under her when a stinging pain shot across her backside; the *fordæmdur gyke* had just struck her across her bare *rass* with the flat of his sword.

Now she was angry. Snarling, fighting-cat angry. Adelais leapt to her feet and took up her guard again, determined to wipe that lopsided smirk off his face.

'Attack when you're angry, mudlark, and you'll always lose to a calmer enemy.'

Fjakk that. He'd showed her at least one good trick. *Íss er árbörkr...* She was muttering rune song to herself as she danced into distance. Raging rune song. *Ok unnar thak... Feint. Begin the overbind*. Was she moving swiftly or had he slowed down? *Ok feigra manna fár...* He started to dance backwards, but feet move slower than hands. *Cut upwards with the wrist from the overbind*.

The last handspan of her sword thumped into his neck, just below the angle of his jaw. On the jugular vein.

Rossignol's eyes flew wide open in surprise, disbelief. Perhaps a little fear.

'Always, *gyke*? Really?' But her anger was spent in that single blow. Adelais breathed deeply, wondering what she'd done. *Ísa*, the ice-rune, to freeze the force of enemies. It had been instinctive, like a bellow from her very spirit. She swallowed, lowering her blade, newly aware of the world around her; the smell of leaf mould, the raucous calling of the ravens.

'Are you all right?' If her blade had not been blunted she'd have killed him.

Rossignol massaged his throat. 'I'll live.' He looked at her with new caution. 'You move fast when the mood takes you. Unnaturally fast.'

'Nah.' She tried to make light of the moment. 'You're getting slow with age. Shall we start again? Perhaps you'd like to find a coif?'

Rossignol nodded and turned for the lodge. 'I'll do that.' He nodded to Elyse, who watched from the top of the steps. Her ravens seemed agitated, flying in and out of the gatehouse arrow slits.

Elyse beckoned Adelais over, took her arm, and steered her into the kitchen.

'What do you think you're playing at, girl? Rune song, for Thor's sake?'

'I didn't mean to, Aunty. I just got angry.' Adelais thought for a moment. 'You *heard* it?' She'd only muttered the first line.

'The ravens did. Think, girl. Rossignol's an Ischyrian, at least in name. Do you really want him to wonder if you're a witch?'

Adelais shook her head.

'And I don't care what he said or did to make you angry. He's risking his life to help you. We all are.' Elyse gripped her shoulders, painfully. 'So whatever he does, whatever he says, you smile and say "thank you, Rossignol", and take it. Yes?'

Adelais nodded, chastened. Elyse shook her.

'You have power. It's raw. It's wild. I've just felt it. Mayhap it's stronger now you have been initiated. You're dangerous.'

4.5 TAILLEFER

It was a short walk across the bridge to the Black Tower, and Taillefer was deeply troubled. He'd never conducted an expulsion. It was a terrible step, reserved for those whose crimes were so foul that they were beyond pardon. And without pardon, that soul could not pass over the bridge of judgement into the arms of Ischyros; they were condemned to fall into the pit of Kakos and be tormented for eternity. Expulsion could only happen after a clerical court had considered all the evidence and interrogated all possible witnesses. If he conducted this act of spiritual execution without prayerful deliberation, he would risk his own passage over the bridge of judgement.

The only available witness other than Ghislain Barthram, the accuser, was Barthram's former assistant, Malory d'Eivet. Taillefer had asked a fellow priest about him before leaving the palace, and had been told he was a young man whose family connections had secured him a role alongside one of the most powerful priests in Galmandie. Yet now he lay rotting in prison. He'd never even faced trial. Something did not add up.

He had little trouble persuading the gaolers of the Black

Tower to cooperate. Taillefer was, after all, a diakonos, second only to an episkopos in the hierarchy of the faith, and he was a de Remy. The gaolers made him wait in a guardroom. 'We'll bring 'im to you, Excellency. 'Tain't fitten, down there.' Other guards stood while he waited, eyeing him with curiosity and perhaps a little resentment.

'Is there a place where I can talk to the prisoner alone? A garden, perhaps?'

The guards became contemptuous. One of them stifled a snigger. 'A garden? In 'ere?'

'You could take him to the battlements, Excellency,' said one more helpful than the rest.

Taillefer nodded, and turned to see a figure being dragged into the room from some chamber below.

Taillefer's first thought was that they carried some stinking animal, a man-sized mole, perhaps, its brown-black coat matted with filth. It hunched away from the light and held both arms across its face against the glare. After a moment Taillefer realised that coat had once been a priest's robe. The lank hair might once have curled but now resembled an abandoned bird's nest.

Taillefer waited until the man could open his eyes.

D'Eivet winced, blinked, and fell to his knees, probably seeing scarlet robes before he could focus on a face. He groped blindly in front of him as if searching for a hand to kiss, but Taillefer recoiled. Even in this poor light he could see the lice in that thatch of hair.

'I am Taillefer, diakonos of Harbin.' He used his 'clerical' voice, quiet but authoritative, to mask his revulsion. He'd never been in a prison before. He had not imagined such degradation. And this had been a *priest*.

'I am Pateras Malory d'Eivet, Excellency.' D'Eivet was still squinting, but his eyes were opening. He seemed strangely calm; a man at peace with himself and Ischyros. 'How may I be of service?'

'Let us walk together. I understand we may use the battlements.'

One guard led them up a steep spiral staircase, and another followed behind. They passed two more high-ceilinged chambers before he unlocked an arched, oak door and waved them through. Beyond, battlements spanned the gap to another conical-roofed tower. To one side a thick, mouldering rope hung between rusted iron posts as the only barrier between Taillefer and a precipitous drop into the central courtyard. Taillefer kept his hand on the castellations to his left. He'd never been comfortable with heights.

'The next door's locked, Excellency, so he can't get away from you. Knock when you wants to come back in.' The door behind them slammed.

Taillefer swallowed the urge to ask for another meeting place, and turned to look outwards, gripping both edges of an embrasure. On that side the walls dropped sheer into the Gaelle, which flowed slick and grey between the Black Tower and the royal palace. The dome of the temple pierced the stinking fog of the city's smoke, the gilded hand on its summit dull. Low, heavy cloud leaked fine but icy rain. Only the southwest horizon was clear; there the breeze came clean across the sodden meadows beyond the city. It was strangely calm at this height; in the streets below the noises were immediate, all-encompassing, but up here the clamour blended into a continuous sound, like a distant, mighty waterfall.

'God bless you, Excellency!' Malory d'Eivet had stepped into the next embrasure and stood tall, an insanely happy smile splitting his face. The wind pushed his hair and beard back from his face so that he looked like a wall painting of an early disciple, or even Salazar Himself. 'Whatever your purpose, you have begun with a gift more precious than you can know!'

'I am making enquiries...' Taillefer looked down, and regretted it. A small boat was spinning in the current below the Great Bridge, and a wave of dizziness pulled Taillefer outwards, towards the void. He straightened, swallowing. 'I am making enquiries about Adelais de Vries, also known as the Vriesian Witch, and about Humbert Blanc, the Guardian who accompanied her.'

Malory turned to him. 'On behalf of your brother, Excellency? You are a de Remy, no?'

The challenge, from an imprisoned priest to a diakonos, was unexpected. And irritating.

'On my own behalf. I seek the truth.'

'But the truth is what your brother decides it to be. Him and the anakritis-general.'

'The Vriesian woman and Blanc stand accused of sins that merit expulsion. I want facts.'

'Accused by your brother and Ghislain Barthram, no doubt. With respect, Excellency, I served Pateras Ghislain long enough to realise that he and your brother are the most evil men I know. I am justly punished for the sins I committed on their behalf. I helped them find all the facts they needed.'

Taillefer struck the parapet in his anger. He'd planned to interrogate this priest, not listen to him insult his brother.

'The anakritis-general says that you let the Vriesian Witch and Humbert Blanc escape from Roquenoir.'

'I could not prevent it.' Malory d'Eivet smiled into the breeze, humble but impenitent. Taillefer began to believe that d'Eivet would keep that inner certainty even if the flames awaited him. 'There was a miracle.' Taillefer's question seemed to have touched some cornerstone of d'Eivet's faith.

Taillefer would not react. The best way to draw out information, he had discovered, was not to confront. 'Why don't you start at the beginning. Assume I know nothing. There was a miracle, you say?'

'Two. One when I saw her hit in the belly with a crossbow bolt, Excellency. It was a mortal wound.' Malory d'Eivet' eyes were watering, whether with the breeze or deep emotion Taillefer could not tell. 'Yet I saw her stand, with blood streaming down her legs, and rip the bolt from her own body. Afterwards there was no wound, only bruising.'

D'Eivet's teeth seemed very white within the dirt. His face shone with wonder at the memory; he spoke the truth as he saw it.

'You saw her body?'

Malory shook his head. 'She was examined by the high priest's own physician, Almundo Torrigiani, at Roquenoir. There was the cut of the bolt through all layers of her clothing, which was saturated with her blood, but there was no wound. He could not explain it.'

'And yet this worker of miracles cursed the high priest.'

Another shake of the head. 'She did not curse him, Excellency, though the anakritis-general wants me to say she did. The Guardian, Humbert Blanc, reminded His Holiness of the grand master's curse, that His Holiness and the king must soon meet him before Ischyros on the bridge of judgement to answer for their crimes. No, Adelais de Vries simply quoted from the Vision of Salazar.'

'She *what?*' Taillefer had not heard that version of the story.

'She said she was one of the Blessèd, and that the shades of all the Guardians would block His Holiness's passage over the bridge. Then she quoted from the Vision: "you fool! Your greed is pointless, for this very day your soul is demanded. And all the gold on Earth will not buy you passage over the bridge." Then there was a thunderbolt, and the high priest died. At that moment.'

'Tanguy's bones!' Taillefer turned within the embrasure, wedging his back against its wall. Malory also turned, now facing him, their roles strangely reversed; now it was the accused priest who had the authority. He smiled benignly, as if his filth was holier than Taillefer's scarlet robe.

'So you let them go.'

'Not then, Excellency. The anakritis-general was preparing to torture them. He believes they stole a holy relic from the Guardians' temple. When His Holiness asked the woman how she could live after a bolt to the belly, the Guardian answered for her, saying she had touched the Hand of Salazar.'

'And what do you believe, Pateras Malory?'

Malory sighed. 'If she was of this earth, she had the protection of Ischyros.'

'*If*? What alternative do you offer?'

'I have had much time to consider, Excellency. She may have had a holy relic about her of such power that she could work miracles, yet she had been searched. She had nothing but her clothes, and if she did not carry a holy relic then she was indeed an angel, one of the Blessèd Ones, sent by Ischyros.'

'And which of those possibilities do you believe?'

'That she was sent by Ischyros. Remember, Excellency, I was at the pyre when Guerin and Cheyne were executed. Just there, on the Isle of Dogs.' He pointed to where the long river-island of old Villebénie tapered into a cluster of islets as the Gaelle flowed on towards the sea. From this height they could see a scorched circle at the centre of the largest of them, only partly recolonised by weeds. No floods had yet swept away the last traces of ash. 'I heard the grand master's curse. And in Roquenoir I not only saw that curse fulfilled, but I saw the temple struck by lightning where the high priest lay, and I stood helpless outside when none could reach him for the heat, until his body was consumed. A curse from the flames, fulfilled in flames.'

Taillefer lifted one hand away from the stone long enough to make the sign of the God. He was beginning to understand the vital importance of finding the witch, if witch she was. So much better to have a sorceress they could burn, if they caught her, than to fuel the rumours that their own high priest had been struck down by the hand of Ischyros.

'You said there were two miracles.'

'Adelais and the Guardian walked free from their cells without my help. They came calmly towards me through the smoke, and she spoke with authority. In that moment I knew that if such divine vengeance was visited upon the high priest, I must share his guilt for I had helped the anakritis-general send many Guardians to their deaths.'

'So you let them go.' Taillefer realised he was repeating himself.

'She had survived a mortal wound, and lived. Then she walked out of that prison, leaving her guards sleeping, as the Blessèd Salazar walked to freedom from the Saradim. Miracle upon miracle. And she unburdened me. She put her hands upon my head, marked me with the sacred ash, and pardoned me.'

'She feigned the sacrament of pardon? A *woman?*' That alone was grounds for expulsion.

'Yes, Excellency, and although she could never be a priest, it felt a holy moment. I felt so truly blessed that I could no more have stopped her leaving than I could have extinguished the fires that were consuming the high priest's body.'

'Did Blanc object? Try to stop the unburdening?' A Guardian should have known.

'No, Excellency. Like me, he saw her holiness.'

Taillefer was silent, staring at a trading vessel working its way slowly upstream; dull ochre sails bellying above small flashes of silver where its oars pulled against the current. He could see now why this priest had never faced a trial.

'You understand that your life is in danger, d'Eivet? I think only your family connections have kept you alive. But the anakritis-general will lock you away until the end of your days rather than let these stories spread.'

'I would see that as a just punishment for my sins, Excellency. And I minister to a small following here in the Black Tower, most of whom are here with much less justification. There is a boy from Arrenicia in my cell whose only crime, as far as I can tell, is to be brother to a Guardian. Perhaps it is the will of Ischyros that I bring comfort to such as he.'

'A just punishment for what sins, Pateras? Why is your need for atonement so great?'

'In my two years with the anakritis-general I helped to inflict pain, Excellency. Terrible pain. Most men would say anything, confess to any lie to end the torture. Others bore it with such courage that I truly believe they were innocent and that the Blessèd Salazar gave them the strength to resist. Adelais de Vries showed me that my work had been to turn lies into truth and to cripple the innocent, and for that I need atonement.'

'There is unburdening, and pardon.'

Malory let out a short, sardonic laugh. 'Oh, we absolved ourselves, we anakritim. Every time we went beyond the prescribed limits, every time a man died, we would unburden to each other. But what value is pardon if it is handed out like a mug of ale after a thirsty day's work? What value if there was no repentance after, only knowledge that the sin will be repeated on the morrow? But this Adelais, the one they call the Vriesian Witch, she saw my remorse and gave me true pardon.'

'Do you not think you committed a sin in letting her and the Guardian go?'

'No, Excellency. I prevented a greater one.'

Taillefer was silent for perhaps five sweeps of the trading vessel's oars. It pulled forwards and slid backwards in the current like the insects he saw crawling on the surface of ponds. One thing was sure: Malory d'Eivet believed his own story.

'If we catch this woman, justice will take its course.' Taillefer saw the absolute necessity of what would happen. 'We cannot have stories circulating about her being an agent of divine retribution.'

'But, Excellency, what if the woman was the instrument of Ischyros, the Lions' Claw, as they are calling her?'

'Then she is assured of her passage over the bridge of judgement, and we will let Ischyros reclaim his own. Can you not see, you fool, the consequences of people thinking that Ischyros struck down his own high priest? The authority of every priest and every diakonos would suffer. The faith would be wounded at its heart.'

'I understand, Excellency, but I know what I saw and heard.'

Taillefer de Remy breathed deeply, exasperated by the priest's stubbornness. This fool was filled with sublime confidence. Taillefer's own, terrible fear was that he believed him. He pushed that thought aside and edged back towards the door.

'I will leave money with the guards for food for you.' Taillefer hammered on the door with his fist, and turned to look at d'Eivet. 'We will catch her, Pateras. My brother the chancellor has eyes everywhere, even as many as the anakritim, so if she moves in Galmandie we will know. Be she Blessèd One or witch, she will then be tried and burned for sorcery, and all those who have helped her will suffer with her.'

As Taillefer stepped through the door into the tower he knew he crossed another threshold. Behind him lay pure, awkward, inconvenient truth. Holiness, in a way. Ahead, as he descended the stairs, was the stinking reality of the need to protect the faith. He had even been granted the perfect excuse. Unburdening was a power reserved to the priesthood. Anyone who pretended to offer such a sacrament, especially a woman, committed a sin that merited expulsion. So did anyone who facilitated such a sin, such as the Guardian Humbert Blanc.

When the expulsion was proclaimed every hand in Ischyrendom would be turned against them. No succour, no conversation, no refuge. Their end would be inevitable. So why was his conscience not clear? Yet every step downwards led his soul deeper into the stink.

4.6 ADELAIS

Adelais sighed with pleasure as Elyse massaged the aching muscles of her forearm. They sat across a corner of the lodge's kitchen table, sleeves rolled back, and an earthenware dish of fragrant oil between them.

'So when have you used rune song before?' Elyse's question brought Adelais back to the moment.

'I didn't really use it today, Aunty. I just got angry. It was like swearing.' And swearing so quietly that even Rossignol would not have heard.

'You swore the rune song of *ísa* and Rossignol slowed, just enough. You swore with enough power to put the ravens into a flap. So when have you used rune lore before?'

'Before the high priest. You know about that.'

'And?'

'Once while we were escaping and the king's men caught up with us. I sang *tiwaz* as we fought.' Adelais didn't want to think about rune lore. She was tired. She'd rather be in the hall above, listening to Rossignol play his lute.

'Did you win?'

'At a cost. Two Guardians died.'

'*Tiwaz* is the rune of sacrificial victory.' Elyse's thumbs pushed into Adelais's knotted muscles as if she was kneading dough. 'But each time you sang rune song with passion.'

'What do you mean, Aunty?'

'It is not enough just to say or sing the words. Runes take power from the singer, so it is the intent or the passion you put behind them that gives runes their power. Anger. Love. Need. That is why you are tired.'

'I thought it was all that time learning swordcraft with Rossignol.'

'That as well. But if you're unleashing rune magic without intent, just because you're angry, then I must teach you more, and quickly.' Elyse rose and wiped the oil from her fingers.

'Why does it happen, Aunty? If I can do this, why can't anyone?'

'In short, I don't know, my sweeting. I have twice your years, and many times the knowledge, but I could not do what you did this morning. Mayhap our little ceremony made the gods more aware of you, but there is something else. Who can tell why one horse is faster than another? A lot is in the blood and breeding. Some is in the training. And some is just fate. The Ischyrians would call it luck, but true luck, what your grandmother would call *harmingja*, is more than an accident. It is like a being from the realm of spirits that comes to us when the gods play in our world.'

'So I'm just lucky.' *Or unlucky*.

'It is your fate. It is your destiny, woven by the Nornir. One day, if we are truly alone, I shall cast the runes for you. That may tell you why you have this gift – or this curse.' Elyse pulled her bag of rune staves from behind the loose stone in the wall and dropped it on the table. 'Runes,' she said, 'are much more than the carved symbol that we call the stave. They are stave, song, and mystery.' She reached into the bag and drew out a thin square of wood about the size of a thumbnail. A rune had been carved into one surface and stained with blood or ochre.

'*Bjarkan*,' she said, looking at it. 'To an Ischyrian, it looks like their letter B, and to them that's all it could ever be. A sound – *beh* – and part of a word. To us it is the rune of the birch goddess, and alone it tells you as little of the earth mother as a fallen leaf would tell you of the tree. If it has been carved, *risted*, with the proper respect and intent, it may whisper to you of the song of the wind through its leaves and how it is one with all that is. This scrap of wood,' Elyse lifted it towards Adelais, 'is but a doorway to the great mystery beyond, for *bjarkan* is the rune of becoming, of renewal, and of rebirth. It is a rune of womanhood, motherhood, and sometimes fertility. It is a caring rune, a rune of unconditional love and of healing.'

Adelais picked up the stave, wondering at the wealth of meaning behind that simple symbol. 'It speaks of your care, Aunty. But when you cast the runes how do you know which of all the possible meanings is right?'

Elyse offered Adelais the bag. 'Because all life is connected and no rune exists on its own. Choose one. Now you can begin to learn how they work together.'

Adelais rummaged and picked out *hagalaz*.

Elyse sighed. 'Not so good. *Hagalaz* is followed by *naudhiz* and *isa*, the three runes that tell us of the Nornir who weave all fates. It warns of terrible change, as unavoidable as the storm.'

Adelais looked up, fearful, but Elyse laid a comforting hand on her arm. 'We are not casting the runes. If we were, *bjarkan* followed by *hagalaz* might indicate the end of a time of safety, but sometimes adversity comes so that good may follow. Without winter there is no spring. This is the craft of the *spakona*, the prophecy-woman, to interpret the runes and know what is fated.'

'Amma Yrsa said all runes are mere glimpses of a great song of life.'

'She spoke well. It is the gift and skill of the *seidhkona* to shape the song itself, and so to influence our fates.' She tipped more runes onto the table and chose one.

'Thus they forge *tiwaz* into the blades of warriors' swords that they might have victory. Never favoured that idea, myself. Much too wide an intent. But a well-risted bind-rune, though, is personal.'

'Like my *taufr*.'

'Exactly so. It is as targeted as an arrow, and so may fulfil its destiny.' Elyse reached for another.

'*Ansuz*, the god-rune, the rune of Odhinn, is powerful in bind-runes. On its own it means many things, but most of all it stands for wisdom. It is most powerful when laid upon other runes, as a king must rule through his lords. Your *taufr* defends you like a knight's shield, but bind-runes can also wield power like a knight's sword. Then it is called a *nidhstick*, and properly risted they can hurl death.

'This is what you are starting to learn, child. Today you only know the runes like single trees, standing alone in the meadow. You know some of their songs and can work simple magic; if you have the power, slowing a man's arm is as easy as making one leaf fall, but it is visible. It will get you killed, and us with you. You must learn not just one tree but the forest, and the streams, and the hills, and the beasts that live in it; all their songs until you can walk among them and sing with them. It is the work of a lifetime. And in Galmandie you must do it quietly.'

'I'm sorry, Aunty.' Adelais looked down at her hands. 'I meant no harm.'

'I know you didn't, my sweeting. But now you know why you're dangerous. With the right training I think you could not only take a leaf off that tree but fell the whole tree, if you were angry enough.'

Adelais idly picked another rune from the table, and turned it face upwards. *Ihwaz.*

She slid it next to *hagalaz*, thinking about what Elyse had said. It was all too complicated. Anger. Passion. Intent. Rune song. The infinite combinations of runes. She picked another, *odhala*, and began to make a pattern with them on the table.

'Stop.' Elyse put her hand over Adelais's. She was staring at the pattern of runes in front of Adelais: *ansuz, ihwaz, odhala,* and *hagalaz*. 'Did your grandmother ever talk to you about the prophecy of the *örlaga vefari*, the weaver of fates?'

Adelais let out a small, humourless laugh. 'I heard of it. I thought it was just a Vriesian thing, cooked up to give everyone hope after the conquest.'

'It's important here, too, among those few of us left who follow the old gods. It holds us together when things are bad, like when my sister died. Her gift was healing. She saved the life of a child and the anakritim burned her for it. She called out to me as she was led away, "one shall come".'

'... born of wolf-kind and of mud,' Adelais added. 'I know it.'

'Who shall roll back the borders of the hungry god.' Elyse finished. 'One who can change the fate of nations.'

'I'm sorry for your sister. But you really think this fate-weaver might be me?' Adelais snorted. 'A weaver's daughter, stuck in a forest two hundred leagues from Vriesland?'

Elyse pointed to the runes. '*Ansuz*, the god-rune. The rune to rule all others. *Hagalaz*, the storm. *Odhala*, for justice and ancestral right. And *ihwaz*. Now that is a strange one. Like *hagalaz*, it means change. New worlds, new ways of living. Even death. That is a powerful combination.'

'I thought we weren't casting the runes.'

'They have a way of speaking, even when we do not ask.'

'So do they say I am the fate-weaver?'

Elyse looked up and made a small shrug. 'You killed the high priest. It's not a bad start, sweeting.'

CHAPTER FIVE

5.1 ADELAIS

When Adelais was a child, before Vriesland was conquered, Yul – the shortest day of the year – was a time of great feasting. Yrsa said the festival was named for Jölnir, one of the names of Odhinn, and on this longest of nights the god was said to ride throughout this world bringing blessings for the year to come. It was the custom for children to hang wreaths of hay on their outer doors for Sleipnir, his eight-legged horse, and to look for a small gift in return; a doll, perhaps, mother-stitched, or a wooden sword, father-carved.

People celebrated the turning of the year even in Galmandie, though it was frowned upon by the Ischyrian faith. Each year the innocent giving of gifts breathed new life into a heathen festival the anakritim had failed to ban. The name 'Yul' was proscribed, though there was a new movement to hold a 'festival of lights' to symbolise the enlightenment that Salazar had brought into the world. The most devout Ischyrians considered it a mark of piety not to feast at all.

Elyse and Sennet would feast; Sennet had brought down a deer with his longbow a few days before. He said Lord Leandre would not object. For Adelais the greatest gift was not the venison but the return of Agnès. For Elyse and Sennet, the joy came in the form of their son Eloi, proudly escorting his chatelaine for the first time and wearing a sword on his hip that, like Adelais, he was still learning to use.

Agnès brought gifts loaded onto a packhorse: fine belt knives for the men, a winter kirtle for Elyse, and for Adelais fine leather boots made to her measure. There was even a cap that could have graced a lord's head; it covered all her hair and hung low on one side in the very latest fashion. When Adelais travelled on, it would be as a gentle. She paraded for them, in her man's cote-hardie, strutting the hall with her nose in the air as if she were a *gyke* noble at Duke Ragener's court, and amidst the laughter Agnès insisted she wear her gifts for the feast.

In the informality of the hunting lodge they all ate at the same table: Elyse and Sennet, Adelais and Agnès, Rossignol and the boy Eloi, though the feast began awkwardly. Elyse was diffident in the presence of her chatelaine and would rush to fetch new delicacies for the table, calling Eloi to help, both of them flustered in their eagerness to please. Sennet hardly spoke, except to offer ever more wine, and Rossignol sat at a slight, self-imposed distance where the shadows hid the disfigured side of his face. He too said little, but would turn his whole head when a horse whickered in the stable. He drank sparingly, and watched Adelais in her finery as if she were a traveller from a distant land whose manners and language he could not fathom.

Adelais felt resplendent, stretching her leg beside the bench as a man might, if only to admire the way her new leather boots folded at the ankle and lay soft to her calves. Agnès followed Adelais's eyes and smiled with the joy of giving, her eyes shining green and bright above wine-flushed cheeks.

The mood eased when Agnès slapped the table and called for music, for Rossignol could truly sing. He swung his lute onto his lap, tuned it, and began a gentle, sweet melody of love, his voice as smooth as buttermilk on a summer's day. Adelais rested her chin on her palm, entranced by the way his fingers danced over the strings, long and sensuous. Their agility seemed to give them a life of their own; press, caress, a gentle shake, jump away. His eye, half-hooded, seemed focused on some point beyond the wall, and all the while a voice to make a woman melt soared around them. When he finished, no one seemed willing to break the silence. Rossignol placed the lute carefully on the table, a hollow resonance that sounded clumsy after the beauty that had gone before. He caught Adelais's look and his own hardened until she dropped her gaze.

'Perhaps that was too sad.' Rossignol's tone was gentler than his look, embracing the wider group. He turned his head to address Agnès. *Such a pity about his face.* 'I believe a vielle and drums are kept here at the lodge. Would my lady care for dancing?'

Yes, Lady Agnès would very much care for dancing. They would all dance! Sennet excused himself by finding a wooden flute, though the results were more of a distraction than an accompaniment to Rossignol's voice. Elyse found a flat, shield-like drum and a curved stick with which to beat it, and Rossignol tuned an old vielle, an oval-bowled instrument, flatter than the lute, which he lay in the crook of his arm while he played its strings with a curved bow. Eloi preferred to watch.

Which left Adelais and Agnès, who was determined to teach Adelais the steps of a courtly dance. They stood side by side, one hand on each other's shoulder, laughing at their mistakes.

'No! One step, slide, pause... then stamp!' The dance made Agnès's hair bounce, dark and lustrous within its golden net.

Adelais stumbled.

'Look up, girl.' Agnès's accent was imperative, as noble as her gown. 'Put your shoulders back. Imagine you are displaying to your lover!' Agnès locked eyes with Adelais and demonstrated, her posture proud, her lips slightly parted, her smile provocative; with the next slide-and-stamp she might almost have been flirting.

Yet around them the drum pounded the beat and the music grew louder, encouraging them, troupe and audience in one. Rossignol nodded with the tempo and did not even look up from his vielle when a horse nickered from the stables. His head had turned a little towards the dancers until the edge of the scar was visible, looking more like a shadow than a disfiguring pit in the fading afternoon light. Adelais faltered at a moment of déjà vu; a memory of a man winking at her while she danced with Agnès. Or was it Humbert? And hadn't the anakritis-general been there?

She must have stood on the hem of Agnès's gown. Agnès squealed and tumbled, pulling Adelais with her. They lay together in a laughing heap on the floor, and the music unravelled like Adelais's memory.

'By all that's sacred, Agnès,' Adelais pushed her new cap out of her eye, 'if you took me to Fontenay I'd have your court at my feet!'

Agnès was still laughing 'Adelais my dear, you wouldn't have to trip them to achieve that.'

The creak on the stairs might have been as loud as a falling tree. Rossignol had drawn his sword before Adelais had spun onto her feet, groping for her belt knife, and for a heart-stopping moment the only sound was the vielle rolling in the rushes. Elyse slowly lowered her drum to the table as a man-at-arms climbed steadily into view. From the guardroom below came the voice of Guy Carelet, calling as he ran in from the stables. *'Wait, messire, I will announce you!'*

But the man-at-arms kept climbing, one step at a time as if a leg pained him. He paused at the top of the steps, lifting his hands from their sides to show they were empty of weapons, though a long-bladed, long-handled sword hung at his side. He wore no armour, but a dirty blue surcoat emblazoned with three silver birds proclaimed his rank. His boots were caked with the mud of a long journey.

'I must apologise for disturbing your festivities.' His voice was old and tired, though he could have lived little more than thirty summers. 'I seek the Lady Agnès de Fontenay. I am sent by Lord Brother Humbert Blanc and my name is Fulke, Seigneur d'Aurillac.'

5.2 BARTHRAM

Pateras Ghislain Barthram knew that Humbert Blanc's arrest would be soon, probably within two days.

But not today, so he need not show weakness by asking Kasim if there was a bird from Arrenicia. He'd have known, anyway, for Kasim would have sought him out, smiling wordlessly, bobbing his head to show there was news.

Reliable news from Jourdaine was still slow, though not for much longer. Soon the cages with his first birds would be there, with a brother trained to use them. Now d'Aurillac had been sent there, he was even more sure that the witch was in Jourdaine. All paths were pointing towards Fontenay.

The witch had shown herself to be resourceful. Kakos himself must be helping her to escape. She was probably living off the land, or was using her dark powers to hide in plain sight. Either way, he saw little benefit in announcing her expulsion throughout Jourdaine; if she was hiding, she'd stay hidden, and if she was with people who did not know her as the witch, it would have no effect. Better by far to wait until he had certain knowledge of her hiding place before he announced it, and then to make sure the net was ready when she ran.

When she did, no hand would help her, not even her friend Lady Agnès. She'd be in the open, and alone.

And he'd be waiting.

He liked this strategy. He could have been a war leader and commanded armies if he hadn't been called to be a man of the God.

5.3 ADELAIS

'Out! All of you!' Lady Agnès de Fontenay was white-faced
with fury. She had climbed to her feet and stood very straight
with her shoulders spread and her fists clenched at her sides as
if she were about to fight anyone who dared challenge her. The
look she gave Guy Carelet, who'd come clattering up the stairs
after the intruder, might have turned him to stone. 'The
seigneur and I will talk alone.'

Adelais glanced back as they filed down the stairs. She'd
never seen Agnès like this; the laughing, bright-eyed confidante
was now a wronged queen, authority personified, and not even
Adelais would have braved that anger with speech. In the
guardroom below they formed a loose, silent group that did not
include Guy. They simply glowered at him and waited for him
to speak.

'He comes from Humbert Blanc,' Guy pleaded, his eyes
darting between each of them.

'And you took it upon yourself to bring him here.' Adelais
was angrier for Agnès than for herself.

'Look, he knows things. He asked for me by name. He

knows I'm the son of Carel de Tour, the Guardian sergeant,' Guy whined.

'So do the anakritis-general and Othon de Remy.' Adelais wanted to kick him.

'They don't know I held the horses during the ambush in the forest. He does.' Guy's shoulders hunched defensively. 'They don't know I killed the Cheyne steward. He does. He knows enough to hang me. If he served the king, he'd have had a troop of soldiers with him when he arrived at Château Fontenay.'

'Were you followed?' Rossignol asked.

'Course not. I brought him because he needed to talk to Lady Agnès quiet-like, away from the château.' Guy glared at them, aggressive now. 'He's got a message for Adelais, too.'

'Which is?'

'By Tanguy's bones, how would I know?' Guy paused. 'He made me bring Brother Humbert's destrier and sword.'

Adelais grabbed her cloak and stood at the door. Outside the sky was fading towards dusk, and a fine mizzle that threatened sleet was falling. Over in the stables Allier turned his head and whickered to her. Maybe the knight had been sent to take him back to Humbert. She'd be excited to have his news if it weren't for the danger that might come with the messenger. Behind her Rossignol was taking charge as naturally as a warrior straps on a helmet.

'Carelet, I'd lay my lute to a child's whistle that you'll be leaving de Fontenay's service,' Rossignol said quietly. 'But until Lady Agnès says we can trust him, we will prepare for the worst. Take the saddles off every horse, if you have not already done so. We must ensure he cannot escape in a hurry. Sennet, bring out what weapons you have. Let us be armed, for there may be murder today.' He spoke with the quiet confidence of one used to command. The way he turned his head to look at

Adelais made him look like a one-eyed eagle. 'Come, *mudlark*, help me shut the gates.'

Adelais bristled but followed him. He walked beyond the gates, scanning the road beyond the stream for any sign of waiting enemies. The light was fading and the rain was misting the trees, but they could see no movement and hear nothing beyond the burble of the stream over the ford. Adelais stood on Rossignol's blinded side, watching him without the embarrassment of discovery. He stood a head taller than her, with light-brown hair that had begun to grey around the edges of his scar, but only there, like a splash of limewash along his temple.

'Let's try those gates.' Rossignol led the way back to the courtyard. They heaved at one of the great gates, but the hinges had rusted solid and it would not move, even with both of them putting their backs to it and kicking against the gatehouse wall.

'It must be years since this place was used as a stronghold.' Rossignol gave up.

'The portcullis works.' As she knew to her cost. She'd been trapped by it in the spring.

'First let us ask Lady Agnès whether she wants to use it. If the mechanism is as ill-kept as the gate, we'll be stuck inside and have to climb over the walls on ropes. I suggest you sit in the guardroom and pray that you don't have to test your new swordcraft on a knight. I'll stay here and watch, in case they were followed.'

The knight remained closeted with Lady Agnès until nightfall, when Rossignol's cloaked form had blended with the outline of the gatehouse. Sennet, Adelais, and Elyse sat in the guardroom with weapons close to hand. Guy sat apart, round-backed, sullen.

They stood when Agnès appeared on the stairs, alone. She seemed calmer but nodded approvingly at the weapons.

'He carries tokens that can only have come from Humbert

Blanc. I believe we can rest easy, but I would like to keep a guard through the night.' She looked at Guy, and her jaw tightened. 'We will speak later, you and I. Messire Fulke tells me you brought the Lord Brother's sword from the château's armoury. Bring it to me.'

There was a difficult silence as Guy ran to do her bidding.

'Will he be staying, my lady?' Elyse asked.

'Certainly for tonight. Make up a mattress where Rossignol can watch him.' She took Humbert Blanc's sheathed sword from Guy and turned back into the donjon. 'Adelais, come. Just you.'

On the privacy of the stairs, Agnès spoke more quietly. 'He was a Guardian, but is released from his vows. He has been tortured, and I believe he shares our hatred for the anakritis-general. With Humbert Blanc's assurances, I am minded to trust him.'

'What news of the Lord Brother?'

'D'Aurillac will tell you. Brother Humbert's words make me think that this Fulke was not of high Guardian rank, and was not admitted to their *inner secrets*.'

Adelais squeezed her arm, understanding. 'So let us be cautious, my friend.'

The knight stood as they entered the hall, his blue surcoat's hem dropping to his knees, its silver birds fluttering downwards. Two chairs had been placed in front of the hearth, and Adelais had the curious idea that he was standing as much for her as for Agnès. She pulled the cap off her head, unsure how she should greet him.

'*You* are Adelais de Vries?' He stared at her clothing, the long boots and quality cote-hardie of a minor nobleman, and then at her face. Only the fair hair of ambiguous length would have given him any clue.

Adelais made a small bow. A man's bow; it fitted how she was dressed. The knight was momentarily stunned into silence, but recovered and waved her to a chair. Adelais glanced at

Agnès for reassurance; they might be friends but Agnès was now a great lady, and it was not fitting that Adelais should sit while Agnès stood, in company. But Agnès was standing at the window, looking out and frowning thoughtfully, cradling Humbert's sword. Adelais sat on the edge of the chair, her hands in her lap, waiting. A woman's posture, though her knuckles rested on the padding in her sling beneath. Sometimes it was confusing, wearing men's garb. The knight eased his left leg in front of him as he sat, as if it gave him pain.

'I bring greetings from Lord Brother Humbert Blanc, who has found sanctuary in Arrenicia.'

'I am happy to know he is safe.' Her words felt formal and stilted in her mouth. 'And I thank you for your journey, sir knight.' Adelais looked up briefly. The knight was travel-stained, with shadows under his eyes, but not unattractive. She looked down again, demurely, as she imagined a lady of Agnès's court might behave before an unknown noble. She no longer felt pride in her new boots; the soft leather sheathing her calves seemed indecent, and she tucked her legs under her.

'I have not yet won the golden spurs,' he made a dismissive wave of his hand, an almost fastidious gesture with his little finger extended, 'so I am simply Fulke, Seigneur d'Aurillac. Lord Brother Humbert speaks most highly of you... mistress. He thinks you are a Blessèd One, sent by Ischyros.'

At that she looked up again. The seigneur had the eyes of one who has suffered. Yet he would be Ischyrian, and she must say the words an Ischyrian would expect.

'The God helped both me and the Lord Brother, messire. That does not make me an angel.'

'And the anakritis-general thinks you are a sorceress, in league with Kakos.' D'Aurillac's scrutiny was unblinking. This time, Adelais returned his stare.

'You know Ghislain Barthram?'

D'Aurillac held up his right hand. The little finger was

rigid, pale, and as lumpy as a badly made candle. 'We are acquainted.'

'Then you know that he is Kakos incarnate. Whose opinion do *you* trust, messire?'

'My opinion is irrelevant. I am merely a messenger.'

Adelais was not warming to this man, despite his good looks. 'Then what is your message?'

D'Aurillac unlaced a purse hanging from his belt. 'Firstly, he wishes to return two gold crowns that you gave him for his journey.'

She kept her hands in her lap. 'That money belonged to Lady Agnès.'

At the window, Agnès turned and shrugged. 'Take it. Keep it for the next stage of your journey.'

Adelais did not move. Fulke d'Aurillac's hand lay open, holding the coins, until he sighed and laid them beside him in the hearth.

'Brother Humbert also wishes to make you two gifts, in thanks for saving his life and, in his words, teaching him more in his autumn years than he realised he had still to learn.'

'That is most kind but—'

'Again, I am merely the messenger. Firstly he asks that you accept Allier, his horse. He saw the friendship between you, and is sure that you will form a bond as strong as any knight and destrier.'

Adelais's hands flew to her mouth, stifling a gasp. She looked questioningly towards Agnès. For the first time since the dance, her friend was smiling broadly. A destrier. *Allier.* 'That is too rich a gift.' Such a horse might be worth her weight in silver.

'Nonetheless, he is yours. Brother Humbert knows you will care for him well.'

'But Allier is trained for war.' Adelais could ride, and ride well, but a destrier was another matter; they were coached to respond to the subtlest touches, to be a living weapon on the battlefield. She had seen Allier hurl himself unflinching into oncoming cavalry. 'How am I to learn his ways?'

'Brother Humbert asked me to stay, with Lady Agnès's permission, and teach you as much as I can. If we work hard, you will know enough within a moon for the horse to teach you himself. After that, I may return to my lands.'

'I am putting Lady Agnès in danger, just by being here. I plan to stay only until the snows of the wolf moon are past, and will ride north with the thaw.'

'Then I will accompany you, if you wish.' D'Aurillac's response was swift, almost a snap.

Adelais sat staring at d'Aurillac, her mouth moving a little but no more words came. *Allier*.

'You have travelled far, messire.' Agnès spoke from the window. The scabbarded sword rattled softly in her arms, steel within hard leather. 'What is your recompense for your part in this great gift?'

D'Aurillac lifted his damaged hand again. 'Under torture I betrayed my order, to my great shame, and I betrayed the Lord Brother, who was my commander. I confessed to heresies that were not true. This journey is my penance, and I do it willingly, with my whole heart.'

Agnès nodded, apparently satisfied. 'You said there were two gifts,' she reminded him, hefting the sword a little.

'Again, I do but speak Brother Humbert's words. He has no son to carry his name, but he saw as much courage in Mistress Adelais as in any knight. He also knows that you are still in great danger. He gives you his sword, knowing that you will wield it with honour if you must, and that if one day you choose a husband who is worthy of you, then he will also be worthy of the sword.'

Agnès, smiling, held the weapon out to her with both hands, flat in its scabbard like an offering.

Adelais stood, still stunned. 'I am honoured beyond measure, messire.' She found her voice as she accepted it. *Sætur Sif* it was heavy. She drew it a little from its scabbard, feeling the drag of the blade turn her wrist.

'My own advice is that you do not try to wield it. A knight is trained to such a weapon as soon as he can walk. If you pretend to be a man-at-arms, you will be killed very easily.'

Adelais slid the blade back into the scabbard. She understood the wisdom of those words, but she did not like the patronising way in which they were said. As the cross guard, the quillon, met the steel-bound rim of the scabbard, it made a slick, oiled sound like the fall of a lock. She found herself smiling, not at the gift of the weapon, not even at the warmth of Humbert's words, but at the realisation that Allier was outside, and that he was hers. She wanted to run out there and throw her arms around his neck, put a saddle on his back, and ride him round the water meadow in the dark.

Would Agnès be upset if she rode north and left the gelding? Knowing Agnès's generous spirit, she'd probably insist that Adelais took both.

Swordcraft. Horsemanship. Runes. She had much to learn. And so little time.

D'Aurillac interrupted her reverie as if reading her thoughts. 'I suggest you find a good night's rest, if you wish to make best use of the coming days.'

5.4 TAILLEFER

'Counsel? Your *counsel*, de Remy,' flecks of spit flew from the Duke of Delmas's mouth, 'brought the chivalry of Galmandie home without honour.'

'My counsel, Highness, brought the city of Baudry into the royal domain.' Othon de Remy had not raised his voice, but his body looked as tense as a loaded trebuchet, ready to hurl violence at his enemy.

Taillefer held himself very still on his chair, making himself as unobtrusive as his scarlet robes would allow. Sweat trickled inside his shirt, but Taillefer dared not move. No one did. Ranged in their order of precedence down the table of the king's banqueting hall, the nobles and prelates of Galmandie stared at the polished oak, not meeting each other's eyes and especially not looking towards the king. This was not the time to be asked for an opinion, not while Othon de Remy engaged the king's brother in brutal, verbal combat.

'We already had Baudry, you fool.' Delmas struck the table hard enough for the blow to send a quiver through his jowls. Further down the table an elderly *episkopos* flinched.

'By treaty only.' Othon's anger, by contrast, seemed to pull his skin even closer to his jaw. 'A treaty that was broken. Yet after this expedition into Vriesland we have left a garrison and a governor in their richest county. For the first time, their taxes will flow to His Majesty, not feed a rebellion.'

Taillefer would have wished himself elsewhere even before his brother and Delmas began arguing. He was honoured to be invited to the table, but it was a day's ride to Villebénie from Harbin and he had a province to run. 'Come, learn,' Othon had insisted. 'See the forces ranged against us.'

Led, clearly, by Delmas. Othon had powerful enemies.

'Taxes, taxes! What are you, some Yddayim in noble apparel, that you always talk of taxes?'

This was supposed to be a jolly, midwinter feast. The 'Festival of Lights', the episkopos called it, though it had no grounding in Ischyrian teaching that Taillefer knew. It seemed to involve burning so many expensive wax candles that they had no need of the fire.

'And perhaps His Highness's head is too thickened by blows to his helmet to understand that armies cost money. It takes the income of four thousand good acres to arm and maintain one knight in the field.'

Taillefer stiffened even further. How was it possible for Othon to insult the king's brother? His reasoning answered his own question: King Aloys, the schemer, did not like his brother Delmas, the warrior. Perhaps he feared him. As Othon had intended, Taillefer was learning here.

Delmas was red-faced with anger. 'Yet we summoned the Council, de Remy. Your honeyed words persuaded the cities and the nobles to raise the money for a punitive assault.'

'Then pay it, messire. All of you.' Othon de Remy glanced sideways down the table. Several nobles found renewed interest in the grain of the table. Only Ghislain Barthram returned his stare, hunched within the black and white robes of the anakritim. 'You all rushed to offer support in the king's presence, but have been tardy to deliver those commitments. You promised gold that we have yet to receive. The treasury is empty.'

'The army could have put down the rebellion and subjugated the whole of Vriesland.' Delmas seemed to find the talk of money tiresome. 'We could have paid the army with the spoils.'

'You thought the same eight years ago.' Othon's voice dropped, though in the silence of the room all men heard him. 'Your arrogance led five hundred knights to their deaths in the mud of Pauwels. Bludgeoned by peasants.'

Delmas leaned his warrior's frame over the table, gripping its edge with clawed fingers.

'And two years later I fucking crushed them at Vannemeer, and took all lands south of the Schilde.'

Othon gave a cold, dangerous smile. 'You crushed them so completely, Your Highness, that this summer Duke Ragener put ten thousand men in the field against us.'

Ghislain Barthram angled his body forwards. When he spoke, his voice held as little emotion as a piece of oiled machinery.

'Yet we hear that many Vriesians secretly tolerate the old gods. They give lip service only to the blessings of Ischyros, and with this rebellion they are falling back into their old pagan ways. Surely the God would be best served by complete reconquest?'

Othon's slow blink was a mannerism he had when he was taken back, a heartbeat-long hooding of the eyes. The question had been typical of a priest, and an anakritis at that.

And yet? The looks that passed between Othon and Barthram hinted at their shared secret: an expulsion. An imminent arrest. If Taillefer interpreted Othon's steady gaze correctly, it said '*unfair. That was not in the script.*' Barthram's humourless half-smile might have meant '*did you really think we could be friends?*'

'Then perhaps the wealth of the fire temples of Ischyros should be used to fund an army, *Pateras*.' Now Othon's look said '*play with me at your peril*'. 'In the interests of the God, of course.'

Othon glanced to his left, towards the king, perhaps looking for support, but the king looked past him, down the table. Was he really going to sacrifice his chancellor?

Vriesland was a running sore, all knew. Half of that cursed duchy spoke Galman and accepted the suzerainty of King Aloys, while the rest, particularly in the northern parts, would beat out the brains of anyone who couldn't speak their own barbaric tongue. And, as Barthram said, there were those who still clung to the old gods. Harbin was close enough to the Vriesian border for Taillefer to have heard the stories.

'Our withdrawal smacked of cowardice.' All heads turned to a new voice. Prince Lancelin, Count of Compeigne, had spoken towards Othon with a languorous sneer. 'Cowardice, I say. Why, they even taunted us with an old hag they said was the Vriesian Witch.' He emphasised his words with a limp waving of his wrist.

A collective intake of breath tightened the atmosphere; every shoulder lifted, every head sunk deeper into fur-trimmed stoles. The king looked hard at his son, and even Delmas leaned forwards to send a warning glance down the table, but Lancelin's eyes were locked on the chancellor, needling him.

'Was that what made you advise retreat, de Remy? An old woman riding in front of our lines, waving her dugs at you and reminding you of the Guardians' curse? What did she cry? "Come, de Remy, let a Vriesian witch send you to the bridge of judgement, just like your high priest! You and all those under the Guardians' curse..."' Lancelin's voice tailed away as he realised his error. His own father, who had led the army in Vriesland, was included in that curse. He could not accuse Othon de Remy of cowardice without equally offending the king. Lancelin looked down and blushed to the same colour as his exquisitely fitted cote-hardie.

Finally, the king broke the silence. His facial expression had not changed, but his flat, quiet tone of voice was laden with warning.

'And was the woman in front of our lines at Baudry the same one who cursed the high priest? Who among us has actually seen her?'

All eyes turned on Ghislain Barthram, who showed no emotion at being the focus of attention save a slight lifting of his eyebrows. His eyes reflected the light like black glass as he inclined his head towards the king.

'I was not with the army in Vriesland, sire, but the witch who cursed the high priest is young. Men think her beautiful.' Barthram pulled his robe closer around him in distaste. The anakritim habit matched his complexion. Black over white. The only colour he wore was the blood-red cap of a pardoner. Barthram often lifted his nose before he spoke, in a single, rodent-like twitch. 'If the woman of Baudry was an old hag, then it cannot have been her.'

'And why, four moons after the death of the high priest, has this witch not been found?' The king's tone was still soft, but without warning he leaned forwards and slammed his fist into the table. 'Am I surrounded by incompetents? Have we no informers?' The king's rage was all the more frightening for erupting out of quietness. 'What reward must I offer for her capture? What punishment for the traitors who aid her?'

Othon de Remy inclined his head to the king, speaking calmly; perhaps he was used to such outbursts. 'The reward is already one hundred gold crowns, sire. And since she escaped from the anakritis-general...' Othon glanced at Barthram in a way that said *that will teach you*. '... escaped, or was allowed to walk free, there has been only one sighting. I fear she is being helped. But if she moves within Galmandie, we will have her.'

King Aloys sank back into his chair, outwardly calm once more, though every noble held themselves still. 'Perhaps she can fly through the air.'

Only the king could say such a thing, for even to suggest the possibility was heresy. There were stories from the newly conquered lands of witches that could fly, and others that went into a trance and turned their spirits into birds that flew over the land, watching for danger. Yet all good Ischyrians knew that these were just old wives' tales. As the silence lengthened the king sighed and looked up to the vaulted ceiling as if for inspiration. 'Do the people talk much of her?'

No one answered him. These nobles never heard the gossip of the streets, but everyone knew of the Vriesian girl who had killed the high priest, and pulled a crossbow bolt from her own belly and lived. Now nervous clerics came to Taillefer, their diakonos, seeking reassurance; was she a Blessèd One, sent by Ischyros to avenge the wrong done to a sacred and noble order? If so, would the God kill the king? After all, Aloys and the anakritim had tortured and sent hundreds of Guardian knights to their deaths. Aloys was known to have seized the Guardians' wealth to fund his wars.

And what about the anakritim, whose zealots had asked the questions and scribbled the answers while the tormentors broke the knights' bodies? Would the God suffer them to live?

Or was it all witchcraft, the work of Kakos?

The silence stretched.

'Find her, and find the Guardian who was with her.' The king stood, bringing the feast to an end. His voice had risen, and as Taillefer rose to his feet with the rest, he realised Othon had been right in his private briefing; the king was afraid. 'She is making fools of us. I want her burned.'

Taillefer was close enough to hear Lancelin of Compeigne mutter 'just like we did to the grand master', with the sneering arrogance of someone who was not particularly intelligent.

King Aloys was already striding to the door, and it seemed he had not heard his son and heir's remark. He turned at the threshold and stared at Othon. 'And before you burn her, strip her naked and shoot a crossbow into her belly. I want all Ville-bénie to see her writhe. I want the world to know the rumours are false.'

5.5 ADELAIS

The snow began during Adelais's first destrier lesson; fat, wet flakes that dropped spots of ice on Adelais's head. It soaked her thighs and knees where they pressed into the saddle, darkening her kirtle. She wished she hadn't left her cloak in the guard-room. One flake hit the ear of Humbert's destrier, making Allier twitch his head. *Her* destrier, now, and Fulke d'Aurillac was fulfilling his promise to teach her the ways of a warhorse. She'd chosen to wear women's garb, a functional kirtle brought by Agnès, even though skirts were a cumbersome barrier between her legs and the horse. It was more seemly, somehow, if she was to be taught by *Seigneur* Fulke d'Aurillac.

'Keep your shoulders back!' D'Aurillac sat on his own destrier, making her ride around him in circles in the hunting lodge's yard.

She thought her shoulders *were* back, in her tight-laced, woman's kirtle.

D'Aurillac had insisted that they begin in the confines of the yard, 'where the horse can't bolt far'. The seigneur seemed more noble in the saddle, with no need to drag his damaged foot along the ground. He too sat very upright, at ease with his horse.

'You and the horse must be of one mind. *He* must be of *your* mind.' D'Aurillac lectured her with the same uncompromising passion as an eldest daughter shouting the teaching of Salazar to novices in a sisterhouse. 'Before he can enter your mind you must enter his. Sit deep. Read him with your body!'

Beneath her Allier danced a little, and she felt the barely contained power of the beast. It was a little alarming.

'Now knot your reins and take your arms away. Direct him with your legs only. In battle a knight has a sword or lance in one hand, and a shield in the other.'

This was difficult. She'd never ridden without reins before, nor ridden with spurs. Allier was dancing unpredictably beneath her, trying to understand signals she didn't know how to give. Although the skirts of her kirtle were cut wide enough for her to sit on a horse, they pulled against her calves, restricting her movement. Riding was so much easier for men. Perhaps she should change back to men's clothing.

'Bend him around your left leg. Hold it against his side. Push your right against his flank.'

That worked. The snow was heavier now, melting on her body, sticking her kirtle to her shirt.

'And wing your arms. Pretend you are a soaring bird.'

The wet seeped through her shirt. She shivered and felt her skin pucker.

'Now turn the other way. Look towards where you want to go. Keep your shoulders square. Trot.'

The donjon tower bounced into view. Agnès sat wrapped in a cloak on a chair in the doorway, out of the weather, watching. Rossignol leaned against the door, fingering his lute. Elyse stood behind them with her arms folded across her chest. Adelais nudged Allier with her other leg to reverse the turn, but the horse mistook the signal and broke into canter. Adelais dropped her arms and grabbed at the reins to slow him.

'Keep him in trot. Slow him with your knees. Arms up!'

Now she could see Sennet, waiting at the yard's edge. He
stood behind a small handcart with a tightly packed bundle of
straw tied to the outside of its front end, and a shield strapped to
that, a part of the lesson that d'Aurillac had yet to explain. This
sitting trot was disturbing; the saddle pounded uncomfortably
between her legs, and her breasts chafed against icy, wet
clothes.

Fulke d'Aurillac came back into view.

'Halt him!'

Adelais sat deeper in the saddle, her arms still winged, but
Allier kept going until she grabbed the reins.

'Ride with your belly, not your hands! Don't hunch.' D'Aurillac tugged his hood forwards. 'Put your shoulders back!'
Again. Her instinct was to fold forwards, not sit straight. The
oiled wool of his cloak seemed to shed water like a duck, while
her kirtle was now plastered to the tops of her thighs.

And elsewhere. Adelais obeyed, glaring at him, shivering,
aware that she was now revealing too much of her body. D'Aurillac was looking at her and yet not looking. He moistened his
lips and swallowed. *Good. This is making him uncomfortable.*

'Sennet will come at you from behind. Imagine that cart is
an enemy soldier. You cannot turn, because you are engaging
another enemy to the front, but you can aim your destrier, as if
you were firing a crossbow over your shoulder. Lift both spurs
when you want him to kick. Keep your weight back or he will
throw you over his neck. Sennet!'

So that was why the shield and the straw were tied to the
cart. But if she couldn't yet control the horse with just her legs,
how could she hope to guide him so exactly that he'd kick the
shield?

She needn't have worried. Allier understood this game.
They waited until the castellan's cart was a lance's length
behind him, and at the lightest touch from Adelais's spurs,
Allier rocked forwards, almost unseating her, to deliver a brutal

kick with both hind legs. One of them connected with the shield with a mighty crack, followed by an oath from Sennet. Adelais found herself bent forwards, knowing that only the moulded saddle grips in front of her thighs had kept her in her seat.

'Good.' D'Aurillac inclined his head. 'Brother Humbert taught him well. Your enemy behind is now on the ground. If you keep your weight forwards after the kick, and rein back, Allier will dance backwards and trample him. Don't do it now; I value Sennet's hospitality. Besides, it is time to give these beasts some shelter.'

D'Aurillac did not speak while they were rubbing down their horses. Adelais glanced at him, hoping some of his reserve might thaw if they were to spend some days together. He seemed more handsome now he'd washed off the road and trimmed his beard. Was there a Lady d'Aurillac? Unlikely, if he'd been a Guardian.

'Why did you leave the Guardians, Seigneur?' She was shaking with cold, but refused to admit it. At least the lean-to stables offered shelter from the snow, if little warmth.

'The Order was suppressed.' D'Aurillac did not pause. He held a fistful of straw, his broken finger sticking out like a hook. Both their horses were steaming.

'Yes, but...' She made that sound like a question. The Guardians she'd known in the spring had still held their vows to be sacred.

'I lost my faith.' D'Aurillac stopped, watching for her reaction. 'I was released from my vows.'

Adelais stared at him. The Ischyrian faith had been the Guardians' reason for living. It was what let them face death with joy on the battlefield. It was their whole lives. What had happened to him?

'Are you shocked, girl? In the anakritis-general's tormentors I saw the evil at the heart of the faith. Aye, and felt it. How can I believe in a faith that sends holy men to the flames?'

Adelais pushed straw along Allier's rump, thinking. The water she smoothed from his hide was already warm. 'Brother Humbert once told me that it is not the faith that is evil, but the men within it. He is a good man, and he believes.'

'He has not endured the anakritim.' D'Aurillac pressed his fistful of straw more harshly into his destrier, enough for the animal to bare its teeth and snap at him. 'You ask too many questions, girl. And I will not be taught by one that men call a witch.'

Adelais was not threatened by d'Aurillac's anger. She sensed that he raged as much with himself as with her, and she thought she detected a vulnerability in him. She turned away from him and bent to rub straw down Allier's legs, feeling a stab of guilt because she knew the backside of her kirtle was particularly wet.

I'm sorry, Arnaud my love, but life must move on.

Her musings were interrupted by Eloi, who'd come to saddle Agnès's horse. He brought Adelais her cloak 'because Mistress Elyse thought you would be cold'. *Bless her.* If Adelais had known that she and Agnès would have so little time together, she'd have asked Fulke to delay his lesson. She helped Eloi lead out the horses and stood holding Agnès's bridle as she mounted.

'You are leaving promptly, Agnès.'

Agnès was frowning and tight-lipped. 'I am uneasy. I do not like being surprised.' She glared over her shoulder to where Guy was mounting a sorry-looking nag. He caught Agnès's eye and looked down, chastened. Agnès gestured vaguely at the snow. 'This will settle and I dare not risk being trapped here. And I will feel easier at Château Fontenay where I know what is happening.' Agnès leaned forwards in the saddle to speak quietly, for Adelais alone. 'Watch d'Aurillac. I do not wholly trust him.'

'Brother Humbert does.' Adelais found it hard to doubt someone who came with such gifts.

'Perhaps he has had time to earn Brother Humbert's trust. He has not yet earned mine. Guy Carelet is sure they were not followed here, but if d'Aurillac slips away without warning, then assume he has gone for soldiers and run, as far and as fast as your fine new horses will take you. Yes, take the gelding as well. You'll need a spare in case one goes lame. Send word when you can.' Agnès straightened in the saddle. 'That is why I am leaving Rossignol with you. You may trust him as you trust Elyse and the castellan, with your life.'

Adelais pulled the trailing edge of Agnès's cloak into neat, decorous folds around her friend's knee. 'I should go, anyway, before I bring you harm.'

'No.' Agnès was emphatic. 'On the road it would be too easy for him to betray you, if that is his plan. Here his only contact is with people I trust, and people who can guard you.' Agnès rested a gloved hand against Adelais's cheek. 'Besides, I can enjoy your company a little longer.'

Since they could not embrace, Adelais gave Agnès's knee a gentle squeeze. 'Come back soon.'

'It may be some days. I need to be cautious. Stay safe, *kjúk-ling*. Be guided by those who wish you well.' Agnès nodded towards Elyse and Sennet, who stood respectfully on the lodge's steps.

'And Castellan, fix those gates!'

Adelais stepped back as Agnès touched her spur to her palfrey's flank, sending it trotting through the archway. She rode straight-backed, the chatelaine of great estates, with her cloak fanned perfectly over her horse's rump. Adelais preferred the laughing confidante of their private moments. Guy and Eloi followed; Eloi proudly, Guy quietly. The yard seemed empty and quiet without them, though four others had watched the departure: Elyse, Sennet, and Rossignol from the lodge's door, and Fulke on his own from the stables. Rossignol glared across the courtyard towards Fulke, his hand on the sword at his hip.

It wasn't a practice sword.

CHAPTER SIX

6.1 HUMBERT

'One flag, Lord Brother!'

Brother Thanchere's shout at the scriptorium door interrupted Humbert Blanc's concentration. He breathed deeply, suppressing his irritation, and continued to shave a slender half-moon from the edge of his quill. Had the quill been full of ink and touching the parchment, such a noisy intrusion could have startled him into an imperfect letter or, worse still, a blot on the page. Hours of work could have been ruined in an instant. Thanchere was a good knight and a fine lieutenant, but his manner and voice were more suited to the battlefield than the commandery. Humbert said nothing, and only looked up when the quill was trimmed to his satisfaction.

Thanchere sounded wary but not alarmed. One flag for caution; armed men were near. Humbert sighed and laid down his quill. The copy of the *Vision of Salazar* he was creating must wait a little longer. Fine legacy though it would be, it would probably never be finished, at least not by his hand. If the God willed, there would be a new high priest and a new order to protect the Hand before long. Younger eyes than his would finish this work.

'One flag,' Thanchere repeated. He was letting cold air flood into the scriptorium; Humbert had been quite snug with a charcoal brazier behind him and the warmth of a lamp on his desk to boost the light from the waxed-linen window, now shut against the winter's chills.

'And Brother Ricard is coming to tell us what he has seen.' The door framed the mill on the skyline to the north. A single rider, almost invisible at this distance but for his white surcoat, had left the mill and was riding down the hill towards them. The fields either side of the road were dusted white with snow, though the road was still brown mud; at this distance the rider looked like a galloping snowflake.

'Will you flee, Lord Brother? Your horse is ready.'

Into the hills again, in the snow? He was too old for this. 'No, Brother. It is but one flag. I will wait for Brother Ricard's news.'

Yet he left his desk, for the commandery's yard was now full of brothers arming themselves, pulling hauberks over their heads and strapping swords around their waists, and for a moment he felt the old anticipation of the call to arms. A brother hurried towards him, urgency tightening his face, bearing a sword and belt for Humbert to wear. Humbert waved it away, surprised to find he still carried his quill-paring knife in one hand. Its blade was no longer than his middle finger, and he felt a little foolish to be carrying something so toy-like amidst the weapons of war. He pushed it into his boot as another brother led a horse from the stables, ready-saddled and with a pack tied to its rump that Humbert knew would be provisions. He accepted its bridle but did not mount, watching the horizon instead. There was a view of nearly a league from the mill. That gave enough time for Brother Ricard to reach them, and for Humbert to ride into the forest above the commandery if necessary before his flight could be seen.

Brother Ricard arrived in a drum roll of iron-shod hooves on the frozen earth of the courtyard.

'By his arms, it is de Mauriac,' he called, even before his horse had come to a snorting halt. The local seneschal's chevrons in the wasp colours of black and yellow were distinctive even at a distance. 'With an escort of three. No helms or lances.'

The brothers seemed all to exhale at once, the tension easing away in their steaming breath. The seneschal could have many reasons for riding through his own domain, and would always ride with an escort. There was no immediate threat. Besides, if it came to a fight, ten armed brothers now stood in the yard. Humbert handed back the reins of the horse.

'I shall wait in the temple until they have passed. And if by any chance they seek me, I shall claim sanctuary.' The seneschal may have chosen not to notice the growing numbers of brothers at this particular commandery, but he was still the law, and an element of caution was appropriate.

Humbert found a cushion to soften the temple's rush-covered floor, and rested his back against the wall, near the door. What was enforced idleness but an opportunity for reflection? Opposite Humbert, the figure of Salazar had been painted onto the plaster where the Blessèd One might greet all who entered, the fingers of his right hand raised in benediction. The mutilated left wrist dripped blood that the years had faded to brown ochre. From beyond the door came the sound of Brother Thanchere whetting his sword, giving himself an excuse to be there, on the chapel's steps, and armed.

The sounds of hooves grew steadily; a busy trot rather than an urgent canter. This was encouraging.

What would Salazar have said about the persecution of the Guardians? Was it indeed the God's punishment for losing Alympos to the infidel Saradim? Yet the Guardians had fought on when kings like Aloys had turned to easier conquests on their own borders. They had been impossibly outnumbered at the end. Was it the God's punishment for their Guardian pride, then? Of that they had all been guilty. But did it merit such an evil humbling? And was it the God's will that the Order should rise again?

Humbert heard the riders turning off the road into the yard. Other than their hooves there was quiet, as if everyone at the commandery waited for thunder.

Salazar taught it was better to bring good out of evil than to suffer no evil to exist. But what good had come from their persecution?

'I seek Humbert Blanc, who was once Guardian Grand Commander of Arrenicia.' Humbert straightened his back against the wall as the seneschal's voice reverberated around the yard, echoing a little between the stone buildings before settling into the dust.

Horses pawed at the dirt, their harnesses ringing.

No one else spoke.

'Come, we all know he is here.' Seneschal de Mauriac sounded tired, as if he did not enjoy this duty.

Humbert slumped. He was not worried; four could not fight ten, but now he must move on, and find another home. Find another base to gather his knights. His copy of the *Vision* would never be finished, though his own vision, of a new order to protect the Hand, would survive.

Thanchere's whetstone was drawn along his sword blade, in a ringing screech more threatening than any words.

'Then hear this.' The seneschal's voice became louder, higher, and more formal as if he read from a proclamation, though the tone was flat with regret. 'Know ye, that for the grievous crimes of sorcery, and of sacrilegious violence against the most holy high priest, by the grace of Ischyros, the prince of our faith on earth, that Humbert Blanc, formerly a member of the dishonoured Order of Guardians, and the woman Adelais de Vries, are pronounced expelled from the faith.'

In the profound silence that followed Humbert could hear his own heartbeat. He understood the words, but could not absorb them. His mind grabbed at them the way a falling man might grab at tufts of grass as he slipped over a cliff, though his body was slack and heavy as if he had already fallen.

'All conversations with the aforementioned persons are prohibited,' de Mauriac continued, 'as are all tokens of benevolence, marks of honour and respect, and any form of contact except that necessary for their arrest and punishment. Henceforth no Ischyrian may share food with them, pray with them, or offer them any kind of succour, on pain of themselves incurring automatic expulsion.'

Still the silence, as if every brother had been knocked senseless, a stillness broken only by the rustle of a parchment being re-rolled, followed by the snap of a saddlebag's flap. Humbert could not stand. He stared at the image of Salazar, needing to believe that painted benediction applied even to him.

'By whose order are they expelled?'

Humbert recognised the voice, even with those hollowed, faltering tones, but in the shock of the moment he could not name the brother.

'By order of Taillefer de Remy, diakonos of Harbin.'

Humbert found the will to roll onto his knees and rest his forehead against the wall's cold stone. Slowly, using the wall as support, he managed to stand, blinking away the black spots that flitted like bats across his vision. He swayed a little, looking at the temple's sanctuary. He would have traded a year of his life to have received the blessing of pardon before stepping out. Would he ever again be allowed inside a temple? Would they allow him to unburden before they burned him, or must he indeed fall from the bridge of judgement into the pit?

The brothers parted for him as he walked across the yard,

all of them wide-eyed and slack-jawed. One of them fell to his knees, holding his sword flat before him.

'*Ischyros be merciful and shine upon us—*'

The brother called the first line of the chant as loudly and clearly as any fire temple cantor.

'*—and lift his hand to bless us.*'

The others took up the call. Humbert was humbled by their love. They could not pray with him, but they could pray together, sending him on his way with the Guardian prayer ringing in his ears. Around him all the brethren also fell to their knees.

'*That the way of truth may be known among all nations.*'

Only Thanchere remained on his feet, his sword tip fallen to the ground, his face stricken.

'The mantle falls on you, Brother Thanchere.' There was no prohibition on Humbert speaking, nor on Thanchere listening. He was still close by on the temple step, and Humbert pitched his voice so that only Thanchere could hear. 'Continue the work. Gather the brethren. The Order will be reborn. Make yourself known to de Fontenay.'

Brother Thanchere fell to his knees, bowing his head.

'*Thy saving health among Thy faithful.*'

Humbert opened his arms wide to show he held no weapon, and joined in the chant.

'*Let all the people praise thee!*' He broke no temple edict, and jeopardised no one. He was praying with the brethren, not them with him.

He paused in front of the seneschal, who looked uncomfortable with this duty. They knew each other; like all the great lords of Arrenicia, their families had intermarried over the generations.

'How?' None of the brothers would have betrayed him.

The seneschal paused, his face not unkindly.

'D'Aurillac was watched,' he whispered, risking his own expulsion.

Humbert closed his eyes at the pain of betrayal.

'That Thy way may be known upon earth.'

And staggered anew at the realisation that he himself had sent d'Aurillac to Adelais's only possible refuge.

The seneschal dismounted and drew a knife from his belt, though his eyes showed no threat, only sadness. 'I must do this, Lord Brother. You are not permitted to wear the marks of a sacred order.'

Humbert was too preoccupied with terror at what he had done to Adelais to feel any humiliation as the badge of his adoptive order was cut from his surcoat.

They brought him the horse that had been prepared for his escape, swapped its bridle for a lead rein, and bound his hands. From its saddle he looked around the kneeling, chanting brethren, and they looked back at him with their shoulders shaking as they wept. So much unsaid. So much did not need to be said.

'May Ischyros bless us until the end of days—'

Humbert shut his eyes as they led him away, savouring the fading sounds of the chant. His *brothers'* chant, for there had been as much brotherhood in that farewell as on any field of battle.

'—and we sing the songs of eternity beyond the stars.'

He tried to pray, but the wisdom of Salazar eluded him. He knew only the sick weight of betrayal and the certainty that d'Aurillac would find her, if she was there. With Humbert's tokens and words, d'Aurillac would be trusted.

It was only a matter of time. It may already have happened.

6.2 ADELAIS

They managed to move one of the lodge's two gates by pouring melted goose fat into the hinges, and applying the combined strength of Rossignol, Sennet, and even Fulke d'Aurillac while Adelais used an old spit as a lever between its ends and the gatehouse. It took almost as much effort to open it again to work more hot fat into the metalwork.

But the hinges on the other were already buckled and rusted. Their efforts snapped one completely, letting the door fall further against the wall where its mighty oaken weight proved immovable. Sennet shrugged; he'd done his best. Now it would take many more men than they had, and a good blacksmith, to fix it.

Rossignol stared at the wreckage and swore. 'So we take watches,' he announced. 'Me, Sennet, Adelais. One of us to be on guard at all times, day and night.'

'I can watch,' Fulke d'Aurillac offered.

'Perhaps when we know you better.' Rossignol's refusal stopped just short of an insult. 'Come, mudlark, we will continue your training in the hall. Sennet, you have the first watch.'

. . .

Adelais borrowed a dry kirtle and overdress from Elyse and kilted them over her sword belt to leave her legs free to move. She did, however, wear Agnès's long boots to save herself the embarrassment of showing her calves. Somehow that seemed important if Fulke was watching. They used the practice swords and wore gauntlets and mail coifs for protection.

'Remember, come just into distance, no further.' Rossignol danced backwards in his defensive half-shield stance, drawing Adelais onwards. 'Cut with the tip, dance back. Don't hack.'

'You will get her killed,' Fulke d'Aurillac said, a statement of fact, without anger. He sat on a bench by the fire with one leg stretched in front of him.

'On the contrary, messire.' Rossignol did not relax his guard. 'I may save her life.'

'All this limp wrist work,' d'Aurillac imitated them, sneering, 'how will that punch a sword through chain mail?'

'It will not, messire. If Mistress Adelais tries to fight like a man-at-arms, she will indeed be killed.' He dropped his guard and moved alongside her to demonstrate. 'Men-at-arms grip their swords hard enough to strike through armour, thus.' He closed his fist on her sword hilt above her hand, like a hammer, and demonstrated the start of a powerful, crushing blow. 'But *you* need to fight with speed and agility, not brute strength.'

Rossignol took up his guard again. 'I'll show you a trick you can use with a man-at-arms. Strike downwards at me, mistress. Slowly, so you see the movement.'

Interesting. Alone, she was 'mudlark'. In d'Aurillac's presence, she was 'mistress'. Adelais moved into distance and cut slowly downwards towards Rossignol's head. Rather than take the blow on his blade he moved his buckler across his sword forearm to stop Adelais's blade and push it to his right, while thrusting *underneath* his left arm into her face. He pulled his stroke just before the point struck her cheekbone.

'That, mistress, is called a "thrust strike". A soldier who is used to a heavy shield will not expect you to cross your arms and defend your sword side with the buckler. A simple, fast movement has blocked his sword and exposed his face to your thrust. This is what you must learn. Stay light on your feet and *think*. Then you may have a chance.'

D'Aurillac made an exasperated sound and lifted his hand in a contemptuous, dismissive gesture.

Rossignol smiled at Adelais as if they shared some private jest. His smile was even, unlike his eyes.

'Why do you help me, Master Rossignol?' Adelais remembered how he'd lost that eye.

Rossignol shrugged. 'At first, because my lady so commanded me. Now also because a man like Humbert Blanc does not give his sword and his destrier lightly.'

'You know Brother Humbert?'

'Only by reputation.'

'And again, *minstrel*, what should she do against a man wearing a great helm?' Fulke d'Aurillac now stood near them, his hand resting on his oversized sword hilt in a way that asserted his authority.

'Run, Seigneur!' Rossignol spread his arms, laughing. 'Run until the weight of his armour has exhausted him, then turn and aim for the eye slits. Give him a wound like mine!'

'She has been given a knight's sword. It should be wielded with honour.'

'Neither of us could teach her the ways of arms in a few days, Seigneur. But I can teach her two or three tricks that she can learn well enough to surprise an enemy. They may save her life.'

'You fight like a peasant, minstrel.'

The smile faded from Rossignol's face. In one breath he

seemed to grow taller and broader. 'A Vriesian peasant taught me a hard lesson, *Seigneur.*' He touched his face. 'One you yourself may learn, before long.'

Adelais looked between them, stunned by the speed with which their animosity had developed.

'*Quiet!*' Elyse hissed at them from the top of the stairs to the guardroom. The low menace in her voice stopped the argument instantly. In this new quiet they could hear voices outside; Sennet and an unknown man. Elyse stepped towards the tall windows overlooking the courtyard, beckoning to Rossignol. Adelais followed, keeping well back, newly aware of a commotion of ravens.

Below them at the gatehouse Sennet was talking to a mounted man shrouded beneath a hooded cloak. Snow had settled in miniature drifts in the folds of his cloak, and his face was hidden within the black cavern of his hood. His horse was not a destrier but good quality, and the tip of a scabbard hung near to his boot. The beast beat the ground with a forehoof, impatient, as the men talked. The words were indistinct but the set of Sennet's shoulders was unwelcoming, even aggressive. The rider touched his leg to his horse's flank as if to send it forwards into the courtyard, and Sennet stepped in front of him, arms raised as a barrier. The hood tipped forwards to peer through the archway, sending clumps of snow tumbling from the shoulders to the ground, and Sennet grabbed the bridle, blocking him.

'I will go.' Rossignol swapped his practice sword for his sharpened blade. 'The rest of you stay here. All of you.' He glared at d'Aurillac as he clumped down the stairs, making no attempt to mask the sound. He strode out to stand beside Sennet, his hand steadying his scabbard, indicating that he was ready to draw.

The rider was saying something; the face was still hidden but puffs of breath steamed in the shadowed space beneath the

hood, icy grey against black. Rossignol lifted his sword arm and
pointed towards the ford across the stream. Sennet released the
bridle and slowly, apparently reluctantly, the rider turned and
disappeared from view. Rossignol returned to the hall but
Sennet stayed watching the path.

'He said he was a messenger from Orval way,' Rossignol
clearly did not believe that. 'Said he had a message for Lady
Agnès at Château Fontenay. Got lost. Someone told him there
was a château this way.' He brushed snow from his sleeve.
'Wanted to come in out of the snow and stay the night. I showed
him the way.'

'Did he have an Orval accent?' Adelais asked.

Rossignol shrugged.

'Why don't I saddle up and follow him?' d'Aurillac asked.
'Make sure there aren't more surprises out there in the forest?'

'No.' Rossignol was emphatic. 'But Sennet should go.'
When d'Aurillac protested, he added, 'A castellan would have
many reasons to visit his lady. You are a stranger.'

Adelais looked out of the window. Sennet was stamping his
feet to keep warm under the archway. 'Do you think I should
leave? Run now?' She wanted them to tell her not to go; the
snow had begun to settle. Only a desperate fool would travel far
in this weather.

'He did not see you. I think we can wait to ask Lady Agnès.
But I'm sure of one thing...'

Adelais turned to look at him, lifting an eyebrow.

'He was lying. That man was a scout.'

6.3 BARTHRAM

Ghislain Barthram turned away from his servant to unroll the flimsy scrap of paper. It was not that he feared Kasim would learn his secrets – the man was illiterate, after all – but he had an irritating mannerism of biting his lips when he was nervous, the way others would lick them. It was a mute, if unintentional reminder that he'd had his tongue cut out. Perhaps Kasim sensed Barthram's displeasure; out of the corner of his eye Barthram saw Kasim lift the cradled bird in both hands until he could scratch at his mouth with a thumb.

No matter. Such petty annoyances were a worthwhile price to pay for information, and to be aware of events before all others was power indeed.

The news unfolding in the scroll caused Barthram to smile, and *truly* smile, an event so rare that Kasim bobbed and grinned with him, displaying an array of very white but lopsided teeth. Barthram dismissed him.

The seneschal of Arrenicia had Humbert Blanc.

He wouldn't tell Othon de Remy. Couldn't tell him, not without explaining how he came by the information, and then de Remy would try to take Kasim from him. And every noble in the kingdom would soon be sending messages that couldn't be intercepted.

Blanc's arrest meant that his focus could switch entirely to Jourdaine. The methods he'd used to take Humbert Blanc had proven themselves effective: first find the hiding place, and then have soldiers on hand when expulsion is pronounced. Now he'd wait until he'd found the witch's hiding place, and serve notice of expulsion with the soldiers he sent to arrest her. D'Aurillac would be there by now. Barthram might even have news of him when the first bird was sent from Moutâne.

With the God's help and a little tormentor persuasion, he would soon be able to do the faith a great service and prove that the Guardians had been in league with Kakos to strike down the high priest. He might even have enough evidence against de Fontenay to recover the Hand of Salazar, if that was indeed the relic they'd stolen from the Guardians' temple.

They'd burn together, Blanc and the witch. The king's requirement that she first have a crossbow bolt fired into her belly was masterful. In a way, it was a pity that Barthram's vows prevented him from shedding blood, at least in so public an arena as a burning.

But he could watch. Perhaps in that moment he'd find the grace within himself to pray for her soul.

Unlikely. But at least he could be seen to say the words, even if he did not believe them in his heart.

6.4 ADELAIS

In the evening of the unknown rider, Adelais bathed her aches in water that Elyse had warmed over the kitchen fire; enough to cover her lower legs and lap against her navel as she sat in a half-barrel. The sound of a lute and a tavern song dropped through the boards from Rossignol and Sennet in the hall above. Sennet had followed their unknown visitor until he took the road to Château Fontenay; much of his story rang true, but they were left with a sense of unease.

'Not much we can do, anyway.' Elyse shrugged.

'I could go,' Adelais offered. All her instinct was to flee, even in this weather. 'Take the horses and run.'

Elyse snorted. 'In this snow? You'll lame them within ten leagues. Besides, Lady Agnès is the law in these parts. What's he going to do?'

Adelais momentarily forgot the stranger as Elyse poured another jug over her neck. Some of the water ran between her breasts and down over her belly, sensuous as a lover's kiss.

'When you poured water over me in the woods, Aunty, it made me feel...' She struggled for the word. '... womanly.'

'Like you wanted to lie with a man?'

'No!' That wasn't what she meant at all. 'More... I don't know. Nurturing.'

'That's good.' Elyse refilled her copper jug from a barrel and set it to heat on the range. 'I sang the *lœgr* rune as I sprinkled you. Mayhap you felt its power. *Lœgr* is the water-rune, the source of all life.' She wrapped a cloth around her hand and lifted another warmed jug from the fire.

'*Lœgr er vellanda vatn,*' she poured a trickle over Adelais's back, '*ok vidthr ketill,*' and again, as if anointing her, '*ok gloemmungr grund...*'

'Water is the eddying stream, and wide fountain, and land of the fish,' Adelais murmured. 'But why does it make me feel that way?' She rested her chin on her knees, thinking.

'Women give life. That's why the Ischyrians hate us. It's the one power they cannot take.' There was a sharpness in Elyse's voice. She was pulling coarse drying cloths from a rack by the fire and folding them. She dropped one by Adelais's barrel and knelt there, where they could talk quietly, faces close.

'In the time of the old gods men had their might, the force of steel and muscle, but women had their own power. To us was given the wisdom of the runes, and that was respected. Now a prophet writes down what we are to believe in a sacred text and we're burned as witches if we stray from his path, or heal the wrong child, like my sister. Giving birth is the only power the priests have left us.'

'You really hate them, don't you?'

'My sister was a good woman. One day I'll have my revenge for what the anakritim did to her.'

'But some women have power, Aunty. Think of Lady Agnès.'

'She is a lord's wife. Under Ischyros a woman belongs to a man, either as wife or daughter.'

'Unless she's shut up in a sisterhouse.' Adelais smiled, trying to soften Elyse's anger.

Elyse snorted and pushed herself to her feet, groaning a little as she straightened her knees. Both of them looked up as an argument broke out in the hall above. Fulke d'Aurillac and Rossignol were shouting at each other, and Sennet was trying to calm them down.

'The sooner that one goes, the better,' Elyse muttered.

Adelais reached for the drying cloth and stood, cascading water. 'I think he's rather handsome, when he's not frowning.'

'I saw you batting your eyelids. You're aiming high.'

'I'm aiming nowhere.' Adelais began to dry herself. 'Besides, he glowers at me as if he's hungry and I've stolen his food.'

'Take care, sweeting. He's a dark one.' Elyse found another drying cloth and moved behind Adelais.

'If he goes, so shall I, as fast as those horses will carry me, snow or no snow.'

'Then mayhap we'll have to detain him so you have a head start.'

Adelais slowed her drying, thinking. 'Aunty, you remember you said you'd cast the runes, when I was ready?' The thought of d'Aurillac above made her uneasy in different ways. Could she trust him? And might he like her? She told herself she didn't want him, not really, but there were times when there was a hunger within her, and it had been half a year since she'd last lain with Arnaud.

'I will, sweeting, if you are sure you know why you want to ask.'

At that Adelais turned in the tub, her feet still submerged in the warm water.

Elyse looked up at her, unsmiling. 'A seeress must first know herself. How else is she to know what is her own will and what is the wisdom of the runes?'

Adelais breathed deeply and found the point of calm where she could ask herself that question. When she opened her eyes Elyse was still staring into her face.

'I want to know whether I am bringing Agnès into danger by staying here. I want to know whether I should take the horses and run, now, without even waiting to thank her. I want to know if I will ever reach safety.' She did not know why it felt right to seek her fate now, when it had not before.

Elyse held her gaze. 'I must warn you that I am no great seeress. There are few *seidhkonur* left to learn from in Galmandie, and my mother and sister knew more of the healing skills than of prophecy. I may give you more questions than answers.'

'Please?' Above all, Adelais needed to know whether she should flee into the winter.

Elyse nodded, perhaps reluctantly. 'Very well. Dress, then. I will bolt the door.'

Adelais stepped out of the tub, shivering as the draught cut across her wet ankles. 'My grandmother Yrsa cast the runes for me, the night before I was sent away from Vriesland.'

'Do you remember them?' Elyse spread a linen cloth over the table.

Adelais pulled her shirt and kirtle over her head, thinking. 'Yrsa had me pick runes and lay them in the shape of a boat, with me at the centre, and the Nornir about me.' She drew a boat shape in the air with her hands, gesturing to the realm of each of the divine weavers of fate. 'Urdhr to the right, who weaves that which has become. Verdhandi below, who weaves that which is becoming. And Skuld to the left and towards the "bow", for that which may yet become.'

'I cast the runes rather than choose them, but otherwise it is the same.' Elyse pulled her drawstring bag of runes from behind its stone. 'What did Yrsa's runes reveal?'

Adelais closed her eyes, picturing the runes laid out before her.

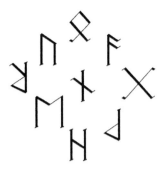

'*Naudhiz* the need-rune at the centre, for the uncertainty of that moment. In Urdhr's realm, *ansuz* the god-rune to show that my own power had placed me in need.' She kept her eyes shut, reciting the runes like a story she had learned by heart. '*Gebo* for love, *wunjo* inverted for the loss of joy. *Hagalaz* for terrible, unavoidable change.'

'And in Verdhandi?'

That which is becoming.

'*Ehwaz* the horse-rune for travel, *raido* inverted for difficulties. Finally *úruz*, which Yrsa did not expect. She said it is normally a man's rune; it speaks of a warrior's courage.'

'What lay in the realm of Skuld, who weaves what may become?' Elyse spoke softly, as if in wonder. 'What is your destiny?'

'*Odhala*, the rune of ancestral right. This is why she thought I might be the *örlaga vefari,* the weaver of fates.'

'She was right about other things. You have travelled far, dressed as a man, and have fought. Do you remember that night when you made patterns with runes on that table?' Elyse nodded across the room. '*Ansuz, ihwaz, hagalaz.* And again, *odhala.* I have seen that you are drawn to some runes, or some are drawn to you. *Odhala. Ansuz. Thurs.* These are runes of power. Mayhap your grandmother was right.'

'Amma Yrsa also made a prophecy, one that I fear, Aunty.

She said I was like a tall tree on a hilltop that draws men to its shelter, but also draws the lightning. Those around me may be killed, even those I love.'

'Like your man Arnaud.'

Adelais opened her eyes. 'Yes, like Arnaud.' By Freyja, she missed him; his strength, his gentleness, his desire. 'And I fear to cause the death of others I love. Agnès. You. But Yrsa also said that the gods can play with us. They can foretell our doom in a way that makes us run towards it, not away.'

'She spoke a lot of sense, your grandmother, though she and I cast the runes in different ways. In a moment you will scatter the runes. What falls to your right is the realm of Urdhr, who weaves what has become. To your left is Verdhandi, what is becoming; and furthest from you is Skuld, what may become. In that we are the same. What falls will be different.'

Elyse held the bag out to Adelais. 'Take a handful. As many as you can hold. Good. Put your hand palm-up in the centre of the circle. Throw the runes lightly into the air, and see if you can catch some on the back of your hand.'

Adelais only caught one that way.

Ingwaz, the rune of Freyr, consort of the earth mother.

'Does that matter?' she asked.

Elyse shrugged as she put *ingwaz* back in the bag. 'It would if your fate was intertwined with *bjarkan*. But I suspect you are most aligned with *thurs* and *ansuz*, Thor and Odhinn. And, as I say, *odhala*. That is a powerful combination.' She rested both forearms on the table, leaning forwards to study the pattern, and was silent for so long that Adelais had to stop herself fidgeting. Eventually Elyse sighed and sat back.

'Tell me again what your grandmother foretold.'

'That I was like the tall tree on a hilltop. People will come to me, but tall trees also draw the lightning and the people around me may die.'

'She spoke well.'

Adelais became very still. 'And if I stay here, will I draw the lightning upon you and Agnès?'

Again it took Elyse a long time to answer. 'Little has fallen into the realm of Skuld.'

And Skuld wove that which is to become. 'So I don't have much future?'

'It means that your future will depend on what happens soon. It is not yet fated.' Elyse hesitated.

'Tell me, Aunty.'

'There is nothing in Skuld's domain beyond *kaunaz*. What do you know of *kaunaz*?' She pointed to the dog-legged rune.

'It is the rune of lovers.' But the love that starts low in the belly, not high in the heart. She'd made that mistake with Jan, back in Vriesland.

'Yes, it is the rune of lust, but it is first the rune of fire. Fire of the mind, and the fires of making as well as the fires of the loins.' Elyse spoke quietly, almost reluctantly. 'What is already fated ends in fire.'

Adelais swallowed, though her mouth was suddenly dry. Was she fated to die by fire, as a witch? 'But should I run?'

Elyse lifted one of the rune staves and peered underneath.

'When a rune falls face-down, its meaning is opposite. You have *úruz* face-up near the centre of the wheel, at the core of your being. *Úruz*, the bull, is the rune of health and strength. If you were sickly it would be further out, or reversed. It also implies wellbeing in other ways.' Elyse gave Adelais a knowing smile.

Adelais simply raised an eyebrow in response.

'A man would be a fool to stray far from your bed.' Elyse's smile became a throaty chuckle. 'And don't blush. Only the Ischyrians think a woman's pleasure is shameful.'

'Yes, but should I run?' Adelais repeated her question.

Elyse's hands moved over the circle, lifting some staves to look beneath but always replacing them in exactly the same position. Her eyes were drawn repeatedly to *ehwaz*, the horse-rune.

'A red rider has unleashed powerful forces against you. His fate and yours are linked. You cannot defeat him, and you cannot run from him. If you flee, you will flee into his path. You can only deflect his might onto another.'

Adelais laughed nervously. 'If I cannot run from him, I may as well stay here.'

Elyse lifted another stave to look beneath, and became very still.

'Aunt Elyse?' Adelais did not like the sadness that was pulling at the *seidhkona's* face.

Elyse did not answer, but looked beneath another. And another.

'Tell me.'

Elyse swept her arm across the circle, destroying the pattern. 'Prophecy is not my skill.' She scooped the staves into their bag with a cupped hand.

'But what did you see?'

Elyse fretted at the drawstrings of the bag, her face slack with worry. Eventually she sighed and whispered a single word.

'Lightning.'

PART FOUR

THE WOLF MOON

CHAPTER SEVEN

7.1 TAILLEFER

A thaw came when the wolf moon was a quarter full; a trickle of messengers reaching Villebénie from the king's nearest cities showed that the roads were open, though the fields were still blanketed by snow. Taillefer announced his intention to return to his much-neglected duties at Harbin. Privately, he had had his fill of the vicious politics of the court; the verbal blows of Delmas and the warrior lords slipping over his brother Othon's oily surface; the acid nastiness of Prince Lancelin's popinjays to any courtier outside their circle. And in the snowbound capital they were all forced into each other's company far too much.

Othon 'counselled' Taillefer to stay. Counselled most strongly, in fact. Provinces, he said, have a way of governing themselves. Kings, however, need advice. Influence. Flattery. 'Oh, and fresh air, which means the king will ride out today. And you, my brother, are a fine horseman. Besides,' Othon added, 'I have something to show you.'

He would say no more.

A circular route of just two leagues was agreed, and servants were sent out on great plough horses, dragging whole pine saplings to clear the roads of snow. And of course most of the nobles must attend upon the king, so a great flock of courtiers assembled outside the royal stables, their exotic plumage muted by fur cloaks, their too-easy laughter steaming the air. It was madness. Their horses had also been confined and were restive, dancing on the icy cobbles. Many needed to be held while their owners mounted; some curvetted under their riders.

Taillefer walked his mare around the fringes, reassuring her with a steady pressure from his thighs and calves. She was too highly bred to be restrained; the contained energy within her must erupt before long. He held his hand against her neck, gentling her as one of the Lancelin faction was bucked onto his backside, triggering guffaws of laughter from de Fontenay and others of the Delmas camp. By the God, he wanted to be free of this nest of snakes; just point his mare at half a league of good ground and let her go. Alone.

Impossible, of course. The king must lead, and the ground was still treacherous. Taillefer managed to restrain his mare at the back of the group until Othon rode past on his placid, dependable palfrey. They brought up the rear of the party, trailing by several horses' lengths. Taillefer glanced at his brother; it was unlike Othon to willingly let the court come between him and the king.

'You have news, brother?'

Othon wore a slight, knowing smile. 'Sometimes, it is so useful to have men in my employ who do the smallest tasks. Servants. Craftsmen. The people we ignore, but who know our lives.' He was particularly pleased with himself.

Taillefer waited. Othon was fond of demonstrating his cleverness.

'Why, do you think, would Lady Agnès de Fontenay order fine boots to be made that would not fit her?'

'For her lord?'

'They wouldn't fit him, either. And he is here, not in Fontenay.' Othon pointed a gloved hand at one of the figures ahead of them. De Fontenay's fur-trimmed cloak hid his red surcoat with its golden flowers, but he was unmistakable.

'A lover, then?'

'That is the local story, and she took great care to ensure she was not followed. She set out one day with one man and came back the following day with two, in the first of the snow. My informant found the tracks of three horses leading out of a forest, and traced them to the hunting lodge where she was caught last year. A lodge known to be empty but for a castellan and his woman, yet there were horses in the stables. Good horses. My messenger has earned his gold to bring me this news through the snow.'

'There could be other explanations.'

'It seems that she has been sending supplies to this lodge. Clothing. Delicacies. I think we can be sure that eight days ago, the witch was hiding in one of de Fontenay's hunting lodges in Jourdaine.

'Then demand her arrest!'

'Remember de Fontenay is seneschal there. He would deny everything to protect his wife, and the witch would be gone. She must be snatched, quietly and swiftly.'

'Then send troops.'

'King's men invading the Duchy of Jourdaine, without the duke's permission? I think not. I have something more subtle in mind. Which is the closest province to northern Jourdaine, brother?'

'Compeigne.' Taillefer felt like a child being taught his lessons.

'And who rules Compeigne?'

'Prince Lancelin, of course.'

'And what have you learned of Prince Lancelin in your time at court?'

Taillefer watched the young prince. There was some altercation happening between him and de Fontenay. Lancelin wore no cloak, but a fur-lined, full-sleeved, waisted cote-hardie, cut short-skirted; his hose-sheathed backside showed as he trotted. By the God, that must be cold.

'He speaks without thinking. He is vain and a little stupid.' Taillefer paused, wondering how much to say, even to his brother. 'He seems particularly fond of his equerry. Perhaps unnaturally fond.' Taillefer had noticed the small gestures, the eye contact that hinted at intimacy. He'd known priests like that, both good men, and had to counsel them about discretion; the legal penalty in Galmandie was castration.

'True. What else?'

Taillefer remembered the way Lancelin watched the king. There was a need there, and when the king showed his wrath the prince had the hurt, pleading look of a beaten cur.

'He desires his father's love.'

'So we will give him an opportunity to ingratiate himself. What did you think of Malory d'Eivet?'

Taillefer's surprise at the change of subject must have shown. Othon smiled at him knowingly. 'At least he convinced you to expel Blanc and the witch. How else did he impress you?'

Taillefer swallowed, choosing his words.

'He is a dangerous fool. He thinks the witch is a Blessèd One of Ischyros.'

'But he knows her.' Othon lifted out of the saddle and broke wind, sighing with earthy pleasure; he seemed particularly happy today. 'I want to be sure we burn the right one, before our enemies parade another yellow-haired woman and Aloys fills his royal loin cloth. Now watch, brother. Watch and learn.'

Othon spurred forwards and reined in alongside Lancelin, greeting him with the honeyed words and mindless pleasantries of a courtier until the rest of the court rode out of earshot. 'I think, Highness,' he finished, 'that I may be able to help you make your father a gift for which he will be grateful beyond measure.'

'And what is the nature of this gift, de Remy?' Lancelin spoke in the lofty, slightly forced tones of an insecure royal who needed to assert his superiority.

'The Vriesian Witch.' Othon smiled ingratiatingly.

'That would be a gift indeed. Why do you not make it yourself?'

'She is hiding, we believe, in Jourdaine, on Leandre de Fontenay's lands.'

Lancelin's slow-spreading smile was evil. *The God help Galmandie when this one is king.*

'So,' Othon continued, 'it is not simply a matter of asking the local seneschal to arrest her. De Fontenay *is* the law in those parts. And in his absence it is his wife, the witch's friend.'

Lancelin stared ahead to where de Fontenay rode behind Delmas's blue cloak. 'But a small expedition from my lands in Compeigne could seize her before she was warned?'

'His Highness has a fine grasp of strategy.'

'And what is your price, de Remy, for pinpointing her hiding place?'

'I wish merely to question her, Your Highness, before she is burned. She may know where a precious relic is hidden. I will willingly trade the honour of her capture for the chance to extract that knowledge.'

'Is she guarded?'

'Not at all, Highness. A trusted man-at-arms and four or five soldiers, well-mounted, would suffice to seize her. They would be back in Compeigne before the alarm was raised. But I would counsel speed, lest she finds another hiding place.'

Lancelin stood in his stirrups and shouted for his equerry, a fine-featured, muscular young man wearing a tight-fitting surcoat beneath his cloak. 'D'Essoyes will be ideal,' he said, settling back into the saddle. 'His lands border Jourdaine. How will he find the place?'

'We can send a priest with the party. He knows the place and can identify the woman. I will have him brought to you immediately.' Othon had the same humourless smile as Lancelin. 'But he is not to be told the purpose of the expedition, nor trusted with any part of the capture.'

'Very well. Attend me this evening and we can arrange details.'

Lancelin's equerry came at a canter, showing his mastery of riding by making his horse dance beneath him, and sending the skirts of his surcoat fluttering in the wind of his coming. It was green, emblazoned with five golden stars, and d'Essoyes held one hand open to the side, aware of how fine a picture he made.

D'Essoyes greeted his prince. 'A poor day's riding, Your Highness.'

'On the contrary,' Othon muttered, 'I think it has been a most excellent day.'

Othon reined back, allowing Lancelin to talk privately to his equerry while he and Taillefer rode together.

'It is unlike you to give away an advantage, brother,' Taillefer said.

'The king will know his son could not do this alone. A word in his ear will be sufficient.' Othon put his hand on his chest and bowed in the saddle, as if to the king. His eyes were bright with humour. 'I am but the humble servant of his family.'

'And one imagines that the anakritis-general does not know of this?'

'Do you really think Pateras Ghislain Barthram has told us all he is doing? What is the merit in telling him when the prize is almost in our grasp, without his help?' Othon laughed. 'The anakritim already have far too much power. The question, my brother, has never been *whether* the witch will be captured, but *when* and *by whom*. Now it will be soon, and by us.'

7.2 BARTHRAM

Barthram stared at his pigeon loft as if his will alone could bring a bird. He did not need Kasim's headshake to tell him none had come. Again. The absence of new knowledge gnawed at his guts as he hurried to the fire temple. He fell to his knees before the skull of the Blessèd Tanguy. Surely, on the holiest spot in Galmandie, his prayers would be heard by the God? If he poured all his faith, all his fervour into the asking?

The brother he'd trained and sent to Moutâne with the first pigeons understood his mission: keep them caged. Replacements will be sent every five days. Release one when you receive another even if there is no news, lest they become accustomed to their new home. Watch for the d'Aurillac arms of three silver birds on blue. The brother was dependable; the failure would not be there.

His flaw was that Fulke d'Aurillac had reached Château Fontenay before the brother. The first pigeon had brought a simple message. *The silver birds arrived one day ago and left the same day with a de Fontenay retainer. Current whereabouts unknown. Searching, as are all brethren.* D'Aurillac had been seen, and remembered, but had not been thought remarkable in the stream of visitors to Château Fontenay. Barthram cursed himself for not broadcasting his plans more widely.

Since then, nothing. His instruction, sent with a replacement pigeon, had been emphatic. *Find him, at all costs. Ask all who love the God to do the same.* Yet there had been no word. The messenger might have been held up by the snow. Or had the bird been taken by a hawk? Such things happened.

D'Aurillac cannot have made contact; there had been two pigeons in that first consignment. Barthram would have heard.

Barthram prostrated himself on the cold marble, his arms outstretched in supplication. Behind him in the temple, worshippers made the sign of the God and wondered at his piety.

7.3 ADELAIS

Adelais's training had settled into a pattern as structured as the devotions in a sisterhouse.

They'd wake with the light, though here in the forest the dawn office was announced by a crowing cock rather than temple bells. Adelais, Sennet, and Rossignol would sweep any overnight snowfall from the courtyard and scatter the straw from the stables over the hard ground; after half a moon it had been trampled into a compacted mat that saved the horses from slipping and lameness on the frozen earth beneath. Brushed drifts were piled against the outhouses and beneath the gatehouse, serving as an improvised barrier.

Adelais had ventured outside the gatehouse only once; deep snow on the meadow squeaked under her boots as she trod. The air was crisp, invigorating, and the silence was wonderful after the arguments within the lodge. She'd stood there, nose lifted, inhaling air cold enough to hurt her throat, until Rossignol called her in and pointed out her tracks, plain for any passer-by to see.

After breaking their fast d'Aurillac would teach her horsemanship in the courtyard. When the sun was halfway to noon

Rossignol would claim her for a sword-and-buckler lesson, demonstrating one new attack and defence each day, slowly at first, then building up the repetitions until they were instinctive and combat-fast. No one observed the offices, but after noon and a light meal the pattern would be repeated.

Around the time of the Lighting of the Lamps they would all gather in the lodge's kitchen, sharing the heat. Rossignol might play the lute. Fulke seemed either lost in his own world or fretful and snappy. Rossignol or Sennet were with him at all times and their distrust clearly rankled. Adelais sensed a great hurt within him, and wished he would let her come close. Let anyone come close. He set himself at a distance, seeming to feed on his own pain.

There was too little private time for runecraft with Elyse. When it was Adelais's turn on watch, Elyse would sometimes join her in the gatehouse tower and they'd talk in low voices, their eyes turned outwards, their thoughts inwards. Elyse would draw a rune in the frost and talk of the mysteries.

'*Jera*, the rune of plenty, one of the three runes of the cycle of the sun. *Raidho* is the sun's daily cycle, *jera* her year, and *sowilo* the sun herself. *Jera* is the rune of Freyja, and is invoked for a good harvest and for fertility. In runecasts it is the sign of rewards for honourable deeds, as spring follows winter.'

They saw almost no one. Twice, a woodsman passed on the track, once with a great bundle of firewood strapped to his back. Sennet and Elyse knew him; a half-wild man who lived from what he could kill or gather in the forest. He had a shelter two leagues away and kept himself to himself. He was harmless. Some said he was holy. Another time, a hunter passed with a great hound ranging around him, sniffing at the tracks of deer. No one called at the lodge.

Agnès did not come, and Adelais understood why; she would be too easily tracked. Yet Adelais missed her; that easy camaraderie, the rich laughter, the sisterhood, the need for each other's company. She threw herself into the training and by evening would be hurting in so many places that all she wanted to do was to lie flat on the big feather bed in the lord's chamber. Sometimes Elyse would rub scented oils into aching muscles.

She fought and rode in women's clothes, not lordling's finery. It was more seemly with the men watching, even though clothes had a way of changing her behaviour. In a kirtle and overdress, she was a woman, engaging with those around her as a woman. While Rossignol taught her swordsmanship, she'd kilt her skirts over her belt because the crouching guard position dropped her hems low enough to trip her. That naturally left her boots exposed, but she still moved as a woman. From time to time she'd put her shoulders back to distract Rossignol in a way that only a woman can, and Rossignol's wry smile told her that he knew exactly what she was doing.

Flirtation never worked with Rossignol. He'd drop into one of the guard positions, forcing her to fight, but even then she moved in a way that hinted at the foreplay to a coupling; her eyes would lock on Rossignol's ravaged face while their sword tips flirted with each other, steely tongued. And always, Fulke watched. And Sennet watched Fulke so he could not slip away unobserved.

At least these days she had a good supply of clean, tight-fitting hose.

The sound of the stream signalled the melt in rising, tumbling notes, though at first they saw little sign of it apart from landslides of snow from the angled roofs of the stables. A day later patches of brown appeared under the trees, where the snow had always been thinnest. The track turned to mud in the sunshine, streaked with white in the ruts, and bounded by leaking mounds of snow on its shaded banks. Adelais almost regretted the thaw; it would soon be time to move on. She'd miss them all, even Rossignol. Agnès, of course, most of all. Elyse had also found a special place in her heart; hopefully Adelais would find another *seidhkona* in Vriesland who'd teach her rune lore, but Elyse had become the mother she'd never known.

And on a day when there were deer on the meadow, pawing their way through to grazing beneath, Fulke announced that Adelais was ready to ride out on her destrier. 'The bond was already there between you,' he said, 'but now he is truly listening to you, trying to understand.' So Adelais dressed to ride away from the lodge as if she were d'Aurillac's squire, in a lordling's hat and herigaut, with all traces of womanhood smoothed away and her legs sheathed in her new boots. In this guise she truly became a noble, manly and proud. Humbert's sword swung on her hip, its weight pulling at her belt. On the ground her hand would fall naturally to the top of the scabbard, steadying it against her thigh. On horseback it hung more easily; pure, sheathed authority. She sat tall in the saddle, widening her shoulders in a way that displayed her confidence, not her sex.

'Just remember you are wearing spurs,' d'Aurillac warned her. 'Always know how you are placing your legs.'

'An important lesson for every woman, messire.' Adelais lifted an eyebrow at him, teasing. Perhaps she was not yet wholly masculine despite her clothes. Or would she have dared say such a thing in a kirtle? *And I have made one who was a Guardian blush!* It dawned on her that d'Aurillac did not know how to be around a woman. Was he, too, more comfortable with her pretence of manhood?

Clearly d'Aurillac had expected them to ride out alone; the excursion nearly ended before Fulke had even mounted, when Rossignol announced that he would accompany them.

'You touch upon my honour, minstrel. Mistress Adelais is safe with me.'

For a moment Adelais feared that d'Aurillac would draw his sword.

'And I touch upon my lady's safety, Seigneur.' Rossignol was calm but firm. 'You are a guest of the de Fontenays. If we ride out, we ride together.' The insistence was respectful but Rossignol's distrust was plain.

They stared at each other and the silence stretched.

'Please, messire?' Adelais leaned forwards in the saddle, making her voice as soft and feminine as she could. 'I yearn for wide spaces, beyond these walls.'

It was several heartbeats before d'Aurillac moved. His eyes locked on Rossignol and his face clenched with anger, but after several breaths he mounted and led the way along a newly brushed path through the melting snowbanks under the gates. No one spoke until after they had forded the stream, and then it was only Rossignol who called to insist they turn away from the route to Fontenay and ride deeper into the forests, not towards the roads and town. Adelais saw d'Aurillac's hand become a fist against his thigh at that. His shoulders were high and crossbow-tight.

Rossignol fell back, as far as a servant behind his master, but he was too intent on surveilling their surroundings for conversation. Adelais trailed behind d'Aurillac, confined between the noble's sullen back and Rossignol's watchful eye. Now she was out of the lodge, she wanted to enjoy the day. Laugh a little. Perhaps even give their horses their head, where the ground was safe to run. Allier began to dance under her, making her wonder if the horse was truly entering her mind. After half a league Adelais nudged him alongside d'Aurillac and held him there so that Allier cantered on the spot. D'Aurillac glanced at her with a face as dull as a blunted axe, but she grinned her challenge, refusing to be cowed.

A clear track stretched in front of them, soft after the melt, with just the occasional puddle of white where snow had slipped from the branches of a fir. The horse wanted to go. She wanted to go. *Sætur Sif, let's live a little*. It took the slightest squeeze with her leg and a giving of her hands to release Allier's energy into the morning. Now they'd have to follow.

But she was still learning the strength of a warhorse. She'd ridden all her life, but had never known this power. It was not so much the speed – although that was fast enough for the rush of wind past her ears to drown all noise except the drumming of the hooves – it was the sheer force of the beast. Muscles bunched and stretched in Allier's shoulders as he ran, and Adelais knew that she would not be able to stop him unless he consented to be stopped.

He didn't. Particularly when d'Aurillac drew alongside, racing her. He even managed to pull ahead, crouched over his saddle with the wind lifting his cloak like a flag. He only reined in when the track entered a sheltered defile and snow blocked their path. Adelais let out a great whoop of joy as they came to a bounding halt, and even d'Aurillac smiled. He actually smiled. The grin split his face unstoppably, almost reluctantly, and became laughter.

'I yield, sir knight!' Adelais was breathless. The snorting of the horses might have been her own gasping, but she felt more intensely alive than she had for months. What was it that Agnès said? A gallop was the next best thing to a coupling?

'The last time I raced like that,' Fulke d'Aurillac said, also breathing heavily, 'was with my Guardian brothers. Life was not all chants and warfare.'

D'Aurillac smiled again at the memory and circled his horse, letting him walk loose-reined, blown. It was as if a shell had crumbled from Fulke like rusted armour, leaving the man exposed. Rossignol was nowhere to be seen; they had long outrun him.

'The minstrel will find us.' Fulke seemed glad to be out of Rossignol's company. 'There has been no forking of the path.'

The track was cramped enough for their legs to touch as they circled, sparking a moment of awkward apology. Afterwards, the quiet held a different, more welcome tension.

'You have done well, girl. More than I expected in the time we have had. You and the destrier have bonded.'

Adelais knew that to be true. She could feel Allier's happiness, the way he danced for the joy of being out and galloping. They were in tune, just as Rossignol and his lute were in tune.

'You will need those skills,' d'Aurillac added. 'I have tried to teach you all I can, but there is so little time...'

'And I thank you, messire.' Adelais paused, not sure how to start their first real conversation. 'You are newly released from prison?'

'Newly enough that I still wonder at the smell of the forest.'

If there was joy in his freedom, she had not seen it before that moment. Adelais risked a more probing question. 'Does the memory of the Black Tower weigh heavily upon you?'

'The Black Tower, and what happened there...' He breathed as if he'd been about to say something, and then swallowed his words. Eventually he lifted his right hand, the one with the rigid little finger. 'They used hammers, at first. It hurts more, the second time, when it is already broken. Later, it was enough just to twist the fragments against each other.'

'You do not have to tell me this, messire.' It was too personal. Adelais regretted starting this line of talk; they'd jumped from a happy moment into a dark memory.

'And they continue, with fire or hammers or whatever is convenient, until you say what they want to hear. There is no other way to end it.'

'Sweet Salazar!' Adelais swore aloud in the name of the Ischyrian prophet.

'Oh, it is done with prayer, that a sinner might see the error of his ways and be received back into the faith. They do not inflict pain themselves, these priestly anakritim, they have *tormentors* who do that, just as we do not gallop, we have *horses* that do our bidding, beasts trained to our will.'

'Why are you saying this, messire?' Adelais sensed he had something beneath his remembered pain that was more important than the pain itself.

'Because I wish to warn you, Mistress Adelais.' He rarely used her name. 'If you are ever taken by the anakritis-general, the truth does not matter, no matter how much you scream, no matter how innocent you are. Pain becomes a foul fiend that is your constant companion, that knows you better than your own mother. Eventually you will say anything, confess to anything, betray your dearest friend, just to leave that fiend behind for an hour. And you will feel guilty for the rest of your life, for that weakness.'

There was heavy meaning in his words, and Adelais realised he'd snatched at this moment alone. Was this their first time without Rossignol, or Elyse, or the castellan watching?

'Why is this warning so urgent, messire?'

He swallowed again.

'I have a brother...'

A shout interrupted him. They both twisted in the saddle to see Rossignol trotting ever closer. His face was thunderous.

'You lost your hat, mistress.' Rossignol held out the nobleman's hat.

'Swept off by a branch.' Adelais put it back on her head, a little reluctantly. Her hair had grown enough for her to feel the wind through it as they galloped. 'I was going to pick it up on the way back.'

'And you were seen by the woodsman.'

'Were we?' Adelais hadn't seen him in the madness of that gallop. He must have been off the track, in the woods.

'I must ask that we stay together at all times.' His tone was crisp with fury. 'Even if our horses have different capabilities.'

Adelais smiled her apology. It *had* been silly to ride around with blonde hair flying free, but oh, such fun. She lifted an eyebrow towards Fulke, the way she might to a friend caught together in naughtiness, but his face was once again a mask.

7.4 HUMBERT

Humbert had had half a moon with little to do but think, incarcerated in Seneschal de Mauriac's castle while they waited for the roads to open. All conversation was prohibited, although the seneschal interpreted the ban on 'tokens of benevolence' loosely, providing a generous supply of food and even wine, and a bed in a secure storeroom rather than the cold depths of the dungeon.

In the first hours after leaving the commandery Humbert had agonised about how Fulke might have been watched. He'd been with them for over a moon, and had not ventured out until his departure for Fontenay; he'd had no opportunity to summon help.

Humbert had his answer on that terrible first day. Wandering clerics were commonplace; they preached outside temples and at town crossroads, claiming hospitality from brotherhouses, commanderies, and local lords in return for their prayers. Humbert hardly noticed the anakritis who'd drawn back onto the verge to let them pass, about a league from the commandery, not at first; he stood there with his hood tugged forwards against the cold, but as the cleric lifted his hand in benediction his eyes became visible, glinting within the hood's cavern, and they were locked on Humbert's bound wrists. The ghost of a smile told Humbert all he needed to know.

Not one informant, a whole order. How many anakritim had eaten at the commandery's board during d'Aurillac's stay? More than enough for a message to have reached Villebénie, and for the order for Humbert's arrest to have reached the seneschal. And if d'Aurillac was watched here, he would be watched in Fontenay. Humbert raged inwardly at his inability to warn Adelais.

One morning Humbert smelt a cold dampness in the air rather than the crispness of frost, and he knew they would be leaving even before he was led out into a dazzling courtyard. There an escort of a sergeant and two men waited. De Mauriac stood at his own gates and lifted his hand in benediction or farewell as they left, a gesture heavy with regret; so much could not be said.

Riding with bound hands was uncomfortable. Like any man-at-arms, Humbert could control his horse with his legs and weight, leaving his arms free for fighting, but he'd always been in control of the horse. The beast he sat on was being led, and so would lurch into unexpected and unbalancing trots as the lead rein jerked. Every league carried him towards a dread fate, but he was more concerned at the certainty that he had put Adelais in mortal danger.

Humbert kept his demeanour deliberately mild, portraying himself as a wronged brother who nevertheless accepts the will of the God. He made a point of chanting at the proper times, and the soldiers' caution gradually eased even though they were not permitted to talk to him. They spent the first night, and the second, in the stables of wayside inns. In each they kept him bound and tethered to a post or a cart. One of them was always awake and watching. Before they left the second inn they let him buy a flask of the strong, distilled spirits of the region, for the nights were freezing and the cold was settling into his bones. They were not, it seemed, unkindly men, particularly when he hinted that he would share his purchase.

They now travelled across an empty land, and when night fell the only shelter was a dilapidated hovel, in a hamlet where perhaps thirty souls scratched a living from the soil. A denier bought them a small fire and a leaking roof, but there was no food to be had save what they brought with them. After this thin meal, Humbert opened his flask of liquor, sipped the fiery liquid, and sighed his pleasure before offering it around. The soldiers did not hesitate. After that he only pretended to sip as it circulated. A simple lamp gave a companionable if evil-smelling light, and after the men forgot the ban on speech the evening became almost convivial. When the lamp died, they finished the liquor by the light of the glowing embers.

Humbert feigned sleep with his back against a damp wall, his bound legs in front of him, and his backside on an even damper dirt floor, cushioned only by his cloak and a layer of disintegrating straw. Through half-closed eyes he watched two of his guards wrap themselves in their cloaks, leaving their boots to warm by the fire. The third sat with his back against the opposite wall, his sheathed sword across his knees, watching Humbert with heavy eyes. His head slowly tipped backwards against the wall, but as Humbert began to move the guard snorted, once, and jerked awake. The man licked his lips, blinked, and shuffled into a more comfortable position. This time, his head fell forwards.

When the man's snores joined his companions' Humbert lifted his feet with a hunter's caution so that the straw did not rustle as he brought his ankles to his hands. He kept his eyes locked on the guard, drew the small quill-paring knife from his boot and held it in his teeth to cut the ropes around his wrists. He took his time with the last strands, lest they fall to the ground and make a noise. When he cut the bonds around his legs he was able to use his spare hand to ease them away.

Yet still he hesitated, long enough to say a prayer. He had killed many men but always in battle, their faces often anonymous behind great helms. They'd been men who were trying to kill him. Trying to kill this guard felt like murder. It was not chivalrous.

The men all slept with their swords close as lovers; the sitting one held his gripped in his lap, another protected his blade under a trailing arm, the third slept with it wrapped inside his cloak. If he tried to take any of them they'd wake. He might fight two, once he had a sword in his hand, but not three. He reversed his little blade, gripped it in both hands, and stood astride the sitting guard's legs.

Evlogiménos Ischyros, Pateras ólon... Humbert prayed silently. *Parakaló mou.* Grant me Pardon...

The man's hand twitched, and a snore stopped abruptly in mid-snort. His neck tensed, and Humbert guessed his half-sleeping, befuddled mind was trying to make sense of the boots either side of his legs.

Humbert brought the knife down with all his strength into the base of the skull between the tightening tendons. The man's limbs collapsed as if his whole head had been severed, but his torso slumped forwards, trapping the sword between body and legs.

Both the others' heads came up from their cloaks. One, more awake than the other, swore a mighty oath and reached for his sword. The other, mumbling his confusion, stayed tangled in his cloak.

Humbert yanked the dead guard's body sideways until the sheathed hilt of the man's sword was upright, then drew the blade. He managed one hard thrust into the thrashing cloak and felt the twist and jerk of his point biting into flesh before he danced backwards, giving himself room to fight.

Dogs began to bark in the hamlet, one setting off several others.

The sergeant had his sword out and was crouched, ready, blinking away his sleep. They glared at each other in the near-dark, and the flashing whites of the sergeant's darting, fear-filled eyes gave Humbert the measure of him. The sergeant had known him as a mild, ageing cleric. Now he saw the shadowy outline of a former Guardian with a sword in his hand.

The bubbling cough of a chest wound joined the dog's chorus from the cloak on the ground, and they both knew the sergeant was on his own.

The man turned and ran, calling for help, though where he hoped to find it in the hamlet, the God only knew.

Humbert took one stride, enough to swing his sword as the sergeant reached the door, and to bring its edge down on an ankle. A crippling wound, not a killing one. He'd done enough killing for one night. The man toppled sideways as his leg gave way, trying to steady himself against the wall with one hand. The other hand still gripped his sword as he fell. His eyes showed bright white in the darkness.

'Please!'

'Drop the sword. I don't have to kill you.'

The sergeant heaved the sword at Humbert as if it were a spear, a last desperate attempt to incapacitate him. But Humbert had seen the shoulder move and caught the blade on his own. It clattered off into a corner.

'You should learn when to yield, man.' Yet Humbert sheathed his own sword, honouring the sergeant's act of courage.

The guard he'd struck with his knife was dead. Humbert had to brace his knee against the man's head to pull the tiny blade out of his skull.

The soldier in the cloak was grey-faced and dribbling blood. Humbert offered to hear his unburdening before he left, but the man only snarled at him until another cough creased him over. So be it. He would pray for their souls.

Outside, in the thin light of clouded stars, the horses were milling in a cattle pen, spooked by the smell of blood. If he took all four he could hope to outrun the news; he'd sell two on the way to fund his needs. He doubted if the hamlet possessed a horse, so someone would have to walk for help. Shawl-wrapped peasants formed a wary half-circle as he saddled a horse. One of them bore a flaring torch and he used its light to search the soldiers' baggage for coins, food and anything else that might aid his journey. He would have three, possibly four days' ride to Fontenay. He had at least a day before any pursuit began, probably more.

As Humbert rode away, tugging at the string of horses, the peasants closed in on the hovel, presumably to look for anything of value that he had not taken. He wondered if they'd let the crippled sergeant live, or whether the lure of two swords and their clothing would be too great. If so, there would be no pursuit; he would simply disappear.

The night had added much to his burden of sins, a burden he must carry until the bridge of judgement, unless his expulsion was lifted. But at least the sergeant's death would not be numbered among them.

CHAPTER EIGHT

8.1 ADELAIS

In the milky light of dawn a wolf trotted along the margin of the meadow. Adelais watched it from the gatehouse tower, wondering if this was a portent. It made no signal that it was anything other than a forest wolf ranging though its territory; no gaze towards her, no blue-eyed glance inviting her to follow. Just a wolf. Going north.

Maybe. Perhaps it was time to go. The roads would be open. When would Agnès come? Adelais wanted to see her before she left.

The wolf may not have been a warning. The ravens definitely were.

Adelais and Fulke had taken their morning destrier lesson out onto the meadow where the snow had melted to leave a wet, muddy turf that squelched under Allier's hooves. She had dressed as a lordling, just to be safe outside of the lodge, and she relished the closer contact with the horse without the skirts of a kirtle or robe. Fulke stood in the middle of the meadow, calling instructions, moving with an awkward, lurching gait when he had to. She wondered if he would offer to accompany her, when she left, and she wondered if she would want that. There had been a distance between them, as if they faced each other across a chasm, until that gallop. She'd glimpsed a warmer man within that shell. He'd started to reach out and reveal his hurt. She liked that.

Allier came to a halt, his nose in the air and pointing towards a commotion among the ravens; they flapped around the gatehouse and made forays towards the woods. Did Allier also see this as a sign, or was he reading her mind? Adelais looked questioningly towards Elyse and Sennet, both hurrying through the gatehouse, frowning with worry, their eyes on the birds. Rossignol followed them carrying his sword but seeming more curious than alarmed until he saw something that launched him towards the trees at a run, his edged blade drawn.

'What is happening?' Fulke said, irritated by the interruption.

'We are watched, I think.' Adelais stayed focused on the trees where Rossignol had disappeared under the lattice of branches.

'How do you know?'

'The ravens.'

'That is witchcraft!' Fulke sounded affronted.

Adelais did not turn. 'If a dog barks, is that witchcraft too?'

Rossignol came back, still running. 'Footprints,' he called. 'Lend me your horse, mudlark. It is the only one saddled.'

It was a sign of the deepening bond between her and Allier that the warhorse put his head into her shoulder for reassurance as Rossignol mounted; a known human but an unknown rider.

By the time Rossignol returned, storming into the courtyard as he fought to control Allier, Adelais had saddled her gelding and loaded it with saddlebags of clothes and provisions for a journey. They all had weapons to hand.

Rossignol shook his head. He seemed keen to dismount.

'Lost him. There were horse's tracks through a snow patch. I went as far as the edge of the forest, but there were several riders on the road beyond. It could have been any of them.'

Their midday meal was subdued. In the silence Adelais came to a decision and laid her bowl on the table.

'It is time for me to go. In the morning, I think; the roads are open. Say farewell to Lady Agnès for me. She will understand.'

Elyse, Sennet, and Rossignol breathed out, an audible release of tension. D'Aurillac looked as if he had been about to say something but thought better of it.

Yet Agnès came that afternoon, escorted by Guy Carelet. She received the news gravely, but insisted that there was no need for Adelais to leave immediately. After all, if the owner of the footprints had been a spy, he would need to send word to the authorities. In the absence of her husband she *was* the authority in northern Jourdaine. A message would probably need to be sent all the way to Villebénie and the king. By the time any force was gathered Adelais could be long gone, perhaps even be in Vriesland, so that night they would feast her departure. And while the light remained, she wished to watch Adelais fight in her new finery and see how her lessons had progressed. 'Sword-craft if you please, not riding.' She knew Adelais could ride. Agnès positioned herself on a cushioned stool at the top of the lodge's steps to watch, wrapped in her cloak. Elyse stood behind her, arms folded, like an aproned chancellor behind her queen.

Adelais was still dressed as a lordling, in a quality cote-hardie that fell below her knees but which left her legs free to move. Beneath it she wore the quilted doublet that Elyse had fashioned, laced tight to her chest.

It was liberating, this freedom of arm and leg, this flattening of her shape. She might loosen the lacing across her chest, that was all; it restricted her breathing a little. Men's clothing

allowed Adelais to concentrate on the lesson, not the encum-
bering folds of her skirts, and she so wanted to display her new
skills. She also wanted to show Guy that a woman could wield a
sword, and she wanted to tease Fulke d'Aurillac again, just a
little. He was standing apart, as always, but eyeing her in a very
male sort of way.

Not so Rossignol. His look had not softened. He had the
same, calculating stare behind that probing sword point. They
knew each other now; his attacks would start with the slightest
narrowing of his eye as he 'moved into distance', entering the
space where his blade could do damage.

Or hers. He'd had her practise 'distance' over and over again
against a log he held in his gauntleted hands, until she could cut
with the crucial last handspan of the blade. Now they mirrored
each other's stance: legs spaced wide (that too had seemed indecent at first) but light on the toes; bent at the waist, leaning
forwards; their swords and bucklers extended and pressed
together in a defensive V. How like a dance this was; circling,
hard-smiling, like snarling cats who don't know whether they
are going to scratch or mate. Adelais could sense that she had
Fulke d'Aurillac's full attention.

Perhaps she was overconfident. Perhaps she was thinking
more about displaying than fighting. It was late in the day and
certainly she was tiring. Rossignol's blade pushed hers away,
and she responded with too much force, hacking downwards
towards the neck and inadvertently opening up a gap between
her sword and her buckler. Rossignol deflected her blade easily,
and this time his sword flicked through the gap and she felt the
rasp of its blunted edge against her shoulder. Worse, he
followed through, managing to hook his leg behind hers as she
danced backwards *out* of distance, and punched her chest with
both his buckler and the hilt of his sword. Adelais fell heavily
onto her backside, cursing, and found herself staring up the

length of the blade he held to her throat. On the steps Agnès made a small cry of alarm.

Adelais let her head fall back, humiliated. 'I yield.' She let go of her buckler and held her right breast where the hard end of Rossignol's quillon had struck her. Even through Elyse's padded *jacquet*, that had hurt.

'Are you wounded, mudlark?' Rossignol taunted, lowering his blade.

Adelais shook her head and held out her hand. She didn't blame him. Their understanding, from the beginning, was that he should make no concessions to her sex; if she ever had to fight for real, her opponent wouldn't.

Rossignol pulled her to her feet. 'Slice meat with your sword, don't chop wood.' He sounded a little angry. 'If you are leaving on the morrow you should not still be making mistakes like that. If you hack and your attack fails, it leaves you open and it's hard to recover. Remember, always kill with the wrist, not the shoulder.'

Adelais nodded; it was a hard lesson, well-learned. She picked up her buckler and backed away, holding her chest. She saw Agnès was on her feet, mouth slightly open with concern, and at the gates Guy Carelet was sniggering. She'd like to wipe that smirk of his face. She dropped into guard, wanting another chance to prove herself.

'Enough!' Agnès interrupted them. 'You are making me thirsty, just watching. Let us have wine, and meat, and music.'

Adelais straightened. It seemed she was not going to show her new skills. But perhaps it *was* time to stop; it was late in the day, and *sætur Sif* she was stiff and tired as she walked towards the steps, though she still had her shoulders back. There was something about having a sword on her hip that made her swagger a little, even after Rossignol had bested her, even though she ached everywhere. Worst of all was her forearm and wrist, for Rossignol insisted that even at rest she practice moving the weight of a sword's blade with just a flick of the wrist.

After they had eaten Elyse sat Adelais at one end of the hall's table, rolled back the cuffs of her shirt, and kneaded her salve of fragrant oil into Adelais's forearm with her thumbs. Adelais shut her eyes and groaned in pleasure.

'If you were a cat, *kjúkling,* you'd be purring.' Agnès was sipping wine beside them. She had washed away her cares of Château Fontenay with several glasses of wine; she was already a little flushed. Near the fire, Rossignol cradled his lute, filling the hall with sweet, mournful songs of impossible love. Sennet sat near him on a bench, his back to the table, clasping a goblet to his belly. Guy had drawn the first watch and was outside. Fulke d'Aurillac sat further away, the pale outlines of his surcoat's heraldic birds looming in the shadows.

'D'Aurillac keeps himself apart.' Agnès lifted her goblet towards him.

'He and Rossignol find it hard to be in the same room, my lady.' Elyse turned Adelais's hand over and began pushing oil deep into her palm. 'Rossignol does not trust d'Aurillac, yet Mistress Adelais teases the lord as if he were a suitor.' She grinned at Adelais; a knowing, woman's look.

'Me?'

'Don't play the innocent, my sweeting.' Elyse's thumb made a valley along the inside of Adelais's forearm.

'I'll be gone soon, and then it won't matter.' Adelais sighed. She still didn't know if she'd accept if Fulke offered to ride north with her. She frowned towards the shadows. It was impossible to tell if Fulke was looking at her. She wished they'd had longer alone after the gallop; surrounded by the others he seemed locked inside invisible armour.

A log fell within the fire, scattering sparks, and Elyse rose to stamp them out. She knelt to build up the fire again, muttering about idle men as she poked at embers. Rossignol shifted his feet to give her room, without interrupting his playing.

Agnès picked up the dish of oil and held it to her face, sniffing. 'What is this?'

'One of Elyse's concoctions. Vervain, betony, and rose petals soaked in oil.'

'Does it work?'

'It's soothing. I don't know whether that's her touch or the herbs.'

'Let me try.' Agnès copied Elyse's technique, sliding her hands up the forearm. She looked up at Adelais's face, watching for the effect. 'Don't leave yet,' she whispered. 'Stay a few more days with me, at least.'

'But if we have been discovered? You'll be ruined.'

'We have half a moon at least before troops might come. No one in Jourdaine would take up arms against me.' Agnès worked her fingers into Adelais's arm, though she did not have Elyse's skill; her touch was a caress that smoothed the muscles beneath rather than eased their knots. 'You cut a fine figure as a young gentle, *kjúkling*. Why, if you had a man's shaft I'd take you to my chamber.'

It was said lightly, but there was a loneliness in Agnès's eyes. She covered Agnès's oil-slick fingers with her spare hand and squeezed. 'Agnès, my friend, if I had a shaft you'd have been fighting me off long ago.' Adelais used the same bantering tone, but wasn't sure if that sounded quite as she'd intended. She knew only that Agnès was high-born and beautiful; green-eyed, dark-haired, and full-breasted, a woman any man would desire.

'I might not have fought too hard,' Agnès said in the same joking, knowing tone, a flicker of a smile crossing her face. But she dropped Adelais's arm as if suddenly embarrassed.

'Is there any word from de Fontenay?' It was the first question that came into Adelais's head.

'None. He is still in Villebénie, as far as I know, courting the Duke of Delmas.'

By the fire, Elyse had been persuaded to sing; a lusty, peasant song.

> *My love is like an ash tree, tall and strong,*
> *I sleep beneath his branches, his root it loves me*
>   *long...*

Her voice was surprisingly sweet, low and warm as a smoky hearth. Adelais's eyes began to close as wine and music and hard effort caught up with her. She waited until Elyse finished her song and stood, applauding with the others.

'I'm going to take my aches to bed.' Adelais put both hands into the small of her back and arched around them, trying to stretch out the knots from the constant half-crouch, pivot-and-dance of sword-and-buckler work. 'I'm moving like an old crone.'

Agnès hesitated a moment before she picked up the dish again. 'Would vervain and betony help?' Her smile was wine-bright and impish.

'I'll miss you, *kjúkling*.' In the lord's chamber, Agnès eased off her golden net, letting her hair tumble to her waist. She sat in her shirt at a small table, holding a polished silver hand mirror.

Adelais picked up Agnès's brush. 'I must go.' She moved a candle to light her task. Agnès did not travel to the lodge with a maidservant, so like sisters they brushed each other's hair before bed. Agnès's took much longer. 'And you have already risked much to help me.'

'You'll ride north?' Agnès sipped wine, and lifted the goblet for Adelais.

'North, yes. And no more wine, thanks. Too much dulls my

responses with Rossignol.' Agnès's hair was lustrous. It flowed through the brush like moonlit water over a weir. 'You and I will both be safer when I am beyond King Aloys's reach.'

'I will worry about you, alone on the road.' Agnès spilt wine as she put her goblet down.

'But I will be a young noble, on a mighty destrier with a sword at my side!'

'All the same...' Agnès stood, turning. 'Take care.' Agnès's hug was fierce, her head fitting naturally into Adelais's neck and shoulder. She swayed a little and she pushed herself back. 'Drunk too much. Time for bed.'

When Agnès first visited, Elyse had set out a servant's straw mattress for Adelais in the lord's chamber, though it had never been used. They slept together as sisters in the great feather bed, but that night for the first time Adelais was truly aware of their nakedness. Until Agnès fell asleep there was a new tension between them that was also a shy excitement.

In the night Agnès rolled over, still asleep, and hooked a leg over Adelais's thigh. Her head rested into Adelais's shoulder, a limp hand came across her chest, and a breast pushed against Adelais's ribs. She was bed-warm and soft, and squirmed a little, enough for her bush to scratch against Adelais's leg.

'Wish you had a prick,' Agnès mumbled.

They both became very still, and newly awake.

Adelais slid from under Agnès's arm and crossed to the window. She opened the shutter a crack; the crisp moonlight had cast patterns onto the forest of black and silver, charcoal and ash. Behind her came the sound of Agnès moving, swinging a cloak around herself, but Adelais did not turn until her friend stood beside her, close enough for Adelais to feel her heat. They did not touch. If Adelais had made any contact, offered any gesture of intimacy, she feared she would change their friendship. She wasn't sure if it would survive.

'It is time for me to go, my friend.' Adelais said the words as gently as she could. 'For many reasons.'

Agnès swept her cloak around Adelais, covering them both. 'I think I had too much wine.' She rested her head into Adelais's shoulder but did not press her warmth any closer.

Adelais did not move. 'I would rather be your friend for life than your lover for a night.'

'I will always be your friend.' Agnès's hug was sisterly, despite the way it pushed her curves into Adelais's side. 'And I hope you will be mine.'

Adelais relaxed enough to put her arm around her, returning the hug. 'Never doubt it.'

Agnès's hair held traces of some exotic fragrance. Another, mustier scent rose from her body. 'Wait one more day. I will bring a purse for your journey, or send one if I cannot come.'

'You have already been generous beyond measure.' And Adelais felt ungrateful to be standing so stiffly.

'If you ride as a noble, then you must be able to lodge like one. You don't want to spoil your new finery by sleeping in a hedge, do you?' Agnès emphasised 'finery' by brushing the backs of her fingers against Adelais's body. The knuckles against her breast were not quite a caress.

The draught through the window was cold; soon Adelais would have to find the warmth of a bed. For the rest of this night, perhaps she'd take the servant's mattress. Perhaps. As if understanding, Agnès lifted onto her toes to kiss her on the cheek.

'Come then, my friend,' Agnès said, with a gentle emphasis on 'friend', and tugged Adelais back towards the bed. She lay near the far edge, yielding safe space to Adelais.

That night Adelais dreamt of the wolf. It stood at the forest margin, watching her, wanting her to follow, and she ran after it through black trees until she was lost and alone. The trees looked low and hunched, little bigger than a man, and they formed an impenetrable ring around her. She spun, searching for a path, and the trees straightened, unfolding until they became hooded anakritim and the white trunks of their habits hemmed her in like the bars of a bear cage. Through their midst came a rider in red silk on a bay mare that leapt at her so its hooves struck her on each shoulder, knocking her backwards and pinning her to the ground. She woke on her back, gasping her panic, to find Agnès sitting over her, gripping her shoulders to shake her awake.

'Bad dream?'

Adelais nodded, as breathless as if she'd just run a league. 'I must leave.' The wolf had been warning her. 'With the dawn.'

The moonlight through the window edged Agnès's curves with silver. She rolled off Adelais as if suddenly aware of the renewed intimacy of their bodies, and they both lay awake, staring upwards, sharing a bed but frightened to touch.

'Stay one more day, kjúkling. Just that, so you can take gold for your journey. We'll say our farewells in the morning, just in case I cannot return myself. You'll see either me or Guy Carelet by nightfall.'

Adelais reached out a hand, beneath the covers, and Agnès clasped it, both giving and needing reassurance. Adelais lay listening to Agnès's not-yet-asleep breathing for as long as it took for the band of silver light between the shutters to narrow and fade to nothing.

Adelais slipped from the bed at cock-crow, dressed swiftly in her lordling's finery, and was putting Allier through his paces on the meadow when Agnès rode through the gates with Guy following behind. She reined in while Adelais cantered over to join her.

'Leaving so soon?'

'I will try to return before sunset.' Agnès spoke a little stiffly, in her chatelaine's voice. Adelais did not know whether that was for Guy's benefit or whether a barrier had come between them. Agnès did not hold eye contact and Adelais knew her well enough to see awkwardness beneath the hauteur. There was a moment of silence before Agnès touched a spur to her palfrey's flank. 'We will talk tonight,' she called, without turning her head.

8.2 BARTHRAM

The noon office had passed before Ghislain Barthram managed to speak to Othon de Remy, and the bird from Moutâne had arrived just after dawn. Half a day lost. He needed soldiers quickly, while the witch was still there, and only de Remy could provide those. Barthram had no intention of revealing the true source of his information; it could have been a mounted messenger rather than a bird. He would have to tread carefully.

First de Remy had been in Council with the king, and Barthram was sent word that the king wished to unburden before hearing noon office in his private chapel. As the king's pardoner, Barthram must wait, knowing that even when de Remy emerged he would have neither the time nor the privacy to speak. He stared through the windows of the antechamber and forced himself to remain calm, despite his eagerness. He found himself muttering a praise chant while he stared at the bare-branched orchards across the river. This was a good day, even if he was being made to wait.

Finally, a group of nobles left the council chamber with the Duke of Delmas at their head. Othon de Remy followed, talking with courtly deference to Prince Lancelin, and he did not even lift his head to acknowledge Barthram's presence – a pointed act of disdain or contempt. The first niggling concern entered Barthram's mind, but he could not interrupt. Already he was being called to the king.

In all his years of service to Aloys, Barthram had never grown close to the man beneath the crown, even as his pardoner. Unburdenings for Aloys had been a ritual, a process, like a spiritual ablution. Aloys held few regrets, and did not even notice the incidental damage caused by the onward march of his kingdom. The wrecked lives were like trees felled to build a ship; necessary, not worth his notice, and therefore not matters for unburdening. Yet now there was a matter on which the king needed constant reassurance: the death of Bastien Guerin, the last grand master of the Guardians and a man who had counted Aloys as his friend.

From this antechamber where Barthram and the king now knelt together, Aloys had watched Guerin die, bound to a stake and burned on a small marshy island below the palace. No amount of reassurance, not even the confessions that Barthram's tormentors had extracted from their Guardian prisoners, could wholly persuade Aloys of Guerin's guilt.

But the greatest evidence of all, Barthram repeated, was the death of the high priest. The Guardians must be in league with Kakos, the Destroyer; how else could the witch have struck at the heart of Ischyrendom?

'Unless the high priest's death was the God's vengeance for what we did to the Guardians,' Aloys responded, as always. In Council, in front of his nobles, the king would beat the table and rant at their failure to bring the witch to justice, but here, at his unburdening, the insecurity surfaced. Beneath it all, the king's niggling doubt: 'What if I was wrong? Must even I fall from the bridge of judgement?'

'I may have news soon, sire. Perhaps before this moon is out. I may have found her.'

Aloys seized his arm, his face lifting with hope.

'Now is the time for caution, sire. It is like the hunt. You see where the boar is hidden, but the quarry is not yet surrounded or killed.' Barthram would not allow himself to say more; it was foolish to overcommit with King Aloys. But he allowed optimism to creep into his voice.

'Bring her to me, man.' In his impatience, Aloys knocked Barthram's hand as he pressed the sacred ash of pardon onto the king's forehead. 'You will have her weight in gold.'

'I do not desire gold, sire. I live only to serve my king and the faith.'

Though temporal power is essential to do the work of the God, Barthram mused as he closed the silver box of ash, and gold bought power.

When Barthram was finally free, Pateras Octave was waiting for him. The mountainous anakritis had followed de Remy, as instructed, and now reported that the chancellor had gone from the Council to noon office in the great fire temple of Villebénie, where his family had been waiting for him. De Remy was not a man to worship quietly, unobserved by any save Ischyros, not when the mighty splendour of the fire temple was nearby. His path to and from the temple would be cleared by mace-bearing sergeants who'd beat the road clear if necessary. De Remy himself would stroll at ease surrounded by an inner guard of soldiers, with a steward nearby to block petitioners.

Barthram and Octave waited beside de Remy's route home, listening for the sound that marked the chancellor's progress. It was a whispering surge like the passage of a great fish beneath the still waters of a pond; a wave that swelled, was crushed against the buildings, and faded behind the great man, and its sound was the awed whispering of a name. '*De Remy*'. Did the chancellor see the look in the eyes of the people? Did he recognise their fear? Did he ever turn, and catch also the unmasked loathing in an unwary face?

Today de Remy's wife walked at his side, one hand resting on his arm, while his children trailed behind like a string of ducklings. Barthram stepped into the road, knowing he was one of the very few who would be allowed through that inner guard.

Their greetings were brief, scarcely interrupting the forward pace of the entourage; the steward moved ahead, joined by Octave. Madame de Remy made a brief curtsey and slipped back to join her children. Their conversation would flow discretely within the moving wall of people.

'I have found her,' Barthram announced quietly, masking his satisfaction.

He expected joy, surprise; anything but that supercilious smirk.

'How?' De Remy's tone was merely polite, hardly even interested.

'She was seen by a woodsman, a man of the God, who told his priest, who told the anakritim. She is harboured by Agnès de Fontenay. We can prove collusion between de Fontenay and the witch.'

A faint inclination of the head acknowledged the achievement. Still no comment. Not even a question.

'The witch is at a hunting lodge near Château Fontenay.' Barthram's unease rose towards a terrible understanding.

Another polite nod.

'You knew, didn't you?'

De Remy's enigmatic smile was infuriating.

Barthram's mind raced. If de Remy knew, he would have taken action. 'Have you sent soldiers? When?' Anyone but the chancellor or the king would have been terrified by the menace in Barthram's voice. The anakritis-general of Galmandie was not accustomed to being played in this way.

De Remy slowly unfolded one finger after another,

pretending to count days as if the matter was of little consequence. He ended with a grunt of satisfaction. 'Prince
Lancelin's men will probably take her today, if the God wills.
Do not worry, Pateras, I have warned them to avoid your man
d'Aurillac, should they find him there. Three silver birds on
blue, I believe? Though I must say he has been slow in sending
you word. Do you think he might have fallen under her spell?'
De Remy's tone was teasing.

The staff-wielding retainers ahead of them turned into the
street leading to the de Remy mansion. The short journey from
the temple was nearly over.

'You know about him?' Barthram's anger was cold as iron.
He spoke softly, almost a whisper; it was quieter away from the
major thoroughfare, and harder to talk discretely.

'Do not forget, Pateras, that the Black Tower belongs to the
king. You might make liberal use of the tormentors, but they
know who pays them.' De Remy spoke as if he was still
competing with the noise of the crowd; he did not care who
heard these words. 'Me.'

They had reached the de Remy house. The chancellor
turned to face the anakritis-general, pulling his face into the
smile he reserved for political opponents like Delmas in
moments of triumph in Council.

Barthram swallowed, a physical attempt to push his fury
deep into his body so he could think. 'Then you had better let
me see her before you parade any yellow-haired woman in front
of the king. I *know* her, remember. You do not.'

'Ah, I thought of that too, my dear anakritis-general.' De
Remy lowered his voice. 'I took the liberty of sending your
former assistant with them, young Malory d'Eivet. I am sure he
will be most helpful. He was pathetically pleased to see the
light of day.' The chancellor held out his arm for his wife, and
the de Remy entourage streamed past Barthram until he stood
alone with Octave.

8.3 ADELAIS

'Watch your horse's ears as you strike; that blade will take them off.' Fulke d'Aurillac gestured at Humbert's sword, now upright in Adelais's hand. She held Allier's reins in the other, containing the destrier's energy as the great beast danced beneath her. This was another game Allier understood; to take his rider within a sword's length of a target, and keep the line steady to allow an accurate blow. The target was a cabbage, balanced on a pole at the height of a foot soldier's head in the water meadow. Fulke's warning was serious; today for her final lesson she used Humbert's sharpened weapon and was learning to combine the skills of riding and swordcraft. It was harder than she expected; Allier would sidestep in response to small shifts in her weight as she swung the blade. Fulke stood nearby, calling instructions, with his hand-and-a-half sword braced against his hip.

Adelais found it hard to concentrate; Agnès's farewell had disturbed her. And was it only her? Even Elyse had been fretting all morning, saying the ravens were unsettled. Adelais could see her beyond the lodge's gates, throwing grain for chickens and peering at the sky as if she expected rain.

Rossignol and Sennet squatted on the meadow side of the gates, watching Adelais ride. Rossignol wore a protective gambeson in preparation for the lesson that would follow; bucklers and blunted swords rested against the wall. Adelais wished she had gifts to repay their kindness. She'd miss them all when she left.

Allier made a small, impatient buck.

'You won't kill it by looking at it.' Fulke prompted.

Adelais nudged Allier into a trot. Humbert's sword had a different balance to the practice weapons – finer somehow; less like a weight and more like a weapon. Her hand moulded naturally around its grip, which had been bound with the coarse skin of some great fish so that it would not slip, and the blade's edge rising past her eye was honed until it shone like the sun lining a summer cloud. She sighted along it and squeezed Allier into a canter.

She would not use a swinging blow – that, she'd learned, would leave her body unprotected if she missed – but would thrust as if sword and arm were a single lance. Adelais brought the tip down until she was aiming at the cabbage, leaned forwards in the saddle, and gripped hard with her legs to steady her strike.

Allier bucked at the accidental command and the saddle smacked into Adelais's *rass* with enough power to punch her clear over his neck. She bounced on the turf and lay there facedown, winded, slightly stunned, staring into a miniature forest of grass by her nose.

'On your feet, woman!' There was no sympathy from Fulke. 'Your enemy is coming to finish you off!'

Adelais pushed herself onto her knees and groped for her sword, but Fulke already stood beside her, the skirts of his blue surcoat flapping against his boots. He held Humbert's sword out to her by the base of the blade, smiling without humour. Allier was trotting through the gates, trailing reins, where Sennet was trying ineffectually to block his passage back to his stable.

'Why?' Her vision spotted as she stood; little leaf-sized flecks swirled against the forest like black snow. Her head spun and she didn't understand why the normally well-behaved Allier had thrown her.

'He merely did what you asked. You put both spurs into his belly in a way that told him to clear enemies behind. If you'd have been sitting back for a swinging blow, you'd still be in the saddle.'

Adelais groaned as she took the sword. She wished she had tutors who agreed on the merits of slice versus strike.

'Did you really expect to learn it all in a few days? It takes years! Now go and bring him back. We'll try again.'

Larger black spots hovered above the gates, and Adelais blinked again until her vision cleared and they resolved into ravens, flapping and cawing around Elyse's head. Adelais stopped in the middle of the meadow, disoriented, for the drumming of Allier's hooves on the hard ground beyond the gates had become a growling thunder, and now he was splashing through water, as loud as a whole herd. Then round the corner of the curtain wall from the ford came a mounted, cantering troop of soldiers.

Adelais stared at them, too stunned to move. At the gates Rossignol drew his sword and the castellan rushed to arm himself, but Adelais turned to Fulke d'Aurillac, hoping for guidance. He stared back at her with sadness or regret in his eyes, and took a step backwards, distancing himself from what was to happen.

She started to run towards the gate, but everything was moving slowly, as if she ran waist-deep in water. Her vision now seemed unnaturally clear; light flashed along Humbert's blade with each pump of her arms, with each pace. The soldiers were led by a noble in a green heraldic surcoat; she could even see that the stars on his surcoat were *embroidered* with golden thread. He rode a beautiful, dark bay gelding with a white blaze between its eyes, and he waved one man out onto the meadow, sending him wide to come between her and the woods. *Why am I registering the quality of the gauntlet on the noble's hand?*

Adelais slowed to a walk, assessing now, rather than panicking; the riders would reach the gates before she did. How many soldiers were bunched behind the noble? Five? Six? She could not see the rear of their column around the curve of the wall. And was that a priest at their back, with the packhorses? The soldiers wore bascinet helmets but no chain mail; just quilted-cloth gambesons like Rossignol's. These men rode light, for speed, without even the weight of shields. Rossignol and the castellan both now held drawn weapons; Rossignol his own sword, and the castellan a practice weapon, which he hefted with nervous unfamiliarity.

The noble halted in front of the gates. Adelais glanced at his heels, seeing silver spurs of one who had not yet won the golden symbols of knighthood. No helmet, so his hair flowed free; light brown, almost as long as Adelais's, and so well-groomed he must have combed it that morning. He looked first at Fulke d'Aurillac, beyond Adelais on the meadow, noble to noble. *But is that a sneer?* His gaze passed to Adelais, and the slight parting of his lips told her he liked what he saw, even if she was dressed as a boy.

'State your business, messire,' Rossignol growled. 'You are on de Fontenay land.'

The noble did not answer but stared around the group seeing, no doubt, an old man who hardly knew which end of a sword to hold, an old woman who'd armed herself with a buckled iron spit, a one-eyed veteran, and a pretty, beardless boy. Plus a noble who hadn't drawn his sword or moved to join them. And he had six trained men behind him, not counting the priest.

Adelais edged towards the gate. Why was Fulke staying out on the meadow, where he couldn't help?

Finally the noble spoke. 'I am Gerard d'Essoyes, and I seek Adelais de Vries, also known as the Vriesian Witch.'

So the moment had come. Rossignol spun a buckler towards Adelais, flicking it low over the grass, spike upwards, in the way he might skip a stone over water. She stamped on it to stop its roll and slid her hand into its reassuring grip. As she straightened, Rossignol held her gaze and drew one thumb backwards across his neck. She nodded, understanding. Slice, don't hack. She swallowed, but her tongue was soft stone within the dryness of her mouth.

Rossignol turned back to Gerard d'Essoyes. 'And by whose authority do you seek anyone on my master's lands, messire?'

'I do not need to justify myself to you, peasant. Drop your weapons, bring me the witch, and no one need die.' D'Essoyes turned to shout down the line of his soldiers. 'Where's that priest?'

The hooded priest they ushered forwards seemed to be as much a prisoner as a companion. He was hunched in the saddle, his hood flicking nervously from side to side, but when he saw Adelais he sat suddenly upright, made the sign of the God, and pushed his hood back from his head.

Adelais found herself staring into the eyes of Malory d'Eivet. 'You!' But oh, how changed. The immaculately groomed young anakritis that she'd known in the spring was now haggard, with the matted, tangled hair of a hermit. He seemed as shocked to see her as she was to see him.

'I did not bring them, mistress,' he faltered. 'Believe me.'

'*That's* the witch? The boy?' D'Essoyes looked from d'Eivet to Adelais, and tilted his head as if the sight of a woman in men's clothing was a novel and exciting perversion.

'She is no witch, messire.' The surprise on d'Eivet's face had turned to wonder. 'She is an angel, sent by Ischyros.'

D'Essoyes ignored him. 'Seize her!' Three men behind him

dismounted, drew their swords, and spread out to encircle Adelais. Two others held the horses.

'By the gods, you will not!' Elyse was the first to strike. She swung her buckled iron spit into one man's side. It struck with a sound like a beaten blanket and the soldier growled, hunching over his left arm and spinning to punch Elyse viciously in the side of the head with the hilt of his sword. She dropped like a slaughtered beast and lay against the bank below the curtain wall, her eyes bulging and her mouth twitching.

Sennet bellowed his rage and swung his blunted sword at the man who'd struck Elyse, but the soldier brushed the attack away as if Sennet were a raging infant. He thrust his own, sharp blade into the castellan's chest, casually, as if he were simply pushing him away. The old man dropped to his knees, eyes wide.

'The fucking cow broke my elbow,' the soldier whined, cradling his left arm to his side, ignoring Sennet as he toppled onto his back and coughed gobs of blood at the sky.

'I want the witch alive,' d'Essoyes called from his saddle. 'Kill One-Eye if you must.'

Rossignol tugged Adelais backwards, though her eyes were locked on Sennet. She was vaguely aware that Elyse and Sennet's sacrifice had bought her time to reach the gate. 'You can't help them,' Rossignol muttered. 'Get in the archway. Stop them getting behind us.' Adelais let herself be dragged, fighting the instinct to help her friends.

Three soldiers faced them on foot, though Sennet's killer hung back. Adelais glanced towards a metallic tapping sound coming from the two with the horses; they were hammering tethering pegs into the ground, unhurriedly, as if they were making camp. The mounted one stayed in the meadow, ready to ride anyone down who tried to run. He paid no attention to Fulke d'Aurillac who still stood, sword sheathed, a slingshot out into the meadow. He clearly believed that Fulke was no threat.

'You brought them!' Adelais screamed at Fulke, heavy with the leaden certainty of betrayal. Fulke looked down, not meeting her eye. 'Where is your honour, d'Aurillac? Where is your chivalry?'

'Put the sword down, girl.' A sword blade angled towards Adelais, interrupting her. The stubbled face beyond had the leering confidence of a tavern brawler. He was totally unthreatened. 'Now.'

Adelais wavered, lowering her point. If she surrendered, would it save the others? Were Elyse and Sennet alive to save? She took a deep breath, reaching for the calm that had helped her in other fights, though few so menacing as this. *Sætur Sif, help me.*

'Don't even think it, mudlark. They will torture you before you burn.' The word 'mudlark' held respect, for once. It was a call to arms. Adelais would have been pleased if she wasn't so frightened. '*Wrist!*' he added, emphatically. That one word was enough. It was an instruction to fight and a reminder of how to kill.

Adelais dropped into the crouch that he'd taught her. One more breath and she'd found the icy focus she needed.

'I said drop it, witch!'

'Try taking it from me.' Adelais even managed to smile at the soldier as if this were all a game. That was always the trick; pretend to be confident, even if your heart is pounding inside your chest.

He snorted and slapped her blade aside with his own, just as Rossignol had done time after time, with a piercing ring of steel on steel. And just as Rossignol had taught her, she rolled her blade on top of the soldier's, pushing it downwards, sword and buckler together. She held it there with the spike of the buckler as she twisted her sword wrist to bring the tip of her blade up against his throat. So fast, now so instinctive, just like practice. *Slice, don't hack.* One push and, unlike in practice, the soldier's neck split like over-ripe fruit. For a frozen instant she stayed crouched over his blade, staring at the bursting wound, appalled at what she'd done.

The man yelped and jumped backwards, his blade rasping against her buckler, as a jet of dark blood squirted from the wound. And another. He passed his sword into his left hand, brought his right to his throat, and stared at her with wide, incredulous eyes. She should strike again, now, while he was shocked into stillness, but she couldn't. She wanted to apologise. The soldier lifted his hand away, looked down at his own blood saturating his gauntlet, and another spurt shot out. He clamped his hand back and staggered away, dropping his sword and hunching his head into his shoulder as if that would stem the flow of blood pissing from his neck.

'Good strike!' Rossignol's praise was as calm as his comments in a lesson.

Adelais could not answer, but watched the wounded soldier drop to his knees in the meadow, crying, calling on Salazar to save him.

Did I really do that? The red smear on her blade's tip was gory proof.

'Keep your guard up, mudlark.'

Her point had dropped. How could Rossignol sound so calm? Five soldiers and a noble still faced them. Plus the priest, who stared at her wide-eyed. The noble's horse, a riding horse and not a battle-trained destrier, was snorting and dancing away from the twitching body in the grass. Some part of Adelais's mind was still able to flit across such irrelevancies and focus on the mounted soldier in the meadow. He had his back to d'Aurillac. The soldiers knew that Fulke, the man she'd begun to think of as a possible lover, was no threat. As the fighting line formed in front of her and Rossignol, Adelais bellowed her anger across the meadow.

'Traitor!'

8.4 HUMBERT

Humbert Blanc reached Château Fontenay as the temple bells were tolling for noon office. He was not surprised to see anakritim at the crossroads; if they'd been watching his commandery, they would be watching Château Fontenay. They ignored him. Again, he expected nothing else. He would have outrun any news of his escape and he wore no insignia: to them he was just an ageing, travel-stained man-at-arms with a twenty-day beard, riding one horse and leading another. He'd look like the kind of veteran who can afford two unremarkable mounts but not a servant; a man who'd spent his journey sleeping not at inns but in barns when he could, and under the stars when he couldn't.

The château crowned a long, narrow ridge that rose like an axe blade from the valley floor. Humbert had been here the previous year as a guest of Leandre de Fontenay, but he decided there was little chance of him being recognised now outside the private apartments. He remembered from that visit passing a tavern on the single road that ran like a spine within the walls; it had looked like the kind of place the garrison would go in search of a wench, somewhere he could blend in with the crowd, watch and listen.

He paid for water and hay in the tavern's stables, but kept one horse saddled, just in case. There was a table outside where the innkeeper had lit a charcoal brazier to encourage custom, and where Humbert might sit with his back to the wall, dipping bread into thin morning ale, and observing the flow of people. All his years of campaigning told him to be cautious, and to know his ground before he moved.

'Come far, 'ave you, messire?'

The woman bringing his jug of ale was a full-blown rose; ruddy cheeked, broad-hipped, decently but not cleanly dressed in chemise, under-dress, and kirtle. She smiled at him, her face morning-fresh and pleasant, creasing into the folds of her middle years. The 'messire' was probably mere courtesy, but just to be sure Humbert flattened the nobility from his voice and slurred a little Arrenician patois into his words.

'Oc, far enough. My lord is dead and I seek another.' Humbert tried to sound like a veteran down on his luck. Even though he was expelled, he felt no qualms about speaking with her; *knowing association* was the faith's measure of guilt, so if she did not know, he did not risk her soul.

'Poor love.' The woman polished a leather mug on her apron and set it before him. The apron looked as if it had also been used to polish the table tops. 'Only, Lord de Fontenay's away in Villebénie with the king.'

'If you have another of these,' Humbert lifted the mug, 'would you like to join me?' He gestured to the bench opposite. Now he did feel a twinge of guilt; the woman wore a lifetime of disappointments in her eyes, and he'd kindled the first flicker of hope. She simpered a little as she sat.

'Well, just for a little while...'

'What about Lady Agnès?' He'd already guessed Leandre de Fontenay was away; no banner flew from the château.

'Oh, she's around. Some of the time, anyways. In an' out, she is, like a soldier new home from the wars.' She giggled, glanced at his face, and blushed.

'Is she here now?'

'She don' tell *me* when she's goin' out.' The woman rested her arms on the table and leaned towards Humbert, making her kirtle bulge over her chest. 'Though she rode past 'ere this morning on her way back in. Word is, she's got hersel' a lover. And her jus' married an' all.' She frowned as if fearing she'd said too much. 'D'you know her?'

Humbert shrugged. 'Only at a distance. Bit grand for the likes of me.'

The woman looked relieved. 'Not that I'd blame her, what with Lord Leandre being away all the time, and her such a pretty little thing. Such a waste!'

'There was one in her service that I did know. A boy, Guy Carelet, who came with her from Villebénie.'

'Guy? Guy? Oh, I know 'im. 'E was with Lady Agnès this morning. 'Andsome young man. Got a bit of a swagger about 'im...' She stopped as Humbert slid a silver coin across the table to her.

'I would speak with him. Tell him Humbert the Black requests an hour of his time.'

The name was a spur-of-the-moment inspiration.

'Black?' She looked at his head. The only dark hair he had was on his eyebrows and upper lip; the rest was wholly grey.

'It was, once. Now find Guy for me, will you? Bless you.'

Humbert had not seen Guy Carelet since the day in the summer when he and Adelais were surrounded by King's men in the courtyard of the hunting lodge. Arnaud, Adelais's lover, had been cut down but Guy had escaped, rather bravely, and brought word to Leandre de Fontenay. He had hopes for the lad; he was young, both in years and mind, and they'd had their differences, but Guy had shown courage that day, so Humbert smiled warmly at the youth who slid onto the bench opposite.

His smile faded at Guy's expression. The boy's eyes darted fearfully to each side, his head was hunched into his shoulders, and his whispered greeting of 'Lord Brother' was almost a hiss, his discomfort palpable.

'Just Humbert. An old soldier seeking a new lord.' Humbert sat back against the wall of the tavern, scanning the street beyond Guy's shoulders. Crowds milled, hawkers touted their wares, and a blacksmith crouched over a horse's hoof, tapping. No one was watching. Humbert lifted his hand towards the retainers' badge of de Fontenay sewn to Guy's chest. 'You have a position. Good.'

Guy's grunt was loaded and implied '*and I want to keep it*'.

'You don't seem pleased to see me.' Humbert had expected a little more warmth from the boy.

Guy paused as the pot-woman brought him a mug of ale, and waited until she left. 'You got me in big trouble, *Humbert*.'

'D'Aurillac arrived?'

'Aye. And I took him to Adelais.'

Humbert closed his eyes and took one long breath. 'Where?'

'The hunting lodge. She will leave tomorrow. Lady Agnès will go back there this afternoon to say her farewells. I am to escort her. Again.'

Humbert stood. 'I must go there, now. I made a grave mistake with d'Aurillac; he is not to be trusted. Make sure it is safe before you let Lady Agnès approach.'

Guy swore, and looked fearfully over his shoulder. Humbert leaned forwards to speak into Guy's ear.

'We may not meet again. Nor may I speak or ride with Lady Agnès.'

Guy looked up, frowning, as Humbert lowered his voice to a whisper.

'I am expelled. So is Adelais.'

It was the first time he had said those words, and they unlocked such a rush of emotion within him that he hunched, gripping the table for support. His life had been spent in the service of the God. All that service, all the honours, had been taken from him. So, more importantly, had his hope of crossing the bridge of judgement into the arms of Ischyros and the company of his martyred Guardians. He took one deep breath and strode away before he shamed himself. As he called for his horse he was aware of Guy reaching across the table for his unfinished ale.

8.5 ADELAIS

Fulke d'Aurillac had flinched at Adelais's cry of *'Traitor!'*, but stayed in the field, unmoving, beyond the mounted soldier.

The three soldiers facing Adelais and Rossignol crouched with their swords ready, but seemed reluctant to attack. They'd probably expected an easy capture, and they carried no shields. Now one of their number lay twitching, soaking the grass with his blood.

'By Salazar, must I do it myself?' The noble dismounted, drew his sword, and called to the one still in the meadow. 'You! Get over here!' He turned back towards the gate, so he didn't see Fulke draw his hand-and-a-half sword, but Adelais did, and her heart sank at the sight. The odds were already impossible. Three fit soldiers, one more with a broken arm, and a noble. Plus the one with the horses. The soldiers didn't need d'Aurillac, yet he came lurching across the grass towards them.

The mounted soldier had just leaned forwards, preparing to dismount, when Fulke strode past and thrust his sword up into his body. The soldier's face widened into a scream at the twist and wrench that followed, and which dragged him half out of the saddle. The horse lurched forwards and he hung there, creased over, bouncing, until he toppled into the grass near Pateras Malory. The priest fluttered his hands in front of him, saying 'no, no', but Adelais wasn't sure what he wanted to stop.

All three of the soldiers at the gate looked over their shoulders, and in that moment of distraction Rossignol lunged, taking the nearest in the side. The man bellowed and staggered away, holding himself.

'Watch for your chances, mudlark.' Rossignol was back on his guard before the man fell. 'It's them or us.'

Adelais heard the implied criticism that she, too, could have struck.

'D'Essoyes!' Fulke came limping across the meadow, lifting his blade; a clear challenge, noble to noble.

'D'Aurillac? You are with the witch?' D'Essoyes sounded incredulous. 'You are setting yourself against the king!' He held his arms wide in appeal until Fulke swung his hand-and-a-half at his legs. D'Essoyes danced backwards to take a defensive guard.

This was madness. In the time it took to drain a glass, an amiable riding lesson had become bloody murder. Pateras Malory knelt beside Sennet and Elyse, making the sign of the God; did that mean they were both dead? The soldier that Rossignol had hit was on his belly, crawling away from the fight like a lizard and leaving a gory trail in the mud. The one Adelais had wounded now lay still on his side in the meadow, his head in a puddle of blood. Two surcoated nobles were circling each other, and Adelais did not have to be an expert to see that d'Essoyes's lightness on his feet gave him the advantage. He'd dodged Fulke's swing with ease, and seemed keener to remonstrate than fight.

'She is expelled, you fool! She and your master Blanc, and all who aid them!'

D'Essoyes's words slid home like a knife. Adelais lowered her guard, dazed. *And Brother Humbert?* Ischyros was his whole life. Expulsion would destroy him. Even Rossignol took a step backwards, his guard wavering. *And all who aid them.*

The distraction was enough. The two men in front of Adelais rushed at Rossignol, but for several heartbeats the scene was unreal, and she was drawn to Pateras Malory smearing sacred ash onto the forehead of a dying soldier. *He can never do that for Humbert, now.* But Fulke shrugging off d'Essoyes's words and resuming his guard –*that* was real. The fight had not ended, and she turned to the blows and oaths beside her, still drunkard-slow.

Rossignol was staggering backwards near the gate, hard pressed. A red stain was spreading down the inside of his thigh and the soldiers had parted to come at him from two sides. Rossignol stumbled again; it would be near impossible to ward himself against both. The nearest to Adelais, *within distance,* Rossignol would say, was the one with a damaged arm and the castellan's blood on his blade. That made it easier. Forgetting all her training, she swung her sword in a scything swipe that bit deep into the back of the man's leg, just above the knee. He screamed and fell over, flailing, like a mummer's puppet whose strings have been cut. His leg folded over her blade, tugging it with him, and he screamed again as she wrenched it free. Her bemused mind told her that worked rather well. *How can I be so detached?*

How swiftly the tables were turned. The remaining man in front of Rossignol backed away, trying to cover two assailants with one blade.

He died swiftly. Adelais feinted from one side, he guarded, and Rossignol thrust from the other.

Out in the meadow d'Essoyes was down. Adelais hadn't seen him fall, and she did not want to look too closely at the new, gory crease where Fulke's longer blade had cleaved his skull. Fulke was lurching towards the horses. There, the only remaining soldier had pulled his mount clear of the herd and was swinging into the saddle, fumbling in his panic.

Fulke d'Aurillac thrust upwards into his back as he was wheeling his horse. The man rode clear, arching in his agony, and toppled to the ground before his horse reached the stream. He did not move again. To Adelais, that looked like murder; there had been no need for that man to die. She turned away, and saw the first blessing in the chaos; Elyse was sitting up, white-faced, but alive. She groaned, rolled onto her knees, and crawled towards Sennet's body.

Adelais knelt beside Elyse and put her arm around her shoulders. Apart from the blood around the castellan's mouth, he might have been sleeping. Elyse leaned forwards, dry-eyed, to wipe the mess from his face. She spoke so quietly, so calmly, that she might have been talking about a distant relative. 'He were an idle sod, and overfond of his drink, but he were a lovely lad in his youth.' Her voice tightened. 'And he were my man.' Only when Elyse had composed the body did she allow herself to be pulled into Adelais's arms. She slumped there, so still that Adelais thought she might have lost consciousness again, though she stirred when the priest came to stand at Adelais's elbow.

'Ischyros has delivered you again, mistress.' Malory d'Eivet looked at her in wonder. Rossignol limped closer, bending to hold his leg wound closed. He watched the priest suspiciously.

'Pateras Malory.' Adelais acknowledged him. She was too numb to feel surprise. Too numb to feel anything except a sick revulsion that she'd just killed a man. She blinked at the priest, trying to think. In the spring he'd chased her over half of Galmandie. Persecuted her. And he'd just described her as an angel sent by his God. 'I think I was saved by these friends, not Ischyros.' She tried to swallow. 'The noble said I was expelled.'

'You, Brother Humbert, and any who help you. It was not of my doing.'

'So my friends cannot receive pardon for this.' Adelais

waved her hand around the carnage. The only soldier left alive had backed against a gate post, where he hugged his wounded leg to his chest with one arm. It was bleeding badly, enough for a puddle to be forming beneath him. The other arm hung slack beside him and his eyes darted fearfully between them.

Malory d'Eivet shook his head. 'Yet I cannot believe the expulsion was just; the God is still protecting you.'

'It was not the God, Pateras, it was surprise.' Rossignol sat down heavily on the bank, his face pale. 'They did not expect a fight.'

Adelais stared at Rossignol, forcing herself to think. His wound needed treatment. She cut a strip from a soldier's surcoat and wadded the cloth into a pad to press against the gash. It had been a thrust below the gambeson that had gone deep into the muscle; it would not kill him but it would need stitching. Rossignol would not be teaching her to dance with a sword for a while. She looked up at the priest, who still stared at her as if she were some vision of his god.

'In particular, they did not expect the Seigneur d'Aurillac to fight. Why do you think that was, Pateras?'

When the priest did not answer, Adelais glanced at Fulke, who was cleaning his sword on a rag. She felt dazed; why was it so hard to think? One thing was sure, though; d'Aurillac might have turned the tide for them, but *by Odhinn* he had some questions to answer.

8.6 BARTHRAM

Barthram walked back towards the palace deep in thought, knowing that Pateras Octave would be behind him.

It had been hard to conceal his fury as the last of de Remy's retinue streamed past them into the chancellor's residence. So hard. But Barthram would reveal no hint of emotion to the soldiers who had turned to guard the de Remy doorway. They would undoubtedly be asked for their observations, later. Instead he'd breathed deeply and opened his arms, as if all was well with the world and he was shepherding his fellow anakritis away from the door.

All was not lost. If the next bird brought news of her arrest, he'd know long before de Remy. He could be the first to tell the king.

Better still, he could ride out to meet her on the road, and be *seen* to be the one bringing her back. He knew enough of young Lancelin's perversions to use them as currency against the young prince and demand prominence in whatever story he told the king. Lancelin would want to make a huge show of bringing the witch back to the capital, and Barthram could intercept this procession. She should be in a cage, on a cart, with an escort of anakritim.

By then he would be able to parade Humbert Blanc, similarly caged. Linking the Guardians so openly with witchcraft would be brilliant politics.

Where was Blanc? His captors should have brought him to Villebénie by now. Perhaps the snows still lay on the high ground to the south. If only he had more birds and more trained priests to handle them.

But what if the capture of the witch failed? She'd flee, and she'd probably be well horsed, thanks to her friend Agnès de Fontenay.

But flee *where*? Undoubtedly towards Vriesland. He should have a fallback in place. The king's library would be an ideal place to plan; it had maps.

And if the raid did not succeed he could be the one to tell the king of de Remy's failure. Oh, that would be powerful news. It would teach de Remy never to work behind his back again.

But first he needed hard information. And that would arrive in his dovecote, many days before that scheming de Remy knew what had happened.

The waiting was the hardest part. The God grant him patience.

8.7 ADELAIS

After the urgency of dressing Rossignol's wound, a strange, staggering numbness settled on Adelais. She walked in a dream world, seeing, but detached from it; as if she strolled on a stage after mummers had finished their play but fallen asleep in their costumes.

Behind her d'Aurillac questioned Malory d'Eivet in a crisp, warrior's voice: 'who sent you, how did they know?' While at her feet the soldier she had killed lay in a slick puddle of blood, a discarded effigy with a wax face. Yet an effigy wouldn't stink of blood and shit. Adelais dropped to her knees and vomited in the grass. When she rocked back on her heels Humbert's sword still trailed from her hand; she knew she had to clean it before it could be sheathed, but a crushing weight of tiredness made even that light task impossible.

'You need to wipe your blade.' She hadn't heard Fulke arrive beside her. Had the thought come to her before his words, or was she thinking that slowly? When she didn't move he took her sword and crouched by the dead soldier's body, folded the edge of the gambeson over the blade, and cleaned away the blood. He had to pull her to her feet and sheath it for her. 'You did well, girl.' D'Aurillac looked her in the eye. His were the dark brown of ripe chestnuts. *Why am I noticing such things?* She had to look up; he seemed even taller, this close.

A man's scream made her turn. Elyse stood over the injured soldier who'd killed Sennet. She'd just kicked his wounded leg straight and now trod down on the thigh, flattening it and releasing a new gush of blood from the great wound behind the knee. The man looked up at her, begging, but Elyse simply said, 'He were my man.' Someone, perhaps Rossignol, must have told her this was the soldier who killed Sennet. When the man tried to push her foot away with his one good arm, she trod more heavily.

This was a new Elyse. That gentle, caring soul had found a terrible hardness. Yet only Pateras Malory remonstrated as the soldier weakened. The others just watched, accepting Elyse's right to vengeance.

It took him some time to die. When Elyse finally lifted her foot, she said again, 'He were my man,' and staggered a little as she stepped away from the body.

'Come.' D'Aurillac touched Adelais's arm. 'We must clear up and prepare to leave.' By what right was he taking charge? She shrugged her arm away.

'They knew you were here. They thought you were on their side.' She breathed deeply as she glared at him, trying to force her mind to think more swiftly. There were cleaner, colder smells on the air, above the aftermath of battle, the scents of land newly released from snow.

'I did not bring them. I told no one.' Yet he looked guilty.

'But they knew you.'

'I will fetch the cart for the bodies.' D'Aurillac strode away from her through the gates. She let him go. She was not yet ready for fast movement. Or thought. Rossignol sat on the bank, watching her with the heavy-lidded look of one on the edge of sleep. Elyse also stared at her from beside Sennet's body, the hem of her kirtle russet with blood. Adelais heard her grand-mother Yrsa's words. *You are the tall tree that draws the light-ning. Those around you get burned.* Only the priest was busy, visiting each of the bodies in turn with his box of sacred ash and the words of the Office of the Dead.

Move, girl. Adelais put one foot in front of the other until she was able to totter, then run after d'Aurillac. She found him pushing the handcart out of a stable and stopped him by bracing herself against its front. Less than a moon before, Sennet had hung a shield there as a target for Allier's hooves. Now they were about use it to carry his body.

'How did they know you, *messire?* The noble called your name.'

'He must have recognised my arms.' D'Aurillac waved a hand at his surcoat, emblazoned with the three silver birds. 'I did not know him.'

Adelais pushed down on the cart's rim hard enough for the handles to jump in d'Aurillac's hands. 'But he knew you'd be here. He did not expect you to fight.'

'He was equerry to Prince Lancelin, who is in league with Othon de Remy, the chancellor. That is what the priest said. I have no dealings with either of them.' D'Aurillac tried to push Adelais out of the way. She stood her ground.

'Then who *do* you have dealings with, messire?'

D'Aurillac straightened, letting the cart's handles fall. For a moment his face had the same stricken look as Elyse's. 'I will tell you, on the road. But now, we must bury Sennet and leave, swiftly.'

'On the road? Why should I trust you enough to ride with you?' Adelais struck the cart's rim again. Her numbness was turning to anger.

'Because I have just saved your life?' D'Aurillac closed his eyes and swallowed. 'And because if my part in this day's work becomes known I will have condemned my brother to death.'

They buried the castellan by the ruins of the old temple, next to Arnaud's grave. D'Aurillac dug and the others let him, standing a little apart as if this was his penance. Fulke attacked the earth with such violence that sparks flew from the shovel's tip when it struck a stone. He'd stripped to his shirt and loin cloth for the work, and Adelais was surprised that she noticed the way his shoulders bunched and flexed. Surprised, too, that she was making comparisons. He was taller than Arnaud, without the armourer's packed muscle, but there was a dangerous beauty in his brooding fury.

Could she ever trust him?

Malory d'Eivet pressed sacred ash into the castellan's forehead, though Elyse muttered that it would mean nothing to her man. She climbed into the grave before they filled it and clasped her husband's dead hands around the hilt of the practice sword he had been wielding. 'That he might be chosen,' she whispered to Adelais, 'though he was mayhap too mild a man for Odhinn's hall.' Rossignol hobbled to the graveside, saluted with a wine flask, and dropped the rest by the body. Adelais left nothing, but wished she believed in the Ischyrian rite of unburdening. She wanted to leave her guilt.

Afterwards they stood around the grave, reflecting.

'We must leave. Now.' D'Aurillac thrust the shovel into the loose earth. 'It would take too long to bury the rest.'

'We?' Adelais challenged. D'Aurillac was still assuming too much.

'He cannot ride.' D'Aurillac pointed at Rossignol. 'And the priest must not be allowed to spread this news. You would be alone on the road.'

'Not alone.' Elyse turned away from the mounded earth,

smearing her hands down her apron. She was still dry-eyed. 'Seven more dead men behind us, one of them a noble, and a priest to tell the tale. I do not think even Agnès de Fontenay can protect me from this. I too must flee.'

Adelais folded her arms around her, hugging her close.

'Mayhap I'll get to teach thee after all,' Elyse whispered. 'Now I must pack for the journey. Come with me, sweeting.' They linked arms, leaving the men at the graveside. As she walked back to the lodge Elyse's shoulders were slumped and her back bent in the way of a much older woman.

In her private room off the kitchen Elyse reached into a deep, narrow hole in the stonework and drew out her staff. As she lifted it to her forehead Adelais saw the rune-work carved into its length, covering the whole surface in an intricate dance of meaning. This was the ritual staff of a *seidhkona*, a staff-woman, the symbol and instrument of her power.

'I'll run,' Elyse said, 'but not before I've laid this to rest in living water.' She wrapped it in a cloak with a shovel and led Adelais out across the meadow, following the line of the stream. Behind them d'Aurillac and the priest had made a chair with their hands, and were carrying Rossignol towards the hall. If they wondered at Elyse and Adelais's purpose, they asked no questions; everyone moved in a daze.

In the grove where Elyse had conducted her ceremony, she and Adelais stripped off their boots and hose and waded into the stream. The cold gripped their ankles like frozen iron as they scraped a trench in the stream bed, and weighed down the staff with rocks. 'It cannot be kept hidden on a journey,' Elyse said, 'and I'll not leave it to be found.'

They stood together on the bank, staring at the spot. Adelais put her arm around Elyse and hugged her.

'Was this the lightning you saw, Aunty?'

Elyse shook her head. 'This is just the beginning.'

· · ·

In the lodge they found Rossignol sitting at a bench, ashen-faced, with his wounded leg resting on a cushion. As Adelais put food and wine within his reach he gripped Adelais's arm so hard she thought he was in pain, until he made eye contact.

'Do not take d'Aurillac with you.'

Fulke had heard. 'Two women on the open road? They would not survive.'

'But can they trust you, messire?' Rossignol eased his leg, grunting.

'I think Mistress Adelais should decide that.' D'Aurillac turned to her. He sounded indifferent to her decision, but his look was almost pleading. 'You will ride as a noble, Elyse as your serving woman, and I as your escort.'

Adelais held his stare, considering. He did not look away. 'I will trust you, messire.' *For now.* The look in his eyes told her this was important to him. Very important. 'Until I have heard your explanation.' And even then, by Odhinn, she would watch him.

Rossignol groaned. 'You take too much risk, mudlark. D'Aurillac is right about one thing, though: you must go, and now. Leave the dead inside the walls, out of sight. When Guy Carelet comes they must simply disappear, with no blame on the de Fontenays. Which means you, too, must disappear, *Pateras.*'

'I will say nothing.' If Malory feared for his life, it did not show.

'We will let Lady Agnès decide how your silence can be assured. Until she arrives, there is a perfectly comfortable cellar here.'

'In comparison to the Black Tower, it will be a palace.'

Adelais knelt beside Rossignol when they were ready to leave.

'You look the part, *messire*.' Rossignol swept his cap from his head in as much of a bow as his position would allow.

She smiled her acknowledgement, knowing he was right. Three moons before she'd been barefoot, hungry, and running. Now she was dressed in a lordling's cote-hardie and fine leather boots, with Humbert's sword at her side. Waiting outside, ready-saddled, was a knight's destrier and the fast gelding that Agnès had given her. There was food in the saddle bags and coin they'd stripped from the equerry and soldiers. If fate was kind, and the roads were open, she'd be safe in Vriesland before another moon had run its course.

'I wish I could thank Lady Agnès myself. Tell her...' She could not form the words, not in a way that would sound right in Rossignol's mouth. Besides, there was too much unresolved after the last night.

'She will know.' Rossignol squeezed her forearm reassuringly.

'I will ride for Vriesland by the fastest road, and send word when we are safe.'

'Go back to the high road. Head for Orval, then Bellay. That is your quickest route. Move swiftly, and you can outrun any news that leaks here.'

'You taught me well, Rossignol.'

'Remember: dance! Use your agility. Kill with the wrist, not the shoulder.'

'I shall remember, but I hope never to use your teaching again.'

'And watch your back.' Rossignol flicked a glance at the doorway. Fulke waited at his destrier's head, dressed in gambeson and helmet. He did not wear his heraldic surcoat.

'I shall miss you, *master*.'

'And I you, *mistress*.' His smile at her lordling's clothes made light of the honorific.

'Thank you, Rossignol.' She bent to kiss his cheek, on the scar, and again on the lips.

'All debts are now paid. Go, little mudlark.' And this time he spoke the insult with respect.

8.8 HUMBERT

The only noise from the old hunting lodge was the raucous cackling of crows. No wind, no other birdsong, no human movement. Humbert knew that sound and it was enough of an alarm for him to tie his spare horse to a tree and ride on with his sword drawn, unencumbered by the lead rope. He had learned from many battlefields that the first scavengers after a slaughter were always the birds; crows and magpies, usually, tugging at soft flesh and the lips of loose wounds. Later, in darkness, wolves and foxes would come to tear and gorge.

As he emerged from the forest there was a single fresh grave beside the ruined temple, so if there had been a fight then someone had lived to dig it. Humbert's horse danced nervously, and he had to nudge it up the rise from the ford. By then he could smell blood, and as his eyes drew level with the water meadow he saw the stains in the grass. Still no other signs of life.

Inside the archway, seven bodies lay in a line against the wall. One wore a richly embroidered surcoat with five golden stars on a green field. The noble had the kind of deep, sharp-edged wound that can only be inflicted by a longsword or an axe on an un-helmeted head. Bulging eyes stared upwards either side of the gash. Someone had composed the corpses' limbs, and all had a thumbprint of ash on their foreheads, so a priest had given them the Office of the Dead. And the birds pecking at their eyes were ravens, not crows.

The lodge's yard was empty enough for his horse's hoof-beats to echo when they struck stone, but a line of horses were tethered in the stables. They whickered in greeting at his own mount. Someone had taken enough care to unsaddle them and leave them hay, while their masters' bodies lay unburied. A hasty departure, then, but no panic.

Humbert was standing in the doorway to the lodge when he heard the slow drawing of a blade from its scabbard. He froze, guarding himself. In the gloom within he could make out a man hauling himself to his feet, using a table for support. One leg was caked with blood, and he wore a quilted gambeson with the retainer's badge of de Fontenay on its breast: three golden flowers on a red field.

'If you serve de Fontenay, I mean you no harm.' Humbert sheathed his own sword and opened his hands away from his sides. The man could not attack him anyway.

'I am Rossignol.' The man dropped his sword onto the table, where it clattered amidst bowls of food and a flagon of wine, though it remained within reach. He lowered his backside onto a bench, grunting. 'And you are?'

'My name does not matter. What happened here?'

'Well, messire does-not-matter, I will tell the Lady Agnès what happened, when I can, and ask if she wishes to share the news.'

Humbert snorted. He'd have given a similar rebuff.

'I am told there was a young woman here, and a noble, Fulke d'Aurillac.'

Rossignol stared back at him without answering.

'You are alone?' Humber asked a broader question.

'There is a priest in the cellar who came with the soldiers.
But I cannot allow him to go free.'

'With your *permission*,' Humbert put enough emphasis on
the word to show he didn't need anyone's permission, 'I shall
put him to work digging a grave. So many dead men would
prove embarrassing for Lady Agnès. And I can stand guard.'

The head that emerged from the cellar steps was strangely
familiar. The beard split into a smile, revealing white teeth
within a dirty face.

'Lord Brother Humbert!'

Now here was a curiosity. The priest he'd known as an
anakritis, and assistant to the Angel of Death, was greeting him
like an old friend. And casually revealing his identity to a
stranger.

'Pateras Malory.' The last time Humbert had seen this
priest he'd been on his knees beside a burning temple, after
Adelais made the act of pardoning over him. Back then Malory
had seemed transformed and had let them walk free, but had
that heretical act really turned the torturer into this wide-eyed
zealot? If so, Adelais must indeed be one of the Blessèd.

'*Lord Brother?*' The one with the wounded leg struggled to
rise, though Humbert waved him down.

'We both have news to share, it seems, Master Rossignol.
But for now Pateras Malory must wield a spade.'

Humbert let the priest do the work. For one thing, it meant that
he could ensure Malory d'Eivet had no ideas about escaping,
and for another he was getting too old to dig graves. There had
been a time when he'd leapt from his bedroll to chant the dawn
office, but these days he rose groaning and stiff from nights on
the ground. And he'd had too many of those of late.

The priest accepted his task with smiling goodwill.
Humbert did not even have to ask questions, just sit nearby and

listen. Before the grave was half-dug Humbert knew the identity of the dead noble and who had sent him. The priest did not know how Adelais had been found, but he could assure Humbert that she was unharmed, had left some time after noon dressed as a young nobleman, and that both Fulke d'Aurillac and the castellan's wife were with her.

Humbert looked at the sky. On fresh horses, they would be three or four leagues away already. He had no chance of catching them before nightfall, even if he knew the route they had taken.

'And I am expelled.' Humbert found even saying that difficult, as if the words were too heavy to rise up his throat.

'And all who help you.' Malory threw another shovel-full of earth onto the pile by the deepening grave. 'No food, no shelter, no speech.'

'But you are talking to me.'

'I do not believe the expulsion is just.' Malory grinned as he threw soil.

'Yet by the rules, you too would be expelled. You set yourself against the faith.'

Malory leaned on his shovel, clearly eager to begin a theological discussion, until Humbert waved him back to his task.

'The rules are made by men, not the God. Men like Ghislain Barthram, who was my master. For two years he dragged me ever deeper into his evil, and I felt its weight until Mistress Adelais unburdened me. I truly found Ischyros on the day she pressed ash into my forehead. Now I serve the God, but I find him more in my heart than in the directions of the anakritim.'

'That thinking will get you burned, priest.'

'But who will Ischyros welcome over the bridge, Brother *Guardian*? Murderers wearing an ash thumbprint, even if that ash was pressed there by a servant of Kakos? Or one who can walk tall and say he has lived his life with honour?'

Humbert stared at the dirt-streaked man, now waist-deep in the pit. He so wanted to believe those words.

Agnès arrived long before the grave was dug, riding hard and ignoring Guy Carelet's shouted pleas to let him scout ahead. Humbert held up his hand to stop her speaking.

'I am expelled. You must not talk to me.' Humbert stared at his niece, unable for a moment to say more. The look in Agnès's eyes made his own fill. He swallowed and forced himself to stand a little taller. 'But you can listen. Go inside, niece. You must not be seen here while there are still bodies to be buried. Tend to Rossignol, who is wounded. He will tell you what has passed. And Guy, take over here. Pateras Malory needs a rest from spade work. He and I will start bringing down the dead.'

It was a strange, stilted conversation in the lodge's hall, with Humbert announcing that he would ride after Adelais along the road that Rossignol had said would be her fastest route; the high road to Orval, then Bellay, and on into Vriesland itself. Rossignol also said he had advised Adelais against accepting d'Aurillac's company; he might have fought for them, eventually, but Rossignol did not trust him.

Humbert turned to Agnès. She could offer no assistance, but perhaps he could steal some provisions?

Agnès insisted, talking through Malory d'Eivet, that Humbert steal not only provisions but a purse of gold that she laid on the table. 'Look away,' she told d'Eivet and Rossignol. 'You haven't seen this.' And she hugged Humbert close.

'Go with Ischyros, Uncle,' she whispered in his ear. 'If you find Adelais, tell her... just tell her I will always be her friend.'

Humbert tensed within her embrace, lifting his head at the faint sound of hooves nearby. It sounded as if it was coming from beyond the walls, yet all their horses were in the stables. He backed away from Agnès, drawing his sword, and ran for the steps. Guy stood at the gates, staring back towards the ford.

'Anakritis. Just one. We must have been followed.'

Humbert closed his eyes as the implications sank home.

'Did he see the bodies?'

Guy nodded. 'Then he galloped off. We could chase him.' He lifted a hand towards his mouth, remembering the ban on speech.

Humbert shook his head. 'Our horses are unsaddled. We would not catch him before the high road.' Besides, could he really kill a priest? He turned, knowing Agnès was behind him. Her green eyes were fearful yet defiant, showing the steel within. He rested his hands on her shoulders. Did that break some holy law, now?

'You must find your husband, urgently. Try and reach him before the anakritim; he must be warned. You both will need powerful allies, and soon.'

'I will go to Villebénie. I'll take that priest, too. He seems willing to speak for us.'

In the fading light of a winter's day Humbert chose the best horse he could see; a glossy, dark bay gelding so fine that it must have belonged to the dead noble lying outside. He would take just this one horse and leave the two troopers' mounts he arrived with. He packed the bare essentials for a journey into bags he tied to the saddle; he could move more swiftly without dragging a lead rope. All reason said he should spend the night at the lodge and ride with the dawn, but he might still put a league or two behind him before full dark. When he mounted, the beast curvetted beneath him, sensing his tension. He could do nothing more for Agnès, but he could confront Fulke d'Aurillac and protect Adelais. D'Aurillac might still betray them, either deliberately or accidentally, just by being with them. He was watched. Even if he did not wear his heraldic surcoat he was distinctive; a man-at-arms, lame on one leg, with a wrecked right hand.

And, by Salazar, with a horse like this he had a chance of catching them.

CHAPTER NINE

9.1 ADELAIS

Fulke had led Adelais and Elyse in a fast trot to the forest's edge. There he slowed to a walk, lest their haste attract attention. He also insisted that Adelais lead as they joined the great road, playing her part as lordling. Adelais sat erect, shoulders back, letting her fine destrier, her escort, and the servant behind shout her rank. She kept her nose on the horizon, pretending indifference to other travellers; merchants, mainly, rumbling slowly past towards Moutâne on laden wagons. She rode in a daze, still numb, though her heart beat faster within her padding when she saw the black and white robes of an anakritis. She twisted to look over her shoulder after they'd passed and the anakritis had also stopped and turned. Perhaps he was intrigued by Elyse's stricken, tear-streaked face.

The afternoon was fading towards dusk and Moutâne was three leagues behind before the road was clear. Adelais reined back Allier until d'Aurillac and Elyse were alongside.

'Well?' she said to him. His explanation was overdue.

But d'Aurillac avoided her question. 'While the way is clear we must make speed. The night will serve for talking. With the

God's help we will make Orval in four days.' He spurred his horse into a trot, taking the lead.

Adelais fell in beside Elyse, who was bouncing along at the awkward jog of someone unused to riding. To maintain her disguise as a serving woman, Elyse also had to hold the lead rope for Adelais's baggage-laden gelding, which tugged her off balance.

'I brought the storm, Aunty.' There was no one close enough to hear. 'Can you forgive me?'

Elyse came back into the moment slowly, from far away. She turned to Adelais as if she had only just realised she was there. 'Child, you can no more stop what happens around you than the wind can help bending the trees. Sometimes one falls. What is fated will happen; what matters is how you face it. My man was fated to die today, but it is hard. It will be hard for our son, too. And he must hear the news without me.'

'How long had you been together?'

Elyse might not have heard. 'He were lazy, and a bit fond of his drink, but oh, what a laugh he had. Laughed me into bed, he did, nigh on twenty year ago.'

'Eloi will worry about you.'

'Lady Agnès will ensure he has a place. He's old enough to make his own way, now. But when we're safe I'd like to send word.'

'I'm sorry.' Adelais was repeating herself.

'Mayhap I was always fated to teach you, sweeting.'

'What did you see, Aunty? In the runes, I mean?'

'Nothing clear about that one, for sure.' Elyse looked to where d'Aurillac had tugged his spare horse behind him, out of the way of a passing wagon. 'And much that worried me.'

'Which was?'

Elyse shook her head. 'The gods play with us when we play with runes. They make us think we can change our fate, when all the time they are driving us towards it like a dog drives sheep. And I have no skill as a seeress.' She paused while they passed a cleric; the man leaned on his staff and raised a hand in benediction.

'One thing I saw and will share,' Elyse continued, 'is that our fates are linked. I have the skills of a *seidhkona* but no more power than anyone else would have from a lifetime of learning. You have power because the web of fate flows strongly through you, but no skill with which to wield it. If it is my destiny to teach you, then I am content.'

'I wish I could have spared you the cost.' Adelais reached over and squeezed Elyse's forearm. 'But will you not need your staff?'

'The drum will serve almost as well.' Elyse sounded as if she was trying to convince herself. 'That too is rune-marked, beneath the skin.'

Adelais had wondered why Elyse had been so insistent on bringing her drum. It was tied to the baggage in an oilcloth sack; it weighed little but it resonated when they trotted.

'I'm not sure I want to have a great destiny,' Adelais mused.

'So what do you want, child?'

'I want to walk free, as a woman, in women's clothes, speaking my mother tongue. I want friendships without risk or falsehoods. One day, perhaps a man who will love me as his equal.'

'Is that why he is with us?' Elyse lifted her chin towards d'Aurillac's back.

'No.' Was her denial too swift, too strong?

Elyse's silence was eloquent. It was several strides of their horses before the *seidhkona* sighed and spoke. 'Fate may have other things in store for you.'

As night was falling they came to a wayside inn. It was a humble affair, offering stabling, an uncertain stew that had probably been warming by the fire for several days, and two rooms; one each for men and women. Adelais and d'Aurillac would have to share to maintain the pretence, but at least there were no other guests.

D'Aurillac let Adelais take the bed. She removed her boots but nothing else, and sat hugging her knees while he spread his cloak on the floor. A single tallow candle lit the room, guttering in the draught.

'So can I trust you, messire?' Adelais spoke quietly, in case they were overheard. It was only after she'd spoken that she realised he might think she meant because they were alone in a chamber together.

'No.' He too spoke softly. His denial was almost a sigh.

Adelais stared at him, waiting for more.

'The anakritim hold my brother. He is sixteen and innocent. He will be killed if I do not deliver you to Ghislain Barthram.'

Adelais swallowed and glanced at her sword, resting against the wall, trailing its belt. D'Aurillac followed her glance.

'Do not worry. You can sleep well tonight.'

'Yet you fought for us.'

'Those men were not sent by the anakritim.'

'You did not know that when you drew your sword.'

D'Aurillac sat back against the wall, his face a pattern of flickering shadows; beard, skin, and hollowed eyes. Lips.

'You called to me. Reminded me of my honour.' His white teeth flashed; he was actually smiling. 'The Angel of Death would say you bewitched me.'

That was almost a flirtation. Adelais felt her body relax. 'So would you fight for me again?'

'I have asked myself that many times today. There would only be shame in surrendering you, and, at the moment, I do not think I would betray you. I hope to see you to safety. I have decided to ask the Count of Arrenicia to intercede for my brother with the king. The d'Aurillacs have been loyal to his family for generations. I should have done that as soon as I was released, but my mind was not thinking clearly. I thought finding a witch would be a surer route to his safety. Now events have taken a different turn. When you are safe I will hasten south... But I have to warn you; if Barthram stood before me now, and I knew I could save my brother by giving you to him, I think I would choose my brother.'

At least that was honest. 'And why should I not kill you as you sleep?'

'Because that is not your way. And, of course, you would have the whole country on your heels at daybreak.'

He was right, on both counts. Adelais wrapped her cloak around her and blew out the candle.

A little later he whispered in the darkness. 'What are you, mistress? Am I saving a witch?'

Adelais feigned sleep.

9.2 BARTHRAM

Barthram paced the corridor outside Chancellor de Remy's offices, too agitated to accept the chair that had been offered. Besides, he needed to think, fast.

Of the news, he was certain. How to convince de Remy of the urgency, that was the problem. As far as de Remy was concerned, there was no way short of divine intervention that Barthram could know that Adelais de Vries had been spotted, riding free and armed, along a road in Jourdaine yesterday. And he would not give that snake of a chancellor the secret of his messenger birds. One day, he might be forced to explain. That day had not yet come.

Finally, he was granted admission. He brushed rudely past a departing functionary into de Remy's presence.

'Pateras Ghislain. What an unexpected pleasure.' As usual Othon de Remy sat with the light at his back. He waved graciously towards a chair but Barthram walked further into the room before he turned. He needed to see de Remy's face.

'Your mission to arrest the witch. I believe it has failed.'

A flicker of concern, a moment of calculation, and de Remy's features were once again calm.

'They would have taken her yesterday, at the earliest, seven or eight days' ride away. What could possibly cause you to believe such things?'

'I had a dream. A vision. The Blessèd Salazar came to me as I slept. The witch is powerful. They all died.'

De Remy made the sign of the God, a ritual response, but his face smirked with disbelief.

'And what do you expect me to do with this terrible news?'

'She will flee north, and there is only one logical road. They must cross two great rivers on their way to Vriesland; the Gaelle at Orval and the Fauve, probably at Bellay. We must be waiting for them.'

'Them?'

That had been a slip. Barthram had received two birds; the first reported that a noble youth, a man-at-arms, and a serving woman had joined the Orval road from the direction of the hunting lodge. They were all well-mounted and equipped for a long journey. That was too much detail to reveal to de Remy. The second bird came after his anakritis had investigated and found the aftermath of a fight. Two birds. They had sent all they had. There would be no more news from Moutâne for some days, and he did not know if d'Aurillac was the man-at-arms with the witch or was among the dead.

'In my vision she was escorted. Helped.' Barthram heard himself stumble and breathed deeply, forcing himself to stay calm. He was near the window and a draught around the frame was cold and surprisingly free of the river's stink. That helped Barthram to think.

'So on the basis of a dream you want me to send soldiers to head "them" off?' De Remy's smirk told Barthram that he was playing with him.

'I will go with them. I know the witch.'

'I think not, Pateras. I do not have enough men to chase after dreams.'

Barthram felt his hands fisting. He took a deep breath, forced them open, and chose to release a little more detail. 'You will regret that, de Remy. My dream was very clear. Seven of Prince Lancelin's men died. They were led by a noble bearing the arms of five golden stars on a green field.' That had been in the message. 'Perhaps you recognise the arms?'

Now there was real shock on de Remy's face, though it was quickly masked. Of course, Barthram could have been told about the equerry and the troops.

'I have nothing to gain by deceiving you, de Remy. Will you help?'

The face that stared back at him was blank, professionally blank, but the eyes betrayed the racing thoughts behind the mask. Yet still de Remy shook his head.

So be it. 'Where is Prince Lancelin?'

'With the king, who as you know is hunting the forests to the east.' De Remy was shaken, yet he still managed to hint at the burden of state that rested on his shoulders while the king chased wild boar. 'You are at liberty to ride after them but you do not hunt, do you, Pateras? If you wish to wait for them at Harbin they plan to be there within half a moon?'

No, Barthram did not wish to wait half a moon for Lancelin to arrive at Harbin with the king. He inclined his head. 'When Prince Lancelin's men do not return you will have questions to answer.'

He was at the door before de Remy had formulated his response.

'And if your vision proves to be accurate, Pateras, I imagine *you* will have questions to answer.'

Barthram turned.

'Surely the faith would wish to investigate such a miraculous intervention by the Blessèd Salazar?' De Remy's smile was cold.

Barthram breathed deeply outside the chancellor's office.

Yes, he would ride, but he would waste no more time chasing Lancelin. The king himself, perhaps. Aloys would send half his army if he believed the witch was escaping. Yet that encounter with de Remy had been bruising, his disbelief palpable that the Blessèd Salazar had visited Barthram in a dream. Barthram would deny it, of course; there had been no witnesses. But there was no way back from a lie to the king. And the king would demand news of the former Guardian, Blanc. Where was the man? He should certainly have been brought to Villebénie by now.

No, Barthram would do this himself. And if it was down to him to rouse a local garrison, then he had better do it where he could be sure of being ahead of the witch. That ruled out Orval. Too risky; they might already have passed by the time he reached the city. Bellay, then. He'd study the maps.

Pateras Octave waited in an antechamber with his lead-weighted staff cradled across his knee. He stood as Barthram approached, and Barthram heard the muffled ripple of chain mail.

'Prepare for a journey, Pateras. A long one.'

Octave lifted a questioning eyebrow, but Barthram would explain as they rode.

'The God needs us.'

9.3 ADELAIS

It was Allier, the destrier, who first noticed the rider behind them. Where the road crested a rise he spun beneath Adelais without warning, lifting his nose and snorting towards the southern horizon to test the wind. Adelais could see nothing that should alarm him; a farm wagon rolling south, a mendicant cleric they had already passed, and in the distance a lone man-at-arms trotting in their direction. It took an angry tug on the reins and a touch of a spur to turn Allier back, although he looked regularly over his shoulder.

On the next rise Allier spun again, and for the first time refused to obey her commands; he danced beneath her as if he was about to be unleashed into a gallop. It took all her skill to hold him; one touch of the spur and he would have hurled himself towards the oncoming man-at-arms.

He was close, now. Close enough for realisation to dawn, and as she recognised Lord Brother Humbert Blanc, Adelais let out a wild whoop and released Allier's energy with the merest caress of her leg. Allier gave one mighty joyful buck and ran. Adelais brought him to a bounding, curvetting halt beside Humbert and turned him, deliberately now, so they could ride alongside. Allier pushed his muzzle at Humbert's thigh and Humbert dropped his hand onto his former destrier's poll to scratch the spot between the ears.

'Hello, old friend.' But his eyes were on Adelais. 'And lioness!' His private name for her made her blush. He'd once said she reminded him of a caged lioness, growling at the world, always ready to fight.

'Lord Brother.' Such inadequate words. She wanted to hug him. Ask him how he came to be there. Gush a thousand questions that she was too breathless to ask. She hoped her smile would speak for her.

'Just Humbert, now. Not even Brother. And I see you have learned to master Allier.'

Not quite; the horse had known its true master. Adelais just nodded.

'It does me good to see you free.' Humbert glanced down the road to where d'Aurillac and Elyse waited. Adelais had never seen d'Aurillac look so uncomfortable. 'Though I hesitate to say *safe*.'

'He fought for us.' She'd found her voice.

'I heard. He chose sides. I am saddened that he needed to choose.'

'It is so good to see you.' Adelais touched his wrist, and the touch became a clasping of hands, a gauntleted grip that emphasised the look between them.

'We have much to tell, Adelais. But first I would talk with the seigneur. Alone.' Humbert trotted his mount forwards. Adelais noticed that he placed his horse to the left of d'Aurillac, where he would have the advantage if they drew their swords.

They rode together for some time, leaving Adelais and Elyse to follow. There was no easing of their pace; they trotted when the winter-wet road allowed but even then their argument could be seen in tense shoulders, gesticulations, and sideways glances. When Humbert finally reined back beside Adelais, Elyse dropped behind them, giving them space, although Humbert was grim-faced and silent for a while. Adelais watched the way his sword-hand fisted and flexed, and asked no questions. This was a matter between Guardians. At least they hadn't killed each other.

Humbert's mood slowly eased. He made small, sideways glances at her. One of them caught the wry smile she offered in return and he snorted a short laugh.

'You look very fine, young lioness. Quite the noble.'

'Why thank you, my lord.' Adelais smiled at him under lowered eyes. Why was it so easy to flirt with Humbert? He was an old man. He was safe. And...

'I've missed you,' she blurted.

'And I you.' Humbert covered the moment by reaching over to stroke Allier's ears. Allier looked up as if to ask what he was doing riding another horse.

'Would you like to take him back?' She hoped he wouldn't say yes.

'He is yours now.' Humbert almost mastered the catch in his voice. 'But perhaps I might ride him once more? For old time's sake?'

'As much as you wish. I think of him as yours.' Adelais glanced at him. 'It was cruel that you were expelled. You have given your life to Ischyros.'

'I had plans. My former knights were gathering. Now I must be a nameless wanderer.'

'I know how that feels.'

They laughed together, an easing of his tension.

'I hope, like me, you find good friendships along the way.' She touched his arm again. It seemed natural for them to touch. They rode through uplands where there was little traffic and they were free to talk. 'Where will you go?' They were walking their horses down an incline into a valley. Ahead of them the road forked; a parting of ways. The world seemed a large, empty place with endless possibilities.

'I will see you safe to Vriesland, first, then take a ship for Saxenheim. Even now there are friends there who would hide me, under a new name.'

'Or you could stay in Vriesland?' Now he was back in her life she did not want to lose him again. They were easy together, and he'd become more of a father to her than her own had ever been.

Humbert shook his head. 'I cannot set my faith aside, even though the faith has expelled me. There are one or two Ischyrian brotherhouses in Saxenheim that would accept a wanderer and ask few questions.'

'Can the expulsion not be lifted?'

'Only by the diakonos who ordered it, or his superior. And that diakonos is a de Remy. I cannot even plead my case; if I was arrested I would be tortured until I confessed to their version of the truth.'

'Will Agnès be expelled?' That thought had been worrying her all the way from the hunting lodge.

'Unlikely. "Knowing association" is the faith's criterion. She did not know. And of course she is noble, with powerful connections.'

Adelais blew out her relief.

'But she is not safe,' Humbert continued. 'While this king lives, no one you love is safe. You are proof of the lies he and the anakritim concocted. If the truth were known about what he did to the Guardians, no honourable knight would follow Aloys into battle. Delmas would probably take the throne.'

Humbert reined in his horse and made the sign of the God before a wayside shrine at the junction of roads. D'Aurillac had already set his horse at the left-hand, north-westerly path; the other led north-east up the valley floor; a substantial road, wide enough for two carts to pass, although clear of travellers on that winter's day.

'What lies that way?' Adelais stopped herself calling him Brother, but his name alone still seemed disrespectful. It was an idle question; her mind was still full of Humbert's comment. *While this king lives, no one you love is safe.*

'Theignault. A rich county, they say.'

Adelais stared up the northerly road, remembering the time when she'd told a cobbler that Theignault was her home. Was it only three moons ago? So much had happened. That day she'd stolen a priest's sandals. Now she wore Agnès's gift of fine leather boots.

She did not see the wolf until a flock of sheep panicked and ran up the hillside as if they, too, were newly aware of its presence. It stood in the middle of the Theignault road, on an island of turf between muddied ruts, where the way curved into low scrub. The wolf was watching them, its white chest very clear against the bushes beyond. Their horses became restive beneath them, nervous at the sight of a predator.

'Can we reach Vriesland that way, messire?' Elyse moved alongside Adelais and Humbert. She too was staring at the wolf.

Humbert shrugged. 'It is a long way round. It would add perhaps four days to our journey.'

The wolf turned and trotted away. It paused at the limit of their vision and looked over its shoulder as a wolf had done once before, as if to say '*are you coming?*'.

'Humbert...' It was the first time she had used his given name. 'I think we should go that way.'

He did not laugh. 'Does that wolf have meaning to you?'

Adelais glanced at him. She was on dangerous ground. 'To my family.'

'Adelais,' Humbert spoke as he might to a wayward child. 'It is not Ischyrian to believe in such portents.'

'And yet...'

D'Aurillac had halted his horse within shouting distance on the Orval road, and twisted in the saddle.

'Why have we stopped?'

'Mistress Adelais wishes to take the Theignault road,' Humbert called.

'Why, in Salazar's name?' D'Aurillac nudged his horse closer.

'I believe there is danger ahead of us.' She could say no more. Not even with Elyse nodding her encouragement.

'Every day is dangerous until you are in Vriesland. No messengers, *no one* has passed us so far, but they will if you add days to our journey.'

'It is a road no one would expect us to take.' Adelais knew she sounded stubborn, even petulant.

'And I wish,' d'Aurillac added, 'to ride south and plead with the Count of Arrenicia to intercede for my brother. I will not delay.' He turned his horse and trotted away down the Orval road, ending the discussion.

'The seigneur is right.' Humbert followed. 'Come.'

The howling behind them began as soon as Adelais turned her horse's head away from the Theignault road. It was an eerie, winter's moon baying and it startled Humbert's horse into a sudden gallop until he brought it under control.

It was Elyse's turn to reach over and touch Adelais, trying to reassure her, but her eyes betrayed concern.

'It may have been just a wolf, sweeting.'

Adelais shook her head. 'It was a warning. It—she—was *fylgja*.'

9.4 TAILLEFER

'Talk to me about visions.' Othon de Remy clasped a goblet of wine to his stomach with both hands, spread his elbows on the arms of his chair, and watched his younger brother expectantly. They sat in Taillefer's office within the palace of the diakonos at Harbin. Candles illuminated a pile of documents awaiting Taillefer's attention on his desk. They cast enough light to show that Othon was listening intently.

'Visions, brother?' Taillefer played for time. The chancellor's arrival was unexpected, or at least premature. The king was not expected in Harbin for several days, not until he had hunted all the game to be had in the forests further south. Then the whole court would descend upon the palace, expecting to be fed, wined, and watered. Taillefer's stewards were already slaughtering and preparing. But Othon, alone except for his escort, had come much too early. Here he sat in the fading light of the day, mud-spattered, and asking about visions.

'Visions. If a man came to you claiming he had seen things in a vision that he had no way of knowing, how would you react?'

'I would think he had drunk too much wine. And if he

insisted, I would seek proof.' Taillefer was cautious. His brother had ridden twenty leagues in winter to ask this question.

'What is the faith's teaching on the matter?'

'Proven cases are as rare as miracles,' Taillefer admitted. 'If a rich woman claims that the Blessèd Salazar has told her to establish a sisterhouse at a sacred place, no one is going to complain. If a king claims divine blessing before a battle, few priests would be brave enough to say he lies to inspire his army.'

Othon de Remy sipped wine, his forehead furrowed in thought. Taillefer wished he'd come to the point; there was much to do, and once the king arrived the only business would be hunting, hosting, and politics.

Othon leaned forwards. 'So, *diakonos*, what if a priest, a holy man, came to you with information that he could not have known by any natural means?'

'It would probably be dismissed as guesswork, imagination, or most likely coincidence. A priest might pray for guidance, and in following his instinct take an improbable course of action. When history proves him right, he may claim to have received divine guidance.'

'But information—incontrovertible, factual information that could not have been acquired through natural means—must have been acquired through supernatural means, yes?'

'Yes, I suppose.' Taillefer steepled his fingers, thinking. 'Do you have evidence of such a "vision"?'

'Not yet, brother. And in truth I hope that I never do.'

'We had another unexpected visitor last night.' Taillefer watched for Othon's reaction. 'The anakritis-general, no less, claiming a night's lodging for himself and another anakritis. They left early this morning, going east. They seemed to be in quite a hurry.' He had his brother's attention. 'Would your visits be related?'

9.5 ADELAIS

'I never thanked you, Seigneur.' Adelais was still not sure what to call d'Aurillac. 'Fulke' would be too familiar, but she was finding ways of saying 'seigneur' that implied informality; not quite the tones of a handmaiden, but just a hint of intimacy after four days on the road together.

'For what?' Fulke took a swig of breakfast ale. It had been warmed with a hot poker and steamed a little in the morning air. They were both leaning on a fence, staring into the paddock where all their horses except Humbert's grazed. Humbert had pressed on to Orval, an hour's ride ahead, insisting that he scout the way before risking the bridge and town.

'Fighting for us at the hunting lodge.'

Fulke snorted. 'I could not have lived with myself otherwise.'

'But thank you.' Adelais touched his arm. The contact did not have the ease it would have with Humbert. Fulke looked down at her fingers as if unsure of how to react. It was strange, having this time to talk. It was the first time since Humbert had caught up with them that they had been alone, and the first time they had not been either pressing forwards, or eating, or falling asleep exhausted in some inn at the end of the day.

'Don't count on it again,' he answered, too gruffly, 'not if the Angel of Death is watching.'

Adelais turned to rest against the fence, hooking her elbows backwards over the top rail. It was a man's stance. Or perhaps a woman's if she wanted to display her curves, but Adelais's figure was bound tight beneath her *jacquet*. Ahead of her now was a small market square. Elyse sat on a bench outside the inn with a hunk of bread and her own pot of ale. Small birds waited hopefully at her feet. Adelais worried for her; Elyse still moved as if in a dream, grieving for Sennet, missing her son. Perhaps she too had memories of killing that she'd like to forget.

'You could leave now, and ride south to your count. Humbert will protect us.'

'I'd thought of that.' Fulke sighed. 'Brother Humbert thinks I should seek an honourable death.'

Adelais looked at him sharply.

'If I am dead, you see, the anakritim have no hold over me. He does not believe even they would burn an innocent boy, just for vengeance; they too want to cross the bridge of judgement.'

'And will you?'

Fulke looked down at his hands. 'I thought I had lost my faith, but I find myself more reluctant to die now I am apparently expelled. We Guardians were taught to welcome martyrdom as a certain path to the arms of Ischyros. It is easier to face death courageously if you are sure of what lies beyond. For now, I will follow the Lord Brother and hope that I might find favour in his eyes, if not the God's.'

For a moment Fulke seemed so vulnerable that Adelais wanted to put her arm around his shoulders.

'When you are safe I shall turn south,' he continued. 'Have you been to Arrenicia, mistress?' Fulke also managed to weave hints of intimacy into the formality of 'mistress'.

Adelais shook her head.

'It is a land of lush river valleys and rocky hills. The wine is rich and strong, and tastes of hot stones.'

Fulke's smile and distant gaze hinted at the man he might have been before the anakritim did their work.

'I'm tempted to ride south with you.'

They both knew she wasn't serious, but with Vriesland so close she was starting to wonder what she might do with her life when she was safe.

PART FIVE

THE SNOW MOON

CHAPTER TEN

10.1 BARTHRAM

Ghislain Barthram surveyed Bellay the way a commander might view a field of battle. It was a walled town of reasonable size; he could see the domes of at least two temples as he approached along the Harbin road. It sat on a hill on the north bank of a great bend in the Fauve, like the hub to the river's wheel. There were no slums against its walls, which suggested either a strong seneschal or regular floods. There were two gates on the side facing him, both commanding bridges over the Fauve; there would be at least one more astride the road north. As Barthram clattered over the Harbin bridge his eyes were drawn to the other, carrying the Orval road. *Surely he was not too late?*

The seneschal, the gate guard told him, had chambers in the great tower overlooking the Orval bridge. 'Not that he's there. With Prince Lancelin, he is, and he's with the king.'

Barthram and his escort were greeted by a grizzled sergeant, the kind of veteran whose stocky competence could keep a town in order in the absence of his lord. He seemed more unsettled by anakritim than he would be by marauding Vriesians; the man littered his speech with awkward pieties. Barthram declined his offer to escort them to the town's main temple and insisted that they talk privately. He was shown to the seneschal's own chamber, which filled an entire floor of the tower. In times of war it would be a fighting platform, with embrasures cut for archers radiating around the wall. In these more peaceful times waxed linen had been stretched across the openings to admit light and soften the winds. Barthram declined a seat, chose the embrasure closest to the Orval road, and opened the linen shutters. Beyond the bridge the road crossed a floodplain before rising through woodland; none of the traffic he could see would be the witch. Barthram turned back into the room.

The sergeant was eyeing Barthram's escort. Pateras Octave shifted slightly, and the ripple of chain mail sounded beneath his robe.

'How many men do you have, sergeant?' Barthram asked.

'Ten, Pateras. And by the grace of the God, all good men.'

'Mounted?'

'We have four horses in the stable, but our duties lie largely within the town.' The sergeant carried his helmet in the crook of his arm and shuffled awkwardly.

'Sergeant, you have the chance to do a great service to Prince Lancelin, to the king, and to Ischyros. You know of the Vriesian Witch, no doubt?'

'Indeed, Pateras. Spawn of Kakos that she is.'

'Quite. Some days ago Prince Lancelin sent men into Jourdaine to arrest her. They failed. They died. She is now fleeing north towards Vriesland. I believe she will pass through Bellay. Soon.'

'We are but ten, Pateras...'

'And she has but one man-at-arms with her. I would like you to gather all your men.'

The sergeant fiddled with the aventail of mail hanging from his helmet. 'Pateras, the seneschal should know...'

'I understand. He is your lord, and you do not take orders

from a priest. Send a messenger, of course, but by the time he has found the seneschal and returned, the witch will be gone.'

The man nodded, reluctantly.

'Good. The shameless woman has disguised herself as a young noble*man*, and she also has a servant woman with her. I shall stay in this room and alert you when she passes; you are to have at least half your men always at this gate, and a man within my call.'

Barthram could do no more. Now he must watch, and pray that he was not too late.

The days passed slowly. Barthram moved a chair into the embrasure and stared out over the Fauve towards Orval. The river widened between the bridges to form a small harbour; the bank had been reinforced into a wharf below the town's walls. He wondered at the purpose of a stone pillar set into the pool above the Harbin bridge, trailing a cork-floated rope, until the crew of a laden barge seized the rope and used it to haul the boat through the central arch of the lower bridge. The outfall, apparently, was squeezed into a fast-flowing current between the bridge's supports, too strong for oars alone.

Opposite the town, between the Orval and Harbin roads, was a grassy plain perhaps a bowshot wide and thrice as long. A boy who brought the garrison food told Barthram it was the place for the great autumn fair, when Vriesian cloth was traded for Compeignois grain or exotic silks and spices from distant lands. Beyond the fair ground the land rose in a grassy slope to a wooded ridge. The outlook might have been pleasant for a brief time of reflection. After two days it was tedious.

Barthram and his anakritis observed the offices of the God on their knees in the chamber, declining an invitation to worship at the temple. The temple bells were sounding for the second office, at the start of their third day, when Barthram began to despair; had the witch really been so swift as to be ahead of him? He fell on his knees in the embrasure, imploring Ischyros to send her to him. Yet the Orval road stayed stubbornly empty, save for a lone man-at-arms who ambled slowly towards them; well-mounted but grey-bearded; quilted armour only with a mail coif thrown back from his head.

Barthram stiffened. Impossible. Humbert Blanc should be in Villebénie by now, awaiting the tormentors in the Black Tower, not riding down a road in Compeigne. And if Blanc was here the witch must be close, but where was d'Aurillac? Barthram pushed himself to his feet, making the sign of the God. If ever a prayer had been answered, it was now. How it came to be so would be discovered before long but, as he turned and called for the guard, his heart was filled with joyous thanks. He was truly blessed.

Blanc fell into their hands as sweetly as a ripe plum in summer. He was not expecting trouble; he walked his horse steadily through the gate, relaxed in the saddle. The only sign of unease was the way he looked around, registering soldiers, perhaps counting them. He would see nothing unusual for a town's gate near an unsettled border: two guards on the gate, one on the tower, a sergeant pushing himself out of a doorway, apparently calm.

'That's a fine horse, messire.' The sergeant stood in front of Blanc, blocking his way, and stroked the horse's neck. 'Distinctive. Had him long?'

'Long enough to learn his ways.' Blanc eyed the sergeant. He sounded cautious.

'Strange, though, that when I last saw him he was the mount of Gerard d'Essoyes, whose lands are nearby.' His hand strayed to the bridle and gripped it tightly. 'Can I assume that Messire d'Essoyes is no longer in the best of health?'

Blanc tried to rein back but the sergeant had the bridle fast, and when Blanc twisted to draw his sword he found himself looking at the point of a lance. Two, in fact; one each side. And two more soldiers emerging from the tower, swords drawn. He lifted both hands from his sides to show his surrender and dismounted slowly. He probably thought he was being arrested for stealing the horse.

Barthram waited until Blanc had been disarmed before he stepped out of the shadows. The expression on Blanc's face at the sight of him was exquisite; that draining of the flesh to chalk, the slack-jawed disbelief, would have been worth many times the hours Barthram had spent watching. Best of all was that instinctive flicker of the eyes back down the Orval road, swiftly masked, which told Barthram that the witch was nearby. Blanc was merely scouting the road for her. And if she was watching from those distant woods, the arrest had happened far enough inside the gates for her not to have seen.

Barthram did not waste time with gloating. After all, he and Blanc would have endless hours together, alone except for the tormentors, before Blanc was burned. And Barthram would only grant that release when he had all the evidence he needed. Perhaps not even until de Fontenay had yielded the relic. It was much more important now to secure the witch before she suspected anything was wrong. As soon as Blanc was bound and bolted into a secure storeroom, Barthram summoned the sergeant to the top of the tower. Below, the Fauve curved between the bridges. Barges unloaded on the wharf. Another was being hauled beneath the Harbin bridge, hand over hand. Snatches of song carried to him on the wind, a slow beat in time with each pull. Life continued unaware of the drama within the town's walls; there should be applause, not the rumble of rowlocks. Barthram did not turn. An idea was starting to form.

'Sergeant, the witch will be close. The man you arrested was scouting the way.'

There was silence behind him. Barthram turned and once again saw reluctance in the man's eyes.

'If you were the witch, where would you be waiting?'

'There is a village, less than a league away, with an inn. Bellay's gates are closed between the Lighting of the Lamps and dawn office, as you know. If I arrived too late to enter the town, and I had the coin, I would lodge there for the night.'

'Excellent. I would like you to take three men and search that inn. See if you can surprise her.'

'My men have other duties, Pateras...' The sergeant's eyes were fearful.

'You require *four* men to take two women? She was travelling with only one man-at-arms and we have him.'

'She's the Vriesian Witch.'

'Just think, sergeant; what you have already done will earn you rich reward. The man we have captured is Humbert Blanc, formerly a Guardian Grand Commander, who was with the witch when she killed the high priest.'

'I hear six good men went with d'Essoyes. Are they all dead?'

'Only Ischyros can tell. What is more certain is that the king has offered the witch's weight in gold for her capture.'

Greed replaced fear in the sergeant's eyes.

Barthram continued. 'She is unprotected, and not expecting any attempt to arrest her. Seize her, and half of the king's reward will be yours, to share with your men as you see fit. But if you cannot take her easily, I want you to give her a message. If she wishes Humbert Blanc to see the sunset, she will meet me on that field.' He pointed towards the fair ground. 'His life is now in her hands.'

Pateras Octave cleared his throat. 'Shall I go with them, Pateras?'

Barthram had almost forgotten him. Strange how someone so large had the ability to fade into the background.

'No. I have a task for you here. We must prepare an appropriate welcome.'

Barthram looked down the curve of the town's wall towards the Harbin bridge. The battlements would afford an excellent view for the townsfolk. By this night no one would doubt who had taken the Vriesian Witch.

He had seen the bond between Blanc and the witch when he had them both in his hands in the spring. Blanc had just proven it again, somehow escaping capture and crossing half of Galmandie to be with her. Barthram was about use that knowledge to his advantage. Malory d'Eivet's time as his assistant had been disastrous, but he had left one excellent technique behind him: achieving results through *indirect* pain on a loved one, rather than the *direct* application of torture. Quite brilliant. If the sergeant could seize the witch quietly, that was good, but his fallback plan might even be better.

And rather more enjoyable.

10.2 ADELAIS

It was easier to be in Fulke d'Aurillac's company when Humbert was not with them. The nights had been difficult, with Adelais required to sleep in the same chamber as the men when they stopped at roadside inns, while Fulke and Humbert eyed each other like feuding cousins. On the road the conversation flowed with each of them, individually, but never with them both together. With Humbert it was as deep and steady a friendship as she could imagine between a man and a woman who could only ever be friends. With Fulke there was now the occasional glance and a smiling hint of something private that made Humbert stiffen in disapproval if he saw. Adelais realised she was going to miss Fulke's company when he turned south. He seemed more reconciled with himself, now he had a plan.

She was a little relieved when Humbert went ahead into Bellay, as he had at Orval, scouting the way over the last great barrier before Vriesland. The tension left with him, like a sigh. They'd spent the night in a room that was little more than a platform set into the roof of a modest inn; a plank floor laid on the beams of the communal room below, warmed at first by a central fire pit below, but freezing by dawn. A thin partition and a door gave some privacy. A small dormer window set into the thatch had been shuttered against the night but now stood open to a sun that promised the end of winter.

When Fulke returned to the room with Elyse to pick up the last of their bags, Adelais was wearing a shirt and her padded *jacquet* but had yet to don her cote-hardie; a state of partial undress that sparked a certain *awareness* between Fulke and Adelais. Elyse glanced between them and said she'd wait by the horses. Adelais knew she'd stay there, guarding the packed animals. And then there was a new, shy tension in the room; she and Fulke were always together and so rarely alone.

'It smells like spring.' Adelais filled the silence with useless words. Suddenly she didn't know what to say. She stood by the tiny window, looking out onto the road. Her heart beat a little faster.

Fulke came to stand beside her. He needed to put his head close to hers to peer out. 'Two more nights and you will be in Vriesland,' he whispered. Sound would carry easily from this room. 'What will you do?'

'Find somewhere to hide.'

'You will not be allowed to hide. You are too important. You must find Duke Ragener. Seek his protection.'

'And you will turn south, to find the Count of Arrenicia.' She looked into his face. He was very close.

'I must try to save my brother.'

They looked at each other for a long moment, and his face came nearer, slowly, until their lips touched. His were surprisingly soft and yielding, though the beard that had been growing since Moutâne tickled at her face.

Adelais withdrew, gently enough for it not to be a refusal. She did not love this man. Was it so wrong to feel desire? Just desire, with a touch of friendship? She looked down as his fingers tugged at the lacing of her *jacquet*. Perhaps she would permit a little intimacy, a promise of what might be, one day.

'I will miss you.' Adelais felt torn between the wanting and the fear of wanting, of letting it happen, but she did not stop him sliding the *jacquet* from her shoulders. She held his gaze, and felt his hand upon her breast. His thumb traced a nipple through her shirt, and the wonder that filled his face was more arousing than the caress itself. That tender innocence told her she might have to teach him to love her, if they ever found a more private place. Here they could not even speak without being overheard, yet as he slipped his hand inside her shirt she felt her resolve weaken. Could she stay silent? She'd lifted her face to be kissed again when the clatter of horses outside broke the moment as emphatically as a dropped pitcher.

'Kakos take them!' Fulke pulled back from the window, though Adelais wanted to tell him not to stop. She felt a little dizzy. Surely the riders would not bother them?

Riders? *Soldiers.* A sergeant and three others. One was being sent around the back of the inn. Three coming in. If they were looking for her, she and Fulke were trapped in this upstairs room.

Fulke backed into the corner by the door, leaving her by the window, exposed in every sense. There was nothing between her and the door. If anyone came in, she was half-dressed; she was breathing heavily and she knew that her breasts would be pushing at her shirt. Beyond the door, down the steps, men were shouting. Her sword was on the bed beside her and she reached for it.

'Take off your shirt.' Fulke's voice was still thick with desire, but she must have misheard.

'What?' That moment was already shattered. There were soldiers below. They were arguing with the innkeeper.

'Take off your shirt,' Fulke repeated. 'Distract them.'

Swiftly, furiously, she obeyed, holding the shirt high over her chest.

'Lower. Please?'

She glared at him as she bared herself. Almost as an afterthought she bent, drew her sword, and kicked the scabbard out of sight. There were boots on the stairs as she straightened; the floor shook with their stamping. By the time the door burst open, swinging back on Fulke, she was holding her shirt in front of her sex, and behind the shirt was the sword, its point to the floor.

A soldier stood just inside the door, hefting his sword but licking his lips with his eyes on her breasts. Adelais retreated, drawing him further into the room. The clump of his boots on the boards was slow and ponderous. His sword point began to drop. Adelais looked for a point to strike. He wore a chain-mail coif beneath his helmet. *So I can't go for the neck.* The bucklers were with the horses; she couldn't use Rossignol's tricks, either. Behind him a second soldier craned for a view. Adelais shook her head, letting her fear be seen.

'No, please...' she whimpered like a frightened woman. *That was easy. One more step. Padded armour only, no body mail.* Did she have the strength to punch her sword through a gambeson? His blade would parry before she struck. *And another step.* She was in the corner now, both men in the room.

Fulke kicked the door backwards against its frame, and the second soldier let out a terrible, dying groan with Fulke's thrust deep in his body. He twisted as he fell, ripping the sword from Fulke's hands.

The one in front was turning, lifting his sword to strike at Fulke, when Adelais hacked her blade across the back of his knees. She'd learned that strike at the lodge. His blade went high and wide as his legs folded and he fell with his head against the wall. He began to flail at her from the floor with his sword, and she flicked her own blade sideways with her wrist to block it. It wasn't even a proper defence. All Rossignol's training was forgotten. Yet the tip bit deep into the man's wrist, almost severing the hand and releasing a spray of blood that splashed hot across her skin.

The door had not latched; it swung slowly open, still shaking. Adelais dropped into guard facing it, holding her sword two-handed against anyone who came through. The blood was slick between her breast and bicep.

'Enough, witch!' The sergeant was at the bottom of the steps, staring up at her. He sounded frightened. Nothing in this veteran's experience could have prepared him for the sight of an almost naked, blood-spattered woman with a sword in her hand standing over one of his men. They stared at each other. Adelais made no attempt to cover herself. *Show no weakness, girl. Play the part.* A man and a woman appeared at the sergeant's shoulder, peering fearfully upwards; the innkeeper and his wife. Adelais crouched and hissed at them like a cornered cat, and they fled out of her sight.

At her feet the wounded soldier rolled onto his belly, crawled to the top of the steps, and fell down them, arcing blood.

Adelais looked over her shoulder. Fulke had retrieved his sword and was again behind the door, flexing his fingers around the hilt in a two-handed grip, and she realised the sergeant may not have seen him. *This might be important.* She felt more naked in Fulke's presence than in the stare of the stranger below. The remaining soldier's body stared at her ankles with sightless eyes.

'This one is dead,' she said, quite calmly, as if she killed people all the time.

'I have a message for you, witch.' The sergeant grabbed his crippled soldier by the belt and hauled him clear. 'From the anakritis-general.'

. . .

Time was marked by the *drip, drip* of blood through the boards. The world was newly silent save for the faint splashes into the rushes below. They slowed and Adelais waited for the next, feeling as if she was coming awake from a deep dream. No, a nightmare. Humbert taken. Ghislain Barthram here. She found herself staring down the line of her sword to where its point rested on the boards. There should have been more staining on the blade; it still shone. From outside came the sounds of two soldiers trying to lift a third into a saddle. She straightened and turned her back on Fulke, newly embarrassed at her nakedness. There were droplets of blood spattered in a line over one breast and smeared on her side. A few moments before he had stared at that breast with lust and wonder. Now his eyes held no desire, only horror.

'See if Elyse is safe. Please.' Adelais dismissed him, and kept her back to him as he left. There was a pitcher of water and a bowl in the corner, and she bent to mop the blood from her body.

'You will go to him?' Fulke had spoken from the door.

She did not turn. 'We must all choose our own paths, now.'

They rode together to the edge of the forest, and halted where the land fell away towards the river, keeping themselves hidden within the trees. To their left the tree-crested escarpment curved away as if they stood at the edge of a great, grassy bowl with the walled town of Bellay at its centre. They were within a bowshot of catching up with the soldiers, who moved slowly. One of them walked, steadying another in the saddle, while a third led two riderless horses. More soldiers were running towards them from the town's gates. Behind Adelais a crowd of curious villagers had followed; they too now halted in the road, watching to see how events might unfold. They scattered when Fulke spun his horse, drew his sword, and cantered at them.

Adelais knew that was an empty threat; he could scarcely grip it one-handed.

'Are you all right, Aunty?' Adelais was concerned for Elyse. The soldier at the rear of the house had been sent to guard the door and had seemingly failed to realise that Elyse was part of Adelais's group, but the ageing *seidhkona* had clearly been shaken. Fulke had found her clutching a small axe in one hand and a stool in the other, ready to wield it by one leg like a cumbersome club. Fulke clearly thought she was deranged; before they mounted, Elyse had smashed the legs off the stool and brought the seat with her.

'All right, sweeting? For now,' Elyse replied. 'Though this is a day when we will all be tested.'

When Fulke returned, Adelais led them off into the forest, keeping far back within the trees until they found a place where they could tether the horses and watch from hiding. 'Watch and learn,' Humbert had taught her. 'Always watch and learn before you approach the enemy.' She dismounted, holding Allier's head. Elyse stood beside her, still carrying the axe and the remnants of the stool.

'You will meet him? The Angel of Death?' Elyse sounded as if she already knew the answer.

'I think I must listen to what he says.'

'He will kill you both.' Fulke spoke from behind them. 'You know that, don't you? He will relish your pain.'

Adelais turned to him. His face still wore a shadow of the moment in the chamber when lust had turned to revulsion. 'So what would you have me do, *Seigneur*?' She emphasised his rank, putting distance between herself and the man who was almost her lover.

'You could ride west. Leave the baggage and ride fast, before word spreads. There is another bridge at Harbin. Then strike north into Vriesland.'

'Abandon Brother Humbert?' Adelais made that an accusation. 'And Elyse?' Adelais might be able to outrun news, but Elyse could not.

Fulke looked away. That morning he had put his hand on her breast. He had kissed her. Now he would not meet her eye.

'Ask yourself what he would want. The Lord Brother's death is inevitable, now. Yours is not.' Fulke's voice held regret but no shame.

'And you, Seigneur? You are well-mounted. You could ride south. Find your count and have him plead for your brother.'

'I might.'

'Or you could don that blue surcoat and ride down there with me. Ensure that I am taken and save your brother that way. The time for concealment is past.'

In Fulke's instinctive recoil she saw that he still did not know what he would do if put to the test.

'Well I'm too old to go galloping around the country.' Elyse was calmer than either of them. 'I'll make my fight here.' She put the broken stool seat against the bowl of a tree and began trimming it with the axe.

'With a piece of wood,' Fulke snorted.

'Good yew wood,' Elyse replied. 'Yew, the wood of magic.' She brought the axe down again and began to sing the song of *ihwaz*, the yew-rune. '*Ýr er bendr bogi...*'

'You are a witch!' Fulke's eyes flew wide in shock.

'That is not a word we use. I am *seidhkona. Ok brotgjarnt járn...*'

Adelais knew Fulke should not see this. Besides, he would spoil Elyse's concentration. He'd disrupt the all-important *intent*. 'If you want to be useful, Seigneur,' she told him, 'you could stand between us and the road and make sure that no Ischyrian bigot from the village tries to stop her.'

'But *I* am Ischyrian,' he protested.

'Not if you are expelled, you're not,' Adelais snapped. 'You were also a Guardian, sworn to stay pure, yet this morning you would have bedded me. Today we must all find our own way of fighting. This is hers.'

He went. Adelais squatted beside Elyse. This might be the last day of her life, or at least of her freedom, but she could still learn. She could even share the rune song.

'*Ýr er bendr bogi, ok brotgjarnt járn, ok fífu fárbauti...*'

'The yew is the bent bow and brittle iron, and the giant of the arrow...'

Elyse hacked the seat into a rough lozenge shape, and sat with it resting between her crossed legs.

'The yew-rune is powerful defence. It hardens the spirit.' She picked up a small, sharp knife, her risting knife, and began to carve into the flat surface. 'If you live, child, never do this lightly. I am weaving more than your protection; this is a curse, a *nidhstick*, and my *intent* is the death of your enemies.'

Adelais swallowed, watching the yew-rune take shape.

She was in awe of the *nidhstick*'s power even before it was carved.

Below them two anakritim had appeared through one of the town's gates and were walking down a wharf that stretched all the way from one bridge to another along the bank beneath the walls. It was too far to make out details, but their black and white robes were clear. One of them was huge, and walked with the wide-spread gait of a wrestler. Four soldiers followed, with a prisoner between them. Adelais was sure it was Humbert.

'*Íss er árbörkr, ok unnar thak, ok feigra manna fár...*'

Elyse was carving rune upon rune. Now it was *ísa* the ice-rune, a single upright line.

I

A rune to freeze the power of others, a rune to bind foes. 'Ice is the bark of rivers and roof of the wave, and the destruction of the doomed...'

The prisoner and the big anakritis boarded a small boat from the wharf. Two men climbed in with them. Why row him across when they could use either bridge?

'*Oss er algingautr, ok ásgarðs jöfurr, ok valhallar vísi...*'

Ansuz, the god-rune. It would harness the power of Odhinn. 'The most powerful rune to bind others,' Elyse had once said. 'As a king rules through his lords.'

'Aged Gautr and prince of Asgard, the lord of Valhalla...'

The two men rowed the boat out into the river and tied it to a pillar that poked out of the middle of the stream. There it swung in the current, waiting. Two soldiers were keeping people clear of the lower bridge. The sun shone on metal beyond the castellations on the towers; probably helmets. Distant pinpricks of colour on the battlements were probably the hats of onlookers, waiting for the show. The figure of the smaller anakritis crossed the Harbin bridge and stood on the bank below her, level with the boat and Humbert. The four soldiers formed a protective box around him; six armed men were outside the walls, none of them mounted.

They were ready for her. It was as the sergeant had said. The town's gates would be shut to show her that she would not be surprised by a sortie. She could approach on horseback, and only soldiers on foot would be there to defend the anakritis-general. The fate of the former Guardian would be in her hands. He had not said that Humbert would be protected by the river, like an unbridgeable moat.

Adelais stood. 'I shall go and hear what he has to say.'

'Wait.' Elyse was still carving runes with murderous intent, wounding the wood with deep, straight cuts.

Both roads were filling, now the town's gates had been shut. It looked as if the villagers had made it past Fulke; the Orval road carried a cluster of people on foot. They were shuffling forwards, watching, waiting.

Down in the town the temple, bells were sounding the noon office when Elyse drew her knife across her palm and dripped her blood onto the runes, singing in a low, venomous snarl as she smeared it in. She dripped and spread more until every rune was filled with red. Only then did she push the end of the *nidh-stick* into the ground so that the bind-rune faced the bridge. 'It is done.' She stood, taking several deep breaths before she relaxed.

Adelais embraced her, letting their foreheads touch. 'Thanks is too small a word, Aunty.'

'I think this will be the most foolish thing you will ever do. It may also be the last, but the gods love courage. They will honour you for this.' Elyse lifted her head until she was looking into Adelais's eyes. 'Remember what happened with the high priest; power came to you because your anger unleashed it, not because you sought it. Power comes when you forget yourself. Let it come.'

Adelais kissed her on the forehead, unable to speak.

'Now pass me my drum, sweeting. And whatever you do, whatever he does, don't yield.'

10.3 HUMBERT

Humbert had been allowed to sit on a rower's bench in the middle of the boat with his wrists bound behind him. He faced forwards, staring at a giant of an anakritis in the bow. A rope stretched from the bow to a pillar in the water, through an iron ring, and back again to a cleat at the anakritis's elbow, holding them in place in the stream. The priest toyed with the loose end, constantly coiling and uncoiling it, and he stared at Humbert with the implacable menace of one whose profession is torture.

Humbert wondered if they really worshipped the same God. Yet this man was of the faith. At his feet was the satchel all priests carried, and in that satchel would be a silver box with the sacred ash. On the bank on the meadow-side of the river, protected by four soldiers, stood Ghislain Barthram. The Angel of Death. Both priests had the power of pardon, while Humbert was expelled.

Humbert closed his eyes. *Holy Ischyros, if you can still hear my prayers, do not let her come.* He knew how this would play out, for behind him a noose had been strung from the central span of the bridge. It hung just low enough to put around his neck if he was made to stand. She would be told to surrender or watch him die. It would be a false promise; he would never be released.

Strangely, he did not fear his inevitable death, even though he was denied passage over the bridge of judgement. He feared for the new order that he and his brethren had planned that would protect the Hand; would Brother Thanchere be adequate to that task? But his greatest fear was not for any great matter of faith and mission, it was for the agony that would be inflicted on Adelais, if she came; she who was both friend and daughter, in all but blood.

The boat rocked as the anakritis shifted on his seat, and the two boatmen in the stern cursed. Their role as rowers done, apparently they needed to sit back there to balance the great weight of the anakritis in the bow. Humbert risked a glimpse at the men, and they seemed sullen and resentful of their task. He wished he could have comforted them.

Humbert watched the Orval road, from whence she would come. If she came. The road was crowded now. People were watching. Townsfolk lined the battlements. The anakritim were putting on a display. Yet the four soldiers he could see around Barthram on the Orval bank were frightened. He'd overheard them saying that the witch had killed two of them that morning, stark naked. Humbert didn't believe that. *Strange how quickly stories grow.* 'She weren't natural,' they'd said.

The temple bells were sounding. Noon office. Humbert tried to run through the ritual in his mind, but the only chant that came to mind was the Guardian chant.

Ischyros be merciful and shine upon us.

A lifetime of service to the God, and yet in the time of greatest stress he could forget even the comfortable ritual of the noon office.

Yet the Guardian prayer was still strong in his mind.

And lift his hand to bless us.

Somewhere a drum was sounding, a slow, steady beat.

That the way of truth may be known among all nations.

'Stand, Guardian!' The anakritis's tone smeared that glorious name.

Thy saving health among Thy faithful.

The boat rocked again as he stood, and the noose was placed around his neck.

Let all the people praise thee!

The drum was resonating at about half the pace of a walk, and he looked for the source of the sound.

Adelais was coming. He'd been watching the road, and she was already halfway down the slope from the woods. On Allier. Two dear friends together. *Holy Ischyros, let it not be.* The horse was prancing in time to the drum, alternate beats, stepping high, arched. *Sweet Salazar, old friend, thou art beautiful.*

Allier had seen him. He made an impatient buck, briefly breaking Adelais's composure, and picked up speed. Gone was the proud bearing of a captain's mount on a victory parade; now he was a knight's destrier on the verge of battle. Adelais reined him in within hailing distance of the boat. The soldiers backed away, swords drawn.

'Welcome, witch!' Barthram sounded almost affable.

'The torturer-general.' Her voice was high and clear across the water. 'Do you enjoy your work?'

'Your life for his, witch. He can take your horse and go.'

'Run, Adelais!' Humbert bellowed. 'Do not trust him!'

'One more word, Guardian, and we'll choke you as she watches.' The anakritis in the bow stood, unsteadily even in this broad-beamed working boat, and untied the rope. He let it out, just a little, but enough for the boat to drift backwards in the current and for the noose's slack to tighten. He kept the end in his hand, one foot braced against the bow, his eyes on Barthram, waiting for a signal.

Can she not see I am dead already? Yet she hesitated, even nudged Allier a little closer. She had to be made to run.

Humbert made his decision in a moment, as fast as the parrying of a blade. It was no decision, really; simply an instinctive movement. He gathered his strength and kicked the huge anakritis in the backside so hard that the priest pitched over the side with a childlike gasp. The boat rocked violently and bounced upwards at the loss of his weight, and rose on a great spray of water as the man hit the surface. A single, flailing hand rose as he sank. Humbert had forgotten that the man was wearing chain mail.

And he'd just killed a priest. Another soul for him to carry onto the bridge of judgement.

Time moved slowly as the boat slipped backwards, first in finger-widths, then in hand-widths as it was picked up by the stream and the rope unspooled over the side. Pateras Ghislain turned on the bank, calling a desperate 'no!' as the end fell into the water.

So slow, and yet too fast. There was time to consider consequences before the noose tightened. Humbert looked as steadily as he could towards Adelais, breathing in short, desperate gasps. As the noose began to lift he knew that although he might be denied the company of his Guardians in the afterlife, this sacrifice was a noble act of which they would be proud. Did not the Blessèd Salazar preach that the God's martyrs feared neither death nor pain? Ischyros triumphed in them, said Salazar, and they, who lived not for themselves but for the God, found in death itself the way over the bridge to eternity. Some buried corner of his mind resumed the Guardian chant.

That Thy way may be known upon earth.

Adelais's heartfelt scream filled him with warmth at the certainty of her love.

The wrench when it came was brutal, dragging him from the boat by his neck. His legs struck the boat's gunwale then thrashed at the water as he tried to turn himself. He wanted to see her.

May Ischyros bless us until the end of days

For Adelais and Allier had erupted into a leaping, slashing, kicking partnership before which the soldiers crumbled, and together they were magnificent; pure harmony of hoof and sword. As darkness claimed him his heart swelled with pride until his chest could no longer contain the pounding.

And we sing the songs of eternity beyond the stars.

10.4 ADELAIS

Rune song followed Adelais down the slope towards the further bridge, hammered into the warp and weft of fate by Elyse's drum. Allier danced to its slow beat, his energy contained between her legs and her fingertips so that she did not bounce *on* him but moved *with* him; together they made a single body.

Sól *er* **ský**-*ja* **skjöl**-*dr* − *ok* **skín**-*andi* **rödh**-*ull* − *ok* **ís**-*a* **aldr**-*tregi*...

Sowilo, the sun-rune, the lightning-slash victory-rune. 'S*ól* is the shield of the clouds, and shining ray, and destroyer of ice.' The liberator of bonds.

There were people at the bridge; travellers and merchants from Harbin and beyond, denied entry to the town by the barring of the gates. They backed away into the meadow beyond as she approached. More people were leaking onto the fair-ground field from the Orval road behind her, and the battlements were thick with onlookers. She was alone in a crowd, watched by all; she could feel the fear and awe around her. She held Allier poised, directed towards Ghislain Barthram and the four soldiers guarding him. She knew that their fear was her greatest weapon,

Then Allier saw Humbert, standing in the boat with a noose around his neck. He gave a small buck and surged forwards, and for the first time Adelais knew the power of a warhorse with its blood hot. That too was frightening; she lived, she rode, she would fight, only by harnessing the destrier's will.

By the time she managed to rein him in ten paces in front of Barthram she knew that the situation was hopeless. She did not need Humbert's shout to know that Barthram could not be trusted. Even if she managed to cut her way through the soldiers, Humbert would be dead before she reached him.

Adelais drew her sword. *Humbert's* sword. She'd salute him with it before she turned away. He would not blame her; he would not want her death.

For a moment she did not understand the splash as the anakritis hit the water. But the boat began to move backwards beneath the span of the bridge, the rope snaking over the side, and Humbert, calm at its centre, gave her the gentlest smile she had ever seen.

Adelais moved in a way that was beyond instinct. There were screams, and the loudest of them were hers, but there was a groundswell of noise from the crowd as she and Allier surged into a divine madness. There were four soldiers and a priest between her and the bridge and any hope of saving Humbert. Four *cowering* soldiers, who were no longer men, they were barriers. Obstacles. And Allier knew that. He reared high on his hind legs, and brought his iron-shod fore-hooves down on the first one's head. Adelais rocked in the saddle as he threw his weight onto his forelegs to spin and kick with the hind. And through it all, Adelais stayed balanced at the heart of fury, guiding with a touch of the spur. Only one of the men came close, and he went down from a lunge-thrust-recover manoeuvre that she had never been taught.

She was through. Adelais threw herself from Allier's back in the centre of the bridge, spinning on her heel to look for more danger. One guard was banging at the gates to be let in and Allier was rearing at him, teeth bared. Three were down in the field and not moving. One was crawling away, bleeding badly. Another staggered away with one arm hanging useless. Ghislain Barthram was on his hands and knees, howling, trailing a leg that was clearly broken. And across the meadow Fulke d'Aurillac came galloping towards her. *Too fjakkinn late.*

She could not shift the rope. Not with Humbert's weight on the end of it. She leaned over the parapet and tugged uselessly, feeling she was wounding him more by pulling. He spun beneath her, his legs trailing their own little wakes in the water. The flow gave him movement so she could convince herself that he still lived, but those distorted features could not be Humbert's. Only the grey hair and grizzled beard were his.

The wood balustrade beside her jolted as if struck by a mighty hammer, and she glanced back to see the flights of a crossbow bolt embedded in the wood. Still she tugged, ineffectually. Humbert was not conscious. Might already be dead. If she cut the rope he would drown.

Fulke arrived beside her, also peering downwards. From high above them on the tower came the steady *tick-tick-tick-tick* of a windlass crossbow being re-spanned.

They could lift the body between them. Just. Adelais wrapped the rope's slack around the rail and held Humbert's weight while Fulke reached over and heaved him onto the parapet, groaning with the effort. Humbert hung there with his legs over the water, dripping, and his head lolling downwards, while Fulke gasped for air and shifted his hold.

Humbert was dead. She could see that, even before the next crossbow bolt slammed into his back. She stared at it in disbelief

for several heartbeats before she screamed gutter Vriesian up at
the tower.

'*Thú fjakkinn svín!*'

Tick-tick-tick-tick.

'Come, Adelais.' Fulke gathered Allier's trailing reins, and
the sword that she'd dropped, and pushed them into her hands.
Adelais looked back as he tugged her away. It seemed wrong to
leave Humbert there, slumped in the roadway. He should have
honour, and a priest of his faith to smear the sacred ash and say
the words. She backed away into the field, tugging Allier's reins,
staring at the sodden body in disbelief, and almost fell over
Ghislain Barthram. She couldn't even remember the blow from
Allier's hooves that seemed to have shattered his shin. He was
blubbering curses as he crawled towards the road. He was probably also the reason why that crossbow hadn't fired again. All
her rage unleashed into a kick to his guts that lifted him onto his
side.

He screamed again as Fulke picked him up bodily with one
arm under his chest and one between his legs, and threw him
onto his own destrier's saddle.

'Why?' Adelais could not imagine any reason for slowing
themselves down with a crippled priest.

Fulke bent to repack Barthram's satchel where its contents
were spilling into the mud; a silver box of sacred ash, a stop-
pered bottle of ink, sealing wax, quills, and a small knife with
which to sharpen them. The tools of one who might need to
send messages, now tumbling alongside a spare shirt and hose.
A few precious sheets of paper fanned from its flap, fluttering
on a gentle breeze. 'Because he is going to sign my brother's
release.' Fulke stuffed them back and held the satchel towards
her as if it was sufficient explanation.

'You'll burn in the pit first, d'Aurillac.' They were the first
coherent words she'd heard Barthram speak since the fight.

'I think not, priest. You taught me a lot about pain, remember?' Fulke kicked Barthram's dangling leg. The scream that followed was as high as a woman's.

Adelais mounted Allier with a sense of failure. She looked around at the town gates, expecting to see a sortie of soldiers coming for them, but they remained closed. The bodies of the men she'd killed were humped in the riverbank's mud. Humbert lay face-down on the bridge, his outline disfigured by the bolt. It was a betrayal to leave him there, untended, unheld. She needed to touch him. Cry over his body. She and Allier were of one mind; at first he would not move, but whinnied towards his former master, his body shaking with the force of his calls. Adelais had to use the spur to turn him.

On the road the people parted for them, backing away. Most made the sign of the God. None offered any threat, but most surged for the town when the gates opened, pausing only to stare at Humbert's body. Still no soldiers emerged.

She and Fulke waited on the road until Elyse joined them, leading the baggage-laden gelding. She looked exhausted.

They walked down the Harbin road, ignoring the crowd's stares, until a bend of the road took them out of sight of the walls. Adelais led. She didn't want to have to look at Barthram. She wished she'd killed him outright. That would have given her a vicious pride. As she'd launched into that fight she'd felt such fury within her that she might have blown him clear into the water with just a snarl. But Barthram was in agony, his leg swinging to every movement of the horse, and his pain made her feel tainted.

'For *fjakk's* sake, leave the little *skit* by the roadside,' Adelais pleaded after another whimpering groan from the anakritis. She didn't turn her head. She knew Fulke walked at her heel, leading his destrier.

'Not till I have that release paper.'

'So where are you taking him?'

'Far enough to be beyond rescue and beyond hearing.'

'Was that why you showed yourself? To capture the anakri-tis-general?'

Fulke did not answer until she turned in the saddle to look at him.

'Humbert was my commander. He was also my Brother.' Fulke stared back at her. There was a frightening determination in his eye.

'You could have escaped. Ridden south to Arrenicia.'

'No Guardian could have watched and done nothing.'

Beyond Fulke's shoulder Ghislain Barthram's grey face, distorted with pain, was locked on Adelais and filled with enough venom to blow away her pity. Beyond Barthram, Elyse rode slumped in her saddle, her eye lidded, her mouth slack.

'I taught you well, Adelais. I saw you, on the riverbank. You fought like one trained from birth. Better, even.' Fulke's respect had a note of surprise.

Adelais shook her head, overcome by her own wave of exhaustion, and with the exhaustion came memories. Those soldiers had been ordinary men. They had not chosen to be there. Yet she'd taken their lives as mercilessly as she'd once lifted weeds from around a crop. They had been between her and Humbert. More than a father. Dying on the end of a rope like bait on a fishing line. That was all the reason she needed to kill, and she'd killed so efficiently, beyond any training. What had happened to her?

They should have been across the river by now, the last great barrier before Vriesland. Adelais sat straighter in the saddle, forcing herself to think.

'Where is the next bridge?' By the sun, the road was heading west and a little south, away from Vriesland. And soon the countryside would be raised against them.

'Harbin,' Fulke replied. 'Ahead of us. Two days' easy ride if the road is good. Perhaps just one on horses like yours.'

'They will send a messenger. Harbin will be alerted.'

'You could ride on, fast. Abandon the baggage. Beat the message.'

Adelais glanced at Elyse, who was already swaying. Adelais remembered how spent her grandmother had been after working *seidhr*; she would expend as much effort working her magic as a soldier would spend in battle. To stay ahead of the news she'd have to abandon Elyse as well.

Adelais shook her head. 'No. What about looping back to that other place the Lord Brother said?'

'Theignault. But the Fauve turns south beyond Bellay; it's a longer way round. And do you really want to ride back past Bellay?' Fulke paused where a track led off the road into the forest. 'I think it is time to disappear.' He led the way into the trees.

'Thank you, child.' Elyse touched Adelais's arm as they followed.

'You heard?'

Elyse nodded. Adelais had the strange idea that beneath her tiredness Elyse was almost happy, or perhaps just relieved.

'Was that what you foresaw, Aunty,' Adelais pointed back towards Bellay, 'when you cast the runes?'

Elyse closed her eyes, letting her horse find its own way. Her body swayed with the motion. 'I saw the untimely death of one who loved you. Until the Lord Brother arrived I thought that must be Lady Agnès.' A half-smile softened her face. 'Now all you have to do is find the red rider.'

10.5 ADELAIS

A league from the road they came across an abandoned hut and barn, probably used for summer pastures; patches of forest had been cleared around it. There was at least an hour of light remaining, but the chance of shelter was too good and too rare to pass by. There were even bundles of hay stored in the barn's loft. '*Harmingja*', Elyse muttered, though Adelais wondered what kind of luck put them on the wrong side of the River Fauve, moving away from Vriesland, with Humbert dead at Bellay.

There was an awkward moment as the three of them looked at Barthram, still sitting on Fulke's destrier. The Angel of Death's face showed disbelief. Denial. Affront. And then, a wide-eyed recognition of his deadly peril.

'D'Aurillac.' Barthram began to bluster. 'You will burn for this. You and your brother.'

'Let us talk about that, Pateras.' Fulke smiled insolently upwards and dragged the priest violently out of the saddle. Barthram's fury ended in a terrible scream as his leg hit the ground. Fulke pushed him face-down, knelt on his back, and used Barthram's own belt rope to bind his hands behind him.

He then seized a handful of the priest's robe where it was falling over his neck, lifted his head the way he might lift a puppy by the nape, and flexed his crippled hand under the Barthram's nose. 'Remember, Pateras? Would you like to know how it felt?' He stood, breathing deeply, visibly containing himself.

'Messire!' Adelais tried to call Fulke away. She sensed that once the violence began it would be hard to stop, and she wasn't sure she wanted to be part of what might be coming.

'Don't weaken now, child,' Elyse growled. 'Remember what Pateras Malory said; this man was going to shove a red hot iron up your backside. Or was he planning to use the other entrance?'

Adelais was shocked. This was Elyse. *Aunty*. 'But *torture?* We'll be no better than him.'

'But for him Sennet would still be alive. And anakritim burned my sister.' Elyse spoke loudly enough to make sure Barthram heard.

'You're really going to do this, aren't you? For vengeance?'

'Not just that. There's powerful magic at work here. How else was he able to get ahead of us on the road? *How did he know?*'

'Maybe he was just there. Coincidence.' Adelais knew the implausibility of her answer even as she spoke it.

'No.' D'Aurillac was emphatic. 'The Angel of Death only emerges from temple or torture-room to lick the king's arse. He knew. Somehow, he knew.'

'And if he does have an explanation, we'll find out.' Elyse followed d'Aurillac into the hut, where they began setting a fire. A big fire. D'Aurillac emerged briefly to drag Barthram into a position where he could watch them.

'What was it you once told me, Pateras? Anticipation is key. Your victims had to know what was going to happen to them.' Fulke went back inside with an armload of wood.

Adelais squatted against the hut's outside wall and looked up at the sky. How normal the world seemed. Fading light. The moon rising already in a clear sky; it would be a cold night. Was it wrong that could she be so detached?

'So how *did* you know we would be at Bellay, Pateras?' Adelais asked. 'How were you ready for us?'

'Witch! You'll burn!'

'So you said. You say it all the time. But just now I'm more worried about you burning. I don't think I can stop them, you see.' Adelais closed her eyes, but an image of Humbert's dead, twisted mouth filled her mind and she winced away, screwing her face into her shoulder.

'You wouldn't dare!'

Adelais looked up. Barthram was glaring at her.

'I see it in your eyes, witch. I smell your lies! Remember I know how this works.'

'A good, decent man died today because of you.' *Others too.* But somehow the soldiers didn't count. A whole army wouldn't add up to Humbert. 'And I know he would pardon you, even now, if he had the power. He was more holy than you have ever been. Ever will be.' Humbert would want no part in torturing anyone, even this piece of *skit*.

Fulke emerged from the hut and pulled Barthram towards the fire, letting the priest's broken leg drag along the ground. 'Sitting in your dungeon, we Guardians compared your methods.' Fulke's voice held a bright madness. 'With me, it was the hammer and the boot. Others, of course, had their feet held in the fire.' His own fire was now blazing.

Adelais pushed herself to her feet and followed. Barthram was already white-faced and whimpering with pain. 'Let me go, d'Aurillac.' He was gasping into the dirt, pleading now. 'She has bewitched you. It is not too late for pardon.'

Fulke seemed not to have heard. 'First you used to smear their feet in pig fat. Makes them burn like torches, I'm told.'

The set of Fulke's face told Adelais that this was no act; he really was going to torture the priest.

Barthram saw that as well. He began to whimper. 'You'll spend eternity in the pit!'

Fulke bared his teeth in a sneer. 'I am already expelled for helping Mistress Adelais. You have no greater threat to make, anakritis.'

'Messire?' Adelais ignored Elyse's warning look. This was enough. 'Brother Humbert would not want this. Let us kill him cleanly and have done with it.' Adelais was beginning to feel sick. She was already part of it, but she could not sink further towards Barthram's level.

Fulke shook his head. 'By the time this night is over that man will have signed my brother's release or he will be dead. He taught me well, you see. If you keep working broken bones, then break a few more and work those, before long one part of your mind floats off on its own and watches the rest of you go mad.' Yet the madness was already written over Fulke's own face. 'But you always know that you could stop it all with a word. A confession. A signature. Isn't that right, *Pateras?*'

Barthram looked pleadingly at Elyse, who stood by the fire, fists on hips. 'Just in case you think I'll plead for you, priest, I watched my sister burn.' Elyse spoke without emotion; loud, clear, almost conversational. 'She were a gentle soul, a healer, but she sang the songs of healing over the wrong child, and the anakritim burned her as a witch.'

Adelais swallowed. 'I cannot do this.'

'But I can.' Elyse wiped her hands on her kirtle as if she was working in her kitchen. 'And I want to know how that man knew. I need to know what magic is ranged against us.' She looked up, watching the smoke drift beneath the thatch; the wood was a little damp. 'I think you should go back to the road and make sure our smoke cannot be seen.'

When Adelais did not move she added, 'Go, child,' in a voice with the power of a *seidhkona*'s drum.

Adelais left, despising herself. She was several hundred paces away when the screams began. They tore at the fading day like the cry of some fearsome animal, or a pack of animals, for so much noise could surely not be contained within a single body. Allier tensed under her, reading her, and she urged him into a trot, risking injury among the shadowed roots until the noise faded behind her.

She should have realised what was going to happen. With Fulke, she might have expected it. By the gods, if she'd been tortured like that she might be tempted herself. But Elyse?

And between them they were tainting Humbert's memory.

She could have ridden on alone. Abandoned them. Perhaps been across the river at Harbin before the news shut the bridges.

But that wasn't her way, any more than torture.

And now the news would have overtaken them. Elyse's rune lore might be useful. She would know which runes to combine to work spells of concealment, or to confuse enemies.

Sætur Sif she was tired.

The sun had set by the time she reached the road, which stretched empty in both directions. The snow moon was full and bright, so she rode half a league towards Harbin. There was no sign of the fire; no reflected glow, no smoke, no smell, no sounds. She saw no one; no travellers, no messengers. Slowly, tiredly, she swung out of the saddle, rested her cheek against Allier's neck, and wept. She wept a little for herself, for the whole bloody, dirty mess that had been her life since the hunting lodge, but mostly she wept for Humbert. As if understanding, Allier bent his neck over her shoulder until his muzzle reached her backside, and began to groom her in that gentle way that horses bond. It helped. A lot. Enough for her to remount and ride a league in the opposite direction. Still no sign of the fire. When the moon began to set she made her way back to the hut while there was still enough light to see her way.

She stopped when another scream split the night. And another. More, as regular as a man can be when he must suck air before he can bellow out pain, and will turn himself inside out in the effort to push the agony through his mouth. She dismounted and stroked Allier's neck to calm him. Was she being a coward, to absent herself from an atrocity she had not tried hard enough to prevent? *Could* she have prevented it? And was she content to reap the rewards, if they were successful? When the screams faded she led the horse forwards, having found no answers.

They had dragged Barthram clear and cut him loose outside the hut. He lay curled on his side with his knees drawn up, blubbering like an infant. Adelais tried not to look at his feet. The clearing stank of burned meat; she remembered that smell on the clothes of Malory d'Eivet after the execution of the Guardian's grand master. How many moons ago had that been?

Fulke and Elyse sat inside, unmoving, hunched under their cloaks. Adelais sat opposite them where the fire would light their faces. They looked back at her with haunted eyes that flickered in the firelight, as if they were already in the pit.

'Did you get what you wanted?' Adelais wondered that she could talk calmly when she felt so weak, so shamed.

Fulke lifted a sheet of paper. 'My brother's release.'

Adelais looked at Elyse, who would not meet her eye.

'Birds,' Elyse muttered, her voice numb. 'He trained birds to carry messages. No magic.'

There was a gulf between them. Among them.

'We have become what we most despised,' Adelais said. The 'we' was deliberate. She was complicit.

'It is no more than he has done to hundreds of better men.' Fulke stood, crossed to Barthram, and tugged a signet ring from the priest's finger. He used a burning twig to dribble sealing wax onto the paper, and pressed the anakritis-general's seal into it. 'I shall leave for Villebénie as soon as it is light enough to see. I will go south, then east across country in case the word is already ahead of us.'

Elyse lifted her head. 'Then do one thing for us. Visit his house and release the birds. Take that servant with you, the one he said knows birds. Show him that ring if you must, but leave no trace or knowledge of this art for others, or they will be ahead of us always.'

Fulke nodded and put Barthram's ring in his scrip.

They carried Barthram back into the warmth of the hut for the rest of the night, as if they sought to make amends for their abuse. Adelais even splinted his leg, binding it to a plank she tore from the barn and hacked into shape. She doubted if anyone slept.

At dawn they broke their fast on food they had plundered from the inn outside Bellay, then Adelais helped Fulke strap his bags to his destrier. She touched him on the arm before he mounted.

'Farewell, riding master.' The man she might once have bedded deserved more than 'messire' in farewell.

Fulke kissed her lightly on the cheek, like a brother, and looked at her steadily. 'We would never have been comfortable together.'

He was right, she knew. But there had been attraction.

'Will you marry, now you are released from your vows?'

'I shall look for a wife, yes. One who...' Fulke did not finish.

'Wields a needle rather than a sword?' Adelais tried to make light of the moment, but did not feel like smiling.

'Who wants to be the wife of a lord. You are a beautiful and courageous woman, mistress...' *Mistress.* Not even her name. Two days before he'd wanted to plough her.

Adelais finished for him. 'But just a little frightening. *Seigneur.*'

He was right. Whatever spark there had been between them had died for him when he saw her fight, near-naked, the blood splashed over her breast. And it had died for her at the fire behind them.

'What shall we do with the anakritis?' Adelais nodded towards the hut.

'I still fear the pit and will not kill a priest. I shall leave him to your conscience. Mine is already over-burdened. Think of it as an act of mercy.'

Strangely, Adelais did not think she could kill Barthram. Not now, not in a cold act. Not when the Angel of Death was curled and crying like a baby. In all her imaginings she had not foreseen putting the tip of her blade against a weeping man's throat and slicing. What would Humbert have done, in this moment?

Simple. He would never have let the torture happen, not even to the persecutor of the Guardians.

Beside her, Fulke mounted. 'How will you cross the Fauve? The bridges will be guarded, and soon the countryside will be crawling with soldiers.'

Adelais shrugged. Perhaps she should rely on *harmingja*, which Ischyrians would call 'luck', but which meant so much more in Vriesland. She only knew that she and Elyse must keep moving forwards, even if the path to Vriesland meandered more than a great river.

'Go quickly, Seigneur, in case we are taken.' All words seemed too mundane for the moment.

There was no other farewell.

Adelais picked up a stick and crouched to scratch at the soil, thinking. Only luck would get them through, or powerful rune magic. Yrsa had told her that *harmingja* was like a spirit that visited followers of the old gods when the gods played in this world, and *perthro* was its rune. Adelais drew more forcefully, inscribing *perthro* in the dirt.

She did not sing its song, for *perthro* was also the rune of fate, of *örlog*, the great, wild unknown. Perhaps soon she would find out if she was indeed the *örlaga vefari,* the weaver of fates.

CHAPTER ELEVEN

11.1 ADELAIS

Adelais sat by the fire in the hut staring at Elyse, who stared back at her wide-eyed, quivering a little. She stank of smoke and guilt. Adelais knew that they would both carry the burden of this night for the rest of their lives.

'If you're going to kill him,' Elyse lifted her chin towards Barthram, 'get it over with. I cannot.'

Barthram had begun to crawl on his elbows towards the barn and the horses, one agonising handspan at a time, dragging his splinted leg. Adelais didn't think he'd be able to stand if he got there, let alone mount. She shook her head and hunched deeper into her cloak.

'If you let him live it would be the biggest mistake you ever make. Perhaps your last,' Elyse said.

'You do it, then. I've had enough of killing.' It was surreal, to be discussing a man's death while he wept nearby. They hadn't even bothered to tie him up, but then he couldn't walk. Might never walk, so her conscience crawled in the dirt. She hadn't felt this wretched about any of the men she'd killed, and she'd hardly even touched this one. But she'd let others do it. She almost wished she was Ischyrian, able to lay a sin before a priest and have it taken away with a daub of sacred ash.

Perhaps the blessing of pardon had made the anakritis-general what he was; able to inflict endless agony and have his soul wiped clean every evening. He'd lost his need for a conscience. She wondered what he was thinking now as he endured what he had inflicted on so many. He'd managed to crawl halfway to the barn, but toppled sideways on the slope and rolled onto his back. He held his unbroken leg off the ground, like a stranded beetle.

'Let us go, child.' Elyse pushed herself to her feet. 'We're wasting the day.' She had to step around Barthram on her way to the horses.

Adelais swung her scabbard behind her and squatted, facing Barthram, just beyond his reach. He seemed to look at her *through* his skull, not *with* it, buried behind a mask of agony, and taking short, panting breaths. The last time she'd seen eyes like that had been in Carel de Tour, the tortured Guardian that Barthram had brought to the sisterhouse the year before. She took a swig of water from a skin and spat the taste of the fire from her mouth. Then another. This time she swallowed.

'Well, Pateras. What am I to do with you?' The weight of the sword on her hip told her what she must do.

But this was Humbert's sword, a gift that came with the instruction to 'wield it with honour'. Killing a defenceless priest, however loathsome, was not honourable. The Lord Brother would say it was not *valiant*, not worthy of chivalry.

'I want you to know something, Pateras; I was never a witch. If you'd left me alone I might have been an *adeifi* by now in the sisterhouse at Montbeauvoir, if I hadn't managed to escape back to Vriesland.'

Barthram whimpered a little, and made the sign of the God.

'But I have learned that there is power in rune song, and I intend to learn how to wield it. If you live, know that you and your *fjakkinn* anakritim have turned me into that which you most feared.'

Adelais stood and steadied the hilt against her hip. For a moment she was still tempted, and his eyes followed her fearfully. The wrong word from him and she would still have swung that sword at his neck.

'Please?'

She dropped her hand, stretched her back, and swore the filthiest word she knew. No. Fate was also a matter of consequences, and though she would carry the burden of his torture she would not compound it with his death. Elyse watched as she tightened the girths, and gave Adelais a look that said '*on your head be it, girl*'.

Adelais pulled some waybread and a linen-wrapped leg of chicken from a saddle bag, the last of a capon they had taken from the inn outside Bellay. She left it within his reach with the water skin. They had a little cheese but from now on she'd have to hunt. No matter; she'd done that before.

'When we are safe across the river I will leave word where you may be found. It is a better chance than you have given many fine people.' She tightened Allier's girth and mounted. 'Eat sparingly. It may be some days.'

11.2 TAILLEFER

A feast had been laid on trestle tables at this agreed rendezvous by the Bellay road, four trundling hours by ox cart from Harbin, and all so the king and his court could satisfy their hunger in the middle of their day's hunting. The king sat within a pavilion tent and was served on linen, though mere courtiers like Taillefer must stand. They clustered in politicking groups, each subtly different in their manner. Prince Lancelin's set twittered like songbirds and nibbled fastidiously at fowl's legs, held in napkins to protect their fine plumage; a group around the Duke of Delmas were in muted hunting colours, and dared to laugh while they gripped pies in their fists. Those most keen to be noticed and remembered clustered on the fringes, wearing surcoats emblazoned with their arms. Huntsmen in autumn browns, too base-born to eat in the king's presence, held the dogs away from the food and took it in turns to disappear into the woods with portions of the bounty.

Taillefer looked down at the skirts of his scarlet robe. He had no choice in his clothing, for he must at all times proclaim his profession – priest – and his rank – diakonos. He'd had this robe cut with extra cloth so that he might fit decently and elegantly into a saddle. Beside him his brother Othon wore drab, workaday clothes that shouted how little he needed to say to proclaim his power. Othon was briefing Taillefer on the politics of the moment in preparation for the night's feasting in Harbin. He was optimistic; it was a fine day with sunlight streaming through bare branches, yet with a hard frost in the shade, and patches of mist lingering in sheltered hollows. The king was in a magnanimous mood that would be even better if the afternoon gave him a kill.

A galloping horse on the road set the horse lines into a rearing frenzy until the rider realised he'd burst upon the hunt and slowed. At a distance he seemed to be a boy, though – as a servant brought him to Othon to explain himself – Taillefer saw he was a lightly built man, and he was riding a horse that looked to have been bred for speed and endurance; a professional messenger. Othon cut off his apologies with a lift of the hand.

'You are in a great hurry. Why?'

'I have a message for the commander of the garrison at Harbin, messire.'

'And at that speed you will deliver it before the afternoon office. First you will deliver it to me.' He took the horse's bridle and dismissed the servant with a jerk of the head.

'And you are, messire?'

He had balls, this man.

'The chancellor. There sits the king.' Othon spoke quietly, as if he was a little bored by the delay.

The man looked around him, and swallowed. The court of Galmandie watched him back; a diversion while they ate. He leaned forwards in his saddle, talking quietly.

'The Vriesian Witch was at Bellay yesterday.' He hesitated. 'She is a fiend. I saw her kill three men. Veterans. Two more died earlier, and another two will not fight for a while, but the crossing is shut against her. An anakritis also died, but not by her hand. So did a former Guardian who was with the witch, one Humbert Blanc. Worst of all, Excellency, she has taken the anakritis-general captive. The witch was last seen heading towards Harbin, and I am to alert the garrison that she must not cross the bridge.'

Othon had slumped as if he was suddenly very tired. 'How many with her?'

'One man-at-arms and a serving woman.'

Othon dropped the bridle and stepped back. 'Go.' He did not look up. 'Just go.'

Around them the court watched, curious. Taillefer could see the effort it cost Othon to straighten and to calm his face; if the witch was at Bellay, the raid by Lancelin's equerry had failed. 'Will you tell the king, brother?'

Othon considered briefly. 'No. He would run for cover behind the walls of Harbin, and after the debacle of the retreat from Baudry every noble in Galmandie would laugh at him. The hunt must continue. I won't even tell Prince Lancelin until we are almost at Harbin.'

There was something in this news that Taillefer did not understand. Lancelin. Othon. The anakritis-general. 'How did he know, brother?' Taillefer counted days on his fingers. 'Barthram, I mean. How was he ahead of her?'

'Quite. We shall ask him, when we can. Meanwhile I shall return to Harbin and send to Villebénie for more soldiers; cavalry, not garrison foot soldiers. It is easier to tell the king bad news when we have a plan. Tomorrow those with the stomach for it will hunt the witch, not boar.'

11.3 ADELAIS

Adelais and Elyse rode east until they were well out of sight, letting Barthram think they were heading back to Bellay or beyond, and then backtracked towards Harbin, taking their direction from the sun. The forest was criss-crossed with tracks and it was easy to stay off the road. Sometimes they strayed close enough to see it, or to hear the distant rumble of a wagon. To the north was the River Fauve, occasionally glimpsed in folds of the land. Provided they rode west between road and river they would reach Harbin and its bridge. Somehow, they had to cross that river before they could turn north towards Vriesland.

But how to cross? They had no plan. Blunder in under cover of darkness? Hope that Elyse could work *seidhr* to cloak them? Adelais had heard of such magic, but never known it done. 'Follow your fate, sweeting,' Elyse said in one of their rare moments of conversation. 'If you are destined to die in Harbin, then what matters is only the courage with which you meet your dying-day.' It was strong advice, but not very comforting. 'Or mayhap it is your destiny to live and become the *örlaga vefari*.'

Mostly they rode in silence apart from the beat of hooves into leaf mould, with Adelais feeding on grief and the sick sense of guilt within her. The hilltops were bathed in sharp sunlight, while the hollows were chill and streaked with mist. In one small valley, no deeper it seemed than the others, the sunlight was blocked altogether and the leaves dripped moisture in air as cold as snowmelt.

Elyse saw the wolf first this time, or perhaps Allier did. He began dancing sideways as they crossed a stream bed in the valley's dip, and Elyse's horse snorted and broke into a canter up the far slope, away from whatever threat had appeared. Allier stood his ground, breathing furiously, although he turned to face up the little valley. The she-wolf stood at a distance, white-splashed grey among rounded grey stones. Two great trees stood on either bank, arching over her, and framing the misted forest beyond, so that the wolf appeared to be standing at a portal, inviting them on. Allier lowered his head and pawed the ground, quivering, while the wolf lifted her snout, sniffing the air. Adelais had the strange idea that horse and wolf were communing at some deep, unknown level. So much so that when the wolf turned away and trotted up the valley, Adelais could persuade Allier to follow; the prey led by a predator.

'I see it.' Elyse turned her horse.

'Take the gelding.' Adelais handed Elyse the lead rope. 'Would that we had followed her before.'

The wolf loped away, faster than Elyse would be able to follow, though Allier managed to keep it in sight. Adelais drew Humbert's sword and hacked at branches to indicate their path to Elyse; her trail would be clear, even if the ground showed no mark. And the wolf was leaving her in no doubt, bounding along, always in sight, never close enough to threaten, so that Allier settled into an easy lope after her tail.

Long after she had outrun Elyse, Adelais cantered into a grassy clearing, a broad space the size of a city's market square, and found it empty. Around her the dripping trees seemed an unbroken fence, yet Allier's tracks in the grass proved there were ways in and out. No other tracks, not even the wolf's. She circled at the clearing's heart, sword still upright like a knight with no one to fight as she peered towards tree trunks that were shadowed to black. Directly overhead was a hint of sunlight, a blue-white tinge to the cloud, but all else was shades of charcoal and silver. Allier's hooves crunched frosted grass as he danced.

She sheathed her sword and shivered as the sweat of her ride began to cool on her body.

'Amma? Amma Yrsa?' It seemed so natural to call for her grandmother.

Silence. Grey, wet silence. Then, in the distance, the sound of horns.

11.4 TAILLEFER

The hounds found a scent that afternoon. A good trail; a whooping, mud-in-the-air gallop that purged all thoughts of politics or witches from Taillefer's mind as his lovely mare surged ahead of the court.

It helped that he was unencumbered by a boar spear, and so had two hands for the reins. The partnership between him and the horse could be complete; the slightest touch with the leg and opening of the rein that curved them around a tree, the fingertip signals that collected her before she leapt a stream. They became one animal, one madness, one joy, and it would be a rare horseman indeed who could better them one-handed.

There was another good reason why Taillefer never carried a spear when he was hunting boar on horseback; boars were intelligent and courageous animals, perfectly capable of erupting out of the undergrowth if they thought they were cornered, and in his experience there were few horses who would face down such a charge. Even destriers, trained to hurl themselves unflinching at the enemy, were prone to rear and shy when a squealing beast the weight of a fully armoured knight came fast out of nowhere, scything tusks that could rip open their belly. At such moments even Taillefer needed both hands for control.

Better still to kill on foot; boars knew their enemy, and would charge a man whether mounted or not, but would rarely attack a riderless horse. Taillefer would not risk this horse near a boar's tusk if he could help it.

Othon joked that Taillefer treated his mare like a lover.

In any case, most royal boar hunts ended on the ground. The gallop would be over once the 'bay dogs' had chased down and cornered the quarry, when the king would dismount to finish the kill on foot. He'd have at least two huntsmen near, always ready to step between him and the boar; spears had a way of catching on branches or underbrush in that desperate moment when you needed to spin to meet a side attack. Taillefer would be on his own, so he preferred to trust his hunting sword. It was two-handed, for a boar's thick hide could easily turn a thrust, yet shorter than a warrior's weapon; honed to a fine edge, and with a leaf-shaped broadening behind the point that gave him the highest chance of an immediately fatal wound. And on a hunt, unlike a war blade, it was entirely compatible with priestly garb; a priest could not shed human blood, but there was no prohibition on animals.

By the time this day's boar took cover, only the king, two of his huntsmen, the Duke of Delmas, and Leandre de Fontenay were ahead of Taillefer. They had dismounted near a tangled mass of undergrowth that clung to a slope beneath a rocky outcrop. The hounds had surrounded the thicket and were baying at it, drooling, making little runs towards its shadows and then retreating. They knew their job, which was to corner, not to kill. The king and his huntsmen were circling the bushes, boar spears held mid-shaft and levelled, keeping enough of a distance to allow a strike. More dogs had been chained to a tree and were straining at their bonds, barking. These 'bully dogs' were a different breed; short-nosed, broad-shouldered, ugly beasts with a gruff, snarling bark rather than the baying of the hounds.

Taillefer dismounted and drew his sword, but a huntsman held up one hand. 'Do not go closer, Excellency.' This was one of the few times when a commoner could command a diakonos. 'We cannot know which path he will take.'

'Send in a bully?' Even King Aloys only offered a suggestion; out here, the huntsman ruled. 'Delmas, take that side.' The king positioned those near him. 'De Fontenay, over there.' He looked at Taillefer and frowned.

'I am Harbin, Your Majesty.'

The king merely pointed to a place on his left.

A huntsman unchained one of the snarling bully dogs, led it to where it could snuffle at the boar's trail, and unleashed it. For as long as an arrow might fly they could hear it growling in the bushes, moving this way and that.

The growls ended in a piteous scream, and Taillefer froze as the boar burst from the bushes. The bully dog appeared to be impaled on its snout until the boar tossed its head, throwing the carcass high in the air. By Salazar, the boar was huge, like a squat pony. Ivory tusks the size and shape of Saradim daggers curved up from its lip. The flying, dying dog may have distracted the nearest huntsman's aim as his spear merely opened a gash along the boar's neck, and the boar continued barrelling towards him. The vicious head swung again and the huntsman went down, bowled over like a screaming skittle.

Taillefer's heart thundered as the beast came straight for the king, and took Aloys's spear in the chest. Aloys kept his grip but was thrown backwards, and still the wounded beast tried to attack. It pushed itself onto the spear as it tried to reach its persecutor, but was stopped from impaling itself further by the cross guard beneath the blade.

It was not an immediately mortal wound, and as the boar thrashed the king was in real danger. The remaining huntsman was sprinting across towards them, but the king tripped backwards and for a moment his life was in the balance. Only the butt of the spear, embedded deep in leaf mould but sliding backwards, kept the king beyond the sweep of the huge beast's tusks. Now was the time for a hunting sword, but the king was lying on his scabbard and could not risk letting go and twisting to draw it.

Taillefer threw one leg across the beast's back, gripping its bulk with his knees, and rode it like an unbroken horse; it was so huge his feet were off the ground on both sides, making his aim unsteady as he reversed his sword and struck downwards. The boar bucked and the point merely glanced off the spine. Another mistake like that and he might emasculate himself. A moment of near-calm between bucks allowed him to put the tip behind the shoulder blades, and in the instant before the thrust Taillefer made eye contact with Aloys; no longer subject and king but man and fallen man. Taillefer rammed downwards with all the weight a two-handed grip can deliver. The sword's whole length must have passed through heart and lungs, for the boar coughed once, dropped on its forelegs, and toppled onto its side.

Taillefer now lay pinned to the ground by the boar's weight on his leg; its hide was coarse and scratchy, even through his robe. The hilt of his sword rose between his legs like the pommel of a saddle and he let his hands drop from it, gasping. *Thanks be to Ischyros.* The world seemed wonderfully sharp; fine strands of mist were weaving between the branches above him, and he could see each hair on the fur-trimmed herigaut of a noble. There was a growing circle of them watching, some already on foot, others newly arrived on horseback. The novice courtier within him realised that the sight of him straddling a dead boar, in the king's company, would do him no harm. Othon would be most pleased. Taillefer muttered his thanks as Delmas and de Fontenay themselves lifted the boar's body from his leg and the king's own hand helped him up. *But why had Delmas and de Fontenay not rushed to save the King?*

Taillefer pushed through the back-slapping courtiers to stand beside the wounded huntsman. The man's leg had been opened, deeply, from knee to hip, and his partner was trying to slow the blood by winding a cord around the thigh. The injured man was trying to apologise, but his speech was slurring and his face was waxen. Taillefer took his silver box of sacred ash from his belt bag, but the one with the cord shook his head.

'The fool will live, Excellency. If he don' get wound fever.' He nodded at Taillefer with real respect.

Taillefer backed away, and was pulled into a melee of hands reaching for his, congratulating him. He tugged at the wrecked, bloody robe he wore, knowing it had become a badge of honour. Smiling faces with envy in their eyes were all round him, envy that turned to resentment when the king said, 'Ride with me, Harbin,' and mounted. He threw his spear to the ground, signalling the end of the hunt.

Taillefer glanced back at the boar as they left. He was proud of that kill, and although he was being shown great honour, he would have liked a little more time with his trophy. If the dray horses following the hunt could drag its carcass out of the forest in time, no doubt it would be paraded at the night's feast.

There was time to find another scent trail, but the king pointed their horses towards Harbin. At first Taillefer wondered if Aloys had been more shaken than he allowed himself to show. He spoke little, and Taillefer was content to ride alongside in silence, for at this most important of moments, alone with his king, he found it hard to concentrate; his mind was replaying the fight with the boar and his elation as his blade went home. He wanted to tell and retell the story; the swing of the tusks, the leap and plunge of the beast beneath him. Surely the king would also want to tell of how he managed to keep the animal at spear's length, even though he was pushed backwards, ploughing the ground with his body. Yet the king said nothing.

As the silence lengthened Taillefer began to realise that he was there so that others could *not* be, and the cause of the king's mood was probably Delmas's hesitation. Both Delmas and de Fontenay were courageous men who saw hunting as both a noble sport and training for war, and yet they had held back; long enough, perhaps, to see how the boar's attack would play out. And if the king's own brother thought a hunting accident would be convenient, who else among the nobles was plotting? When the king spurred his horse into a trot his face was dark with anger, and Taillefer's certainty grew. Aloys would now want the company of counsellors he could trust; men like his chancellor, Othon.

And then he'd have to be told about the witch. It would be an interesting evening. Taillefer looked over his shoulder as they dropped into a shallow valley. The court were following a bowshot behind. It seemed there were those among them who would not thank him for his day's work.

The mist thickened as they dropped into the valley; the sun seemed to be shining through pale linen. By the time they reached level ground there was little more than a weak brightness above the branches.

They heard the snarl before they saw the wolf. It came at them from the side, a streak of ghostly grey, its fangs bared above a white-bibbed chest, and both horses bolted into a frantic gallop away from its line of attack. For many strides of his horse Taillefer knew more fear than he had fighting the boar; he and his mare were not in harmony; he was balanced atop an animal that was fleeing in uncontrolled panic. He had to duck under branches with his face in her mane, feeling the snag and rip as his robes caught and threatened to pull him from the saddle. Any root, any hidden snag beneath the leaf mould, could trip them and send him flying into a trunk or the ground with the speed of a runaway horse.

He felt slight satisfaction in recovering control before the king, though his mare still snorted and danced, looking about her so the whites of her eyes flashed. He managed to nudge her alongside the king.

'Are you well, Your Majesty?'

Aloys nodded, stroking the neck of his horse to calm it. 'We have lost them.'

He meant the court. He reached for the hunting horn hanging at his side, and had time to blow a single blast before the wolf came again. A new direction now, and their horses panicked beyond all calming. Each fed on the other's fear as they ran side by side, a herd of two fleeing their natural predator. Taillefer and Aloys were powerless beyond holding tight and hoping their mounts ran out of energy before they fell. Taillefer had the strange notion that they were being herded. *Are there more wolves waiting in ambush ahead?*

The chase ended as suddenly as it had begun, with two blown horses staggering into a clearing. They had the energy only to move far enough from the trees to be able to see if another attack was coming. There they stood with their heads drooping on sweat-streaked necks while their breath wove small clouds of fog above frosted grass. Taillefer found himself breathing as heavily as his mare, and straightened in the saddle. He attempted a slight smile, but had to swallow to force moisture into his mouth before he could speak.

'You lead an exciting hunt, Your Majesty.' He tried to make light of the moment. He was trying to find a way of telling the king that he would not speak of this; no warrior would want to be reminded that he had lost control of his horse. Aloys said nothing.

Taillefer looked around them, still panting. Trees stretched away on either side, fading into insubstantial shapes. And at the centre of the clearing, outlined against the mist, was a lone rider. He pointed. 'This one will know where we are.'

He and Aloys gathered their reins and pushed their horses towards him. A young man, it seemed, though nobly dressed with a knight's sword hanging at his side. He was well-mounted on a fine destrier that arched beneath him, dancing a little but held to the spot by the youth's fingertips; the boy was a good horseman. A well-born page, perhaps, to a noble of the court, yet he showed no sign of recognition or respect. Ice-blue eyes stared at them from within a face that had the high cheekbones and fine jaw of the northern provinces. This one would break a few hearts before he was much older.

'This is your king, boy.' Taillefer chose to cast himself in the role of herald. 'Show some respect.' The boy should bare his head. Any page knew the art of a bow in the saddle.

The youth betrayed a flicker of emotion, possibly surprise, but he made no sign of obeisance. He simply stared at the king for several breaths of their horses, then threw his head back and made a dry, humourless laugh in the high tones of a beardless boy.

If the page had been within reach Taillefer would have struck him. 'Are you mad, boy? Who are you? Whom do you serve? This is the king!'

The boy lifted one hand to the fine hat that he wore, and pulled it from his head. But this was an act of defiance, not of deference; yellow hair fell to the fur-trimmed collar of his cote-hardie.

'I am Adelais de Vries, whom you call the Vriesian Witch.'

11.5 ADELAIS

The two approaching riders posed no threat; their horses were spent and they carried no weapons save for short hunting swords. Adelais could out-reach them with her sword and outrun both of them on Allier. She let them approach, for one of them wore the scarlet robe of a diakonos under his cloak. She told herself that she couldn't stop every red rider that crossed her path, but this one rode a bay mare, like in her nightmare, and he was coming to her. Allier was restive beneath her, wound as tight as a crossbow, though she did not understand why; there was no sign of the wolf. She sat very still to calm him, keeping a steady, gentle pressure with her leg.

The rider alongside the diakonos was a richly dressed noble, though both were filthy and caked with blood; it was drying a darker red over the priest's scarlet. They halted a horse's length from her and waited as if they expected something from her. When she did not speak the diakonos leaned forwards in the saddle and pointed at the noble.

'This is your king, boy. Show some respect.'

Adelais blinked. A slow, dry laugh began within her and bubbled its way to her mouth. Oh, the gods were truly playing with them. This man had his entire realm searching for her, then he rides into her path in the middle of a forest and doesn't know what he's found. The laugh turned into a snort. If this encounter was fated, then the fate was woven not by the Nornir but by Loki, the trickster god.

'Are you mad, boy? Who are you? Whom do you serve? This is the king!'

Think, girl. This will be the greatest test of your life. For if this was the king, there would be many others at his call. Soldiers. Servants. Nobles. Her greatest threat now came from the hunting horn at his side. Her greatest weapon would be his fear. She pulled her hat slowly from her head, spilling her hair.

'I am Adelais de Vries, whom you call the Vriesian Witch. And you are persecuting my people.' She meant Vriesland, and she meant the followers of the old gods. It was only after she'd spoken that she realised it could also be interpreted as the Guardians. Humbert. Above all, Humbert.

The diakonos gasped and made the sign of the God. That was predictable; he posed no threat. The king went linen-white and his mouth moved silently, like that of a stranded fish. Would he fight or would he flee? Adelais made the slightest tug on Allier's rein, the half-halt of warning. *Be ready, my friend. It is coming.*

Aloys bellowed as he drew his hunting sword and spurred his horse towards her. At a touch of Adelais's leg Allier spun, threw his weight on his forelegs, and kicked out with both hind hooves. There was a fleshy smack as one of them connected, the scream of an injured animal, and the thump of a falling body. Allier spun again, turning full circle. Aloys's horse was down and struggling to rise; the king himself was on his knees, scrabbling in the grass for his sword.

'He is your king!' the diakonos screamed.

'And he is about to meet his god,' she shouted back. *Frighten him, as you once frightened the high priest.* A touch of the leg pushed Allier towards the king, forcing him away from his weapon. The laughter of Loki was becoming the divine wrath of Thor. This was the man who had crushed the Vriesian army at Vannemeer, the man who'd unleashed the persecution of the Guardians. But for him, Humbert would be alive. So would the four Guardians who had become her protectors and friends in her flight from Villebénie. So would hundreds of other knights, now dead or tortured because of the man now trying to lift a hunting horn to his lips. She barged him with Allier's chest, knocking him down again. 'The Guardians were good men. Honourable men. Sacrificed to your greed!'

Allier's momentum took her past him. When she turned, Aloys had managed to get up and was running towards the diakonos, who was trotting closer, holding his own sword out to Aloys hilt-first. A priest would not shed blood, but he would help his king to do so. Beyond them, the king's own horse scrambled to its feet, winded and coughing.

Adelais had not yet drawn her sword; Allier was proving a better weapon. The spirit of Loki empowered her to bellow at a man before whom her whole sisterhouse would once have knelt.

'Back away, priest! It is not yet your time.' But it was Aloys's, and Humbert would applaud his death at her hands.

She was too late. The king was armed again. But whimpering and staying close to the diakonos's stirrup. From that shelter Aloys lifted his horn and blew the feeble blast of a frightened man; a coward whose lips are dry and whose breathing is ragged.

The cold, calculating vengeance of Thor offered her another name. *Arnaud*. A precious death to lay at this man's door.

Adelais charged, and the fool ran towards his own horse. Aloys did not even try to fight, and Adelais rode him down, bowling him over. This time she did not simply send him tumbling, she spun Allier on the spot and reared him above

Aloys so that the fore-hooves came down on the king's belly. Aloys made one great cough of exploding wind and spittle in which there was the crack of breaking bones, and she knew it was over. Humbert's friends had taken their vengeance. She circled, bringing Allier around to finish the task, but the diakonos had dismounted and was kneeling by his king. Aloys was still alive, but folded over on his side and retching as if he was trying to expel some hidden blockage in his gut.

'At least let him make his unburdening!' The priest looked up at her, begging.

And a change was happening within her. The anger, the killing rage, was flowing out like water from a broken flask. She slumped in the saddle, staring down at this crouching, gagging thing. She'd done that. She thought she might have felt elation, but instead she felt more spent and soiled with each heartbeat. She had become a killer. The riverbank at Bellay, the king in the clearing, she was *executing* those who opposed her as coldly as any steel-bound knight on the field of battle. Where was the woman who'd been loved by Arnaud? No wonder Fulke had looked at her with revulsion. She began to edge Allier away, towards the trees. Soon the clearing would fill with men.

'*What* are you?'

Adelais turned at the diakonos's call. 'The Guardians who live call me the Lions' Claw, a Blessèd One of Ischyros.' Adelais had to play the part to the end. 'And who are you, Excellency?'

'Taillefer de Remy, diakonos of Harbin.'

Oh, this meeting was truly fated.

'Then I demand you lift the expulsion of Humbert Blanc. He has served the God faithfully all his life, and deserves to cross the bridge of judgement. You will find his body at Bellay. He should be buried with honour.'

'And you?'

Adelais shrugged. 'What you will.' She realised he might

think that she was above expulsion. 'But those who have helped me should not suffer. They too are good Ischyrians.'

Taillefer De Remy stared back at her without speaking, and she nudged Allier towards the trees. Behind her came a frantic blowing of the hunting horn, and she squeezed the horse into a trot, then a canter.

11.6 TAILLEFER

It was chaos in the clearing. Taillefer found himself pushed aside by some courtiers and surrounded by others, demanding angrily to know what had happened. He stood dazed in their midst, still trailing the hunting horn, knowing that what he said now would alter history. He could lie. Tell them the king's horse reared at a wolf, threw him, and trampled him as it ran. He was a diakonos; he would be believed.

Or would he? The tracks of a third horse still lay in the frost. Would anyone notice before they were covered by the milling horses of the court?

But if he told the truth he'd widen the mighty wound that had been bleeding since the Vriesian Witch killed the high priest. Leave people wondering if the king, and by implication the high priest, had been struck down in acts of divine vengeance. Either that or Kakos the Destroyer had struck twice at the very heart of Ischyrendom.

Othon would want it to be an accident, Taillefer was sure. Should he be loyal to his brother or tell the truth? The consequences were unimaginable.

The Duke of Delmas had him by the shoulders, looking

fiercely into his face. Too close. 'What happened?' Delmas shook him. 'Tell me, man.'

Taillefer took a deep breath and closed his eyes. *Blessèd Salazar, help me.*

'It was the Vriesian Witch.' Taillefer let out a sigh, releasing words that might change the realm's destiny. 'She kicked him from his horse. Rode him down. Said she was the Lions' Claw.'

There. It was done. He'd chosen truth, but with it what would happen now? Would the faith crumble around him?

Delmas's hands dropped from his shoulders. Taillefer had spoken quietly, but he would not have been the only one to have heard.

The shock on Delmas's face tightened into a more calculating emotion. His eyes searched Taillefer's for signs of a lie. But how could anyone lie about such a matter?

'Tell no one.' Delmas looked around the courtiers who had clustered around Taillefer. 'On your lives, tell no one. I must consider this.'

'Does he live?' Taillefer remembered his role as priest. The king would want to make his unburdening. Taillefer's satchel with the sacred ash hung from his saddle.

'For now.' Delmas looked around for his equerry. 'De Gris. Ride to Harbin. Bring any of the Council still there to the rendezvous on the road. Oh, and the king's physician.' His manner was brisk, almost enthusiastic.

Aloys pissed himself with blood as they lifted him onto a litter of cloaks tied to boar spears. He was semi-conscious, his face contorted with pain as they made a slow, staggering walk to the road; under two leagues, yet it felt much further. Aloys did not even have the breath to groan as his litter lurched. Nobles and huntsmen took it in turns to carry the king, and Taillefer walked at his side.

The sun was sinking when they finally reached the road and laid Aloys on a linen sheet over a bed of cloaks, within the same, brazier-warmed pavilion where he'd feasted at midday. Those with knowledge of wounds peeled back his clothes, looked at Taillefer, and shook their heads. One hip was smashed, and probably several ribs, and the fast-panting belly was black with blood beneath the skin; he was even shitting it now. Aloys reached up for Taillefer's hand and tugged him close. Taillefer had to put his ear near the king's mouth to hear.

'Pardon. Now. You.' Aloys looked at Taillefer with eyes that spoke of a terrible yearning beneath the agony. Perhaps he felt some trust in the man who had saved his life and who must now save his soul.

Taillefer straightened, though still on his knees. 'Out. Everybody. Now.' The new diakonos ordered the greatest in the land with the authority of the God.

They all understood. The king's pardoner was not there, and the king's soul must be saved.

When they were alone Taillefer bent again, putting his face close to the king's in strange, unwanted intimacy. He had to prompt Aloys in the ritual words of the High Tongue. '*Evlogiménos Ischyros, Pateras ólon, dóste chári ston amartoló...*'

And the unburdening began; at first a self-justifying trickle that Taillefer probed, as a priest must, requiring a penitent to acknowledge the truth, and the trickle became a torrent that stank worse than the bloody excrement leaking from Aloys's body. A litany of crimes poured out in small, gasping whispers, each heavier than lead, until Taillefer felt himself forced down, folded double, not only by the need to hear but by the mass of guilt filling the pavilion. He felt he was not so much taking away the sins as helping to carry them.

Taillefer sensed that Aloys stopped through exhaustion, with sins still untold. Did that matter? What was one more death, unconfessed, or ten, or fifty, against these hundreds? Yet Aloys must have felt his life slipping away. Pardon was expected. Now. Demanded, even, for this was a king.

Taillefer rocked back on his heels, unable to do it. Surely some crimes were too heinous for a mere priest to pardon, even a diakonos, but must be referred to the highest of all courts – the God himself. And while Taillefer thought, and prayed, Aloys tugged fretfully at his sleeve, no longer commanding but pleading. When Taillefer looked down he saw not a king but a man, begging him with eyes that held the fear of one who must soon cross the bridge of judgement and knows he will fall. For the first time Taillefer felt the true burden of priesthood: to pardon the unpardonable. He could grant a soul passage over the bridge or condemn them to the pit of Kakos. He fumbled for the silver box of sacred ash, wondering if one thumbprint and some holy words could really outweigh all those deaths in His eyes...

'*Apó ti chári tou Ischyros, sas xefortónomai tis amartíes sas.*' By the grace of Ischyros, I pardon you of your sins. Taillefer pressed his thumb onto Aloys's forehead. '*Zíste mia kalí zoí apó aftí ti stigmí. Sto ónomá Tou, amín.*' Live a good life from this moment on. In His name, amen.'

Though the final words were as meaningless as the pardon. Aloys would be dead before morning.

It was full dark when Taillefer emerged, aching with the strain of kneeling by the king for so long. His body straightened, but his mind still bowed beneath the weight of his new knowledge.

Had he been right to grant pardon? It was his duty and his power to give the sacrament of the ash to those who showed contrition, even if that contrition comes from fear for their souls, not guilt for their deeds.

Taillefer wiped his face with his hands, rubbing the palms into his eyes, sighing. If some of the courtiers around him knew what he now knew, and knew that he knew, he would be killed to ensure his silence. His priesthood would be no protection. Suddenly alert, he surveyed the clearing. The roadside was littered with carts, left to carry carcasses or spears and other

baggage at the end of the day. Flaring torches had been set into
the ground at intervals and servants had lit a great fire. Small
groups of nobles talked by its crackling heat, stamping their feet
against the frosted ground, their breath smoking. These were
the nobles whose rank demanded their presence at the death of
a king. Delmas, with de Fontenay. Prince Lancelin, talking to
Taillefer's brother Othon, who must have arrived while
Taillefer was with the king.

A man Taillefer did not know stood in front of him; he'd
asked a question but Taillefer stared at him, uncomprehending,
until he saw the flask badge of a healer on his cloak. He nodded,
and the man scuttled past into the pavilion. Taillefer had no
hope that he would succeed; Aloys was beyond healing.

The work of the faith was also done. Taillefer crossed to
Lancelin. Now it was time for the son to sit with his father
through his last night on earth. He sensed he was interrupting
an argument; Lancelin was visibly upset. Othon wore his chancellor's chain and the look of studied regret that he used to relay
bad news to royalty. Taillefer didn't ask the cause; he wanted no
part in court politics at that moment. He didn't even want his
brother's company. In fact, he especially didn't want his brother's company; the knowledge he now carried would stain their
relationship forever.

Taillefer turned his back on his brother when he'd delivered
his message to Lancelin, and walked alone until he was far
enough from the fire and flares to see by the light of the moon. It
hung above the forest, bright enough to bathe the trees in shades
of silver and grey.

The faith taught that the stars were a net, woven by Ischyros, and cast there by Him to trap Kakos the Destroyer on the
earth, as it was written in the Vision of Salazar. *That the battle
for Eternity might be fought on the Earth and not in the vastness
of the Heavens. Thus it shall be until all that is evil is destroyed,
and the hearts of men are once again pure.* Yet Taillefer knew

that he had just granted passage over the bridge of judgement to one whose heart was not pure. Men believe what they want to believe, and Aloys had wanted to believe that the Guardians were heretics, practicing foul perversions, for had not his own chancellor told him? And had not the anakritim found proof?

Taillefer had challenged Aloys: if you tell a torturer what to find, they will find it. If you send written details of what you expect them to find to every province, then they will find the same 'heresies' throughout the realm. Did the king not doubt the evidence? What would he say when he faced his God on the bridge of judgement?

And, word by gasping word, the truth had come. Othon's scheming, Aloys's willing acquiescence, and the anakritim's complicity, for their tormentors had found the evidence. And Ghislain Barthram's reward had been power; his ruthless clerics were now in every town in Galmandie.

No wonder kings had their own pardoners. Ghislain Barthram must have heard the king's doubts for years, spoken words of comfort, and pressed the ash. More importantly, he'd have done it with real compassion, not the ritual-cloaked revulsion that Taillefer felt. Barthram could have convinced the dying king that he'd done the God's will. Taillefer could not. Aloys had filled his coffers with the Guardians' wealth. He'd been tempted to remind the king of the same passage from Salazar that the witch had reportedly thrown at the high priest: *You fool! Your greed is pointless, for this very day your soul is demanded.*

Perhaps the girl really was a Blessèd One, wreaking vengeance, for the high priest had not defended the Guardians. The Order were untainted by the hierarchy's venality and so become inconvenient; no high priest wants his soldiers to be purer than the priesthood.

Taillefer sighed again. There were times when the Vision of Salazar seemed as remote as the moon; a vision of a day when the hearts of men will be pure, and the bounds of earth loosed, and all people will cross the bridge of judgement to sing the songs of eternity with Ischyros beyond the stars.

Othon had once told him that the pinnacle of power is slick with blood and shit. Was it possible to exercise authority without compromising integrity? Taillefer looked up at the net of stars, shining faintly beyond the snow moon's light, and resolved that he would try.

Aloys died just before dawn. He vomited blood in the middle of the night, then faded rapidly. By the time the eastern horizon was paling he seemed no longer able to recognise the men around him: Taillefer, Othon the chancellor, Gervais of Delmas, Prince Lancelin, and a physician. They all must have carried their own fears; Gervais and Lancelin for the succession, and Othon for his own survival without his protector. Taillefer feared that all his faith and prayer was useless. Even the physician would have feared that he would be held to blame for not saving his king.

When the king's breathing faded to a point beyond hearing the physician held a feather over his lips, and when that no longer moved he touched the staring eyeball. It did not blink.

'The king is dead, long live the king,' Othon intoned, inclining his head towards Lancelin, who made the sign of the God.

'Not yet, de Remy.' Delmas breathed deeply, his eyes closed. 'First there must be an acclamation.'

And so it began; while the king's body was still warm, his brother and the chancellor squabbled over the succession.

Delmas was correct, though; ever since a brutal civil war centuries before, the tradition was for a new king to be acclaimed by the nobles before taking the throne. It was just insensitive to point that out over the dead king's corpse.

. . .

They made a slow procession into Harbin, carrying Aloys's body on a cart. Messengers were sent ahead, so at least for the final stages the ox cart was replaced with a more regal carriage, and Aloys could be shielded from prying eyes in a wooden coffin draped with the royal banner.

Taillefer tried to avoid Othon, but short of an undignified gallop out of his way it proved impossible. In the last league before Harbin, close enough to hear the slow, distant tolling of the temple's bell, Othon managed to ride alongside him. The procession had stretched out; they could talk quietly.

'So what happened?'

Taillefer looked at him. He wanted to see the impact of his words.

'The witch. She rides a destrier, and rides it well. She kicked him out of the saddle and trampled him on the ground.'

Othon made a hissing intake of breath. 'Who else knows?'

'Delmas. De Fontenay. A few others. Too many to hope for silence, if that is what you are thinking. And too noble to kill quietly.'

At that Othon looked hard at him.

'What else?'

'She said she was the Lions' Claw, sent by the God in vengeance for the persecution of the Guardians,' Taillefer continued. 'Do you know, brother, I am minded to believe her.' If he'd had any doubts, the king's deathbed unburdening had convinced him.

Only the working of the muscles behind Othon's jaw showed how quickly he was thinking.

'We must avoid Prince Lancelin being tainted by his father's mistakes. He must be distanced from this.'

'His father's mistakes? Surely it was your plan, brother?

Yours and the anakritis-general's? You heard the news from Bellay that she has taken him prisoner, no doubt?'

Though Barthram hadn't been with the girl in the clearing when the king was trampled. After the unburdening that followed, Taillefer had no great wish to find him. He also enjoyed seeing the consternation on his infallible older brother's face. Othon's gloved hands had tightened into fists around his reins.

'Now, more than ever, she must be found. We'll make her confess to being in league with Kakos. She can die publicly, as Aloys wanted.'

'And if she is indeed sent by the God?'

'Then we will send her back to Him.' Othon had spoken too loudly. Heads were turning.

'Haven't you made enough martyrs, brother?' Taillefer could not say how much he knew. All unburdenings were sacrosanct, their content known only to the sinner, the priest, and the God.

Othon ignored the question but continued more quietly. 'Aloys will lie in state tonight in your fire temple. Tomorrow he will be borne by barge down the river to the capital. There must be a meeting of the King's Council in Villebénie. I will make those arrangements, then you and I will talk again, tonight.' Othon spurred away. Taillefer watched him overtake the procession in his haste to reach Harbin. He feared for his brother. Soul and body.

The view as they came down the hill into Harbin was too colourful. The castle was too small to accommodate the whole court in the luxury that they required, so a cluster of pavilions had been erected on the riverbank. From a distance they looked like a crop of mushrooms in the meadow. Many flew banners, and more were being raised as nobles returned from the hunt; Delmas's royal sun quartered with a black boar's head, and de Fontenay's golden flowers on red.

Taillefer found it strange how the court's factions had shaped where the nobles chose to sleep; Prince Lancelin's clique in the castle with the royal guards, Delmas and the warrior nobles under canvas. The seasoned campaigners had carpeted their pavilions with waxed canvas sheets and rugs over the cold earth, and hung them with thick drapes. When the braziers were lit they were probably cosier than the castle.

Aloys and his immediate entourage, including Othon, had filled Taillefer's small palace on this bank of the river, though today they would ride on to lay the king's body in the temple. Prince Lancelin led the procession, and Taillefer wished that the prince would show a little more humility, perhaps make at least an outward display of grief. He was smiling and waving to his acolytes as if this was his coronation.

Retainers lined the road as they approached the encampment and the river, their liveried tabards too gaudy for the day. They bared their heads as the cart with the king's coffin approached. More stood on the slatted walkways that had been laid to keep the nobles' fine boots clear of the mud. And alone in front of the de Fontenay pavilion stood a noblewoman who pushed the fur-lined hood of her cloak back to show a strikingly attractive face: high-cheeked, small-mouthed, dark-haired, and with large eyes that looked up at Leandre de Fontenay not so much with love but with hope, almost yearning.

Yet de Fontenay merely straightened as he passed, looking at her intently. His expression was surprised, and possibly not pleased. He said nothing, merely inclined his head as he rode on alongside Delmas. The lady curtseyed in response, the skirts of her gown dipping into mud, her face masking hurt. This must be Agnès de Fontenay, and Taillefer sensed that her arrival was both unexpected and unwelcome.

She might not yet know of the death of her uncle, Humbert Blanc; the messenger from Bellay would have gone to the castle. Taillefer resolved to be the one to tell her, as gently as he could;

the guilt of that expulsion was gnawing at him. Perhaps the lady would like to make use of the baths in the palace. A pavilion was no place for a woman in winter, and Taillefer had maidservants who could assist.

But first he must conduct a proper office for the dead king, in the fire temple. As he turned his head back towards the castle, Taillefer caught sight of a priest in the crowd, standing close enough to Lady Agnès to be part of her entourage; it had taken Taillefer a moment to recognise the man he'd last seen on top of the Black Tower in Villebénie. Pateras Malory d'Eivet. Othon had sent him with Gerard d'Essoyes to capture the Vriesian woman. Now he was here, raising his hand in benediction as they passed. At the king's body? At the nobles? At *him*, a diakonos? Taillefer glared his confusion.

Taillefer's reverie carried him over the bridge and onto the market square in front of the castle. He was exhausted; he'd had a night without sleep at the king's side. He wanted only to conduct a suitable Office for the Dead, bathe, and snatch some rest in his chamber.

'What's that *fucking* puppy doing?' Delmas's shout jolted Taillefer out of his half-sleep. Delmas was pointing at the tower, making no attempt to hide his anger nor his contempt. At some prearranged signal, the golden sun banner was being hoisted as Lancelin passed. It had not happened in Taillefer's lifetime, but he was sure that raising the royal standard now in an assertion of kingship was premature. Presumptuous, even. There was a process to be followed: a proclamation followed by the acclamation of the nobles. A coronation. The oaths of fealty.

Delmas swore again and turned to de Fontenay. 'He would never have done that on his own. Hasn't got the balls. I'll rip the fucking thing down when we've put my brother in the temple.'

Taillefer feared he saw his own brother's hand in this. As if in confirmation, Othon rode out of the castle gates and joined the head of the procession, a suitably deferential horse's length behind Lancelin. Othon must have calculated the risks; if Lancelin claimed the throne, and Delmas refused to accept him as his king, the only outcome could be war.

Delmas nudged his horse forwards until he and Lancelin rode side by side. No one could now wonder if Delmas was ceding precedence. Delmas did not turn his head, but spoke loudly enough for many to hear.

'If that banner is still flying at sunset, nephew, I will push it up your arse on the point of a lance and pull it out through your nostrils.'

CHAPTER TWELVE

12.1 ADELAIS

'You haven't just poked the hornet's nest, my sweeting, you've smashed it to the ground. Prepare to be stung.' Elyse spoke without great feeling; the life seemed to have gone out of her since Barthram's torture, leaving her unsmiling and drained.

Adelais said nothing. She lay on a hilltop, staring down at the point where the road and the river finally met. The town on the far bank could only be Harbin. The dome of a large temple rose above the houses, and a small castle was set in the town's walls like the gemstone in a ring. Beneath her a sweep of the river had cut an undercliff, allowing her to look down into the town square, which was just a thousand paces away and teeming with people: nobles and retainers in bright surcoats and tabards, commoners in drab shades of leather and homespun. There seemed to be some kind of procession crossing the single, wide bridge over the Fauve. On the near bank an unfortified stone manor or palace sprawled between road and river, and a meadow beyond was dotted with bannered pavilions.

Elyse sat behind the crest with her back against a rock, paring slices from a wedge of cheese that they'd taken from the inn. At least her appetite had returned. She was slowly coming out of her flat mood. 'Stung, I say. But it was fated. The wolf led you to him.' She lifted a sliver to her mouth between her thumb and the blade of her risting knife.

'We haven't seen her,' Adelais said. 'Not since before the clearing.' If the wolf had led her to the king, why wasn't she showing her the way forwards?

'Perchance because you are where she wants you to be.'

'Staring at the hornet's nest? It will take the cunning of Loki to cross that bridge.'

'Then mayhap she is busy somewhere else.'

Adelais snorted.

After the encounter with Aloys and the diakonos she'd found Elyse easily by backtracking her own marked path. They cantered eastwards together until the horses tired. They'd heard horns but seen no one. They'd passed an uncomfortable night with just their cloaks for shelter and a fire for warmth, but although exhaustion granted her some fitful sleep, Adelais's rest was disturbed. So much killing. Around her. By her.

There had been a moment at Bellay when a soldier had run at her, swinging his sword in a two-handed grip. Allier had danced sideways, *into* the attack, inside the blade, adding his momentum to her thrust so that her point buried itself in his face. That violence could not have been her. No one had taught her that harmony of horse and sword. And the woman she had once been would never have felt that cold pride at her own instinctive prowess.

But the man was still screaming, still falling. She flexed her fingers at the memory of the jolt as the blade struck.

And she still heard the crumpling of the king's bones under Allier's hooves while the other woman inside her bellowed her vengeance from the saddle.

They'd moved on at first light, riding in a daze between road and river, until they'd reached the point where they could go no further.

'How do you escape a swarm of angry hornets, Aunty?' That bridge was their only route to Vriesland.

'Oh, that's easy. You become a hornet.'

Adelais groaned, slid down the rise, and sat next to Elyse. Twenty paces away their horses grazed contentedly on a patch of grass. Allier lifted his head and looked at her, ears pricked. Did he feel guilt about the fighting? If so, it didn't show.

'What's happening to me, Aunty?' Adelais slumped against the rock. 'I'm killing people. I don't even think about it any more. It's as if they don't matter.'

'Until afterwards?' Elyse offered her a slice of cheese, but Adelais shook her head.

'I don't feel like a woman. When the anger takes over I'm like a siege engine, throwing death.'

Elyse reached into her bag with her spare hand and pulled out the *nidhstick* she'd carved outside Bellay. 'I risted these runes to bring death to those who wish you harm; both the king and his faith. *Seidhr* does not just happen, child, the fates must work through people. I would say they are working very well through you. Do you think you could have done what you have on your own? Did they teach you swordcraft and riding that well?'

'I am not just an instrument of the fates. I chose to do those things.'

'Some people just follow their fate, like cattle that are led to grazing or slaughter, but you have more power than you know. You *change* fates. The threads of many destinies flow through you.'

'Yrsa said that, too. But I do not want this power, Aunty. I want to live peacefully. Speak my own language, in my own country. Perhaps have a man and a family.'

'My sweeting, the power of *seidhr* is not like a gown you can choose to wear or not wear; it is part of you. It comes when rune song is woven with anger, or fear, or passion, and when you forget to be Adelais. You can no more set it aside than you could ask yon horse never to run again. When I work *seidhr* I am no longer Elyse, the old woman, I am a channel for the web of fate. I am *seidhkona*. So it is with you.'

'I do not seek it.'

'Which is why it comes. Those who least want power are the ones best fitted to wield it.'

'Brother Humbert would not approve.' Somehow that was very important to her. *He thought so highly of me. He would have been so disappointed in the reality.*

'You loved him, didn't you?'

'Like a father.' And more. 'He thought I was an angel, sent by his god. It would have hurt him so much to know that I follow the old gods.'

'He loved you for yourself, my sweeting. I saw it in his eyes. If he had seen you at Bellay, he would not have seen witchcraft, but prowess. He would have been so proud of you.'

Adelais choked. Somewhere beneath this numbness was a deep, howling grief that wanted to come out. Needed to come out. She let herself be pulled into Elyse's shoulder as the tears began to flow.

It was not a long hug. Elyse pushed her away and stood. 'No point moping. There will be search parties before long.' She peered over the hilltop towards the town and stiffened. 'The de Fontenay banner is there.'

'Can you be sure?'

'I can't see to thread a needle any more, but I can see like an eagle that far away. The de Fontenay banner flies over one of those pavilions, and I think I see Lady Agnès's palfrey.'

Adelais spun onto her knees. She could see a red banner, with splashes of gold that might be the flowers of de Fontenay. Horses. But Agnès? If so she must have made a forced journey from the lodge; she would have ridden to Villebénie and then on to find the court. With any luck the chancellor now had more to worry him than the fight at the lodge.

'Do you think she might help us?' It would take either powerful *seidhr* or a very good friend to cross that bridge.

'I will go to her. Alone.' Elyse turned to look at Allier. 'You can hide yellow hair under a hat, you can hide a woman's body under men's clothes, but you can't hide a stallion like yours. Not one that fine. On my own, I might reach her.'

Elyse was right, of course. Allier was so very recognisable, and the diakonos would surely have passed on a description.

'Then take the gelding and the baggage. I may need to ride fast.'

Elyse picked up the priest's discarded satchel and pulled out a sheet of paper. 'While I am gone I want you to do something that may help us both.' She dipped a quill in ink.

'You can write, Aunty?'

'I can neither read nor write, but I can rist the runes. If Lord Leandre is there I am no longer sure of my welcome. I may be taken. Lord Leandre may even surrender me to the king's men. You are going to rist your first *taufr*, with runes of protection. For both of us.'

'I have not learned such things.'

'Then listen well. You will have a year of learning in the time it takes to walk half a league. This,' Elyse tapped the *nidh-stick* she'd carved at Bellay, 'was meant to kill. It worked. Now our intent must be to confuse, or persuade, or hide.' She held the quill awkwardly, as one more used to wielding a needle or a paring knife. Her first mark on the paper was blotched, looking more like spattered droppings than a rune. She practised until she could draw a single line, upright as a limbless pine.

|

'*Ísa*, the ice-rune, to constrain the will of those who oppose us.'

A second line appeared, angled down across *isa* from high left to low right.

'Now *isa* has become *naudhiz*, the need-rune. It will direct your intent.'

Elyse drew an arrowhead angle between the top of *isa* and the crossing point.

'Both now lay under *reidhr*, the rune of justice. You know its song?'

Adelais nodded. '*Reidh er sitjandi sæla...*'

'Not now. Sing it with intent, and with the beat of your heart, for it is also the rune of the chariot of Thor, which may carry us through.'

If it had been Yrsa sitting there she'd have added '*mynn litla Sif*', my little Sif, the golden-haired wife of Thor. Elyse turned the paper at an angle to draw another line from the bottom of *naudhiz* to the bottom of *isa*, creating a second arrowhead below the first.

'*Bjarkan.*' Adelais knew that one. Elyse had used it at her initiation.

'It is the earth mother, and like a mother she will conceal

and protect her children when they are threatened.' She handed the paper to Adelais. 'And since that dawn in the woods, by the lodge, you are the child of the earth mother. Carve that with good intent, and you will see us through.'

'We could turn back, and find a road through Theignault?'

'I am old and tired, sweeting.' Elyse touched Adelais gently on the cheek. 'I'd rather take my chances with the de Fontenays. Go back from the town a ways. Find a place where you can watch the road, and wait a day. If Lady Agnès or I don't come for you, it means I have failed and there is no way to cross at Harbin. Then you'll have to go east, alone.'

Elyse stood, letting the satchel drop. 'Best not to take that.' They embraced awkwardly.

'Give Agnès my love. Tell her I desire her friendship, always.'

Adelais found a stand of trees with water and grass nearby, tethered Allier on a long line, and cut a piece of wood the size of her palm from a fallen ash tree; ash was a powerful wood for *seidhr*. She climbed to a branch where she could watch the road, several bowshots away; far enough for her to stay hidden, yet close enough for her to recognise Elyse's horse. She settled against the trunk, rested Elyse's *nidhstick* across her knees as a work bench, and began to carve.

Íss er árbörkr, ok unnar thak, ok feigra manna fár...

Her knife was double-edged and the blade too long for the work, even for a mark as simple as the ice-rune. She had to cut a new block of wood to protect her hand when she pushed down on the edge, near the point.

Naudh er thýjar thrá, ok thungr kostr, ok vássamlig verk...

It was hard to keep her balance. The need-rune focused her will, but if she was distracted her intent would not flow into the carving.

Reidh er sitjandi sæla, ok snúdhig ferdh, ok jórs erfidhi...

Adelais found a rhythm with the riding-rune. It flowed like the stride of a horse in a gentle canter. **Reidh** er **sit**-*jandi* **sæ-**la.

She had time. Elyse would need to find Agnès and they would have much to discuss before she could return.

Bjarkan er laufgat lim, ok lítit tré, ok ungsamligr vidhr...

She found herself settling into a trance-like state as she carved rune upon rune.

Place the point where the cut must be made. Íss er árbörkr. Press down on the edge with the loose block, turning the knife into a chisel. Ok unnar thak. Prise out another flake of wood. Slowly the composite bind-rune appeared:

Around noon a troop of soldiers came from Harbin towards Bellay. They carried packs across their horses' rumps, perhaps supplies for a journey. A search party? A whicker from below gave her a sudden stab of fear; if Allier should call, and be heard, all would be lost. Adelais made shushing noises and Allier dropped his head to graze.

She returned to her carving. *Concentrate!*

Reidh er sitjandi sæla...

Her trance deepened. She forgot to be hungry. She sat high above the ground the way a true *seidhkona* sat on her platform, seeing beyond this world. Her heel tapped the time against the tree the way Amma Yrsa's staff had beaten rune song into the warp and weft of fate. *Bjarkan er laufgat lim...*

Adelais added a little magic of her own; another arrowhead cut and she could overlay the whole bind-rune with the *thurs* rune, the rune of Thor, the battle god. It had worked for her before, when the thunder had come and the high priest had died. It was personal, *mynn litla Sif*, for Sif was the woman of Thor.

Thurs er kvenna kvöl, ok kletta búi...

But no thunder came. She paused, trying to remember what her grandmother had told her about the *thurs* rune. Wasn't it also a rune of love magic? Or was it simply important to know the *intent?* Her intent was the confusion of their enemies, not that they find love. Knowing half of what she needed could be dangerous, but she shrugged and continued carving. *Ok vardhrúnar verr...* Already the moon was rising above the trees, the faintest hint of a silver coin against a cloudless afternoon sky. It would be another cold night.

Done, but it looked raw, the angles imperfect. Adelais started again, sharpening the runes. The blood from several small cuts seeped into them as she carved.

Íss er árbörkr...

Adelais jolted awake as she began to fall from the branch. She managed to grab it in time, though her knife and the carving fell tumbling into the leaf mould below. It was already sunset.

And Agnès had not come.

12.2 TAILLEFER

By the time Taillefer met Agnès de Fontenay he craved sleep.

The Office of the Dead for Aloys had been devoid of grief. Lancelin had tied black ribbons around his shield arm in a way that merely enhanced his finery. The sycophants standing behind him could barely mask their elation. Delmas and the warrior lords stood glowering or whispering among themselves, their eyes murderously on Lancelin's back. Taillefer himself delivered the words without emotion or conviction; how could he intercede on behalf of a man who had sent the God's own knights to their deaths, just to fill his coffers?

Afterwards he sent his steward with a message to Leandre de Fontenay, inviting him and his lady to move into the palace for as long as Lady Agnès chose to stay; there was a newly vacated chamber, the very best, which they might find more amenable than a tent.

Lord Leandre replied, politely, that while he himself would stay in his pavilion Lady Agnès was welcome to avail herself of the king's former chamber, particularly if she might bring a woman servant to attend her.

Which meant, thought Taillefer, that politicking with

Delmas was more important to de Fontenay than sharing his wife's bed, even after moons of absence. A fact sad enough for Taillefer to question the basis of their marriage, though it was not his role to intervene. He simply asked the steward to ensure the linen was changed and that water was heated for the lady. The steward huffed that he would do that in any case and did his Excellency know how many nobles were arriving after the king's death, all expecting to be housed and fed? They would have lords in the stables before nightfall... Taillefer waved him away.

He began a letter to the episkopos at Villebénie, the most senior priest in Galmandie and his direct superior, who would receive the king's body and carry it to the fire temple. There Aloys would lie in state beside the relics of the Blessèd Tanguy. Taillefer's eyes grew heavy and his head fell forwards.

A sharp knock at the door jolted him awake. The steward announced Lady Agnès de Fontenay, who wished to thank him for his hospitality. Candles had been lit in the room while he slept; he had missed the Lighting of the Lamps.

She was clad in a rich velvet gown that matched the green of her eyes. A mass of thick, dark hair was constrained by a golden net and she smelt of soap and expensive perfume. Her cheeks were slightly flushed by her bath, a living warmth above the cold shine of emeralds about her neck; such a vision had surely never before been seen in the palace of a diakonos. Taillefer waved her to a chair and poured wine with his own hand. She was going to need this. She sat on the edge of her chair, straight-backed, her manner polite, even gracious, but guarded. She thanked him for her regal chamber with a formality that reminded him of his guilt. And no, Lord Leandre would not be joining her; His Highness the Duke of Delmas had called a meeting in his tent. She believed that Prince Lancelin and Othon de Remy had called a similar meeting in the castle.

Leandre de Fontenay was a fool to decline the royal bed and this exquisite woman.

Whose stare was level, almost hard. He was, after all, also a de Remy, and her uncle's persecutor. 'Lady Agnès, I fear I have sad news to impart...'

Taillefer told her of her uncle's death as gently as he could, and saw her poise soften in grief. That rounding of the shoulders, those filling eyes, made him want to offer more than priestly comfort. By Salazar, this was a woman who showed him the price of priesthood.

A ridiculous thought, of course. He was a diakonos. His door was open so that proprieties were not only observed but seen to be observed; her serving woman sat within view, her hands moving fretfully in her lap.

'How did my uncle die?' The lady's eyes were round and full, and so distractingly green.

Taillefer shook his head. 'I do not know. The messenger only said that he was dead. There seems to have been some kind of skirmish. The commander of the garrison may know more.'

'And he was expelled.' She looked straight at him, accusingly.

'Lady Agnès, I have to admit that I believe a great injustice has been done. I plan to lift the expulsion and to recover your uncle's body from Bellay for an honourable, Ischyrian burial. From what I now know, I believe he will be welcomed across the bridge.'

Oh, how that look softened. He could drown in those eyes. And she was breathing heavily enough for her gown to stretch in ways a priest shouldn't notice. Taillefer shut his own eyes, took a deep breath, and prayed. *Holy Ischyros, spare me this temptation.*

'And what has made you change your mind, *Excellency?*'

Still a note of bitterness.

He looked at her. There was strength there, pushing through the grief.

'The woman they call the Vriesian Witch killed the king. She said she was the Lions' Claw, sent by the God.'

'So it is true.'

She knew. Word was spreading fast. 'She trampled him to death with that black stallion of hers.'

'A stallion that was once my uncle's destrier.'

Taillefer snorted. There was a poetic justice in that.

'And she convinced you of my uncle's innocence?' Agnès prompted.

'Not on her own. I was more persuaded by facts I learned later. These I cannot divulge, my lady.'

Agnès took a nervous sip of her wine. 'You were with the king when he died, I hear.'

Taillefer resolved never to take this woman for granted. She thought too quickly. 'I can say no more. The secrets of an unburdening are sacrosanct.'

'Of course.' Agnès lowered her eyes. 'But did you learn enough to be persuaded of Adelais's innocence also?'

Taillefer rose to his feet and poured himself wine. He needed time to think about his answer. Time when Lady Agnès was not watching his face.

'She is a friend of yours, is she not?'

'Yes. And I believe her to be a good person.'

He stared out of the window. He had real glass in the panes, clear enough for him to see distorted images of men moving outside; the flames of torches glistened wetly through rims of ice inside the panes. There were sounds of an argument from near the bridge, where guards were forcing any yellow-haired man to drop his loin cloth and prove his manhood. Taillefer closed the shutters, lest any draw the wrong conclusions about a woman alone in his office.

'It is a question that troubles me, my lady. I believe that

there was justice in what she has done, but is she truly a Blessèd One, the Lions' Claw? In the death of a king, and the turmoil that will follow, perhaps even war, has she done the work of the God or of the Destroyer? I truly do not know. I will pray for the God's guidance.' He turned back to her. Her eyes were round and pleading.

'If she was captured, now...'

'There would be consequences. Galmandie is dividing into those who want to prove witchcraft and those who want to believe in divine vengeance. Neither side is particularly interested in the truth, still less in letting the other faction have proof of their version of the truth.'

'So she would be killed.'

'Either quickly and quietly, or publicly and painfully.'

Agnès took a gulp of her wine.

'There are those who have helped her...'

'I will lift the expulsion. All of it. That will protect you and yours from any clerical consequences. I cannot save you from the temporal authorities, should they choose to attack you.' Taillefer refilled her goblet; there was a mass of work awaiting him but he wanted to find out more about this Adelais.

'I can ask no more.'

'There is much we do not know about this woman. We heard that she had captured the anakritis-general, but he was not with her when she killed the king. Nor was a man-at-arms who was seen with her at Bellay.' And the biggest unanswered question of all was how the anakritis-general knew to intercept them at Bellay.

'I do not believe she is a witch.' Lady Agnès's manner was softening.

'I saw a priest near the de Fontenay pavilion. One Pateras Malory d'Eivet.' He also wanted to know how a priest sent with Lancelin's men to Fontenay came to be in Harbin. 'He once told me he thought Mistress Adelais was a Blessèd One.'

'I don't believe that either.' Agnès half-smiled, lost in thought for a moment. 'And Pateras Malory travelled here with me. He was present when Prince Lancelin's forces failed to capture Adelais.'

Taillefer sighed. So many unknowns. But here at least might be a few answers.

And some delightful, chaperoned company.

'Perhaps you and Pateras Malory would like to dine with me? Unless you are too tired from your journey?'

Her smile transformed her face.

12.3 BARTHRAM

The God must have spared him for a purpose. It was not the witch who had shown mercy; she was pure evil, the spawn of Kakos, but the God had stayed her hand. Now Barthram had to live that His purpose might be revealed and fulfilled.

He had found a way of moving, using a plank from the abandoned hovel where they had so humiliated him. He'd passed out once, when he tried to crawl, and a second time when he'd tried to lift his body onto the plank, but the God gave him strength and he succeeded. He'd used his rope belt to bind it beneath his thigh so his broken leg rested on it, and now he could move. Slowly, and with terrible pain, he could move, if he lifted his weight onto his hands and shuffled backwards, dragging his legs, one handspan at a time.

The hut had been about a league from the road; five thousand paces or more. This was Barthram's second night and the path seemed endless. It stretched behind him in alternate patches of grey and black where the setting moon sent bars of thin light between the trees. If he twisted to look over his shoulder the view was the same. He feared that he had somehow taken a wrong path, and was condemned to make his slow progress into eternity.

The pain was all-encompassing. There was the steady, gnawing agony from his legs that stirred into terrible spikes when the plank snagged on a root, but it was the little pains that were draining him; his shoulder muscles from the constant lifting of his own weight, and the sharper stabs in his hands where every movement pressed on the raw flesh at the base of his palms. He'd torn strips off his cloak and bound them around his hands to stop grit pushing into the grazes, but it was not enough. Now his backside was also raw where the ground had rubbed his robe to shreds. He stopped to try and wad his tattered cloak beneath him, but in that short pause the cold settled upon him. He could not stop. To stop would be to die.

There were times when he cursed the God. Surely He demanded too much of His most dedicated servant.

But that was weakness. That was Kakos the Destroyer. The God was testing him. He must have a purpose in this. Barthram would be strong. And whatever Ischyros's purpose for him was, it would include vengeance. The witch. The serving woman. D'Aurillac's brother. All of them. The agony he was now suffering would be repaid a hundredfold. They would beg for death. The thought of their coming torture sustained him; the God fed him a feast of imagined retribution when earthly food was gone.

It was dawn, and he was in a clearing when a wolf's howl split the night. It sounded close. Barthram pushed himself harder, not bothering to turn to see his way between each shuffle, so his hands thumped into hard-stalked heather or onto small stones, until the plank caught against an obstruction. He screamed and stopped, gasping.

The wolf was only ten paces away, beyond his trailing feet, a pattern of greys against the first milky light of day, pierced by two eyes that reflected the sky. Barthram whimpered and made the sign of the God.

The beast sat on its haunches, watching him, its snowy bib whiter than an anakritim robe.

Barthram picked up a stone and threw, but it went so wide that the wolf did not bother to move.

Twenty years of piety unravelled.

'*Fuck off!*' he yelled, feeling that in one obscenity he had thrown away his priesthood.

The wolf bared its fangs.

He had the strange notion that it was laughing at him.

He ranted. He cursed. He hurled obscenities, hating himself for his degradation.

Until a pair of boots stood in front of him. And a cloak. And a kindly, bearded face that looked down at him from beneath a merchant's hat.

'Love the God, look at the state of you.' The man squatted for a closer look. He had the fleshy, broken-veined face of a drinker. 'Could hear you all the way from the road.' He swung a leather flask from around his neck and held it out to Barthram. 'Bit early for me, but it looks like you need it.'

Barthram gripped the flask between his fingers, as if praying, to spare his palms. The liquor made him cough and spread fire through his belly.

'You lost, then?'

'Harbin.' Barthram rasped. 'Take me to Harbin right away. I'll pay.'

12.4 ADELAIS

Adelais was woken by Allier blowing in her face, nuzzling her with a whiskery kiss. She reached to stroke his cheek, surprised that she'd slept so well. It was as if all her tension, all her yearning, had gone into risting the runes, leaving her mind free.

But she was cold. And hungry. She stood, sniffing the dawn, and put her arms around the horse's neck, savouring his warmth.

The gods were with her that morning; a pigeon fell to a slingshot at her first attempt, and there was enough dry wood under the trees for her to risk a fire in a sheltered spot. She watched the road while the bird cooked, fearing that some telltale smoke would still rise above the trees, but no one appeared. In the distant town they would still be singing the dawn office.

The sun was above the horizon before the first travellers appeared, all riding east from Harbin; merchants, a mendicant cleric, a messenger, a huntsman with a baying pack of hounds. The dogs did not worry her; it would be hard for them to track her scent on a well-travelled road, but she thanked the gods that she'd lit her fire well downwind. Then in the middle of the forenoon the knight appeared, and she knew it was time for her to make herself known.

At first, it was just one rider, cresting a distant hill towards Harbin; too far for details, but the horse was a destrier, arched and prancing, and the rider wore a red surcoat. Two more riders came behind: a man-at-arms, also surcoated, and a lady. They disappeared into a fold in the land, and when they were closer Adelais was sure. The knight's surcoat bore the golden flowers of Fontenay, and the lady behind could only be Agnès. The man-at-arms looked like Guy Carelet, wearing a plain red surcoat with a retainer's badge. Adelais planted the rune-carved *taufr* at the base of the tree; unlike Yrsa's talisman it was too large to be hidden in her scrip. Best not to be found with that. Nor with the *nidhstick* or the priest's satchel.

Her joy faded as she rode close enough to see the glowering expression on Leandre de Fontenay's face, as unwelcoming as his chain mail. And why was he fully armed? She sat tall, refusing to be cowed, and curbed Allier into as proud an outline as the lord's destrier. Beyond Leandre's shoulder, Agnès gave a weak little smile from a wide-eyed, frightened face. *What has happened to you, my friend?* Guy watched Adelais approach as if she were some strange, dangerous animal, like an unchained bear.

'So this is the witch?' Leandre did not turn his head to his lady.

'I am no witch, my lord.' Though hadn't she just made her first attempt at a *taufr*?

'Mistress Elyse says you killed the king.'

'He died, then? Yes.' Adelais would not grovel. Or lie.

'I should kill you on the spot. And you have been hiding in my hunting lodge.' A statement, not a question. Adelais did not reply. 'I may be stripped of my lands.'

'Not by this king, you won't.' Adelais dared to challenge him.

A momentary crack appeared in Leandre's grim face; a smile, quickly masked.

'And you slew seven of Prince Lancelin's men there.'

'They came for me. I declined their invitation, but I did not fight on my own. Your man Rossignol fought bravely alongside me. So did Sennet, the castellan. He died. And a former Guardian, Fulke d'Aurillac, turned the tide in our favour.'

'If Lancelin is crowned,' Leandre held her eye, 'he won't forgive you that. The noble who died was his equerry.'

'If?' Adelais had heard a faint emphasis on the word.

Leandre relaxed slightly, leaning forwards in his saddle. 'Whatever happens, you are an embarrassment.'

'Then, my lord, you have two choices.' Sleep and food had made her strong. 'Kill me or help me.'

'You are bold, witch!'

'If Elyse and I are captured alive we will be tortured. I cannot promise to remain silent. So I suggest you either kill us both now or help us escape to where we can no longer be an embarrassment.'

'Hah!' Leandre twisted in the saddle and gestured at Guy Carelet. 'Give it to her.'

Guy handed her another Fontenay surcoat. Adelais had to dismount and unbuckle her sword belt to put it on.

'Proper stirred things up, you did,' Guy muttered as she stood by his stirrup. 'Some say there's going to be war between the nobles.'

'If you wear my colours, witch,' Leandre called to her, 'you obey my orders, understood?'

'Understood, my lord. And my name is Perrin Wilg.' It felt strange to use that name again. And he must have made his decision already, to have brought the surcoat. He'd been testing her.

'Well, *Master Wilg*, my first order is that you cover your head with that bascinet.' He nodded at Guy, who handed over a helmet with a broad aventail of mail to cover the neck. 'You will keep your aventail hooked over your face at all times, and you will not speak.' Leandre blinked as she swept off her hat, and her hair fell almost to her shoulders. Adelais sensed that he liked her more as a man.

The helmet was too big; it flopped forwards over her eyes as she re-buckled her sword belt. It had a matted sheepskin liner that stank, but once its aventail was fastened across the face only her eyes would show. The weight of the mail across her nose was uncomfortable, and she was forced to breathe the tang of oiled steel with the liner's stale sweat.

'Do you understand?' Leandre shouted.

Adelais nodded. She was not speaking. Again a flicker of a smile crossed Leandre's face. She could like this man.

'The bridges at Harbin are closed to you. It is too risky. Those without beards are being... examined. You would be taken. So you and Mistress Elyse will ride in my train when I return to Villebénie, and you will cross the river there.'

Adelais bowed her head and bent her knee, feeling weak with relief and gratitude. 'My lord–'

'Silence!'

She mounted, and fell in alongside Agnès as they trotted back towards Harbin. Adelais glanced at her often, needing her reassurance. There had been so much unsaid when they parted, so much unresolved. Were they still friends?

At first Agnès exhaled, puffing out her cheeks, but said nothing. Perhaps the testing of Adelais had been finely balanced. In time, she seemed to relax. Finally, on a stretch of road where both Leandre and Guy were ahead of them, Agnès and Adelais made eye contact, and Agnès's face softened into her mischievous smile. She pulled the edge of her veil across her nose to imitate Adelais's aventail, made big, mock-seductive eyes at her, and fluttered her eyelids.

Their hands touched and squeezed before either of the men looked back.

Adelais tensed again as they rode down a hill into Harbin, where the royal banner of a golden sun on a blue field now flew from the castle's tower. On the south bank, nearest to them, the lines of nobles' pavilions seethed with men-at-arms, and the bridge had been closed by a line of soldiers at the far end; sword-and-shield men standing shoulder to shoulder, with a second row making a hedge of spears behind. More men-at-arms waited in the broad square under the castle's walls. To ride into this mass was madness. Allier caught her tension and began to jog; even when she curbed him he danced under her, ready to spring.

'Steady, Master Wilg!' That was Agnès, offering a thin smile of reassurance. 'For once, they are not here for you!'

'De Fontenay!' A stocky noble pushed his way through the crowd. He was fully armed for battle in a suit of mail, with the coif pushed back on his neck, and wore a heraldic surcoat bearing the royal sun quartered with a black boar's head on red. A squire and two men-at-arms followed, also armed, with their hands resting on their sword hilts. 'You picked a fine morning to ride out! De Remy is forcing our hand. Wants us to swear fealty to that puppy Lancelin now. Here.'

'Today, Highness?' Leandre dismounted; his squire had rushed to hold his horse. 'Surely fealty follows a coronation?'

Highness. This must be Duke Gervais of Delmas. Adelais also dismounted; she felt too visible above the crowd.

'We are to be led, one by one,' Delmas was almost shaking with rage, 'one by one into the castle to swear fealty. De Remy means to pre-empt any discussion about the succession. How many men do you have?'

'What you see, Highness. I came to hunt, not to fight.'

'Three, then?'

Adelais realised she had been numbered with the fighting men.

'Lancelin has forty in Harbin now, and more on the way from Villebénie. A messenger was sent out this morning that they should stop any noble they meet on the road and bring them back to swear.'

Leandre looked down the line of pavilions, each flying a noble's banner. 'How many others are with us?'

Us. Adelais realised she was witnessing the start of a war.

'Let us find out. Have your men ready to fight.'

'Carelet!' Lord Leandre waited until Guy came close enough for them to speak quietly.

'Take Master Wilg,' he jabbed his thumb over his shoulder, 'into the store tent. He is not to leave. He may speak to no one except Mistress Elyse. You keep his sword.'

Guy took Allier's bridle. 'Come on.' His voice was not unkindly. 'Don't worry, I'll look after him.'

Adelais stroked Allier's neck; it was hard to let him go. Harder still to unbuckle her sword belt, like a captive. She allowed herself to be led away, feeling very alone and defenceless in the crowd.

The de Fontenay store tent was cramped, low enough to make Adelais stoop, and filled with a knight's necessities: saddles, horse tack, and chests for clothes. The length of a narrow passage down its centre was filled by boar spears. A mattress had been laid across the chests, and in the gloom of the tent's interior Adelais thought a sack had been piled on top until the sack unfolded, straightened, and lifted a hand to push back a hood.

'Welcome, sweeting.' Elyse managed a wan smile as she opened her arms for a hug. She looked a tired old woman as she stared into Adelais's eyes. 'Did you carve the *taufr*?' she said, when Guy had gone.

Adelais nodded.

'Exactly as I said?'

Adelais did not see any point in lying. '*Íss, naudhiz, reidhr, bjarkan...* and *thurs.*'

'You risted *thurs?*'

'It worked for me in Roquenoir, before the high priest.'

'But, child, runes are not toys to be brought out to play!' Elyse sounded more shocked than angry. 'Arranged in a row because you *like* them! Runes call to each other, change each other. We needed concealment and the confusion of our enemies, not war.' She waved her hand angrily. 'And especially not love.'

A tumult of noise grew outside; men were gathering, calling challenges and encouragement. It reminded Adelais of street sounds in the build-up to an apprentices' fight.

Elyse gripped her hands into fists, and let them drop with a sigh. 'If only you would do as you are told. You had *one* thing to do...'

There was a snap of canvas as the tent flap was flung back. Adelais rapidly re-fastened the aventail across her face before she turned. Guy stood by the pole, bending to see inside. His eyes were bright with excitement as he held Humbert's sword out to Adelais.

'To horse, both of you. We will fight our way through.'

12.5 TAILLEFER

Lifting the expulsion felt like one of the purest acts of Taillefer's priesthood. It was a righting of a wrong, a chance of atonement.

There were just the two of them at the small, private ritual within the sanctuary of the temple: Taillefer and Malory d'Eivet. Lady Agnès had returned to the de Fontenay pavilion before Taillefer set out, and in any case the warlike preparations at the bridge would have made it unsafe for her to reach the temple. Priests, of course, could walk through battle lines with impunity. Taillefer decided that no other invitations were appropriate. When he lit two candles at the sacred flame, symbolising the re-admission of Humbert Blanc and Adelais de Vries into the light of the God, d'Eivet's eyes were full.

They walked back through the town together afterwards, with the noise from the square reverberating through the streets like a market day. Taillefer experienced a glorious sense of freedom; he had made his own decision. He had done the right thing. His brother's inevitable wrath no longer troubled him. He remarked on his new lightness of spirit to d'Eivet.

'I understand, Excellency.' D'Eivet wore a beatific, slightly mad smile. 'When I was imprisoned I raged at first at my helplessness. Then I found meaning in the small acts of goodness that were still open to me. I could still comfort the dying. I could still be a companion to a frightened boy. I found the God even in the dungeons of the Black Tower, or perhaps the God found me. How much more so in a holy act in a fire temple.'

A companionship had grown between them; that half-smiling inward pleasure that comes from sharing in a good deed.

But this was no market day. There were no competing cries of the vendors, no jovial sounds of chatting maids and shrieking children, although many voices were raised. This was deeper, more masculine, and much more menacing.

The town square was crowded with men-at-arms. Bordered on one side by the mighty walls of the castle, and on two others by merchants' houses, it grumbled with their talk and hissed with an undercurrent of moving chain mail. The warriors clustered most heavily on the open side of the square, where wharves lined the riverbank. The bridge itself was blocked by two lines of soldiers; local guards to the front, and spearmen wearing the royal badge behind.

On the meadow on the far side of the river a crowd was gathering, calling to one another, their voices flowing together in a steady current of sound. Nobles moved among them, many with groups of liveried retainers milling about like small herds that would soon become one. The colours of their heraldry were like flowers in a summer meadow, yet never had a meadow been so deadly. Many were mounted and armed for battle, wearing chain mail beneath their surcoats.

Prince Lancelin sat astride his destrier outside the castle gates, armed for war. He'd already had his surcoat altered so that he wore the golden sun on blue of the king; the white, three-tabbed 'label' that denoted the king's son had been picked away. Lancelin looked nervous as he faced the first and perhaps defining challenge to his authority; he held himself rigid as if he feared he might crumble.

Taillefer thought the prince's inexperience was dangerous; the boy might snap an ill-considered order without thought for the consequences. Now was the time for a calm head, and that certainly did not sit on Lancelin's shoulders. A small group of young nobles had bunched behind him, and at his side Othon tried to steady his own mount, his horsemanship tested amidst the palpable tension. The golden chain of the chancellor bounced around his neck, gleaming against a black velvet herigaut.

Taillefer crossed to his brother's side and laid a calming hand on the horse's neck.

'Will there be war, brother?' Taillefer asked. 'Is this really necessary?' This was not a day for conflict. Taillefer felt he had been touched by the God and was filled with grace.

'The king will have their fealty, or their lives.' Othon's horse twisted and he snatched at the reins, grimacing his anger with the fretful beast. 'By sunset I will have the Villebénie garrison at their backs, those that still live. Then they will swear.'

Taillefer lowered his voice. 'King? Surely Lancelin remains prince until acclaimed by the nobles. That is our tradition, is it not?'

'It may have been, before we had a clear bloodline to the throne.' Othon was clearly irritated. Taillefer wondered why his brother's anger did not matter to him any more.

'And is it not also our custom to swear fealty after a coronation, not before?'

Othon hunched over in the saddle to bring his face close to Taillefer's. Taillefer had to dodge the gold chain of office swinging from his neck. 'Stop meddling, brother. These matters are beyond you.'

'On the contrary. I am only just beginning to understand the importance of process. Like the *process* for an expulsion.'

'What do you mean?' Othon's eyes narrowed.

'You rushed that one through, too, didn't you? Well, I've just lifted the expulsion on Humbert Blanc and Adelais de Vries, and my soul is soaring.'

Othon made a dismissive gesture, as if mere expulsions were insignificant in comparison with the great affairs of state.

'You know nothing, little brother. You may be a diakonos but you are first and foremost a de Remy. Now I suggest you take refuge in the castle. We may have to kill a few to persuade the others. This is going to be messy.'

'On the contrary, Othon.' Taillefer's use of the given name was so rare as to make the chancellor's head turn again. 'I know more every day about what makes a man fit to rule.' He stepped back and lifted his hand in benediction. 'And you are not.'

An exquisite look of shock passed across Othon's face, a moment of stunned stillness, before Taillefer turned and walked through the mass of armed men. There were shouts behind him, a cry from Othon to stop them, but the garrison of Taillefer's own town parted for him, with d'Eivet at his heel, creating a narrow alleyway for them to walk; none would arrest a diakonos of the faith, *their* diakonos, not on a day they might die. Not ever. Taillefer stepped out onto the bridge with as much confidence as he hoped one day to step onto a much greater bridge, able to look his God in the face.

The earthly bridge of Harbin was stone-built and wide enough to allow two carts to pass; a lonely path between the two factions even though Pateras Malory followed close behind. It rose high enough over its arches for him to see the entire gaudy crowd, and he paused at its crest. It was a vantage point from which he could preach, if only they would listen, but only the nearest were looking at him. Most were staring towards the Duke of Delmas, who rode towards the bridge as if he and Taillefer were appointed to meet; his horse forged a way through the people like a ship through water, riding a new wave of sound: '*The God save Your Highness!*' Not everyone shouted; some lords looked undecided and hung back.

Taillefer offered a prayer and made the sign of the God. He opened his arms wide to command silence. Slowly, whisper by whisper, the quiet rippled outwards until Delmas turned in his saddle where the bridge met the road, and bellowed in a voice that could command an army on the field of battle.

'Look, my friends, a de Remy has come to bless us!'

The laughter dented Taillefer's assurance a little. His prepared words were fading like smoke. *The God give wings to his voice.* He lifted his head, arms still spread, and shouted more loudly than he believed possible.

'I am Taillefer de Remy, Diakonos of Harbin.' His words hit the castle walls and echoed back over the throng. Now they were listening. 'It is not for a priest to declare who should rule.'

They were all quiet now, waiting for the 'but'.

'And in due course I, as a diakonos and a lord of the faith in Galmandie, will swear temporal fealty to my king.'

Delmas glowered at him. Beyond Delmas, de Fontenay was also mounted. Lady Agnès sat on her palfrey towards the rear, with a group of de Fontenay men-at-arms. She looked fearful.

'And I give you my word that I will swear that fealty...'

Ripples of consternation spread among the warrior nobles around the duke.

'... to a king who has risen to the throne in accordance with the customs of Galmandie since the realm began...'

He pitched his voice towards Agnès de Fontenay, at the back of the crowd. If she could hear, so could all.

'... acclaimed by the nobles...'

The look in her eyes gave him courage; a dawning of hope. Elsewhere a stirring began; the intake of many breaths.

'... crowned by the faith...'

The first applause began near the riverbank and rippled backwards.

'... and anointed by the God!'

An almighty cheer swallowed the last echo of his cry and

threw it at the castle. Taillefer turned, his arms still spread, to face his brother's fury across the square. Othon's venom glanced off Taillefer's smile the way a blade will turn from a great helm, for at that moment Taillefer felt he could fly on the roars of approval behind him.

Enough. He lowered his arms, turned, and walked directly to Delmas, reaching up to clasp his hand. Slowly, the tumult quietened around them. Delmas released Taillefer's grip, stood in his stirrups, and held up his hand for silence.

'You may wonder, my friends, what caused a de Remy to have such views.'

Taillefer stepped back, fearful for what Delmas would say.

'Most of you will not yet know that Diakonos de Remy was present when King Aloys was trampled to death by the woman he called the Vriesian Witch.'

'Do not abuse my support, Your Highness.' Taillefer managed to touch the duke's arm, but it was lifted out of reach as the duke gesticulated. There were cries of disbelief around them, even horror.

'Our late king was killed for his misdeeds by the Lions' Claw. She announced that she was a Blessèd One, sent by the God. Is that not so, Excellency?'

Taillefer closed his eyes, knowing he was trapped. He nodded, reluctantly, and the crowd began to roar, calling questions, shouting at each other. Taillefer stumbled away towards his palace, scarcely hearing Pateras Malory's words of approval and encouragement from behind him. Over his head came Delmas's thunderous words.

'It seems our king suffered the retribution of Ischyros for his deeds. Now the nobles of Galmandie must decide whether his line is fit to wear the crown.'

The crowd was dividing, if only in the opinions they shouted. Some screamed their denial, their refusal to believe. Others murmured, bewildered. Few received Delmas's words with enthusiasm. The noise almost drowned the duke's challenge: *'Would a son of Aloys be pleasing to the God?'* Hands plucked Taillefer's sleeve as he walked, shouting questions, until Pateras Malory cleared a way for him, parting the crowd with the mad, happy eyes of a prophet.

Taillefer almost blundered into Agnès de Fontenay's palfrey. She folded in the saddle to grasp his hand the way a lady might bestow her token on her champion at a joust; a blessing amidst chaos.

'You spoke well, Excellency.'

The touch was warm, almost intimate, yet her eyes were those of a hunted animal, looking everywhere but at him. He sensed that her fear had little to do with the possibility of her neglectful lord going into battle.

'It is done, my lady. Your uncle can cross the bridge of judgement, if the God wills.'

That caught her attention. 'Lord Brother Humbert?'

'I have lifted the expulsion, with Pateras Malory's assistance.' Taillefer wanted to be away from this madness and go somewhere he could do good. A simple, priestly task, perhaps. 'I thought I might journey to Bellay and take his body by boat to Villebénie. I think the temple of the Guardians might be an appropriate resting place. Would you and Lord Leandre like to join me there? A suitably honourable burial?'

'Soon, I hope, Excellency. But today I must follow my lord.'

She glanced over her shoulder to where Lord Leandre was adjusting the girth of his destrier, close enough for them to hear the metallic ripple of cascading chain mail as he moved. His squire held the horse's head, and beside him two more men-at-arms in the de Fontenay livery were already mounted.

And well-mounted. Taillefer looked long and hard at a fine black destrier with a distinctive pale lightening around the muzzle. The stallion was curved and fidgeting in the excitement, and its rider was trying to calm it. He was sure he'd seen that horse before. It threw a small buck and the memory hit Taillefer like a body blow; the same beast snorting fury and trampling the king. Taillefer gasped and stepped backwards; the man-at-arms' lower face was covered by a chain-mail aventail, but Taillefer did not need to look at the eyes beneath the bascinet to know they would be ice-blue.

Taillefer looked around the de Fontenay group, bewildered. There was another young man-at-arms, looking frightened. The squire was handing his lord a shield and lance; a war lance, not a boar spear. And near them a serving woman was hunched on a gelding's back with her hands shaking above the saddle. Taillefer closed his eyes, praying. *Ischyros spare me this choice.* Or had he made the choice already?

One thing was sure: if he revealed the Vriesian woman, she would die. Delmas wanted the story, he did not want talking evidence. And if the Lancelin faction caught her, her fate would be torture and the stake.

When he opened his eyes they were all looking at him. Lord, lady, serving woman, and one who dressed as a man-at-arms. And he knew that they knew he'd recognised her. Taillefer swallowed, taking another step backwards. With that extra distance he could see beyond them to the Bellay road, and coming slowly down the hill was a man, possibly a merchant, who led a horse. Sitting on the horse was a priest in a filthy anakritim robe, slumped so far forwards that he was resting on the horse's neck, with his bare feet dangling clear of the stirrups. Ghislain Barthram raised his head with difficulty, but he was clearly very much alive.

Agnès de Fontenay had also seen, and now she looked unwaveringly at Taillefer, with eyes that were wide, fearful, and pleading.

12.6 ADELAIS

The diakonos walked ever closer, with Pateras Malory at his shoulder, while Duke Gervais roared over the crowd. 'Would a son of Aloys be pleasing to the God?'

Adelais pretended to watch the duke. Anything but catch the eye of the priests. Around them the people were uneasy now, muttering among themselves. Adelais had been little more than a child when the persecution of the Guardians began, and in all that time the people had been told that King Aloys had acted to defend the faith of Ischyros from heresy and perversion. Many might have suspected otherwise, but it would take more than one man's voice to change history, even if that man was the Duke of Delmas.

'And I will not swear fealty until a king is crowned.'

A groundswell of anger was building in the crowd. People near Adelais muttered that if their king had been struck down by the God, then the high priest must have been too. The foundations of their lives were broken. Their rage needed an outlet, be it noble or priest, Lancelin or Delmas.

Or her. If they thought she was the Vriesian Witch, half of them would tear her limb from limb for killing their king and their high priest. Yet, calm amidst the turmoil, Pateras Malory smiled up at her and made the sign of the God. Adelais fingered her aventail, still hooked across her face. Impossible that he knew. *Of course. Allier. Her lovely, proud Allier.*

Adelais twisted in the saddle, looking for ways to escape. Near her was Elyse, clearly terrified. Malory would recognise her too. Closer still was the diakonos who'd been with the king, now talking to Agnès. As Adelais watched he stepped backwards, staring past her towards the unmistakable sight of Ghislain Barthram being led down the Bellay road on the back of a horse.

Adelais slumped in the saddle, light-headed and clammy. Her one act of mercy would come at a terrible cost. Slowly, with great effort, she straightened, nudged Allier alongside Elyse, and laid a warning hand on her forearm.

'You were right, Aunty. I should have killed him.' Adelais nodded towards the approaching anakritis. Now they would all pay for her weakness.

Elyse turned, saw him, and let out a great sigh. Strangely, the sight seemed to calm her.

'If this is our dying-day, then let us meet it with courage.' Elyse hooked the veil of her hat over her face and began tapping the pommel of her saddle. The veil made small dancing movements over her lips as she began a barely audible chant.

'*Íss er árbörkr...*'

Ísa, the ice-rune, the binding rune.

'*Ok unnar thak...*'

The rune to constrict a hostile will.

'*Ok feigra manna fár...*'

They sang it together, so quietly they might have been praying; Elyse behind her veil, Adelais behind her aventail of chain mail, while at their horses' heads Pateras Malory beamed the blessing of Ischyros upon them.

Across the crowd, Duke Gervais still stood in his stirrups,

holding up his hand for silence, though only those closest to him obeyed. 'I will not swear fealty to an unacclaimed, uncrowned king. I intend to ride across this bridge, by force of arms if necessary, and continue on my way to my lands. Who will ride with me?

'I, Your Highness!' Leandre de Fontenay hefted his lance.

'And I!' Another knight, already armed and mounted. *They'd planned this together.*

On the far side of the bridge a solid cohort of warriors awaited them. Shield men. Spear men. Men-at-arms. Nobles on their destriers. She and Elyse had death in front of them and the anakritis-general behind.

And nearby, close enough for Adelais to hear every word, the diakonos was greeting Ghislain Barthram, expressing delight that he lived, and shock at his injuries. He seemed to be keen to usher the anakritis away from the scene towards food, wine, and his personal physician, but Barthram began to shout, though his voice was faint and hoarse; the sounds of a man who has spent long hours screaming in agony.

Adelais risked looking towards him, and Barthram was pointing straight at her. 'It is the witch! That's her! On the black horse!' His voice was slurred. 'I know that horse!'

Those nearest in the crowd stared at her, and Adelais shrugged – *play the part, girl* – but looked for her best route to run. More men-at-arms were between her and the road. She'd have to abandon Elyse if she ran. And she was wearing de Fontenay livery; Agnès would suffer. She chose to brazen it out.

'And her! That woman on the gelding! She's a witch too!' Barthram was almost incoherent in his rage.

The man leading Barthram's horse laughed. 'Gave him a few nips of brandywine to dull the pain; I did. You wouldn't believe the things he's been sayin'!'

The crowd laughed with him, a little nervously; the witch's presence had just been proclaimed, but claims of two witches were less credible. In front of them Agnès stared back at Adelais, fear in her eyes, as the moment hung in the balance. Adelais glanced around. Few others had heard; most were still listening to Delmas.

'I think,' the diakonos said to the one with the horse, 'the pateras is overwrought by his wounds. I will take him to my own chamber and see that he has all that he needs. It may be best to limit his visitors to my physician until he is recovered.'

Adelais watched in disbelief as the diakonos himself led Barthram away, helpless on his horse, though the anakritis-general still looked over his shoulder with hatred blazing in his eyes. He was shouting as loudly as his damaged voice could manage, but Malory d'Eivet walked with them, singing a praise chant to drown out his words. He bellowed so loudly that those nearby stared at him as if he was deranged. Adelais exhaled, only just remembering to breathe. *Takk til gudhanna.* Thanks be to the gods. In a moment of light-headed irreverence Adelais remembered a filthy gesture she'd seen soldiers use and she gave Barthram the finger, with relish, wishing that her face was uncovered.

In the tension of the moment she'd almost forgotten they still had a river to cross, through a wall of spears. Lord Leandre was calling them forwards. Perhaps a dozen knights had joined the duke, with as many squires, though few had shields or war lances; the rest must make do with boar spears. Some had suits of mail but none had great helms; they had not, after all, come to Harbin to fight.

The bridge in front of them was blocked at its far end by perhaps twenty soldiers in two ranks. Behind them were as many men-at-arms and a scattering of nobles. Heavy odds.

'Ranks of four,' Duke Gervais called. 'Those with lances and shields to the fore, with me. De Fontenay, de Rissac, once we have punched through, stay with your men and hold the square. The rest ride on with me in case they have blocked the western gate. De Fontenay, follow with your lady when all is secure. Now I suppose I had better go and reason with the fools.'

Someone offered Adelais a boar spear as she joined Guy in the third line, but she waved it away. She'd never handled one, and she wanted to be sure of her balance to manage Allier. Ahead of them the duke walked his horse onto the bridge, his lance upright and his shield still slung on his back. He stopped at the crest.

'No one need die today.' There was near-silence now; Gervais's voice echoed off the castle walls. 'A royal duke demands passage to his lands. Stand aside, or we will fight.'

'Then swear fealty, uncle.' Prince Lancelin's voice was high and strained. 'And you may go on your way.'

'When you are acclaimed and crowned, puppy!' It was a ritual exchange, the outcome certain. 'If that ever happens.'

Beyond the duke, Adelais could see the faces of the soldiers blocking the bridge, pale and nervous beneath their bowl helmets. This was not their fight. The second line, all spear men, wore the royal badge on their chests and looked more resolute.

'No. Now.' Lancelin had nothing else to say.

'Then these men's deaths are on your head.' Gervais turned his destrier and rode back to their line.

The moment felt unreal. Every detail was crystal clear; even at the distance of a three-span bridge she could see a front-rank soldier swallow nervously and look from side to side. Another nudged his companion and lifted his chin towards the castle gates, which stood open, framing Prince Lancelin. She could imagine the soldier's sneer; *'Ready to bolt for safety.'* Chancellor de Remy was already within the walls. Around her came the hard sounds of preparation; shields being swung into position, girths and straps tightened, and the metal-on-leather rasp as those without spears or lances drew their swords.

Humbert's was now upright in her hand, its honed edge a gleaming line. In the front rank Leandre de Fontenay looked over his shoulder and glared at her with a face framed by chain mail. His look said *'do not fail me'*.

'From the top, on my command,' Delmas called. The hooves of the front rank clattered onto the stone bridge. They rode knee to knee, filling the width, trotting. The rattle grew as the second rank followed. She could not have stopped Allier even if she'd wished; he was dancing beneath her, curved on the bit, and snorting. There was an awful inevitability about this procession; soon they would hurtle forwards and she had no control of what would happen.

Or did she?

'Thurs er kvenna kvöl...' *Thurs*, the victory-rune. She'd chanted its song the day she confronted the high priest.

Now the third rank, her rank, was on the bridge and the noise of the hooves was like a hail storm on a wooden roof. She did not feel frightened, just detached, an observer rather than a participant. Her world was two lines of brightly coloured, bouncing backs, blocking her view of what was to come, and the voice of an experienced squire on her right who barked 'hold the line' when Allier forged a little ahead.

She did not hear the command to charge. The four lances in the front rank dipped forwards like trees felled in unison, their mounts' hooves echoing the drum roll before an execution.

'Hold, hold!' from her right, as the second line crested the bridge, couched boar spears, and hurled themselves down the slope. They charged into a wall of sound as four armoured knights in the front rank punched into the two lines of men; hammer-blows melded into a single, mighty strike that resounded from the castle walls a heartbeat later in a second thunderclap of sound.

She could not hold. Allier surged forwards into a chaos of men still tumbling over the ground from the impact, a clatter of

swords and shields sent flying over the cobbles. Beneath her
Allier rocked as he jumped bodies, and they were through the
first lines, fanning out. A solid line of soldiers was dancing backwards in front of them, crouched behind shields, until a squire
hammered into them, unable to stop the momentum of his
charge. He went down, his horse screaming, knocking at least
three men over as he fell.

Adelais had wheeled into the gap between the wrecked
lines at the base of the bridge and the phalanx in the square. A
knight from the front rank was down too, trapped beneath a
thrashing horse, and his squire was cantering back to him. A
litter of bodies were sprayed like skittles where the bridge met
the square. Two more soldiers were crawling away. At least half
remained unhurt at the wings of the bridge, and for a moment
both sides held their breath and stared at each other as if unsure
of what to do next. Three young nobles were trying to escape
through the castle gates. Two more, who seemed more disposed
to fight, blocked the road on the far side of the square. From the
bridge came a new thunder as the next ranks charged.

Then the screaming began and the moment of stunned
quiet was lost. The falling squire had broken the shield wall in
the square, and men bunched into protective groups, their cohe-
sion gone. Four soldiers came for Adelais together. She had no
lance, no shield. She would be easy.

'*Ok kletta búi...*'

Afterwards Adelais would try to piece together what
happened from fleeting fragments of memory. She only knew
that she and Allier were one in a dance of teeth and hoof and
sword, and it was a divine madness in which there was no fear,
only a wild joy. For a while she might have been one of the gods,
invincible; the battle had become a mad game in which she
alone knew the moves. The stallion beneath her was a warhorse
from Valhalla, her own Sleipnir, spinning and leaping and
dealing death with his kicks. The soldiers were no longer

people, they were players, testing their skills, and she beat them without even breaking the pace of her rune song.

'*Ok vardhrúnar verr...*'

Too soon, no more soldiers came to test her, though she rode Allier in a circle. They pranced within a low wall of dead and dying men. More cowered beyond, hunched over their shields, their eyes fearful beneath the rims of their helmets. In her madness Adelais hollowed her body and bellowed her challenge. The sound came from her gut and filled the square, reverberating off the walls. It was the screech of a female predator with blood on its claws and fangs, roaring over its kill. What was it that Humbert had called her? *Lioness.*

'Wilg!' Leandre de Fontenay's shout cut off her scream. 'Enough!'

She came back into herself from a far-off place. There were bodies around her, and blood on her sword, though she had no clear memory of how it came to be there. The castle gates had been shut and more soldiers cowered against them, their swords ready but with no fight in their eyes.

'Enough, I say!'

Adelais swallowed, and as she forced herself to concentrate she became conscious of her own breathing and the snorting of the sweat-streaked horse beneath her. She touched Allier's neck with her spare hand; he too needed calming. In the throes of battle she had entered the mind of the horse, and the horse had entered her mind, and perhaps both of them had become one in a higher mind that neither of them would ever understand. Now, in that touch, she acknowledged that partnership and said that she was once again Adelais, mortal woman, while he was Allier, destrier and stallion.

Just Lord Leandre, another knight, two squires, and Guy Carelet remained mounted in the square, and they were all looking at her. Another squire stood with drawn sword by his fallen master, whose horse had died with a spear in its chest.

Two dead nobles lay on the far side of the square and many more bodies lay on the cobbles, leaking small rivers of blood. Hers had not been the only battle. Adelais looked at Leandre blankly, wondering what had just happened.

'Lady Agnès will come across now. We must leave.'

Adelais nodded, suddenly numb. There was a clatter of more hooves and she lifted her head to see Agnès and Elyse staring at her as they rode past; Elyse with what might have been triumph, Agnès with something akin to horror. Adelais followed them out of the square, Humbert's bloody sword still upright in her hand. She let Allier drop his head; he was blowing hard, almost staggering as if he, too, had come back from another world. She rocked in the saddle to examine his legs and flanks; she could see no wound.

The squire standing by his fallen master lifted his sword in salute as she passed.

A league beyond Harbin the road forked and Lord Leandre reined back, allowing Delmas's party to pull ahead. It was a parting of the ways. Leandre pointed at the right-hand fork.

'That way lies Vriesland. In two days' riding you will be in Duke Ragener's domain, but I go left, with Delmas. War is coming, within Galmandie and perhaps with Vriesland, and in letting you go I fear I am releasing a powerful foe. I hope that the next time we meet, *mistress*, it is not on the field of battle.'

Adelais blinked at the Vriesland road, too tired to think or to feel any jubilation that the last great barrier was crossed. She struggled to form the words to reply.

'I do not desire war, my lord. My only desire is to live peacefully and openly as a woman. I thank you for allowing me that.'

'I think war will find you, nonetheless. I counsel you not be swayed by powerful men; you have killed a king, and perhaps a high priest. There are those who will seek to use you for their own ends.' Leandre's gaze dropped to her surcoat, and his eyes crinkled with amusement. 'But perhaps you should not invade Vriesland in de Fontenay livery?'

Adelais's dismount was a weak-legged drop from the saddle. She rested her forehead against Allier's neck, gripping her stirrup leathers to stay upright. He too was spent. Leandre, Guy, and Agnès waited a few paces away, Agnès already dismounted and holding her palfrey's head. Adelais wondered why she was holding back; just Elyse was by her, with her hand on Adelais's arm.

'You can't sleep yet, sweeting.' There was a new message in Elyse's eyes but Adelais was too tired to work it out.

'What happened, Aunty? In the square, I mean?' Adelais didn't open her eyes.

'You danced to rune song, I think. I have heard of it, but never seen it.'

'*Thurs*. I sang the *thurs* rune as I fought. It was like I could fly...' Her mind began to drift.

'And now your body is demanding payment. Soon you will be hungry.'

Adelais nodded, wishing Elyse would stop talking and let her sleep, right there, in the grass.

'Red rider.' A thought came to Adelais like the start of a dream on the edge of sleep. 'De Fontenay was the red rider.'

'It could have been the diakonos.'

'But no fire. You said what was fated ends in fire.'

'I told you, sweeting, prophecy is not my gift.' Still she looked at Adelais with that sad, warning look, and finally Adelais understood.

'You're going with Agnès, aren't you?'

Elyse nodded. 'We had a talk. She needs someone she can trust. And I need to see my son.'

'Does she know?' About the old gods, Adelais meant.

'She isn't asking. But she does know she can trust me with her life.'

'So she does know.' Adelais closed her eyes, wishing she'd had time to prepare the right words. 'Thank you' was too small. So was 'sorry'. A squeeze had to suffice; a hug that crushed them together, cheeks into hair, arms shaking with the effort, then a finger-trailing goodbye.

Agnès's green eyes were misty with her own farewell. Leandre waited a few paces away with his squire and Guy, as if to give them some privacy; he seemed tolerant of their friendship. Adelais pulled off the bascinet and ran her fingers through her hair, relishing the touch of fresh air on her scalp for those moments before she must hide her hair again under a man's hat. She pulled the de Fontenay surcoat over her head and returned Agnès's smile, woman to woman, despite her lordling's clothes. They stood in their own small world of horse sweat and friendship, curtained from all eyes by Allier's bulk on one side, and Agnès's palfrey on the other.

'I watched you, *kjúkling*, in the square.' Agnès looked her in the eye. 'It was beyond my understanding. What *are* you?'

Adelais shook her head. She remembered what she had become in the fight, but she had no words to describe it. She'd sung rune song. Again. What happened after was not *her*, surely? Not the girl who'd drunk too much wine with the dearest friend she'd ever had, and almost become her lover. It was something that had happened *to* her, that's all.

'A friend, I hope?' was all Adelais could say.

Agnès pulled her close, so close that their legs touched along their length, *between* their length, although the padding under Adelais's herigaut allowed no sense of Agnès's curves.

'Always, *kjúkling*. For life, whatever happens.'

Agnès lifted her head to kiss Adelais gently on the lips.

. . .

Adelais lay back on the verge, holding Allier's trailing reins in one hand and her sword belt loose in the other. A silly, trivial thought crept into her mind, a memory of childhood when she'd stacked stools to reach a tub of honey and brought down the whole shelf. She'd stood amidst the debris of broken pottery, looked up at her father glowering in the doorway, and said, 'I think I've been a bad girl.' She giggled at the irrational thought; a flicker of a different madness, and closed her eyes, lulled by the gentle sound of Allier tearing the grass as he grazed. Sweat was cooling on her body and she began to dream of the great kitchen at the hunting lodge, where Elyse had sat her naked in a half-barrel and poured heated water over her.

A whiskery nuzzling woke her as she was drifting into sleep. It was perhaps the hardest thing she had ever done to stand, gather reins, and mount.

Allier stared after the departing horses, still in sight on a far rise, and whickered. He too was losing friends. Adelais touched him gently on the flank and turned his head towards Vriesland.

PART SIX

THE FASTING MOON (GALMAN) | THE WORM MOON (VRIESIAN)

CHAPTER THIRTEEN

13.1 BARTHRAM

They had adapted a chair to carry him; a good one arm with supports such as a lord might use at a feast, but with planks beneath his splinted leg and spear shafts lashed to the sides so that he could be carried. They had also given him a flask of wine infused with opium to dull the pain, and he had slept for much of the boat journey downriver from Harbin to Villebénie.

Barthram was encouraged to drink more before they lifted him from the boat; his bearers might lurch as they carried him through the streets. He swigged, even though he knew it would send him back into a dreamlike state. Later he would wake slowly into a window of time when he could think clearly and when the pain was tolerable, before the drug's effects faded and the agony returned.

He expected a welcoming party of anakritim, but there were only four soldiers and two gaolers from the Black Tower waiting on the wharf. He missed the reassuring bulk of Pateras Octave. Surely Humbert Blanc would burn for eternity in the pit; there would be no healing and no opium for his pain. Barthram greeted the men individually as they roped him to his chair, mildly pleased that he could remember their names through the opium fog. They did not respond. This was strange. One of them laughed when he asked to be taken to his lodgings in the temple grounds, and said there were gentles waiting to speak to him in the Black Tower.

A dark dread grew within him. He pushed his mind to work the way a swimmer might struggle against a river's flow, always fading backwards.

He woke, after a fashion, within the Black Tower when his head fell backwards against the chair; the men were cursing as they edged the poles around the curve of a spiral staircase. They put him down in the room where he'd sent d'Aurillac on his mission. He managed to lift his head, blinking like a drunkard, and found three men watching him across the table: the Episkopos of Villebénie, a young noble of the Lancelin faction, and Othon de Remy. Weak light gleamed on the chancellor's gold chain.

Chain. Chancellor. Official. Barthram swayed his head to the side. Two scribes sat at another table, beneath the window.

'Pateras Ghislain Barthram.' The quills lifted expectantly. 'We are gathered to investigate accusations of sorcery.'

Barthram blinked at de Remy. 'Sorcery? By whom?' No one else was in the room.

'Is this your satchel?' De Remy lifted it.

Barthram managed to nod. His initials were on the flap. So what?

'It was found by the road outside Harbin.'

Oh, that was good. He'd missed it.

'It had this inside.' De Remy lifted a flat piece of wood from it, about half the size of a chair seat and marked with overlapping, straight-line carvings.

'Not mine.' It took effort to speak.

'We have consulted a woman who has admitted to following the old gods, before she saw the light of Ischyros.' The episkopos looked uncomfortable to be talking about such things.

'She tells us these are curse runes. A "bind-rune", she called it, designed to bring death and destruction to the king and to the faith.'

'Not mine,' he repeated. *By the God, think!*

'You will understand the significance of curse runes being found in your bag, near the spot where the king died?' So the noble had a voice.

'Didn't do it.'

'Then will you tell us how you managed to know that the raid to capture the Vriesian Witch had failed, long before the news reached Villebénie?'

Enough sense remained for Barthram to know he had to tell them. 'Birds,' he said. 'Messages on birds.'

The episkopos drew in his breath sharply. 'Like the ravens of Odhinn?' He made the sign of the God. 'Creatures that some call *familiars?*'

Barthram shook his head. 'No. No. Trained birds. Flew all the way home. Ask Kasim.' *Oh. Kasim can't talk.*

'Kasim?'

'Servant. House. Keeps birds.'

De Remy sighed deeply. 'We have searched your house and spoken to those who live nearby. Your servant left with a noble and a boy, half a moon ago. There had been birds, but there are none now. Apparently you are fond of pigeon pie?'

'*Fylgjur,*' the episkopos breathed.

'What?' The noble clearly had not heard the word before.

'It is said that adept sorcerers can send their souls out of their bodies to fly over the land like eagles, to bring word of events far beyond mortal gaze. I have heard of such works of Kakos, but never had evidence of their existence. I had thought them tales to frighten children.'

All three of them made the sign of the God.

'No. No.' Barthram shook his head like a drunkard. 'Pigeons. Trained pigeons. Ask brothers.'

'And who in Villebénie will admit to being part of this sorcery?' De Remy's voice was cold.

'Anakritim. Brothers. Jourdaine. Arrenicia.'

'The evidence is conclusive.' De Remy looked at the others for approval. 'I think this matter must be dealt with swiftly.'

'Appeal. King.'

'There is no acclaimed king, Pateras, though Prince Lancelin is represented.' De Remy gestured at the noble. 'So is the faith. And during the interregnum I am the law.'

De Remy again looked at his fellow judges. 'We are agreed? Guilty of sorcery?' Even the episkopos nodded. *A fellow priest, for the God's sake!* 'For which the penalty is death by burning.'

Barthram stared at them in mute disbelief. *This can't be right. Salazar's wounds, I am the anakritis-general!* By the time they lifted his chair he was raging at them, flailing his arms, demanding to be heard, but he was carted backwards down the steps as part of what must be some terrible jest. It could only be a jest; a lifetime of dedicated service to the God could not be snuffed out in less time than it takes to say the Lighting of the Lamps.

They put him in an empty dungeon to await his fate, leaving him in his chair, facing the door in the darkness. Barthram could not even stand and pace. He had reached the stage where he could think clearly, but soon the pain would return and his flask was empty. At first his mind denied its own evidence. *This is not happening, it is not real.* Somewhere in this cell water was dripping, slowly, maybe once every fifty heart-beats, making a tiny splat on the bare stone floor. It gradually confirmed that this was not a dream.

Surely, then, there would be a rescue. His brother anakritim would not tolerate his execution. They would threaten the judges with expulsion. And the gaolers.

Drip, drip.

As reality placed its icy hand on his soul Barthram tried to call on the God, but they were just words in his mind; he could not pray with a true heart. He found it easier to rage and curse.

He gasped as the bolts snapped open in the guardroom above, and footsteps descended the stairs. At least two people: at least one set of the nailed boots worn by the guards, and one making the softer leather touch his own feet used to make. A yellow, flickering light grew around the door frame, and he gasped again as his own bolts shot back. *Is it now? Already?* In the spill of light he could see his own breath; fast, short puffs of fog that faded quickly, and beyond them was Othon de Remy.

'Don't worry. We haven't come to take you.' De Remy put his torch in an empty sconce and dismissed the guards. 'That won't happen until the morning.'

'Come to gloat, have you?' How could de Remy do this?

'My dear Pateras, I wouldn't dream of it.' De Remy held a gloved hand to his nose. *Yes, it does stink in here.* Barthram could not walk to the bucket. 'I simply wanted you to know this is not personal. It is necessary for the realm.'

'There are others who will speak for me. Tell you how it was done. There was no sorcery,' Barthram pleaded.

'And I shall make the most diligent enquires, I ensure you. Afterwards. For the truth, as we know, is what we want it to be.'

'Why? What *truth* is served by my death?'

'There is to be war, you see. Delmas against Lancelin. We have to sway as many nobles as we can towards the prince. Aloys's programme against the Guardians is now widely believed to have been driven by greed rather than piety. There is even talk of reforming the Order; there seems to be a cluster of survivors down in Arrenicia—'

'This isn't about Lancelin, it's about saving you,' Barthram interrupted.

'Let's just say that it is in everyone's interest if people know that there was an evil sorcerer at the head of the anakritim, who managed to cast a spell on the king and destroy the God's finest warriors. The king is dead, the anakritim will be decapitated, and no taint will fall on Lancelin.'

'Or you.'

De Remy put his hands on his chest and made a mock bow. 'I am the realm's humble servant. I merely carry out my sovereign's wishes.'

'You will fall, de Remy.'

'But not today, Pateras. And if the new king finds me of value, not for a long time.'

Barthram took in a long breath of evil-smelling air and let it out slowly.

'You know she escaped, don't you? The witch? She was with the de Fontenays.'

'Indeed. Duke Ragener of Vriesland is hailing her as the fulfilment of a prophecy.'

'We'd have her if you'd listened. Now the Vriesians have their *örlaga vefari*, their weaver of fates. The one who will unite the north against us. And de Fontenay still has the Hand.'

'If it ever existed. And I'll solve the Vriesland question when I've solved Delmas. Which all means we have to act expeditiously.'

'You're a shit, de Remy.'

'As I said, it's nothing personal.' De Remy picked the torch from its sconce and shouted up the steps for the guard.

Barthram did not even rage against him as he left. It would only have made de Remy happier, and Barthram was just beginning to grasp the enormity of his fall.

Time passed too quickly and too slowly, marked by the intensifying pain in his legs and the steady drip of water. Barthram wanted it over but was terrified of it coming. Yet after an interminable darkness only one set of boots came down the steps and opened his door. Barthram was dazzled by the torch, but through narrowed eyes he recognised one of his own tormentors. He carried a leather mug.

'We'll be coming for you soon, Pateras.' The man spoke in the easy way of one used to suffering and death. 'But you had another visitor. Couldn't let her in, of course, but she left something for you. Wouldn't give her name. Short, dumpy woman, getting old. Greying hair. Jourdainian accent. Said she felt guilty about something, wanted to put it right. Gave me a little bottle. "Two drops in wine will numb any pain," she said. "Five and he'll never wake." I tipped it all in.' He held out the mug as if they were tavern companions.

'Drink up, Pateras. For old times' sake.'

13.2 ADELAIS

A light flurry of snow blew across the fields beside the Schilde; even in the worm moon winter had not quite released its grip. A single flake settled on the fur of Adelais's hood and hung there as she rode, suspended almost too close to see. Six tiny points radiated from its frozen centre, like a miniature bind-rune, until a puff of her breath misted over it and left behind a single droplet of water. The flakes lasted longer on Allier's mane, white on black, and merged as they melted so that he wore a net of jewels.

Her partnership with Allier had changed. There had always been affection there, even respect, but the fights at Bellay and Harbin had forged a bond between them, the way the furnace and the quench harden steel. Perhaps one day they would know that celestial fire again, but in the meantime those tastes had left lasting, total trust between them. They were of one mind. She knew him to be well-rested and keen, and happy to be out in the open again; from time to time his ears swivelled at other travellers and he danced for their horses, proud of himself.

The travellers were merchants, mostly, on this thoroughfare

to the capital. They looked at her curiously, wondering who this great lady might be, riding a warhorse and followed by an escort of soldiers in the ducal livery. 'For your safety,' Duke Ragener's chancellor had insisted. 'There are those who wish you harm, even in Vriesland.' Adelais was not sure whether she was an honoured guest of the duke, or his prisoner. Surely she should be allowed to visit her father, and see if her grandmother still lived? Yet it had taken until the middle of the worm moon for Duke Ragener to let her visit her former home. Perhaps he'd become bored with asking her the same questions.

Did you really kill the high priest?

'No. I quoted the prophet Salazar, threw the Guardian curse in his face, and he died. I also sang the *thurs* rune in my head, but I never touched him.'

Tell me again how you killed King Aloys...

'I got angry. He started it all.'

What did you do at Bellay? At Harbin?

'I sang rune song and things happened. I'm sorry people died.'

Are you the one foretold, the örlaga vefari *who will unite the peoples of the north against the invaders?*

'I only want to live in peace. I will not lead more men to their deaths.'

She was treated with a mixture of awe and disbelief, jubilation and fear. And maybe, among the young noblemen of Ragener's court, a little arousal as she walked among them in men's clothing with her shoulders defiantly back and her corn-gold hair hanging only to her shoulders, like that of their pages. They had jested at the knight's sword that hung so naturally on her hip until one young buck provoked Adelais, thinking he could play with her, and she gave him a flesh wound just to teach him a lesson. She didn't give a *fjakkinn* denier what they thought of her. She just wanted to forget all the killing and start life again.

Whatever 'life' was. Wait for a man to marry her? *No thanks*. Hang around the court as their pet curiosity, dependent on charity? *No, no, no.*

Not that gifts were unwelcome. Some ladies of the court had recently taken pity on her and dressed her in their cast-off finery. The duchess herself was a tall woman and had given her the gown she now wore; she'd even sent her seamstress to fit it. It was blue velvet and too rich for any but a great noblewoman to dirty on horseback, but its skirts were cut generously enough to straddle a horse, and she'd shielded it from the mud and snow under a fur-lined cloak. Adelais was going home in style, with only Agnès's fine leather boots and spurs to hint at a less feminine past.

At a fork in the high road they took the lesser road towards her village. Now she knew every twist in the track, every tree, every house. It was a flat land, where ships slipped along the horizon as if they sailed through the fields, not the unseen river. The scene was winter-wet and unlovely but it whispered memories of childhood to her; memories of bouncing on top of a wagonload of cloth on the way to market; of laughter as apprentices pissed their beer into a ditch on the way home. Family. Svend, the brother who'd died after Vannemeer. A community where all were known. She'd hunted pigeon and pheasant with a sling in those woods. She'd run barefoot races down that track, and beaten even the older boys. They hadn't liked that. And on a day in the strawberry moon, when those fields were summer-dry, she'd taken her father's horse and slipped away to meet the boy she loved, hoping that they would run away together. That all seemed such a childish dream, now.

Jan. Would he still be there? His temple certainly was, with a new, bigger dome rising on the skyline over the houses of her

village. The faith of Ischyros was still tolerated in Vriesland,
even if it was no longer the law.

Jan was there, and he did not recognise her at first. It had,
after all, been three years. He stood in front of his temple
beaming at people; a little fuller around the waist and richer in
that russet beard, a man content with his life. The still-hand-
some cleric who'd taken her virginity with such fumbling
urgency now wore the red cap of a consecrated pardoner.

'Hello, Jan.' Adelais reined to a halt. She didn't know what
she wanted from seeing him. She'd been treated as a whore for
loving him – a cleric – and despatched to the sisterhouse far
away. She'd pined for him there; had that been a symptom of
love, or a young woman's infatuation with the unattainable? She
felt no yearning now. Maybe a bittersweet sense of times past.
Perhaps they could share a cup of wine, and laugh a little?

The only laughter she had was from his expression. Slack-
jawed, wide-eyed; it took many heartbeats before his mouth
closed enough to swallow and stammer.

'You.' He made the sign of the God as if he were banishing
all the works of Kakos. 'Get you hence. You will not bewitch me
again!' Her first love fled within his temple, leaving her with the
wry sadness of lost friendship and might-have-beens.

But she had been seen. A crowd was gathering, large
enough for her escort to push their horses into a protective
barrier either side of her and to clear the way in front. Faces
known and half-remembered were coming at a run, cheering
her, calling her name, and their happiness banished all thoughts
of Jan. Boys she remembered as spotty youths were now broad-
shouldered, light-bearded, and bright-eyed. They pushed
closer, calling questions that she answered with a smile and a
wave of recognition. *Did you really kill the Galman king?*
Over their heads, a once-cherished girlfriend lifted an infant
high in the air, and the child laughed and clapped at the excitement. Adelais was borne like a mounted ship to dock at her

father's door, where he stood to receive her with his hands fisted on his hips. They stared at each other, and Adelais felt her pride stir. He'd sent her away to be shut up in a sisterhouse, and she'd more than survived, she'd triumphed. She'd come home dressed as a noblewoman, riding a horse, *her horse*, which was finer than any in her town would ever have seen, and she'd—

'You're bad for trade, you are,' her father growled.

Adelais stared at him.

'Years it took me to build up this business, and now no priest will buy from me because I'm the witch's father. Do you have any idea what it's been like here for us while you've been running around Galmandie? Do you, huh?'

A gurgle of laughter began deep within her, and she put an immaculately gloved hand to her mouth. If she'd dismounted, her father would have towered over her, but in that moment he seemed such a *small* man.

'Don't you laugh at me! We had anakritim here. Anakritim! I might have been tortured if the priest hadn't spoken for me. Your own father!'

Adelais lifted the glove from her face and turned the smothering gesture into a wave.

'Don't you walk away from me, young woman...'

The crowd followed her to the landing stage, where she dismounted and left Allier in the care of a trooper. Her grandmother Yrsa had lived on a sacred island, Freyjasoy, that was the last solid ground before marshes that stretched all the way to the sea. Before Adelais was sent away the island had been surrounded by a moat of tidal mud that isolated Yrsa from searching Ischyrian soldiers; Freyjasoy could only be reached by boat around high tide, and with enough warning for Yrsa to slip away into the labyrinthine wetlands. Now a causeway of logs had been built, presumably to strip away that defence, and Adelais could walk across. Adelais lifted her fine gown high above the slime and stepped out. She was aware of people following her; troopers were demanding to be let through.

Yrsa's cottage lay against a grove of sheltering trees; oak and ash on the higher ground, with an isolated yew. On the far side of the island, nearer the water, a stand of flat-topped pines encircled the boat-shaped ring of stones, laid on edge, where they had burned their dead in the days before the priests insisted they be put in the ground to rot. The burnings had been almost festive; ale-fuelled farewells before the ashes were scattered on the tide for their final voyage to the other world. Beyond the stone boat was a warren of muddy paths, reed beds, and open ponds where Adelais's sling had taken many a duck. A field large enough to feed a family for half a year lay alongside the grove; once it had been neatly tended and fenced to keep out Yrsa's pigs. Now the fences were broken, and weeds choked the field. Clearly Yrsa was long gone, but no one had found the courage to claim the sacred isle for themselves.

The cottage was empty, as Adelais expected. It was cold, smelt of damp, and was bare of all furniture except the *seidhr*-platform on which Yrsa's high seat had rested. That wooden dais had resonated like a drum when Yrsa had beaten it with her staff, chanting her magic; as loud on this side of town as the temple bell on the other. The high seat itself was broken into many pieces; flakes of it lay scattered where someone had hacked off the runes with an axe.

Adelais turned back to the door and the watching crowd. There had to be someone who could tell her what had happened. Her escort was keeping everyone at a distance, and she resented that. She was home. These were her people, and among the faces was one whose smiles folded her face into the creases of old leather, and whose eyes shone with tears of welcome.

'Estrid!' Adelais reached through the soldiers and pulled her father's house-thrall to her, folding her into a hug that lasted until the old woman pushed her away, demanding that she be allowed to breathe. Two gulps of air, a little laughter, and they hugged again. Thrall she might be in law, but Estrid had filled the void after Adelais's mother died. Adelais tugged her into the house. 'Amma Yrsa's dead, isn't she?' Adelais asked when she had calmed a little.

Estrid nodded, still clasping Adelais's hands. 'Nigh on a year ago. She loved you, you know. Said you were destined for great things.'

Adelais had known, in her heart. She'd known when she'd been licking moisture from tree moss, and a wolf had led her to water. 'How?'

'Let me light a fire while I tell you.' Estrid gathered fragments of the high seat and set them around tinder in the central fire pit.

'We heard that the anakritim were coming. We were warned, but Yrsa wouldn't flee. Said she had a greater destiny to fulfil.'

'They didn't...'

'Torture her? No, *kjúkling*. She cheated them of the chance.'

Kjúkling. She'd taught Agnès that word. Adelais had forgotten that it was originally Estrid's endearment.

Estrid struck flint and steel, and blew the sparks into a flame. 'I think she willed herself to die. All night she sang, beating with her staff, and the town quaked because we knew great *seidhr* was at work.' She rocked back on her heels and watched the flames catch. 'Just before dawn the beating stopped, and the boatman brought me over while the tide was full; no one else dared come, but she was my friend. We met her outside her door; she'd been out into the marshes and she was soaking wet, though she wouldn't say why.'

Estrid crossed to sit on the edge of the dais and pulled at Adelais's hand to sit beside her.

'I have never seen her like that. So tired. Always, when she worked *seidhr*, she would need to rest, but she had spent herself on that magic. Poor thing, she could barely walk.'

Estrid's eyes filled and she fretted at her apron. Adelais squeezed her hand in encouragement.

'She gave me a message for you, though,' Estrid continued. 'She said she carved you a *taufr* before you left.'

Adelais touched her scrip. 'I have it.'

'She said its purpose was to bring you home, and that if I saw you its destiny would be fulfilled. She asked that you burn it in her hearth, in her memory.'

Adelais waited, sensing that Estrid had more to say.

'Your amma said she would watch over you always, and if it was in her power, she would guide you. This was the *seidhr* that she worked that night.'

'*Fylgja*,' Adelais whispered. 'Amma Yrsa became *fylgja*.'

Estrid's eyes widened but she nodded, accepting Adelais's conviction, and patted her hand. 'If I had known how close she was to death, I would not have let her send us away, but she hugged me and told us to go, for she was not yet finished and we might come between her and her destiny. She had one last message for you, though. She said that if the gods found you worthy, *kjúkling*, she would show you the way forwards.'

Adelais did not yet understand.

'As I left, the chanting began again, but quietly now. She had no strength left, and I did not hear her staff beating. When the anakritim came for her on the next tide she was still sitting in her seat, but quite dead.'

Adelais rubbed her face with her hands, smearing tears. 'She chose to die.' She didn't know whether to rage against the anakritim or grieve for her grandmother, or just honour her courage.

Estrid pulled her into another hug. 'She was a great *seidhkona*.'

They squatted by the fire pit and Adelais pulled the *taufr* from her scrip. She wondered if there should be words, or some ceremony, but she simply stroked the carving, kissed it one last time, and laid it in the flames. Fragments of Yrsa's blood that had stained the runes crisped as the scrap of wood flamed, twisted, and was gone. A spark raced through the embers, picking out a glowing, jagged line in a fragile fragment of ash.

M

Ehwaz, the horse-rune, the rune of journeys of the spirit as well as the body, a rune of bonding as between horse and rider, as between one who still lives and one who is their *fylgja*. Adelais watched the rune crumble and found herself smiling.

'Did the anakritim find her staff?' she asked over her shoulder.

'No, *kjúkling*.'

Adelais stood and began kilting her fine gown over her belt to save it from the mud. 'Then I'm going for a walk. Will you help me?'

Outside the door the duke's soldiers were stamping and blowing on their fingers to keep warm. She invited them in, and told them to make as big a fire as they wished. 'I'll need it when I come back,' she added. 'But then you'll have to wait outside.'

'Where are you off to, then?' The squire who led her escort looked at her suspiciously.

'I'm going swimming.'

She enjoyed the shock on his face.

Adelais led Estrid out into the marshes, following her instinct. Amma Yrsa would have laid her staff in living water, but there were so many pools. It would be one where clean water came close to the bank, and where she could step down without becoming stuck in the mud. It would be close to the house, but not in the first, most obvious place.

'We could be out here until we freeze to death,' Estrid grumbled.

'She said she would help me.' Adelais stared out over the endless marsh, grey-brown and bleak under falling snow. She had set out with hope but was beginning to lose heart.

'So are you going to swim in every pond we find?'

There. Adelais had seen a tail waving on the path ahead; the half-moon curve of a wolf's tail. It did not matter if it was an illusion caused by waving reeds and grasses. But just where she'd seen it there was a way down into the water – a log or a root that made a step.

'No. Just this one.'

Adelais stripped naked, festooning Estrid with her clothes. She was shaking before she even put her foot into the water. This was madness. The water was not just cold, it *hurt* with cold. Ripples spread out from her legs as she waded, making the reeds wave. Snow was settling on the seed heads like old men's hair, but melting as it touched the water.

'You need a bit more flesh on you before you play these games.' Estrid eyed her from the bank.

Adelais stepped deeper, searching the mud with her toes, and gasped at the icy shock of water lapping between her legs. No amount of fat would stop *that* hurting.

It was up to her breasts when her toes found something more solid in the mud; a stick, perhaps. She traced its length. A *long* stick, and they were too far from any tree for it to be a root. She took several rapid breaths, braced herself for the shock, and duck-dived.

Yes! Her fingers found carvings, but she could not tug it free and had to surface for air. The water squeezed her chest, forcing her to take short, desperate breaths. Down again to where the cold tightened around her head, making a line of pain from forehead to temples. The staff had been anchored down with a bag of sand but came free, suddenly weightless as she pulled.

Adelais broke the surface, laughing, and pushed wet hair out of her eyes. She waved the staff from side to side under the surface, washing it until it no longer trailed banners of silt, and lifted it reverently to her forehead. This was part of Amma Yrsa, and Yrsa's mother before her, and other generations before that. It was beautiful, it was powerful, it was her Wolf People inheritance and it spoke to her in the language of runes that she was only beginning to learn. It was thicker than a man's arm at its top, tapering through intricate, interwoven lines of carving until it was barely thicker than a thumb at its base. Adelais seized it low on the shaft where her hand would close around it and punched it straight up in the air in triumph. Around them snow continued to fall, each flake a miniature bind-rune, as if in blessing. And in that moment Adelais knew her way forwards.

Staff-woman.

Seidhkona.

A LETTER FROM G.N. GUDGION

Thank you so much for choosing *Runes of Battle*. I hope you've had as much fun reading Adelais's adventures as I have writing them. She's a character that took such a hold on my imagination that I feel we have written this together.

Her story continues in *Blood of Wolves*, so if you want to keep up to date with all my latest releases, just sign up at the following link. Your email address will never be shared and you can unsubscribe at any time.

www.secondskybooks.com/gn-gudgion

If you liked *Runes of Battle*, could you do me a huge favour? I so appreciate feedback, and reviews really help new readers discover the books. Reviews don't have to be long; a few words and a star rating on the website of your retailer is all it takes. Thank you.

Would you like to know the story behind the story? My sources of inspiration? There is a real-life Allier, for example. Or would you like me to talk to your book club? There's a 'contact' page on my website, where you'll also find some free stories to download.

I shall be excited to hear from you.

https://geoffreygudgion.com/

 facebook.com/geoffrey.gudgion.author

 twitter.com/GeoffreyGudgion

instagram.com/GeoffreyGudgion

ACKNOWLEDGMENTS

Many of the people who helped me with *Hammer of Fate* have helped me just as much with *Runes of Battle*; particular thanks to my family for their love and encouragement, and to my agent Ian Drury for his support. My admiration for the team at Book-outure/Second Sky keeps on growing, and particular thanks are due to editor Jack Renninson and his extended team: Angela Snowden for forensically detailed copy editing (and creative input), Alex Holmes, Mandy Kullar, Natalie Edwards, and Lizzie Brien for editorial, Faith Marsland for proofreading, Lance Buckley for cover design, Melanie Price and Ciara Rosney for marketing, and Noelle Holten for publicity.

While building Adelais's world I read many sources about medieval life and beliefs, in particular:

- Geoffroi de Charny, *The Book of Chivalry*, mid-fourteenth century, translated by Elspeth Kennedy (University of Pennsylvania Press, 1996). De Charny died a hero's death as the French standard-bearer at the battle of Poitiers in 1356. He wrote *The Book of Chivalry* as a guide for young knights and it is a wonderful insight into the mindset of a pious, medieval warrior. It helped me to form the character of Humbert Blanc.
- Andrew N. Kenner, *Fencing in the Style of the Walpurgis Manuscript*, 2nd edn, (lulu.com, 2016). I

drew on this book for sword-and-buckler fighting techniques.

- *Whispers of Yggdrasil*, a blog by Arith Härger. There is a wealth of published material on runes and *seidhr*, the practice of sorcery in pre-Christian Nordic cultures. Among the frequently contradictory sources, I have found Arith to be a rich and credible mine of information at both the academic and esoteric levels. A novelist weaves facts into imaginary worlds, and while acknowledging Arith's considerable input, I make no claim that he endorses the warp and weft of my story. https://arithharger.wordpress.com
- Wikipedia provided the public domain, Icelandic versions of rune poems and their translations.

Printed in Great Britain
by Amazon

38972273R00249